# VOX HUMANA

## The Human Voice

A Novel

Mary A. Agria

North Fork NATURALS™
www.northforknaturals.com

This book is a work of fiction. Names, characters, places and incidents are either the product of the author's imagination or are used fictitiously. Any resemblance to actual events or persons, living or dead, is entirely coincidental.


ISBN: 978-1-4303-1759-3

My heartfelt thanks goes out —

—To John, whose unflagging and selfless support on behalf of *TIME in a Garden* opened and continues to open doors that seemed all but impossible and gave me the courage to finish *VOX HUMANA*;

—To the Reverend Dr. William McGill and Ellen whose invaluable input and wise, selfless, patient and repeated readings of this manuscript helped shape this novel in so many ways;

—To fellow AGO member and colleague Kim Palermo-Bogardus, Rebecca Bley, the Reverend Linda Clements, Joyce Giguere, Arline Smith, Karen Weaver and Laurie Zmrzlik, whose input at critical points was so essential and is so deeply appreciated;

—To the staff of McLean & Eakin Booksellers, Petoskey, whose encouragement has meant so very much,

—To my longtime colleague at the Center for Theology and Land, Dr. Shannon Jung, for fostering my faith in the life-transforming possibilities in rural community;

—To Marjorie Schroeder, who let me "sit the bench" with her, taught me so much about pipe organs, and so patiently instilled in me a lifelong love of liturgical music;

—To my weaving teacher, Pat Milford and her husband Bill, for their precious insights into that amazing world;

—And to my mother Lydia and my daughters Adriane, Helice, Kirsten and Shelley, as well as my mother-in-law Rose, for their loving life lessons in the power and grace of inter-generational relationships.

This book is an affectionate testament
to your wisdom and generous support.

THE VOX HUMANA [LATIN FOR THE HUMAN VOICE] IS A STOP ON THE PIPE ORGAN SO-NAMED BECAUSE OF ITS SUPPOSED RESEMBLANCE TO THE HUMAN VOICE. IT IS ALMOST NEVER USED ALONE.

For those who are lucky or persistent or both, there are moments in their lives when *who* they *are*—their inner lives—and *what* they *do*—their external ones—come together. In such moments, they catch a profound glimpse of why they exist and where their lives are headed. Vocal coaches and writing instructors sometimes call it, *finding our voice.*

As for the rest of the time, fortunately, it is not our mistakes that define us, it is our ability to strike that first terrifying note and then just play on, just keep going. The art of life, like the art of music, lies not in perfection but in the grace with which we manage to recover.

# ✣ Chapter One

A day shy of two weeks after my abrupt change in status from Char Howard *civil servant* to Char Howard *reluctant retiree*, I left Philadelphia for parts West, my hometown of Hope, Pennsylvania. The heavens were weeping at the prospect. I had cried myself out days ago.

It was hard either to laugh or cry in my poor hatchback, crammed to the roof with house plants, as I plodded along on autopilot behind the moving truck. From rising to setting sun, Pennsylvania is one very long state—its diagonal from the Atlantic to the Great Lakes just as intimidating. I had plenty of time to think about what was waiting for me on the other end.

Memories rose up and fell behind me like the rain-shrouded waves of the mountains en route, range after range of them—first the Appalachians, then the Alleghenies. Beyond those last foothills lay Hope, a mere stone's throw from the smokestacks of Ohio and the sprawling Midwestern prairie.

It was the Hope of my childhood I was remembering. Idyllic tree-canopied streets clustered around the gingerbread-and-red-brick heart of Main Street. Wispy threads of wood smoke drifted in the crisp winter dawn, and on summer nights, fireflies darted like fairy lights through the tall grass of the encroaching farm fields while tree frogs rasped out their fugues to the velvet sky.

I had grown up in that house. When Gram Grunwald lost her beloved husband to a farm accident, she set aside her own grief long enough to open her home and life to her divorced daughter, my mother, without reproach or complaint. I was only four at the time.

Decades later, again without hesitation, the two of them had offered me their help with raising my girls after my husband died so early in our marriage. Jen was three, Sarah one. It was my choice to soldier on alone in Philadelphia—kept afloat by a civil service job that would have been hard to come by back home in Hope.

But it was not my own strength that I drew on in those dark days after Len walked into the jungles of Vietnam and never came back. Even now I couldn't begin to articulate how deeply that distant homestead and the courage of those strong Grunwald women had imprinted my life.

After all those years, I was going home. Problem was, missing from those life-shaping memories of my youth were the very people who were drawing me there, the family I had loved and lost to time. *Mom. Gram Grunwald.* It suddenly hurt even to name them.

Up ahead I saw the turn-signal light on the moving van—forced myself to fall in behind it as it crept around an even slower eighteen-wheeler. With any luck we would make it just in time for the driver to return the favor and pass us on the downhill stretch. Instinctively, my hands tightened on the steering wheel, anticipating a thunderclap of a *Woooo-sh* as the wake from that monster of a truck buffeted my tiny hatchback.

*Reality check.* Except for my realtor, Todd Rutterbach, I was coming back to a community of strangers.

Moving day, the first day of the rest of my life, had started with a headache. It pounded away in my temples like a harried rookie percussionist I once saw navigating the final bars of the *1812 Overture*—half a beat behind.

*Not an auspicious beginning.* Crawling out of my sleeping bag spread on the carpeted floor of an otherwise empty bedroom in my Philly apartment, I headed for the bathroom. My footfalls echoed on the bare wood of the hallway.

I made a point of evading the eyes reflected back at me from the bathroom mirror as I yanked open the medicine chest. Somewhere in that ragged assortment of outdated childproof bottles I had intended to leave behind, there had to be something that spelled, Relief.

*No sudden moves*, I told myself. *Caffeine.* But then it hit me.

The moving van was parked outside and my driver was already on his way. Under the circumstances, nuking the day-old coffee left sitting in my mug on the kitchen counter was my only alternative. I already had packed most of my utensils along with the coffee maker.

While I waited for the microwave to work its magic, it finally dawned on me that the message light on my answering machine was blinking. Apparently in my volatile emotional state and exhaustion during last night's last-ditch packing, I had not even bothered to check.

I clicked the Play button. The faint sound of shuffling papers gave way to a familiar voice, male and way too cheerful for a Saturday morning.

"Char Howard . . .? It's Todd Rutterbach . . . your realtor. Just checking in. But then maybe you're already on your way. The renters moved out end of last week and I sent someone over to your place yesterday to give it a cleanup and make sure the utilities are turned on when you arrive. Thought you'd want to know tha— "

The voice sped up toward the end as if the agent knew he was running out of time. To no avail. He broke off mid-word, replaced by a sequence of high-decibel beeps, like those rhythmic dinging sounds from the microwave when it finishes a cycle.

For the first time it struck me in the frustrating silence that followed, how obsessed we are about time in our culture, even programming our appliances to remind us that precious commodity is fleeting. Futile, all of it. I never could remember how long it takes to reheat a cup of coffee. More often than not, my own garbled phone messages broke off mid-stream, as unsatisfactory to the caller as to the recipient.

Well, there was no time like the present to find out what my realtor wanted. I punched in the speed dial. After three rings, I started to assume the worst. I was going to be playing phone tag for the rest of the day.

"Hullo . . .?"

Not Todd, that much was certain. The six-or-so-year-old voice on the other end of the phone line sounded suspicious, annoyed.

Boy or girl? I only remembered something about a lot of little Rutterbachs.

"Is your daddy home?"

"He's sleeping."

I looked at my watch. Seven A.M.—retired and perfectly entitled to sleep in at long last. Instead, here I was terrorizing the first working stiff on my list. *Brilliant.* Before I could counsel otherwise, the young receptionist hollered for his dad.

"He's coming. I'm watching cartoons."

"Sorry. I didn't know it was so early."

Somehow that revelation didn't make the voice on the other end of the line sound any happier. Eventually a muffled conversation from the other end of the line was followed by the thud of the phone receiver hitting the floor.

"Todd Rutterbach . . .!"

"Char. Sorry to bother you so early. I got your message."

"No problem. So . . . we're on then, for the move?"

"We leave within the hour. My lease here in Philly expires tomorrow. So it's really good timing, as it turns out."

None of that, I realized, mattered one iota to my realtor, one way or the other. But then I had forgotten how personal small town life could be.

Todd Rutterbach was not just my rental manager, he was Hope's unofficial mayor and operated the town's only surviving retail establishment of any note, a tiny but stocked-to-the-ceiling hardware—a little like the growing mountain of cartons that had been accumulating in my Philly walk-up apartment for a month now, ever since I reluctantly took the retirement buy-out that my boss at the Job Service was offering. Rutterbachs even had a half-aisle of groceries.

"Call me on my cell," Todd said. "I'll have a couple of guys ready to help you unload."

"That's not necessary— "

"Part of the service."

*Lovely.* For weeks now my daughter Jen had been urging me just to throw the stuff in the truck and then do my sorting and discarding on the other end. Tempting, but that was before I knew about these anonymous hired hands my realtor had recruited to help. It would be all over the county in a matter of hours what a thorough pack-rat the new arrival was.

I got off the line, went to rescue my coffee—the timer had protested a long time ago. As I opened the door, dark pools of liquid had boiled over the top of the mug and were spreading over the glass turntable.

"Son-of-a-gun!"

The phone was ringing again. This was getting worse than the Monday morning crunch down at the employment office. Coffee-soaked paper toweling in one hand, I made a grab for the receiver.

"Mom?"

My oldest daughter Jen had put down roots in suburban Pittsburgh with husband Jason and a son and daughter, both under age three. Amazing what parenthood will do to revive mother-daughter relationships. This time, the hour was early even for her.

"Something's wrong?"

"Just wanted officially to wish you a happy retirement."

I told her about dragging the realtor out of bed. Jen laughed.

"Just wait another month," I said, "I won't know what day or month it is, shuffling around at all hours in my bathrobe."

Jen's laughter sounded more tentative now. "Seriously, Mom, you're doing . . . okay?"

"Fine."

My daughter had plenty of practice recognizing evasion when she heard it. During the worst of her adolescence, that particular adverb—*fine*—and the subtle ambiguity it conveyed had been a staple of her vocabulary.

"I'd be happy to take off from work a day or two," she told me. "I'll Just drive up there and help you unpack. It's going to be so great finally to have you living so close."

It was a noble gesture, albeit unrealistic. Jen was new at her job as guidance counselor with the local school district. Personal time right now would not be the best idea in the world.

"I'm really on top of it, Jen. But thanks for the offer."

Truth was, in the entire month since I signed on the dotted line of that buy-out package at the Job Service, my walk-up apartment had looked like a warehouse gone amuck. And right now I couldn't care less whether I ever saw any of the stuff again.

Background noises told me my grandchildren were getting impatient with the lack of attention. I smiled. Time to cut it short.

"You know, Mom . . ."

Jen paused, hand over the receiver while she settled down the troops, "I had my doubts when you told me you were moving back to Hope. That lasted about thirty seconds. Then I thought about that beautiful old house of Great-gram's and all those good times back in western PA when we were little and— "

"A long time ago."

"True, Mom. Although the one thing you always taught us, my sister and me, was how to be survivors. Hang on to the best, let go of the rest, you always said. Just keep breathing!"

I was glad my daughter couldn't see my face. *Out of the mouths of babes.* Our laughter felt good, liberating.

"Okay, so just take a deep breath, Mom. I'm sure you will figure this out— "

"Thanks for the pep talk, honey. I needed that."

*More than my daughter even suspected.* I held the phone in my hand for a good while before setting it down again on the kitchen counter.

By now, my coffee was cold, but mercifully adequate for washing down those three tablets still lying there. My headache had mutated from a percussive annoyance to a vise-twisting cry for help.

Time to pump up the volume a notch, get myself in gear. My ancient boom-box of a radio was one of my last possessions still left in the apartment—the thing took up half the top of my refrigerator. Music had been my passion as long as I could remember and like the pre-set buttons on a pipe organ, my instrument of choice, I had programmed the station pre-sets to my favorite classical stations.

*Instant connection.* Startled, I flinched at the ruthlessly cheerful early Baroque flute concerto trilling away in the stratosphere. I had accompanied a soloist on the piece once, knew where those cascading sixteenth notes were headed.

"Enough of that," I muttered. Flipping the dial, I settled on the languid twang of a country-rock station. "How could you go-o-o and leave me hurtin'?"

Grabbing one of the last remaining empty cartons, I began dumping the few remaining kitchen utensils into the void, dirty dishes and all, and padding the most fragile items with the contents of the towel drawer. I topped off the box with the hand-braided rug from in front of the sink.

All the while my daughter's words kept playing themselves over and over again in my head. *Keep moving—literally and figuratively.*

*Keep moving.* As strategies went, I had to admit, it was pretty primitive.

Still, as I focused on that moving van up ahead of me, right now nothing else seemed to make any sense. My whole life was packed away in that innocuous rental. At this point, there was little for me to do but doggedly follow where it took me.

# ✣ Chapter Two

*Day Two out of Philly.* The gentle mist of a rain became one of those relentless late spring downpours that turns sky and land into an indistinguishable leaden mass.

I had insisted on angling up to I-80 to save on tolls. *A mistake.* Tsunami waves of water crashed over the roof of the car whenever the hulking double tractor trailers overtook our slow-moving caravan—which was often.

Ahead of me in that rental van, my rent-a-driver Marty Santano pressed on with the ethic of the tortoise, doggedly intent on the mile marker at hand rather than the vagaries of the finish line. To look at the guy, that was the last modus operandi anyone would have imagined.

Built like a skateboarder, wiry and compact, his uniform of choice consisted of high-top sneakers, baggies and funk-message tees, topped off by aviator shades whether in sun or downpour. That carrot-red hair was straight out of a bottle, with all the styling of a weed-whacked lawn.

When Marty first showed up on my counseling caseload at the Job Service, he was straight out of college with so-so grades and an equally unpromising sense of self-worth. The degree was his parents' idea. What he really loved was to work with his hands—carpentry, landscaping, fix-it jobs—all of which were tough to come by given the guy's limited social skills and general lack of hustle.

Still, there was something very likeable about the young man. He didn't know what he wanted or how to get there, but the ambiguity rarely bothered him. For months prior to my own unexpected change in job status, I made it a kind of informal mission to hook Marty up with whatever odd jobs surfaced in my computer database. He was embarrassingly grateful.

*As long as the assignment lasted two weeks or less,* I quickly figured out. Of late I had begun trying to push that envelope, to extend the limits of Marty's particular form of work-related attention deficit. My own pink slip intervened.

I had to chuckle at the irony of it all—even as I dodged a shredded tire kicked up by the wheels of that blasted rental Marty was driving. As a career counselor in Philadelphia for thirty years, I helped make sense of life's twists and turns for thousands of Marty's, worn down by unemployment or a lack of purpose in their working lives. And now here I was.

Strange, how unsettling it felt to be forced by circumstances to take one's own advice. But then that was the last thing on my mind that mid-March morning, a month—more like a lifetime—ago.

I was late for work. Rare for me, but there it was.

With a primitive lunch, whatever was close at hand, crammed in that padded I-heart-you tote one of my grandchildren had sent for Christmas, I scurried down the broad front steps of my apartment building. If I took the alley instead of a leisurely stroll through the tiny park down the street, I could shave a good two minutes off my route. My sneakers connecting hard with the pavement, I struck off briskly through block after block of austere brown-brick row houses in the direction of the Job Service office where I worked in downtown Philadelphia.

I liked this neighborhood, had raised both my daughters in this particular urban enclave. History lived close to the surface here. Once a haven for the city's elite, those erstwhile mansions had recast themselves as home to modest walk-up apartments—mine among them.

For all the grime and wear the decades had imposed, I couldn't help but feel a kinship with those tuck-pointed monuments to the passage of time—that, and the human stream meandering through those narrow streets. After all, professional recycling was my life's work. The image fit.

As I walked, the Spring air felt raw in my lungs, cleansing. Around me, Philly was coming alive in a symphony of car horns and the percussive clatter of heavy security shutters unrolling on neighborhood storefronts. High-pitched laughter of children, dawdling along their way to school, pierced through the muffled conversations of their elders crowding the sidewalks—fellow office drones already half-caught up with their overflowing in-baskets and computer terminals.

I felt at home here. I knew this place and myself in it.

And much as I hated rushing to it this particular morning, I loved my work—though of late it was with a weather-eye on the barometer. Transitions may be stock-in-trade with the clients I served, but they can be unsettling in a bureaucracy where structure and certitude are the norms.

For months rumors of cutbacks had been swirling around the copy machine. Still, when my supervisor called me over for a one-on-one, I assumed it was to reassure me that after three decades on the job, I had the seniority to survive any bureaucratic bloodletting.

Grudgingly, I settled into the chair across the desk from my boss Irene. In fact, my mind was already on the stack of mail back in my office.

"Char, I'm sorry to be the bearer of bad tidings."

*That* got my attention. The pinched frown between Irene's eyebrows deepened.

"We've got to cut six staffers by next month. At least two in early retirements."

"You're kidding."

Irene looked down at her hands clutching a personnel file—mine, I assumed. *Charlise A. Howard.* That middle initial was for Amelia. I felt a tight knot begin to build up in the pit of my stomach as I waited for what came next.

"You and Fred Burroughs are the closest to retirement, after all those buyouts five years ago," Irene said. "The incentives are not going to get any better than this."

Numb and disoriented, I reached for the crisp sheet of calculations my boss was extending in my direction—willing my hands not to shake. I wasn't entirely successful. The numbers swam on the page like notes flowing along a staff of music. It took several tries to get the gist of where the cold dollars and cents were leading me.

The proposal was to bring my pension to full- retirement level and help patch my insurance together until I qualified for Medicare. Irene was right. Though it would force me to think about some kind of transitional employment, the offer was generous—and devastating.

"I'm not even sixty," I said.

Fifty-nine, to be exact. Then why, at this moment, did I feel so terribly, irrevocably old? Irene looked down at her desk.

"I could hand you all sorts of platitudes about third age careers," she said slowly.

That formula was our stock-in-trade dealing with older clients. The so-called "third age" before retirement had the potential for being the roughest or the most rewarding, a financial disaster or at last the chance to make job choices based on passion not practicalities. Over the years, as a counselor, I had seen the extremes of both.

"You've been a wonderful counselor," Irene said. "We will miss you. But what would you choose, if you could do anything you always dreamed of?"

The familiar question triggered a rising sense of panic as my boss aimed it in my direction. *Not give all this up*, I wanted to tell her. *Certainly not now—not yet.*

The file drawers of my past were thick with dreams labeled and shelved away in the dark corners of my soul. What would it be like to travel the globe without worrying about the calendar? Or to hunker at the laptop in my makeshift home office and write the Great American novel? Since I was a girl, I had loved playing the organ—sitting at the console and hearing the breathtaking sounds from the pipes thundering back at me. But that too had been "for fun" or as an on-and-off substitute for others who had made music their lives and their livelihoods.

As I shuffled through the options, they took on the distant unreality of adolescence, faded now and tired. It seemed hard to believe that I had ever been that young.

The Muzak oozing out over the office intercom was the ultimate insult—a barely recognizable version of "Moon River". Wistful lyrics about crossing forbidding waters in grand style played themselves out in my head.

*Yeah, right—forget grand junkets.* Right now I would settle for knowing I wouldn't wind up under an overpass somewhere. *Dead broke.*

Detached and dispassionate as if counseling a client, I had done the math over the years. Under duress in Irene's office, I struggled to tick off the short list of assets in my head. *My government pension. The option of mortgage-free housing. A small inheritance. And down the road, Social Security.*

With any kind of luck, the gap between subsistence and a meal out once in a while could be relatively modest. *If I could reduce my cost of living.* That wasn't likely with an urban lifestyle. Worse, agencies in Philly were cutting staff all over the place, not a good bellwether for my finding transitional employment.

My boss Irene was watching my reaction, holding back—waiting. *Just when had our relationship morphed from friends and colleagues to client and counselor?* I bristled, half-resenting the skills that were luring me into the very what-to-do-when-your world-implodes responses that until now I had coaxed from my own caseload.

My mouth felt stiff. "I've been renting out my family's home in western Pennsylvania since they died." I told her. "North of Pittsburgh. Lots of tiny villages strung together out along the interstates and a relatively lower cost of living. I'd always thought about moving back there."

Philly had become a luxury, and apart from a small circle of friends, there certainly was nothing to keep me there. My children were grown and on their own.

My boss nodded. "Lovely country in that part of the state— "

"The house needs a lot of work." I conjured up all sorts of dollar signs on that subject. "After that . . . who knows . . .! I assumed I had at least five years to worry about it."

Irene shifted in her chair. Her smile seemed forced.

"You don't have to decide this minute," she said. "But I need your answer about the package by the end of the week."

So soon. "I guess I can let you know by then."

Who was I kidding? We both already knew what my answer would be. Still, there is a certain dignity in pretending there are options—when in fact, there are none.

I got through that day, the week and then that last month—although how, I can't remember. Friends hosted a hastily-organized round of lunches and an official office party, fraught with the tension of colleagues who half-feared they might be next. On that last Friday on the job, I packed my personal belongings from my cubicle into two file boxes and hauled them down to my newly-acquired junker of a Colt and slammed the hatch lid down on the memories.

*What now?* The route home had suddenly become as alien as a journey to the moon.

Public Radio was running a talk piece on adults and piano lessons, apparently the fastest growing age group for music students. I listened, only half hearing. *Adults find it safer to risk,* the radio announcer was saying, *when learning is on their time and their terms.*

Safety had nothing to do with where I found myself. Nothing at all.

Amid a blare of taxi horns and sirens, I navigated the maze of shortcuts from my office to the parking garage behind my apartment complex. In the muffled silence of those dark concrete walls, I cut the engine and sat staring blankly through the windshield, my hand still clutching at the ignition key. The tears trailed unchecked down my face, hot and stinging in that chill April twilight.

*Be careful what you wish for*, the thought occurred to me. We all 'What-if' about that distant day when we can shuck off the constraints of eight-to-five living and have all the time in the world to live and be as we choose. Fiction had become fact.

I was retired. I was free. I was on my own. And I had never been more terrified in my life.

After all that, there was no way I was going to hire a professional mover. Not given my uncertainty about how far my resources would stretch.

So, that last week on the job when Marty Santano showed up in my office for his monthly pep talk, I told him about my predicament. I needed a driver. Fortunately, the otherwise unexcitable New Jersey native snapped up my offer to pilot the moving van like the Lewis and Clark expedition was about to get underway and he was invited to go along for the ride.

Forget the reality of miles of boring, pot-hole ridden asphalt! *This was a Road Trip.*

Marty's parents had given him a cell phone for his college graduation present. My down-payment on his truck-driving services was to activate the account he had let expire so the two of us could keep each other awake along the interminable stretches of highway. The periodic flashing of lights and whimsical ring-tones Marty programmed into the gizmos gave our trek the unsettling techno-aura of a protracted NASA liftoff.

"Running out of gas," my young companion informed me cheerily as the first signs for a truck stop popped up on the shoulder.

"So am I," I yawned. "My back is killing me. How about we stretch our legs and get some coffee?"

"See ya."

We momentarily went our separate ways, Marty to the truckers' lot and I to the section reserved for passenger cars. I had grave doubts about whether my fifteen-year-old Plymouth even qualified for that distinction.

The roadway in the rest stop was steaming from the humidity, although at least the rain had let up for the moment. I couldn't have made a dash for the facilities if I tried. As I eased myself out from behind the steering wheel, for a split-second the landscape actually swam in front of my eyes.

"You okay, ma'am?"

Bless his heart, Marty seemed genuinely worried. Touched, I chalked it up to that peculiar protective streak in young people who have yet to experience that age hurts, physically and experientially—sometimes with as simple an act as getting out of bed in the morning.

*But then why discourage the young by dwelling on that revelation?* It comes soon enough.

"Sciatica," I told him. "I get twinges when I sit too long."

"Sciatica . . .?"

"An occupational hazard for bureaucrats and people obsessed with keyboard instruments. A royal pain in the butt."

"And truck drivers, apparently." Marty grimaced as he flexed his shoulders "You're not the only one with butt fatigue. The rain was coming down so hard on that last stretch, I just grabbed that old wheel and held on. A couple times I thought I'd go off the road."

"I'd have gone right down the embankment behind you. All I could see out there through that 60-mile-an-hour car wash were your tail-lights."

Marty chuckled, shook his head. "We'd make the 11 o'clock news, for sure."

I was still picturing those streaming headlines across the bottom of a screen as we settled into line at the fast-food counter. The deal was that I pay Marty's expenses so by now—with a full day of polite protesting already behind him—he felt free to load his tray with a formidable helping of burgers, fries and enough other cholesterol-laden "sides" to give the healthiest of circulatory systems pause.

"A hundred-fifty miles to go." He chewed on the notion for a while along with an onion ring. "We'll make it fine by dark."

"Too late, though, to unload."

At that even unflappable Marty seemed relieved. Back on the road, the landscape was becoming increasingly familiar. Up ahead loomed the exit ramp for Bartonville.

"Time to bail, Marty!"

"Maybe you ought to pull ahead at this point," he suggested.

I had already activated my turn signals to change lanes and scoot around him. "Beyond that it's just twenty-five more miles. A piece of cake."

Marty groaned. "Forget the food. What I need now is some quality sack time."

"Sleeping bags on the floor don't exactly qualify but at least there are carpets. In the morning, you can take the car and run down to the mini-mart for donuts before Todd's movers show up."

"And coffee."

I laughed. "And coffee."

"How on earth are we going to sort through all that stuff?"

"You forget," I told him. "We career bureaucrats eat, sleep and breathe organization. I've got a system of box numbers, labels, and a computerized master inventory stashed on my front seat that makes online auction sites look like amateur night in Dixie."

So much for orchestrating the evening ahead of us. Barely five minutes after Marty and I pulled up to the curb in front of the graying hulk of a Victorian in which I had spent all of my childhood years, the rain stopped entirely as if someone up there had thrown a switch.

Barely five minutes after that, Todd Rutterbach cruised into the driveway in his extended cab pickup with two burly companions in tow. Stunned, I just stood there and looked at him.

"You made it," Todd said as he pulled me into an impromptu bear hug. "Welcome to Hope!"

"You sure got here . . . fast!" I said. "It really wasn't necessary of you to— "

"Of course, you'll want your stuff." Todd shrugged, obviously prepared for action in frayed cuff jeans and an overwashed polo shirt. "No problem. Thought you might forget to call me. So, when you passed the State Police post, Agnes Brady phoned ahead and told us you were coming. Ernie and Fred here will help you get all this inside in no time."

Fishing the key out of the rental truck's ignition, the realtor took charge—an aw-shucks version of the Alpha male. Marty just stood there staring at me open-mouthed, as if thrust into a culture so foreign that words fail. Where he came from, this would count as home invasion.

I flashed what I hoped was a smile. "Sounds good to me."

But then Ernie and Fred already were putting their collective muscle to work even as I spoke, opening the rear doors and positioning the ramp. I scrambled for the clipboard with the inventory sheets and barely made it to the front door when the first boxes arrived on the porch. Todd already had used his keys to open the house.

"Those numbers on the carton labels should say where the stuff belongs," I fretted. "Bedroom One is at the head of the stairs, Two next to— ”

“Ma’am, maybe ya’d better put a label on the room doors.” Todd lowered his voice. “And print big. Ernie and Fred here aren’t the best at following oral directions.”

Both men had stopped mid-stairs with boxes in hand, waiting. Hands shaking, I ripped several blank sheets from the yellow legal pad on the clipboard and scrawled out the names of the rooms as they appeared on the boxes. For lack of tape or thumb tacks, I just stuffed the crude labels in the appropriate door hinges then did the same for the rooms downstairs, even the kitchen.

I can’t remember three hours passing as quickly or as slowly as the time it took to empty that rental van. After watching Ernie’s energetic set-down-the-box technique, it also seemed prudent to scour the truck for the more fragile cartons and carry them myself. Marty did his best to help.

The rain had long since been replaced by a sullen night sky that made deciphering my ludicrously elaborate labeling system even more difficult. Ceiling fixtures in the house were few and far between and the chance of finding any table lamps in the shoulder-high sea of boxes was less than zero. Todd, it seems, anticipated even that contingency.

Standing at the front door flashlight in hand, he barked out monosyllabic instructions while Ernie and Fred scrambled to obey. Last off the truck was the sofa bed, which the two movers horsed into the living room while Marty and I frantically shoved aside cartons to accommodate the massive olive green three-seater.

It was only then that I truly appreciated what lay ahead of me. My apartment decor over the years in Philadelphia had evolved into a homey palette of vanillas, greens and earth tones, an urban mix of wicker and pale birch. Here, the walls of the living room were wallpapered in a heinous shade of pink and gray, straight out of the fifties—true, I realized with a shock, of much of the house.

Over the years Todd Rutterbach had been a conscientious rental manager, encouraging major repairs as they were needed. Most of the tenants had been elderly ladies but still—had it really been that long since any major cosmetic re-does on the place? The prospect of making things fit was like trying to impose Martha Stewart on the Cleavers.

In desperation at the worst point in my packing on the other end, I had contemplated just selling it all and starting over. *Sometimes it pays to go with your instincts.*

“Ya gotta lotta stuff there, Char,” the realtor said.

Nothing like stating the obvious. Although they were too polite to push that point, Ernie had pulled out an oversize red bandana handkerchief and was mopping his brow feverishly. Fred just stood there, glassy-eyed, breathing hard.

"I can't find my purse," I stammered. "Or I'd pay you for— "

"For me . . . no need. Part of the service." Todd shot me a conspiratorial look. "Fifty bucks for Fred and Ernie would be nice, though. I'll just handle it now and you can pay me back later."

"A hundred. Fair enough. Will a check be okay?"

*Ridiculously low,* I concluded, for what had just transpired. The realtor's voice lowered to a whisper.

"Fifty—tops—will do fine. You wouldn't want folks to think you're the kind to throw your money around."

I was too tired to argue. With all of our sweating bodies, all that stuff in the living room and no trace of a breeze intervening from outside, the heat index indoors by now had to be spiking in the nineties.

Marty Santano had taken up residence gingerly on the sofa. The poor guy looked ready to fall asleep sitting up. Fred and Ernie were already fidgeting near the door. At my mention of 'check,' I thought I saw Fred scowl.

"I'll come by tomorrow, Todd," I nodded. *"With cash."*

By the time the tail lights on the realtor's car disappeared, I had locked up the front door and clicked off the porch light. I noticed in passing that Marty had slumped over on the couch cushions and was snoring softly.

*Let the poor guy sleep*, I thought.

With some difficulty, I located and took care of the downstairs lights, then headed upstairs to what was intended to be the future master bedroom. Over one of the mountains of cartons, someone had draped the sleeping bag that I had been planning to use. If there was room to spread it out somewhere, it wasn't immediately apparent.

Instead, I dragged the quilted bag into the bathroom and used it to line the huge claw-foot tub. Outside, the wind was kicking up and a low-lying branch was scraping against the bathroom window screen.

As I drifted off into a troubled sleep, it occurred to me there could be a tornado brewing out there. Well, at least in that bathtub—surrounded by an impressive amount of vintage claw-footed cast iron—I was more or less prepared to duck and cover.

My dreams were a dark and murky whirlpool of past and present, swirling toward some unknown center of calm, always just beyond my grasp.

# ✣ Chapter Three

I awoke with a start, thinking it was a nightmare. The morning light was blinding without curtains to soften the glare. Still curled in that wrought iron bath tub, every bone in my body ached and I had no idea whatsoever where I was.

Half-panicked, I waited for my internal compass to stop spinning before gingerly, and with some difficulty, I risked clambering back on terra firma. *Hope. The homestead. Morning.*

I ran out of answers at the day of the week. *Thursday?* The landmarks were getting fuzzy again.

Apparently a front had come through overnight, cooling off the house. Shivering, still clad in the clothes I had slept in, I picked my way downstairs. Marty Santano was still sound asleep on my sofa. Every muscle aching, I stooped to check out the refrigerator.

I shouldn't have been surprised by now, but I was. The contents were modest but obviously fresh. A small carton of orange juice and another of milk, a loaf of bread, eggs and the condiments to go with them.

*Included in the service or not,* I vowed, *I owed that realtor Todd big-time.*

My clattering around in cartons looking for pans was bound to wake up Marty. Instead I opted to steal out through the back door and get the kinks out of my back as I reintroduced myself to the town I had abandoned nearly forty years earlier. Right now anywhere seemed more hospitable than that mess I was leaving behind me.

Hope was laid out on a grid, twelve east-west streets and as many north-south—identified first by numbers radiating out from Main Street in all directions and then farther out, named for common Pennsylvania hardwoods. Even the slowest of power walkers would quickly exhaust the possibilities. I struck off from home base on Elm Street heading in toward the center of town without any plan except to clear my head.

Like the venerable American Elm, Hope had fallen on tough times—except the town's nemesis was not plague or pestilence. In a word, it was a case of lousy connections.

Once a thriving stop along the Erie Canal extension, for a brief five years the town's population soared to over 3,000—until the railroad all but wiped commercial river traffic off the map. No one ever said the townsfolk weren't resourceful. One bleak, mid-winter night about forty of the more enterprising citizens took matters into their own hands. *Literally*. They snuck over to the neighboring town and moved the tracks to Hope.

Of course, it was too good to last. When the Interstate clinched the demise of the railroads, the nearby town of Bartonville wound up with the interchange. Hope's glory days were over.

As I walked the all-but-deserted streets, evidence of that past was everywhere. The landmarks on either side were at once familiar and strangely askew from the Norman Rockwell fantasy in my memory bank. Paint was coming off in hunks on the front of the obviously abandoned Methodist church on Main Street. Most of the brick and ornate wood-trimmed storefronts were boarded up or had For Sale signs in the windows. As I crossed the precariously uneven rail-bed, the once shiny tracks were shrouded in hip-high grass and many of the ties were missing or rotted.

I turned on First Avenue, ambling past several vacant lots. Across the street, the fieldstone Episcopal Church, Nativity, with its squat pseudo-Norman bell tower still seemed to be in operation. It appeared smaller than the childhood parish I remembered, in size more a chapel really, but here at least the bushes were well kept. From behind the building I picked up the high-pitched rasp of a weed-whacker in operation.

After decades of urban living, I didn't expect a response as I fumbled with the latch but after a brief struggle, the glossy red door sprang open to my touch. I stepped inside.

The narthex was dark with that closed-in smell of older buildings where heating is a luxury. But as I wandered from the cramped and narrow entrance hall into the sanctuary itself, I stopped dead still—felt the hair stand up on the back of my neck. *Overwhelmed by memories.*

Tentatively I made my way down the center aisle toward the massive wooden rood screen that stretched across the front of the choir—its intricately carved vines and branches straining heavenward like gnarled and aged hands lifted in prayer. Shafts of light filtered through the stained glass windows while around me prisms of red, green and electric blue danced across the rows of pews and the bare oak floor.

I held my breath. Nestled in front of the screen, where I hoped it would be, sat the unassuming oak case of the organ console. Reason told me it was just the smell of citrus oil in the polish. Still, as I ran my palm gently across the organ bench, for a moment I experienced a gut-wrenching flashback to another morning.

*Sunday. Many years ago. My feet dangling over the pedals. Breathing in the delicate lemon scent of my mother's perfume.*

I shivered, half expected to feel the familiar intake of air from the pipes overhead as the instrument stirred and roused itself. Like some otherworldly organism—a living thing—it was poised and waiting, prepared to pour out its soul into the silence.

I was a child again. A month shy of my tenth birthday, I was sitting on this same bench alongside my mother while she played the service. "Sitting the bench" she called it. Her right hand had just picked out the melody of the *Kyrie Eleison.*

"Lord, have mercy," the congregation sang. "Christ, have mercy."

Hand poised, I waited for the final note. My job was simple enough—to slip my mother's offertory book on the music rack, open to the quiet interlude she had picked out for the Eucharist. I knew the piece, more or less. At her suggestion, I had been practicing around on the little voluntary for weeks.

"I'll head over for Communion," my mother whispered. "Cover 'til I get back."

She was already sliding off the bench. On the rack sat the Celtic hymn-tune SLANE . . . *Be Thou My Vision.* It had been a struggle for me to master those notes on the piano at home, without the use of the sustain pedal—a quick-and-dirty practice technique to develop the fluid touch that separated a true organist from a pianist.

"But I am not ready to— "

"Play!"

I did, holding my breath until light-headed, terrified I would make a mistake. The result was painfully slow. I didn't dare risk adding the pedal. But after what seemed like an eternity, my mother returned and motioned for me to move over on the bench.

She was smiling. "Good," she breathed. Strong praise, considering.

Giddy with relief, I let her take over the piece, easing her hands into position with only the slightest hesitation at the end of a phrase. *Be Thou My Vision*, my inner voice sang along with the line as it unfolded. *O, Ruler of All.*

The images from my childhood scattered in the empty sanctuary like yesterday's rain flowing over the windshield on my hatchback on Interstate 80. Sheer instinct, I tested to see if the organ case was locked. It wasn't.

Accordion fashion, the hinged wooden panels opened to my touch. Instinct, too, I glanced up at the pipes overhead—intimate and reassuring, as only a tracker can be, where the proximity between keys and pipes allows a mechanical rather than an electric action to produce the sound.

It still had to be playable. Someone had left a folio of music lying on the top of the organ case. The instrument's power switch was in plain sight, tempting.

I clicked it on and heard the familiar rumble of the motor and the gasping wheeze as air began to build in the reservoir. Kicking off my shoes, I slid on the bench, my feet carefully suspended above the pedal board. With my second and third fingers wrapped around the stem engaging the pull-knob Principal stop, I drew it toward me and then in quick succession a sequence of fours and twos.

In front of me was a collection of Early English organ music for manuals. I paused at a Pavanne by an obscure composer with a vaguely Italian name then squared myself with middle C. Despite the lack of a pedal line, my feet instinctively hovered about the first combination of fifths in the bass. Right hand poised above the Great and left above the Swell, I began to play.

Pavannes are graceful courtly dances, but here the composer had interjected playful staccato passages that fairly sang out the beauty of a Renaissance night, illuminated with banks of candles and the gleaming fabrics of the courtiers. It was rough going at first. My feet consistently aimed for an A and hit a G.

I grimaced as I flubbed a series of intricate triplets in my left hand. But as the piece progressed, my connection to it became so compelling, I couldn't wallow in technical problems for long.

In my imagination the mood transformed itself from the secular to the sacred—with all the fierce, impassioned energy of the ancient David alone in the sanctuary of the temple, dancing out his love and fear of the Divine. It was not about the notes any longer. I was caught up in the mystery, my feet picking out the counterpoint as the lyrical harmonies flowed on and on toward the final resolution.

One last chord sequence beckoned. *Rallentando.* I savored every note. And then it was over, in a final rich outpouring of sound trailing off into the silence of the empty sanctuary.

As I exhaled, my breath hung in the air like the echoes of that last note. Energy drained from my body, replaced by the familiar mix of relief and sadness.

"Brava!"

The voice was male. I wasn't alone.

A knot of fear rose in my throat—every organist's worse nightmare. My hands balled into fists on my shaking knees.

Years ago I had been practicing late at night in what I thought was an empty church. After a trip to the restroom, I returned to the organ console to find my purse gone. Something had been out there in that darkness, something evil. It was an unsettling memory, even now —decades later and in broad daylight.

"Bravissima."

This time when the voice repeated itself, I also heard a ragged smattering of applause—at most, the sound of two hands clapping. I let my breath out slowly, counted to ten, then turned on the bench to identify the source.

First impressions didn't help much. I took in the denim shirt, the clerical collar and the faint stubble along the chiseled jaw. Piercing gray-blue eyes were half-hidden under a rumpled shock of graying hair.

"You . . . scared me."

"I'm sorry. I was taking a weed-whacker to that jungle out back, came up for air and heard the organ. You play beautifully. But then you always did!"

It was unsettling to think that anybody on earth could still recall my teenage forays on this instrument. I managed a nervous chuckle.

"Rusty as all-get-out, unfortunately," I said. "But thanks. It was fun to try out the organ again. This is a gorgeous instrument. You don't find working trackers all that often."

"I'm told the reservoir may be shot."

The voice and that all-planes-and-angles face finally came together. An athlete's face with at least one broken nose in its history. This was no stranger.

"Robert. Rob . . . Sims— "

"Guilty."

He must have read the rest in my open-mouthed silence. My childhood acquaintance was the last person on earth I would have expected to find decked out in clerical garb in the sanctuary of any church—much less, this one.

"*Father* Sims." His brow quirked as he said it. "Strange . . . I know. But unlikely as it sounds, there it is."

"You're the . . . rector . . . here?"

"Congregation of forty on a good day. Without my corporate pension, I couldn't afford it. As is, I get most of my salary in produce."

"Sounds positively . . . feudal."

"Not really. Though I'll admit the salary borders on indentured servitude." A half-smile teased at the corner of his mouth. "But the pluses more than make up for it. I get to mow my own labyrinth in the back forty behind the rectory. Most of the parishioners are so grateful that the diocese hasn't closed the place, they'll put up with just about anything I come up with from the pulpit."

With every word out of the man's mouth, I was getting more and more confused. This soft-spoken, self-deprecating man of God was most definitely not the Rob Sims I remembered.

His senior year in high school, Rob Sims was the consummate jock—racking up conquests among the female students with the same relentless ease he displayed tallying up touchdowns on the scoreboard. As a lowly freshman, I had not been on that list.

"Scuttlebutt has it, you're moving back here yourself," he said.

"Yesterday."

"Elm Street . . . your grandparents' place. It's been rented for years, if I'm not mistaken."

He wasn't, about that or the rest of the circumstances surrounding my move either. Only a local would know the saga of ownership of that house. And in a place like this, any increase in the population was also big news. I might as well put the cards on the table.

"Early retirement and a government pension. I hadn't planned on retiring yet. So, those dollars will go a lot farther here than just about any place I know."

"And before all that?"

"Philadelphia."

"Music . . . or teaching . . .?"

"Employment counselor."

In my business, you get good at reading people. Rob's eyebrow arched slightly at that revelation. Although a tight smile tugged at the corner of his mouth, it was something akin to sadness—not humor—I read in his eyes.

"Funny how things turn out," he said.

Funny indeed. I suspected Rob never intended to return here anymore than I had. And certainly not decked out in a clerical collar.

"So, here we are." I forced a smile. "Back where we started."

"Well . . . if you're wondering about the up-side . . . with your background, there's plenty to do around here. Unemployment has been double digit in the county for decades. Nativity has been struggling with some programs to turn that around."

Our laughter felt a trifle strained. But I took the hint.

"Thanks . . . thank you. I just might take you up on that," I said. "But right now . . . face it, moving in has got to come first. The place is wall-to-wall cardboard boxes. If you would have told me a month ago that I'd be moving, lock, stock and way too many barrels, I'd have said you were . . . nuts!"

It came out harsher than I intended. Rob caught it immediately.

"A little . . . *shell-shocked*, are we?"

"Try a lot."

"You're entitled, Char. Shrinks rate moving right up there on the old stress meter with— "

"Tornados and earthquakes. I see you read the same cheery stuff in seminary they dole out in the psych department."

"You forgot the interpersonal biggies. Death and divorce!"

Again I caught that half-smile of his. But it flickered and was gone almost as soon as it began. Something told me he was not speaking in the abstract here, but from first-hand experience. His tone had that cynical edge of a man who has pretty much seen it all at one time or another.

The conversation was going downhill fast and I wasn't in the mood for psycho-babble. My excuse to bail was obvious enough. Those mounds of cartons back home weren't getting any smaller. I thanked him again for letting me try out the keyboard. We said our good-byes.

I was already halfway down the center aisle when Rob's voice stopped me.

"Char . . ., it's really good to see you home again," he said.

By the time I turned and looked back toward the organ, the sanctuary was empty. *Welcome home.*

# ✣ Chapter Four

"Funny how things turn out." Rob Sims' words still echoed in my head as I retraced my route back to the house.

The air tasted raw—that exuberant burst of green that comes after a daylong spring rain. A single thought kept pace with the steady rhythm of my stride. *Why? Why this impulse to return to my roots?*

I was never comfortable with gratuitous spontaneity. My daughters always accused me of thinking just about any or every decision to death. All of which made my spur-of-the-moment choice to move back to Hope all the more unsettling.

Running into Rob Sims only compounded the question marks. I grew up in Hope and thought I knew this place. I had spent my childhood with these people—people like Robert Sims—and had presumed to know them.

That was then. Things change. I had changed, just as surely as that classmate of mine must have wandered through some pretty dark valleys to wind up back here as priest of that tiny parish.

The past, it seems, is just that. *Past.* For me that chaos back there in the homestead, that was the *Now.*

I had left this place with music in my soul. Instead, I spent a lifetime listening for the potential music in the hearts and souls of others—my caseload at the job service. As track records go, mine certainly was commendable, by any standards a life of public service. But for all that, it was not exactly how I or others, even relative strangers like Rob

Sims, had envisioned my future.

*We need to learn to take our dissonance like a man*, the American composer Charles Ives once said. I always had a soft spot in my heart for the guy—a quirky, outspoken insurance salesman struggling to sustain his career as an innovative, even radical composer. It made sense. Looking back over the years since I left this place, I wasn't seeing much harmony between my dreams and where I wound up either. Not much at all.

*Small consolation.* Ives and I weren't the only ones contemplating a major soul crisis.

Back in my own living room I found Marty Santano wandering through the mountains of boxes with all the pathos of a lost kid in a supermarket. His spiked hair was even more extreme than usual. Never knife-edge pressed, his clothes by now had an unmistakable slept-in look.

"I thought you'd just decided to call it quits," he told me. "So I turn in the moving van today . . . and what? I walk back to Philly?"

I tried hard not to laugh out loud. Marty seemed so serious, so utterly forlorn, I half-thought he might burst into tears. But then I had a good idea how he felt.

"Hunger," I told him. "It'll do it to you every time."

"Is there even a *grocery* in this . . . nowhere little town?"

"Even better. Thanks to that realtor, we've got a fridge full of food. If you help me locate a pan and something that might work for plates, I'll rustle us up some scrambled eggs and toast."

"With . . . *what* for a toaster . . .?"

"Scouting 101, Marty. Improvise. I'll use a fork to hold the slices over the gas burner."

Marty was looking around the kitchen with the panic of a deer in the headlights. "Even if I dig the stuff out, where in heck are we gonna put it?"

I shrugged. "Not to worry. Todd Rutterbach left us a pair of box cutters. We'll just start slashing and stashing and in no time—"

"Just like that, huh? Well, don't speed up this slash-and-stash too much. I'm not sure I'm ready to make that haul back to Philly again any time soon."

"I would have thought you couldn't wait to get out of here," I laughed. "And once you're back on your home turf, you'll do fine, by the way."

Marty winced. "Yeah, sure. With you gone? Some guy back there in the employment office is gonna take one look at my file and say, Loser."

"You underestimate yourself," I told him. "Look at me. Ancient.

Unemployed. So, I walk out the door on my very first morning in this tiny . . . *nowhere little town* and some guy points me to a job."

"You're kidding."

Marty had caught me in a slight exaggeration. Sheepishly, I gave my young companion a condensed and more realistic account of my encounter with Father Sims, including that bit about the quaint local custom of paying folks off in root vegetables. Still, Marty looked impressed.

"Ya wouldn't think there would be much to do around here."

"Only goes to show . . ."

Just what, I wasn't prepared to speculate. I was hoping, planning, assuming that together my pension and odd jobs would be enough to float my boat for the rest of my life here. And if it wasn't?

Marty frowned. "Like maybe even I could find something to do around here, too?"

That prospect surprised, maybe even shocked me a little. It didn't fit my assessment of Marty as the consummate urbanite. The plan was to spend a week or two helping me unpack and then catch a bus from Bartonville back to Philly.

I tried to let him down as gently as I could. For starters, my relationship with him seemed to be growing just a tad too maternal for comfort.

"You've never lived in a small town before, Marty."

"No."

"It would be a whole lot different from Philly. And your family would be a day-plus drive away."

"Yeah . . . I guess." Marty shrugged. "Still, a guy's gotta do what he's gotta do. Maybe by the time I help you get unpacked, something might turn up."

*Possible*, I had to admit. But not likely. Not with that double-digit jobless rate.

"You could talk to the realtor," I said. "Maybe even Father Sims."

"I'm not Catholic."

"Neither is he."

With some difficulty, I sketched out the main points of difference between Episcopalians and Roman Catholics. Somewhere in the middle of my rusty theology, Marty's eyes started to glaze over.

"I got it!"

He was talking about the spatula he had just retrieved from the carton he was working on. Still brandishing it overhead like a broadsword, he leaned deeper into the box in a one-handed search of a pan to go with it.

*Deja vu all over again.* It seemed like a lifetime ago that I dumped the contents of my utensil drawer into that very cardboard container and topped it off with my grandmother's hand-braided runner.

"My grandmother made that rug, here in this house," I told him. "Faded now . . . but still usable. In Philly, I had it in the kitchen, too."

"Where?"

"In front of the sink."

"Well, then, back in front of the sink it goes."

Emerging from the box, Marty triumphantly handed me pan and spatula. With a great heaving and shoving, he started to clear enough space to lay down the rug.

"Mission accomplished," he crowed. "See . . .? The place is starting to look like home already."

I had to hand it to Marty. He was resilient. As we camped out on adjacent stacks of boxes polishing off our breakfast of slightly scorched toast and passable eggs served off mismatched pie tins, I found myself fixating on the cracked plaster and Stone Age wiring—that, and the syncopated *drip-DRIP, drip-DRIP* of the kitchen faucet.

"Renovating this place is going to take a small fortune," I said. "New drywall. An electrician, if there is even an electrician left in town."

The closest town of any size was arch-rival Bartonville, fifteen miles away. And with two major interstates in their backyard, skilled contractors down there would have their pick of jobs in the Pittsburgh-Youngstown, Ohio corridor. But then Marty, as it turns out, had been pondering his own solution to my human resource problems.

"Ya know," he said, "I could help fix those walls. Forget the drywall. Just a little patching plaster and a fresh coat of paint would do wonders."

Visions of dollar signs danced through my head. My young companion was used to big city wage scales. Although I had agreed to pay him a modest sum to help me with the worst of the unpacking, the old budget was not going to permit even that outlay indefinitely. I told him so.

"No problem." He shrugged. "Room and board are fine, until I find something."

"Marty," I said slowly, "I don't want to take advantage— "

"Gotta eat, don't I?"

True enough. But it occurred to me, ridiculous as it seemed given our age differences, that Marty might also be latching on to some classic client-counselor emotional lifeline here. The responsible thing would be to nip that kind of dependence in the bud.

"We'll think about it," I said. "Meantime, there are a heck of a lot of boxes out there. And we better turn in that rental truck in Bartonville before they think we've moved it on a lot and are living out of the thing."

We had a plan. Together Marty and I made that run to Bartonville to return the van, stopping off at Todd Rutterbach's hardware on the way home for the basics—buckets, scouring and cleaning chemicals, sponges and a jumbo box of rags. Once again my poor hatchback was loaded to the gunwales.

Nothing like breaking rocks in a quarry to clear the old head. While I started opening boxes, Marty scrubbed like a fiend at the cupboards, inside and out, to accommodate all the stacks of dishes and the remnants of my Philly larder that I had been unwrapping. By mid-afternoon it actually was possible to navigate the kitchen without stumbling over cartons.

Even with the cold front and all the windows and back door open, Marty and I sat there on my antique wooden fiddle-back chairs in sweat-through tee-shirts staring at each other. My hands were so sore from lifting that I couldn't even make a fist. Marty looked ready to fall over any minute.

"I sure could use a shower," he said.

He was getting no argument from me—except, of course, that we had been aiming all our efforts at the kitchen. My sleeping bag was still in that bathtub and the towels nowhere to be found.

"If it's creature comforts we're looking for," I said, "maybe we had better switch to the rooms upstairs for a while. Set up the beds. Clear out the bathroom enough to make it usable."

Marty scowled. "The box cutters have run out of blades."

"The hardware won't close for another hour or two. What say we make a run down there and then pick up a pizza at the mini-mart for dinner. At least we won't have to worry about cooking."

It appeared to be the prospect of food that did the trick. Marty stood up, stretched, and with his jaw set, headed toward the half-open back door.

"Anybody home?"

My young helper's hand froze on the door knob. Neither one of us had seen or heard anyone coming.

Smiling at him through the screen was an apparition straight out of the seventies. A large salt-and-pepper-haired woman in a tie-dye tent of a dress had come up the back steps and was standing on the porch. Cradled in her daisy oven mitts was an enormous object that appeared to be some sort of baked goods.

"Rhubarb pie," she boomed. "Welcome to the neighborhood."

Marty's eyes were as big as the pie plate. "What's rhubarb?"

"Later," I whispered.

The woman started to thrust her culinary masterpiece in my hand. Before I could respond, she pulled it back.

"Bad idea. Way too hot," she said. "You don't have mitts."

"The counter's fine. This is really wonderful of you to— "

The woman had set down the pie on a cutting board and was already moving on, literally. Talking non-stop she was checking out the kitchen with all the curiosity of a four-year-old.

"Grace," she said. "Grace Alanson. Your neighbor. Our back yards butt up against each other. Got no dogs to dig up your grass. Deaf as a post but wear a hearing aid, so you don't have to put up second-hand with my choice of radio stations—had quite enough of that high-decibel Jefferson Airplane back in the day, I guess. I've lived in that wreck of a place at least half my life. You need a joint once in a while . . . or just a good jaw over the back fence? I'm there."

It wasn't quite accurate to say we grew up together since she was four years older than I was. My last working memory of Grace was her coming home from college in this fume-belching van spray-painted with rainbows and peace signs. An Earth Mother even then.

"I'm sure you don't remember me," I smiled. "But I'm— "

"Little Charlise. Home from the big city— "

So help me, as I stood there incredulous, the woman actually started to sing. "Take me home . . .!"

I had to admit, it was a creditable rendition of John Denver, though with a healthy dose of Janis Joplin thrown in. The woman must have lungs like a fireplace bellows. Marty's jaw dropped, then he blurted out the only reaction possible.

"Wow . . .!"

"Those were the days, my friend," Grace chuckled. "Even here in little old Hope, Pennsylvania."

"Mom and Gram told me that you had moved back here, Grace."

"They were always good to me." Her face took on a faraway look as she thought about it. "I really missed 'em when they passed. It must have been tough. Less than a year apart, one after the other like that."

"Yes. It was."

Going on a decade later, the pain of that memory still wrenched at my heart. Mom nursed Gram through her terrible battle with cancer, then one night fell asleep herself and never woke up. The Coroner called it Heart Failure and left it at that. The passing of the generations had been sudden and complete. I wept, rolled up my sleeves and went to work, cleaning out the house for rental. Anything rather than sell this powerful reminder of my past.

And so here I was. Back where it all had begun.

"It seems strange," I admitted, "to walk through the house . . . so full of my things now, not theirs."

Grace had a grin as broad as her ample frame. "Bet they'd think it was a hoot finally to see you back here. They loved this old place."

"I wasn't planning on retiring here anytime soon. It just happened."

"Best stuff in life sometimes does." Grace was on a roll. "Learned that the hard way. My folks were so much older than your mom. I was riding the Grand Funk railway . . . starting my own design studio. I never ever thought I'd be back in this backwater taking care of them. But stuff happens. Before I knew it, I was teaching Home Ec at the community college in Bartonville and running a little tailor business on the side. Put in my 30 years and quit. Retired, loving it and then . . . whammo, I find myself right back in the thick of it."

"You're still working, then?"

Grace had to be Rob's age—I vaguely remembered the two of them graduating together, even then as poles apart as two people could be. While the private Rob Sims was anything but readable, this neighbor of mine made it pretty clear what you saw was what you got.

Her sun-tanned face was deeply etched with as many smile as frown lines now. Under that still-thick brillo-pad hair, her blue eyes crackled with life and fun. The smells emanating from that pie of hers were incredible. If she told me she had just opened a bakery, I for one would be a regular. I told her so.

She just laughed, shook her head. "Retired into a volunteer job with the local Carpenter project over at Nativity—Father Rob Sim's baby. Sort of a local Episcopal Joseph-the-Worker program, helping the folks around here find jobs. I'm in charge of the Suit-'em-Up team that puts together work clothes, tools, boots, whatever folks need if somebody is gonna hire 'em."

"I've heard the unemployment rate around here is a real problem."

"Sad." Hand on hip, Grace took up a don't-mess-with-me stance. "But goodness knows we're *trying*. Father Rob said you might be interested in—"

"Thanks, but she's got me," Marty said gruffly. "I can do just about anything when it comes to building and fix— !"

"Relax, sweetie!" Grace laughed. "Don't get your knickers in a twist. Father just thought Char here might want to volunteer for a little counseling once she gets settled in. Goodness knows, we need her."

"News sure travels fast," I said.

It was barely seven hours since I had stumbled on Rob Sims in that sanctuary. But then after my realtor's preemptive help with the moving yesterday, I should have been prepared for just about anything.

Grace laughed. "You have no idea!"

Before either Marty or I knew what hit us, the reinforcements took charge. After about fifteen minutes of chit-chat, good neighbor Grace announced she was going to help. Just turn her loose. She would tackle the bathroom upstairs single-handed.

I was too pooped to protest. While Grace was stacking towels and sheets in the bathroom cupboards, Marty and I horsed enough boxes out of the way in the master bedroom that we could set up my grandmother's ornate brass and iron bed frame and slide the mattress into place.

I had offered Marty his choice of sleeping quarters. Smarting big time from where I had dropped the box spring on his foot, he announced he was going to check out the second guest room. He had already inspected the other option—complete with a turreted bay window—directly across the hall from me. Grace must have noticed him limping down the hall past the bathroom.

"You must need linens, Char!" I heard her bellow. "What's the color . . . blue in there . . .? These blue stripe-y things would fit. Wild. They look like Great-grama's ticking mattress cover. Here, kid . . . if you take 'em to Char, you'll save me a trip."

Loaded down with mattress pads, sheets, duvet and cover, and a trio of more or less matching toss pillows, Marty picked his way back across the bedroom in my direction, stumbling against the remaining stack of boxes in the process. I had been sitting on the bare mattress ever since he left, utterly incapable of putting one foot in front of the other.

"Is that woman on something?" he groaned. " . . . 'Cause if she is, I sure could use some. I'm running out of steam."

My laughter had an edge of desperation, like an overtired four-year-old about to launch into a high-decibel crying jag. It trailed off on a rising note, followed by a hiccup of sound as I caught my breath again.

"You and me both," I gasped. "Hang in there, Marty. Once we get the bed set up for you in your guest room of choice, I'll plead insanity and shut us down for the day."

"Thanks, Mrs. Howard."

"Char," I said brusquely. "You're not on my caseload now. I answer to Char."

Marty grinned. "Okay, *Char.* I can do that."

That's pretty much the way it happened, except Grace wouldn't leave until we promised her that we would accept a casserole she had ready to warm in the microwave. After dinner, Marty ensconced himself in the half-cleared guest room across the hall—complete with a portable TV he found accidentally on one of his box foraging expeditions.

"Darn thing only picks up one channel," he grumbled when he showed me what his nesting instincts had accomplished. "And everything on it looks like we're in the middle of one gosh-awful snowstorm."

I laughed. "This is rural Pennsylvania," I told him, "not downtown Philly. I'm really surprised we even get that good a signal—considering the station is halfway over the mountain."

"They got cable out here?"

Marty had the look of a man reassessing his tentative relocation plans. It had been a good forty years since television reception had been a big issue for me. But I vaguely remembered parade-watching Thanksgiving mornings downstairs in the front parlor.

"Don't know, maybe satellite? In the morning we could check out the roof."

Marty yawned. "Probably would just fall asleep anyway, even if the darn thing worked. This moving stuff is hard."

I couldn't dispute that. Although I had planned to settle into the tub for a good, long soak, I cut it short and after only perfunctory ablutions, crawled into my freshly-made bed.

Waiting for sleep to come, I stared at the bare walls around me with the cabbage roses on the wallpaper thrusting their luxurious blooms toward the ceiling. Here and there, faint rectangles in the pattern seemed to stand out against the faded paper around it.

*Pictures.* That had to be where pictures had hung, for decades from the look of it.

Tired as I was, I couldn't help digging through my childhood memories for images of how the master bedroom had looked in Mom and Grandma's day. I came up with only fuzzy impressions of oversize photographs in thick wooden frames and one especially—a striking oval mirror with beveled glass. Somewhere among my cartons, I had stored the surviving mementoes of those relatives known and unknown.

Giving in to a yawn, I vowed to dust off the best of the treasures and find a way to incorporate at least some of them into my decorating scheme. Whatever that turned out to be.

Bizarre what sticks in your head from all those liberal arts courses in college. *Everyone's life needs some harmony and rhythm*, Plato wrote. My instincts told me connecting past and present was becoming a major issue in making my own world liveable again.

In Philly I had defined my space by my day job—looking for relief from a sterile, cubicle-dominated working environment. The result was simple urban chic with little arty touches like fiber art wall hangings and my studio upright piano to stamp the apartment with my own personality. But here I had no frame—only disconnected objects as my palette.

We can't go home again, but I had. John Denver's country roads ran up hard against Thomas Wolfe as I contemplated the incongruity of where I found myself.

Up until now I had been amused at and even detached from young Marty's struggles to make sense of small town life. With a shock, it came to me that in the end, our situations weren't really all that different. I was a stranger here, too, in my own way—and like Grace Alanson so many years ago, an involuntary pilgrim.

So many rural and small town Americans of my generation had chafed at the confines of our childhood heritage, eager to become part of something larger than ourselves. We left and most of us never intended to return. Unlike Rob Sims, I sensed Grace had made her peace long ago with the eddies that had transported her here.

I found myself wondering what would it take for me to feel at peace, instead of like a displaced person, sleeping in a strange bed in the town and the house that had nurtured my earliest memories. As I clicked off the light, the darkness closed around me.

The house softly creaked and groaned as old houses do—reliving its memories, the joy and the pain of them. *Mine now.* When the moon rose it was casting pale shadows through the bedroom window and fingers of light reached out across the ceiling toward my bed.

*And the evening and the morning were the* . . .who knows *what* day it was in the great scheme of things? *My first one back in the homestead anyway.* My eyelids flickered and closed. I slept.

# ✥ Chapter Five

Maybe mirrors don't lie. Still, I was hoping desperately that mine did. *Day Two, in Hope.*

It was the first time I had ventured to look at myself since my cross-country trek. In my now box-free upstairs bathroom, I stared back at my reflection with the sensation of waking from a long sleep.

I left this house a girl and returned a grandmother. Under the salt-and-pepper hair that depended on cowlicks for its curl were still those high cheekbones I shared with Great-grandmother Grunwald. What could have been my mother's eyes looked wearily back at me, rimmed by their network of laugh lines and dark circles from stress and too little sleep.

After far more decades as a widow than years as a bride, I had struck a tenuous bargain with solitude. In that mirror I was anything but alone. My life, my journey was coming together in this place with those strong Grunwald women who loved so passionately if not always well.

Despite outward appearances, I felt a girl again in their company—caught up in some bizarre time warp, aided and abetted by those chance encounters with Rob Sims and now my neighbor Grace. It was as if my very presence here had thrust me willy-nilly back through the chronology of my life, with all the adolescent uncertainty and angst that went with it.

Out of the blue I found myself transported back to Mrs. Brendorm's high school English class. Could I still articulate—in two concise sentences—my intentions in leaving this place, or now even more so, in returning. Now that it was over, what had that career of mine really meant? What kind of woman would I have become if my husband hadn't died so young?

The memories and questions were as raw and painful as yesterday. The answers seemed as dark and unknowable. And yet there was my reflection in that mirror in front of me, challenging me not just to look but to see.

From my years as a counselor, I knew the symptoms—absolutely predictable. These were growing pains, pure and simple, the inevitable outcome of grief and loss. And I could pinpoint to the second when I first admitted to myself that I was not immune.

*5:07:34 PM.* It was my last day at the Job Service. I was sitting alone in the gloom of the parking garage in my hatchback, the accumulated mementoes of my career stashed in boxes behind me.

Something, most likely a flash of a reflection off the windshield, had pulled my gaze downward from the dashboard clock to the passenger seat where I had tossed my purse and my ID badge.

*Nothing remarkable.* It was just the usual standard-issue security pass, one in a series we had worn ever since the Oklahoma City bombing. Yet strangely disoriented, I found myself drawn to it, only half understanding what it was I was seeing.

Staring up at me from that laminated photo was a woman who, from one minute to the next, no longer existed. *My face, yet suddenly a total stranger.*

The professional in me took over. I knew by rote how to size up someone sitting across that job service desk from me. The makeup in that photo was impeccable, a woman dressed for success—with a subdued gray suit jacket and textured multicolor shell. Discreet silver jewelry picked up the tones in that fashionably short, salon-cut hair.

Those were a counselor's eyes looking up at me, dark and searching under strong, arching brows. The smile was generous and inviting, practiced at putting a client at ease without a single word. The woman in that photo was at the height of her game and knew it. Professionally anyway.

It was my name I read on that badge, but certainly a far cry from *Char Howard the retiree* whose hands at that moment were shaking on the wheel at the very thought of turning that key in the ignition. Life was moving on and I had to move with it.

✣

A lot of bleak miles of asphalt and Interstate stood between that first desperate soul-searching and my face staring back at me from the mirror in the homestead. There was no going back.

My mouth set in a determined line, I ran a brush through my hair and dashed on lipstick and blush. As an afterthought, I even indulged in a hint of lash-lengthener.

*I might look like death,* I vowed. *But it was high time to start thinking, Resurrection!*

Any way I looked at it, it was going to take one heck of a makeover to make my new home habitable. And my life with it.

As I slashed open cartons and unwrapped the past, unpacking began to take on the epic proportions of an archaeological dig. Sifting through the layers of accumulated living is a tough business. The aching that results from the effort is not just in our arms or backs, but in the heart.

It quickly became impossible to agonize over the where's and the why's of every picture frame or wicker basket, every spray of silk flowers or treasured art object lovingly passed down from one relative or another, or crafted by some child or grandchild over the years. *Just do it*, I kept telling myself.

Reconciling all that intergenerational ambiguity could come later. *Just stake a claim here and move on.*

Wielding hammer and picture hooks, I hung the legacy of my past on the walls for safekeeping, however temporary. Furniture by default landed in whatever arrangement it took to get it out of the traffic flow. At least Marty and I now had a chance to sit down when we couldn't stand up any longer.

Under the circumstances, my young friend showed remarkable patience and restraint. If in my anxiety to 'get settled', we shuffled the couch or another heavy object around several times before moving on, Marty rarely complained.

The only source of friction was the choice of radio stations. And even there we arrived at an uneasy truce, with the strains of my Abba and Albinoni one minute and his Green Day and Godsmack the next. When Grace Alanson was on site, her husky contralto belted out anything and everything with a frightening elan. Even with my limited experience with choirs, I couldn't help be impressed by her seemingly limitless range and repertoire.

Best of all, each of Grace's appearances meant more culinary largesse. Baked donuts (they're healthier she assured us), eggplant sandwiches, and zucchini fritters, along with hearty country favorites like meatloaf and mac and cheese. Marty admitted to never having eaten so many "interesting" vegetable concoctions in all his life.

Sunday came and went without my appearance at the Episcopal Church. While I wrestled with cartons, Marty professed howling heathendom and slept until noon. It vaguely occurred to me to wonder whether the good Father Sims would notice or care. On Monday, I found out. I had lived in my new hometown for just over a week.

This time I was in Rutterbach's hardware when our paths crossed. I headed around the aisle crammed with nuts and bolts and fasteners of various shapes and sizes toward the shelving stocked full of cleaning supplies, when out of the blue . . . there he was—in clerical collar, jeans and a faded ball hat with a whimsical Holy Bowlers logo on the front.

"Father Sims . . . hello."

"Rob."

I hesitated. That whole "priest" business still seemed surreal, especially given the graphic on that hat of his—with its bowling ball looking for all the world like a halo.

"Rob, then."

"I heard from Grace after church yesterday that you've really been making great progress over there on Elm Street."

I winced. At least he didn't bookend his news with the observation that while Grace had been out there in the pews, I had not.

"More progress on some days than others," I said. "For the life of me, I don't know how or when I managed to accumulate all that stuff."

"Been there—although fortunately, when I downscaled into the parsonage, community property laws pretty much solved that problem."

*Divorce.* I hadn't been wrong about the battle scars, I found myself thinking. His smile didn't reach his eyes.

"You've been back here a while?" I asked.

"Three years, give or take."

I remembered his mentioning something about corporate pensions. Now that *was* easy enough—picturing him ensconced behind a huge mahogany desk, hand clenched around a phone receiver, all nervous energy, barking out marching orders to some hapless underlings out in the field.

"It must have been quite a switch," I said. "The seminary, and before that . . . what—sales?"

"Close." Rob looked uncomfortable. "Advertising, actually. In

Pittsburgh. There just came a point when none of it made sense any more. I lost my . . .only daughter to a drunk driver. Amazing how your priorities change when your back is against the wall."

"I'm . . . I can't even . . . imagine," I said softly "what I would do if something . . . happened to my two girls."

"They live near here?"

"Jen—Jennifer is in Pittsburgh. Sarah is in Cleveland."

"Nice. They're close."

I chuckled. "But not too close. Mothers and daughters can be a bit intense."

"Trust me, fathers and sons have their moments, too."

"You have sons?" I said.

"One. Ted."

There it was again, that tight and guarded look. *Secrets*, I thought to myself. No one is immune.

All those years ago, if I would have expected anyone to be leading a charmed life at this stage of the game, it would have been Rob Sims. And yet I knew I was not imagining it—that bottomless sadness behind those eyes. The loss of a child was enough to break any man but there was more. I sensed it, couldn't help wondering.

An eager young clerk was hovering at my elbow trying to get my attention, awkwardly shifting from foot to foot in the process.

"Ma'am, d'ja need help?"

"You have no idea," I sighed. "I'm running through rags and paper toweling like there's no tomorrow. Suggestions?"

It was Rob who intervened. "We've got an amazing assortment of factory-reject clothing in the undercroft among the things Grace uses with her jobs program," he said. "Not even fit for free, Grace calls it. You'd be doing the church a favor if you get some of it out of there. All that flammable fabric in the basement is turning into one . . . heck of a fire hazard."

"You're serious?! That's wonderful. Do I need a key?"

"If you want, I'll walk over there with you and show you where the stuff is—although the church is never locked."

"Thanks," I said. "I'd like that."

The teenager on Rutterbach's sales crew had the disappointed look of someone whose commission at the end of the day just took a hit. To his credit Rob noticed and was quick to make amends.

"Just need to pick up a couple of light bulbs for the sacristy," he said. "And while you're at it, Nate . . . will you order some of that industrial sealer for the floor in the undercroft? The sexton has started complaining again . . ."

Fishing several four-packs of bulbs off the impulse-shelf next to the cash register, Rob flashed the price stickers in the young man's direction. Scrambling to jot them down on his receipt book, Nate looked mollified. His morning, it seems, was not a total loss.

Once outside, Rob settled in alongside me as we headed back along Main Street and then turned on the side street leading to the Episcopal church. *A gentleman of the old school*, I smiled to myself. He still made it a point of taking the curb side. Forehead creased in a frown, Rob also seemed intent on steering the safest course around the heaving sections of concrete in the sidewalks.

"I really appreciate this," I told him.

"No problem. Monday is my day off—ostensibly, anyway."

"You don't say Morning Prayer every day, then."

"Tuesdays and Thursdays. We never get much of a turnout, but it's steady. You know, *where two or three are gathered . . .*"

We were passing a sprawling old gingerbread gothic monstrosity of a house with a kayak propped up against the porch rail. Just beyond it along the street, I spotted the familiar red door of Nativity.

"The rectory is right next door?" I guessed.

"Handy, I'll admit, although tough on a guy's privacy."

He shook his head, remembering. "The first week I was here, at least six parishioners let slip in casual conversation that they couldn't figure out why the lights were on way past midnight every night. Oh yes, or understand why I had taken down the clothesline posts out back."

I laughed. "A decadent life style if I ever saw one."

"So, I told 'em my best sermons came to me in the middle of the night. Plus, that clothesline reminded me too much of goal posts. Unless they wanted their priest to start limping around after kicking too many field goals into the neighbor's back yard, I told them, it was a good idea just to remove temptation entirely."

*Enough to make anybody paranoid,* I chuckled to myself. One thing was obvious. Unlike some of my other contemporaries who had been stars on the gridiron, Rob had avoided the downslope from six-pack abs to kegger around the midriff. I was thinking of the kayak. *Good for him,* I thought.

As a late-life convert to regular workouts myself, I knew all too well the effort it took. *The spirit indeed is willing . . . but the flesh?*

"It's depressing what time does to the old bod," I told him.

"Every time I touch a keyboard, the initial reaction is this terrible battle between head and hands. My brain says, *Go*—though my body takes a while to get the message, *especially* if I know somebody else is listening."

"You'd never know it . . . hearing you play last week," Rob said. "Years ago—I remember you were the regular Sunday School organist at Nativity. It sounds like you've kept it up."

"On and off," I shrugged. "Subbing for organists on leave or vacation doesn't take an awful lot of practice—although if I had stopped playing altogether, even that level of hand-eye motor coordination wouldn't last long. Unlike you though, I'm not quite ready to rip out the goal posts yet— "

The laugh lines crinkled around his eyes as he thought about it. It still wasn't a full-fledged smile, but nice.

"Have you ever thought about picking it up again, Char? Professionally, I mean."

"I hadn't—but then again my computer and all my counseling files are still buried in the heap of boxes marked Office. While I'm down here, fooling around on that keyboard . . ."

Maybe, just maybe after all these years, I was finally getting a life. In Philly, looking back on it, I seem to have been on auto-pilot longer than I can remember. If I was honest with myself, there were a lot of things I hadn't thought about, including how nice it felt to have someone to confide in again.

"Anyway, it occurred to me, I should tell you," Rob said, "you're welcome to practice at Nativity any time you want."

"Tempting. Thanks." It was sensitive of him to offer. "Still . . . I'd hate to run into your organist's practice time— "

"Not to worry. Wilma Smoller is ninety and her Hammond at home has to be about the same vintage. It's not realistic for her to crawl down here during the week to practice. As is, her son sits on the bench with her on Sundays to make sure she doesn't get lost in the middle of a hymn."

I laughed. "Face it . . . playing is addictive. There's an old saw that organists tend to die on the bench. And when they do, they'd better be prepared to play their own funerals—because they aren't going to find a sub!"

"We found that out the hard way a time or two." Rob grimaced, remembering. "Until you blew back into town, old Wilma was one of four active organists in the whole county."

"Typical."

"Still, even with the shortage, you didn't choose to make a living at it."

"The operative word isn't *choice* here. It's *living*," I told him. "The number of full-time, decent-salaried church positions for church musicians was always pitiful. Even now with the shortages, most churches just buy a boom-box and a canned year of hymns on disc rather than worry about maintaining organist salaries—or if they have money at all, install organs with digital record-replay devices."

"*Shazaam* . . . just push the button."

I nodded. "And then I suppose places like Nativity probably just try to limp along with a revolving door of minimum-wage volunteers . . ."

"You got that right," he said.

"Even back when, it didn't take the counselors at Hope High to tell me that the prospects were grim. Although they did, with predictable regularity—unsolicited. I fought alternatives tooth and nail, but when I finally had to declare a college major, I had taken more aptitude and career interest tests than my whole caseload of clients the first year working at the job service. Counseling seemed as good a choice as any."

Rob quirked an eyebrow. "You're dead-on, about expectations. Try bucking the myth that All-State athletes belong in business." He hesitated. "Still, I always had you pegged as being so focused. Not the type to— "

"Blunder along, looking for a lightning bolt that never comes? And before I know it, I'm pushing retirement and never quite figured out how I got there!"

"Ouch," he winced. "At the risk of sounding way, way too. . . *pastoral*, I'd say you seem rather . . . hard on yourself."

I felt my breath explode outward in a rush—sheepish at how much of my current malaise I had let surface. Bristling, too, that he of all people had called me on it.

This seemed to be a man who let his guard down rarely, if ever. Was it a legacy of his years on the football field looking out at those linebackers bearing down on him, or of what came later? *Maybe*, I concluded, *a little bit of both.*

"Just honest, I'd like to think," I said slowly. "Some of my hesitation back then was just plain old-fashioned cowardice. I used to get so nervous before I played in public, I'd actually throw up in the bushes."

Rob's eyebrows lifted. Both of them this time.

"You should have seen me when I gave my first sermon. My hands still feel like encased in ice when I'm waiting back there in that sacristy."

I kept trying to picture those strong, sure quarterback's hands intimidated by anything. I wasn't having any luck.

"I wouldn't feel like such a . . . hypocrite," I said. "Except all those years, professionally, I kept counseling my clients, 'Go with your passion'—when I had no clue at all what mine really was. Still don't."

Priest or no priest, Rob Sims was poking around way too deeply in my life story for comfort. Worse, I was aiding and abetting it. I had prided myself on my go-with-the-flow ethos all those years of single-parenthood. Yet in the end, here I was, as alone as I was when I left this place, back where my journey had begun, in this tiny dot on the map in the foothills of the Alleghenies.

Together we climbed the short flight of stairs to the front door of Nativity. Hand on the wrought iron door latch, Rob turned and looked at me. His voice was low.

"When it comes to our life's passion, I've got to console myself," he said, "that we're still young enough to find out."

While I settled down in the undercroft to sort through the potential rag supply, I half-expected Rob to wander off upstairs and do whatever pastors do with another service coming up in a week. Instead, he turned one of the beat-up old wooden Sunday School chairs around, and his arms leaning on the chair back, he settled down to watch my progress.

*Amazing what we can hear when we aren't really listening!* It didn't take much to figure out that Father Robert Sims wasn't exactly a poster child for a purpose-driven life. I suspected, he would be the first to admit it.

And yet here I was—with a little help from that most unlikely of sources—having just admitted what I hadn't wanted to believe when I left Philly. *I hadn't just taken refuge here to nurse my wounds or retreat into the past. I had come here searching for options.*

Even that bleak afternoon of my retirement, as I sat weeping in the parking garage, with the NPR commentator droning on about adults and music, I had sensed doors opening. Out of hand I dismissed, then and now, the prospect of offering piano lessons. That much was clear. When it came to music, it wasn't the theory of the thing I loved but the doing.

Obviously my home parish Nativity already had an organist. But my trusty wreck of a hatchback was reliable enough that if I drew a commute-circle around Hope, I was bound to hit a congregation somewhere that needed one. While the pay would be worse than awful, it should at least handle the gas and a Sunday brunch somewhere afterward.

"When we were kids and I used to drift off like that, I think the expression of choice used to be, *a penny for your thoughts.*"

It was only then I realized that all that time, Rob had been patiently watching me, apparently trying to gauge my mood. I winced.

"Just about what they were worth . . . two cents."

I told him about my very tentative notion about looking around for an organ gig once the dust settled. Rob smiled.

"Smart move," he said. "One of the local churches actually wound up hiring a rock musician who didn't read music because they couldn't find anyone else. Wish we could make you an offer at Nativity. But no such luck. Old Wilma will hang on 'til the Apocalypse, heaven help us."

"Come on now! Nobody can be that bad."

"Mainly slow." He chuckled, shook his head. "So slow that I've arbitrarily started cutting hymn verses to two. Unless memory fails, you always took liturgical music at one heck of a clip."

"I never suspected you were such a . . . fan— "

"Not entirely." Rob paused. "Every time you held forth on that bench, my mom used to point you out as a shining example of the kind of girl she wished I'd be hanging out with."

I laughed. "You're kidding! You must have . . . hated my guts. At least you were 'hanging out'. I was spending my weekends banging away on the family spinet."

"Discipline—there's nothing wrong with that. I always felt most at home out there on the gridiron, too . . . despite all the party-animal rumors floating around whenever my name came up."

"Which was pretty much after each weekend's game."

Rob shrugged. "Unfortunately, my knees gave out in college—which quickly put the brakes on any jock-of-the-year aspirations I might have had."

"And the appeal was the sheer . . . physicality of it?"

"Not really."

His voice had taken on that faraway tone again. "I'd say, the simplicity, the clarity of the game. There was a goal. You saw it for what it was, knew the obstacles. And yet come hell or high water, you just fought to get there—like you and that pipe organ . . ."

"Way too noble," I corrected him, "at least at first. If I practiced, Mom let me out of doing the dishes. And then of course, it's tough to buck the gene pool. Mom was an avid keyboard player. Her folks named her for the patron saint of music, Cecelia."

"And your dad?"

"Bass in a jazz band when he wasn't flying shuttles to one coast or other. Apparently I was a regular strand off the old double helix. Mom claimed that when I was two, I pulled myself upright in front of the keyboard of the piano in my parents' living room and played. And legend has it, it wasn't just the banging of a toddler. I wasn't even tall enough to see what was making those wonderful sounds."

So much for nature. I didn't volunteer that nurture was more ambivalent, starting with my name, Charlise Amelia Grunwald.

I owed that strange legacy to my airline pilot father. The Amelia—as in Earhart—was obvious enough. *Charlise*, quickly shortened to Char, was both his desperation tribute to Lindbergh and a concession to reality. I was not the hoped-for son and heir.

In any case, my mother had other variations in mind. By the time I was four, she saw to it that I was taking piano lessons twenty minutes twice a week from a club musician who taught me to read notes. The man was a recovering alcoholic who periodically exorcized his angst with a frenetic outpouring of Gershwin on the Grunwald family spinet, much to my open-mouth wonderment.

I am told that after my first recital, that same teacher—bleary-eyed but genuinely moved at my rendition of "The Tall Trees"—told my father that I oozed musicality out of every pore. But even the accolades could not change the realities of my parents' marriage. Six months later, citing irreconcilable differences, my father flew the friendly skies from Pittsburgh to who-knows-where and never came back. Mom and I moved back to Hope.

The childhood stirring of regret deep in my guts was easier to suppress now. All that was a very long time ago.

I had buried both mother and father, and with them a lingering world of dashed hopes and broken promises. This one thing remained intact and unsullied—my images of that polished golden wood of the instrument case upstairs in that sanctuary, smooth and responsive under my hands.

Rob was looking at me strangely. Just how long had I been meandering off alone down memory lane again?

"And yet you never gave up, never stopped playing . . . not totally anyway, all these years," he said. "Even though you did the practical thing—got a job, got married . . ."

Subtly he had changed the subject. I already told him about my girls. It occurred to me to wonder whether it was just polite curiosity or a deliberate fishing expedition. I couldn't tell. His own ring finger was conspicuously bare.

"My husband, Len, was in the military. He shipped out to 'Nam and never came back. My kids were one and three."

"I'm sorry."

I managed a wan smile. *Charlise Howard nee Grunwald, widow, single mom.* At first that label had been a way of coping. By now it had become such a reflex, I could almost have been describing someone else.

"You do what you have to do," I said.

A smile twitched at the corner of his mouth. "Tougher than it sounds."

I was getting used to those awkward pauses. Subtle signals, I decided, that I had stepped over some invisible boundary, beyond which Rob was not prepared to let anyone go.

"I'll admit," I said slowly, "the myth of closure is not always what it's cracked up to be. I've had my share of dark moments."

I thought I saw the tight set of his jaw ease a little. He chuckled.

"We can all use a crack-aside-of-the-head pep talk once in a while on the subject of new beginnings," he said.

"Right now, I'm one of 'em. When I came here a week ago, I was still stunned . . . mad, worried . . . cruising down *denial* like a boatload of tourists, for all my platitudes to my clients over the years. Still am, I guess."

"For starters, finances can be tricky . . ."

I laughed. "Tell me about it. Though a government pension helps, even when you're just rank and file. No—I'd say it's more the fear of starting over, a heartbeat away from sixty, no less."

"Change is never easy . . . at any age."

I let out an impatient sigh. "Neither are these blasted knots!"

Rob had hunkered down on the floor alongside me where I was struggling to turn a hideous-looking necktie into a support strap and makeshift handle for the bag of flannel scraps and sheeting I had put together. Every time I tried to pull the knot tight, the overstuffed bag slipped out again. I was getting nowhere.

"I'm going to walk out of here looking like a bag lady."

"Let me," he said.

With some difficulty, I held the bundle steady while Rob worked at securing the knot. Our hands brushed, touched—even together we were struggling. On the third try, the knot mercifully tightened, held.

"S-simple—piece a cake." I forced a laugh. "Are we good or what?"

At that we made eye contact, enough to stop anyone in their tracks. Our faces were inches from each other, so close I could feel his warm breath against my skin. I felt as if someone were cutting off my air supply.

*Dear God . . . this guy is attracted to you!* It had been a long time since a man had looked at me with that intensity, even longer since I had felt myself responding in kind. I felt myself blushing like a schoolgirl, utterly incapable of rational thought.

"Rob . . .?"

My voice shook. I didn't have time to say another word.

Just as unexpectedly as it began, everything changed. It was like that awful moment you realize you've touched a hot stove and that it's going to hurt. *No matter what you do.*

Rob froze, shock and confusion in his eyes—that, and emotions I couldn't identify. Abruptly, he jerked his head away and with the swift, fluid instincts of an athlete, he was on his feet looking down at me. His voice was gruff.

"I shouldn't have . . . that was totally inappropriate," he said. "I'm sorry."

"But n-nothing . . . you didn't—we didn't . . . "

*Nothing happened?* But somehow it had. And even as I frantically tried to distance myself, I realized how ridiculous it was to pretend otherwise.

Rob's face darkened. He started to respond—stopped.

"Take whatever else you need," he said. "Don't bother to lock the door when you leave. We never do."

With that, he turned and headed for the stairs. I could read the tension in his shoulders, the pent-up anger in his stride. *Aimed at himself? Or was it me . . . my response?* One thing was certain—that reaction wasn't just some belated case of scruples because Rob was a priest and I was a potential parishioner!

Hand on the stair rail, he turned—wrestling with something so desolate, so terrible that words failed. My own expression must have been an open book, the tears ominously close to the surface. Rob's voice fell to a harsh whisper.

"It's not you, Char," he said. "All this was my fault, pure and simple. It'll never happen again."

Not long after the echoes of Rob's footsteps on the stairs had died away, I heard the muffled thud of the church door. The sound was like a slap in the face—brutal and final.

# ✥ Chapter Six

*Think, Char. You have to think—focus.*

For once my well-honed survivor skills seemed to fail me. I just sat there on the hard, painted concrete floor of the undercroft. My hands were trembling.

*Cold.* It was getting cold down there—and Marty would be wondering where on earth I had gone. Teeth chattering, I managed to clamber awkwardly to my feet, the bundle of cleaning rags still pressed tight in front of me.

*Stairs. Then the narrow corridor of the narthex.* I ticked off the landmarks around me like the dogged minutia emanating from a dashboard GPS system. The heavy outer door swung open to my touch.

I couldn't even bring myself to look up as I hurried passed the rectory. The rest of the walk back to the house was unsteady, a blur of unformulated questions. I knew this neighborhood like the back of my hand, just a half dozen blocks to home. It seemed to take forever.

When I stumbled into the living room, Marty was unpacking books, stacks and heaps of them. From the look of it, he was trying to figure out just which ones belonged in which of the built-in oak glass-front bookcases on either side of the brick fireplace.

He looked up. His brow came together in a puzzled knot.

"You okay?" he asked.

"No. No, I'm not." I managed a shaky laugh."But I've got to believe it'll pass."

"You've been gone a long time. What happened?"

That's just it. I didn't know. And I certainly couldn't explain it to Marty. One minute I was caught up, even reveling in the first sensually-charged moment I had experienced in a decade, and then—I was standing at the edge of an abyss.

"You ever get hit by a bus, Marty—?"

"Close. But no." He hesitated. "You want some coffee? I made some."

"A good stiff drink sounds better."

Marty put down the stack of books he had been hefting. "What's with the grocery stores around here? I tried to buy us a twelve-pack, no luck. Even the mini-mart doesn't carry 'em."

I chuckled, shook my head. "Don't tell me you didn't pull your share of keggers back in Philly, Marty. Beer distributors—remember? That time-honored Pennsylvania institution."

"I didn't see any of those on any of my trips around town."

"The closest is probably in Bartonville."

"Fifteen miles for a beer . . .?"

"Small town life, Marty. I warned you."

"And if I suggested I drive over there to Bartonville and stock up on some Yuengling . . .?"

"I'd fork over the dough. Pronto."

I was already fishing in my purse for keys and cash, anything but prolong Marty's quiz-show-host probing into my emotional state. Even now, after a multi-block adrenalin-pumping flight, I still felt the aftertaste of danger—the emptiness of loss.

It became the longest day in my recent memory . . . even with the beer. Worse in its own way, I concluded, than the day I cleaned out my office. It was even more unsettling than that cross-country trek in the rain behind the rental truck.

I had lived like a nun for so long, that I had forgotten the havoc rampaging hormones can wreak. On a more rational level, the disturbing part of the whole unfortunate episode, was the "why" of it. And above all, of all people, *why Rob Sims? Where on earth had that come from?*

Marty had set aside my high school and college yearbooks near the closest of the bookshelves, along with several full-to-bursting family albums. Against my better judgement, I singled out the yearbook from my freshman year at Hope High and cracked it open.

The page wasn't random. Until I finished college and moved to Philly, mom had hung on to these souvenirs for safe-keeping. Apparently well-worn from her reading over the years, the yearbook automatically fell open to the Freshman Class directory, mid-G's.

The face that stared up at me from the grainy black and white photo looked impossibly young. *My face.* I winced. It had been a horrendous hair day and the horizontal stripes in my jumper made me look like a chubby convict.

*Charlise Grunwald*, the text under the photo read, *budding Liberace. Keep those fingers flying, Char. Color: Black and white (piano keys, get it!). Favorite song: Moonlight Sonata.*

Even in my current emotional state, I had to chuckle. It was anything but funny at the time.

Flipping through the yearbook, I found myself drawn to the section for the Seniors. There it was, under the S's:

> *Sims, Robert (Rob—Man on the Job). Future NFL Hall of Famer. Color: Green like his Hope jersey. Favorite song: Go, Hilltoppers!*

Caught there in the harsh glare of that anonymous yearbook photographer's lens was a quirk of a grin and the strong, confident features of a young man who believed in the future. *Robert Sims.*

None of that seemed to fit with what came after—including what had just transpired down there in that undercroft. And yet as I continued to stare at the now-fading photograph, I had to admit that things were not as simple as they had appeared, even then. It was something in those eyes that brought me up short—not unlike that "back-to-the wall" look Rob shot in my direction just before he bolted up those undercroft stairs.

Heart and gut, I consoled myself that for a split-second Rob Sims had wanted that intimacy as badly as I did, even though something powerful had intervened. Something far darker than anything in the Hilltopper yearbook.

Whatever it was, I believed the man when he told me that moment of vulnerability would never happen again. Awkward at first, we would pass like the proverbial ships through this tiny rural backwater, making polite conversation, perhaps even collaborating on Sunday services from time to time as rural pastor and local fill-in musician. *Intimate strangers who had let their moment pass.*

Composer Aaron Copland—who perhaps more than any other modern classical musician caught the uniquely American voice in his work—once said that if you write two words about music, one of them is going to be wrong. The same, I was beginning to suspect, is true of our personal histories. That weathered yearbook lying open before me on the hardwood floor of the homestead offered proof positive.

Angry now and frustrated, at myself as much as anything, I shut the yearbook and shelved it. *So much for meandering down memory lane!* We weren't kids anymore—that much was certain. If we never connected back in those simpler times, Rob Sims and I, it sure as heck wasn't any more likely now. And whatever demons were driving the guy, I had plenty of my own to worry about.

*Suck it up—get a grip.* Chalk up the whole unfortunate incident to a bad case of hurt pride and an even worse case of embarrassment! I had work to do.

With an impatient gesture, I snatched up the remaining family albums and shelved them as well, with a satisfying amount of clatter. Nearby I spotted yet another box labeled Books. Dragging it closer to the bookcase and slashing the tape open with a box cutter, I began to relieve the carton of its contents.

*Weaving for Beginners. Mastering Color in Tapestry Weaving.* I smiled as I noticed the titles.

By sheer chance I had stumbled on a carton of my favorite fiber art how-to books. Crammed around them for filling in the box, I even found some of my more fragile weaving tools, wrapped in several of my better woven swatches. I remembered seeing my actual looms upstairs somewhere, still in their cartons—a portable lap loom for tapestries and a used table loom for rag and larger fabric projects.

Compared to music, weaving had been a fairly recent pastime, but I took to it immediately. It fascinated me how in the hands of a weaver, textures and colors interact to a harmonious visual whole—mathematical like music but with the rhythms dependent on sight not sound.

*Fun. Challenging. I couldn't wait to get back to it.*

And then it struck me—one of those weird lightning-bolt moments. I had flashes in my head of that clothing warehouse in the undercroft at Nativity. Off in one corner I had spotted a huge cardboard box sagging under the weight of more yarn ends than I'd ever seen, dozens of dozens of balls of all conceivable sizes and colors.

Through the throbbing in my head, I grabbed the phone and punched in the number scrawled on a sticky-note tacked alongside the base. Three rings later, I heard the familiar voice.

"Grace?" My mouth didn't seem to want to work, but I forged ahead. "I've been depleting the hardware's supply of cleaning rags. So this morning I ran into Father Sims down there and he offered . . . he let me sort through all that reject clothing for something I could use— "

"Great. No problem. I was wondering how on earth to get rid of all that stuff."

"Well, don't, Grace. Don't give up on it. Not yet anyway. I have an idea."

Silence from Grace Alanson's end of the phone didn't last long. What *do* you say when a neighbor you barely know calls you up out of the blue and urges you *not* to clean house?

"Don't tell me . . .," she said slowly. "The future is *plastics*!"

Vintage Anne Bancroft and Dustin Hoffman in *The Graduate*. I had to chuckle. My neighbor may come across like a throwback, but she was also one smart cookie. I could tell she was intrigued.

"Nice try, Mrs. Robinson," I teased, "but I was thinking *rag and tapestry weaving*."

"Rag . . . *what*?"

"After my girls had left the nest, I was fishing around for a hobby that made sense in a walk-up in Philly," I told her. "A friend invited me to a weaver's guild exhibition. One look at those looms and I was hooked."

Grace groaned. "I've tried rug hooking. It's slower than molasses— "

"Weaving is a lot more efficient, once the loom is dressed. It's amazing how quickly you can crank out placemats, runners and scatter rugs. My friend actually started selling her work at a neighborhood fine arts gallery . . . at some pretty hefty prices."

Totally out of character, Grace didn't interrupt—as I saw it, a good sign. She knew exactly where I was headed.

"Grace, how many folks are enrolled in your jobs program down at Nativity?"

"Men or women?"

"Both, about a dozen at any one time. They come and go."

"Ages?"

"Eighteen to eighty. The employment situation is so bad that especially older folks eventually just give up. Some are retired farmers who moved into town, some had small businesses that just couldn't keep up with the mega-stores over in Bartonville."

I took a deep breath, reigning in my excitement. "Grace, we could wait forever for jobs to come this way—when in fact, we just might have the makings of a bonanza here. There's a basement full of rag to get started. We could scrape up the money for a couple of tabletop or maybe even floor looms— "

"Aren't they pretty expensive?"

"Not so bad if they're used. And Marty and some of those old farmers could build lap top tapestry looms for most of the product, plus simple warping boards— ”

“Don't the Carolina artisans have a lock on arty hand-weaving?”

“Not necessarily. I'm not thinking of rugs and utility runners here or even your garden-variety wall hangings. This is an Episcopal parish so a certain amount of ‘high church’ comes with the territory. So, what if we specialized in off-beat liturgical hangings—pulpit and lectern paraments, altar runners, bench and kneeler covers? Add to that, custom anniversary and wedding hangings or runners—and I truly believe there's a potential market out there . . .”

“Father Sims used to be in advertising,” Grace said slowly, “top of the pole in some big Pittsburgh outfit.”

“Helpful. But then my friend in Philly also could help us find customers for made-to-order pieces, even help with training weavers if we asked her. And if any major religious supply catalogs might be talked into carrying our product . . .well, that would be gravy!”

With that I had run out of steam. Even over the phone, I could sense the excitement bubbling up in Grace's voice.

“As plans go, I've heard a lot worse . . .”

“Gee, thanks, Grace. I think!”

“Have you talked to Father Rob about this?”

Silence. “I'd feel a lot more comfortable if you'd do that,” I said.

“It's your idea,” Grace protested.

”No. I'm . . . new here. You know the resources better than I do and could make a better case.”

It wasn't exactly a lie. But then Grace wasn't privy to where I stood with Rob Sims right now. I counted off the seconds as I let her think about my proposal.

“Well . . .?”

Grace chuckled. “You sure know how to rattle the old gerbil cage.”

She didn't know the half of it. Rob's anguished face swam into focus. Closing my eyes, I forced the image back into the recesses of memory.

But then I wasn't the only one staring down a pretty big heap of lemons at the moment. The whole town was. And against all odds, I was suddenly feeling the irrational need to start cranking out lemonade.

“Really, I'd appreciate it very much,” I told Grace, “when you talk it up over there, if you'd bring my name into this only in passing.”

“Don't like it, but yeah . . . if that's what you want. I'll do it.”

She did, quicker than I expected.

# ✣ Chapter Seven

After an all but sleepless night, I was still in bed at nine o'clock the next morning, when I heard the sound of the doorbell. Tentative at first, it quickly grew more insistent.

Even with the worst of the unpacking behind me, climbing out of bed still wasn't getting appreciably easier. Silently praying for ibuprofen, I pulled on the turquoise silk caftan I used as an emergency cover-up. Whoever was down there was not going away.

Marty had traded the guestroom down the hall for the bedroom directly across from mine with that "weird outhouse of a tower", as he called it. From the muffled oath and creak of ancient box springs, I knew the bell had gotten his attention, too.

"I'll get it, Marty," I grumbled.

"What ever . . .!"

Sunlight was streaming in through the parlor windows as I worked my way—still half-groggy with sleep— down the staircase. Through the lace panel over the beveled-glass of the front door, I saw a dark shape standing poised to hit the bell again. Alerted by my rattling of the deadbolt, whoever was out there moved away from the door.

I opened it. After the initial shock, I realized down deep, I was half expecting this.

It was Rob Sims. Hollow-eyed from lack of sleep, he was sporting a growth of stubble along his jaw. The clerical collar was nowhere in sight.

"We need to talk," he said.

I just looked at him, steadying myself on the doorframe.

"I'm not sure that's a good idea."

Rob winced. "Understandable. After yesterday. But at the very least, I owe you an . . . apology, if not an explanation."

Our eye contact was uncomfortable but steady. Reluctantly, I stepped aside enough to let him in.

Almost as if fearing I would change my mind, Rob seized the moment and shot into the room. Halfway across the living room, he abruptly turned and faced me, his hands balled into fists at his side, clenching and unclenching.

*Where next?* Most of the furniture in the room and dining room beyond it was cluttered with odds and ends again that I hadn't gotten around to stashing somewhere. *Leaving no place*, I realized, *even to sit down.*

"Coffee." I said. "I don't know about you, but I could use some."

He nodded his assent. "Thanks."

"It'll take me a minute."

By way of response—though keeping a conspicuous distance between us—Rob followed me into the kitchen and eased himself down at the oak drop-leaf table. I tried to ignore the realization that he was watching me as I ground the beans and got a pot of Colombian premium brewing.

*One hundred percent Arabica beans*, the label read. Why on earth that seemed important right then, I'll never know.

Everything seemed to be happening in slow motion. I reached up into the cupboard for the mugs.

"I understand that it was *your* idea," he said slowly. "About starting a . . . some kind of weaving studio down in the undercroft."

"Grace told you?"

"Brilliant, by the way. Absolutely brilliant. The rest of us have been too close to the heartbreak here to see the possibilities. I've heard of churches that did similar things—opening a coffee shop in an otherwise abandoned downtown storefront, one even running what had been a bankrupt cheese factory . . ."

"I just thought . . . it seems there's an awful lot of perfectly good fabric and yarn down there. And Nativity is already—"

"There's something you should know," he said.

Something in his tone already told me, what was coming next was not about looms and marketing strategies. Mugs in hand, I stopped mid-kitchen, waiting.

"I'm married," he said.

I just stared at him, stunned. I was remembering that off-handed crack of his about community property when we ran into each other that morning in the hardware. I just assumed he was talking about divorce.

"Married?"

It explained everything. And nothing.

"Karin left me . . . just before I moved back here three years ago. Though in some ways she gave up on our marriage a heck of a long time ago."

He looked down at his hands. I recognized the gesture, the way married couples twist at their rings when they're nervous or under stress. Only in Rob's case, the band was gone.

"Which doesn't change things legally, of course," he said, "in the eyes of church and state, we're still . . . man and wife."

I noticed he didn't say, *eyes of God.* Still, the truth of it rose up between us like a wall, hard and insurmountable. What do you say after something like that?

"The coffee's ready," I told him.

I poured us each a cup. We sat for what seemed like a long time in silence, sipping at the dark, potent brew in front of us. I couldn't bring myself to meet his gaze. A dull ache had settled around my heart.

"What happened, Rob?"

I heard him shift in his chair. "By the time I decided to call it quits in advertising, I was an alcoholic— "

It hurt to listen, hurt to look up and see the agony in his eyes. That revelation was only the beginning.

"Not surprising," he shrugged. "With all that wining and dining, and the break-neck pace of the corporate rat race, it didn't take long before Karin and I were . . . let's just say, booze became the strongest bond between us. And then when our daughter Lily died . . ."

His face worked. I thought he was going to break down.

"She was . . . Lily was this beautiful kid, vivacious, smart and she never had a chance—run down in our own driveway by a drunk in a Mercedes after one of our bashes. How in the name of all that is holy do you rationalize or live with something like that? I rarely showed up at work sober. Karin had checked out as a wife and mother in an over-medicated fog while Ted, our son, a teenager at the time, just became even more sullen, withdrawn. The housekeeper started finding empty liquor bottles under his bed— "

Rob caught his breath, exhaled sharply. His face was terrible.

"Finally . . . I had enough. Twelve Steps got me sober, got me thinking about where my life was headed. We . . . the three of us were more or less in family counseling. But still, when I told Karin I'd been accepted at the seminary . . . she stayed drunk for a month— "

"Rob, I'm so very— "

"No. No excuses." His voice was steel. "You need to hear this. All of it. Completing my M-Div was . . . tortuous, but eventually I finished, soul-searching every inch of the way. Even then, I asked to defer taking a church full-time. When the powers that be finally proposed assigning me here three years ago, I thought, okay—it's time. Early retirement from the firm was not out of the question. We certainly didn't need that kind of money . . . "

"And Karin?"

His strangled laugh gave me the answer. "We were still in counseling. I . . . deluded myself into thinking she might come to see it as a fresh start. For both of us, for our son— "

His laughter grated like chalk on a blackboard. I shivered.

"I told Karin at breakfast what I was proposing to do. No tears, no arguments. She just looked at me with this odd little smile," he said. "I told her about feeling called, about needing her support. 'I know,' she said."

Rob sighed, straightened back in his chair. "I got up from that kitchen table, drove to the office and talked to the partners about selling my share. By noon I had accepted the call to Nativity," he said. "That afternoon when I got home from work, without a word—Karin was gone."

"How . . . terrible . . .!"

"When I finally tracked her down, Karin's vocabulary was a lot more . . . graphic."

A grim smile played at the corner of his mouth. "It seems a round collar and some backwater town on the edge of the Alleghenies was not what she had bargained for. By now she was living with this . . . upscale paroled felon—a two-bit stock pusher caught up in one of those mega-scams. I'm told the guy had moved on to *dealing* on the side. Apparently a regular pharmacopeia. Uppers, downers, everything in between. Karin had latched on to an infinite supply."

"Dear God, what on earth did you . . .?"

Rob shrugged. "Talked to the Bishop. And although none of what was going on in my personal life could be construed remotely as healthy family values, in the end the Diocese let my appointment stand. By then my son was in college. I rented out our house in Squirrel Hill, put most of the furniture in storage for Karin in case she wanted it and gave her the phone number of my sponsor at AA. Plus the promise of a monthly check so she could get herself back on her feet— "

He broke off, stared into the depths of his mug. The dark liquid swirled slowly in his hands like a vortex into the heart of hell. Closing his eyes, Rob drained it.

"It sounds like I blame her for what happened. I don't. She was so young, barely in her twenties, when we married. For all that woman-of-the-world veneer she had cultivated, she was what she was—emotionally fragile, self-absorbed, needing me to be what had attracted her in the first place." He drew a harsh breath. "Charitably, I guess you'd call it the mystique of the jock turned hard-scrabble corporate type Karin thought she'd married. Tough and take-charge, sure enough of myself for the both of us . . ."

Chuckling softly to himself, Rob shook his head. "Certainly not some way-too-intense recovering alcoholic in a clerical collar officiating at worship five times a week and hearing confessions from decent folks who have no clue how devastatingly human and . . . addictive . . . real *evil* can be."

*This was the real Rob Sims I was seeing. The depth and the introspection so close to the surface, even in that seemingly cocksure photo in our high school yearbook*. I started to say it, but caught myself.

Karin wasn't alone. Like the rest of this town, I too had never looked beyond the myth of the Golden Boy to the thoughtful, insecure young man crying out to be acknowledged and understood.

Slowly, he raised his gaze to mine. It was all there in his face, no longer hidden in those eyes—the self-doubt, guilt, emotions I couldn't even pretend to fathom or define. What I saw was brutally honest, without a shred of self-pity.

"She . . . Karin hasn't asked for a divorce?"

Rob winced. "Apparently not high on her priority list, though I haven't seen her in nearly two years. At least my checks keep showing up cashed on my bank statements. Not much as a relationship goes . . ."

"But still . . .something."

"Do I still love her? Is that where you're heading?"

He didn't wait for an answer. "We thought we had a life together, Char. By any definition, that life no longer exists, if it ever did."

I had learned to pick up subtle rhythms in silence. The coffee maker was beating out a sequence of mechanical clicks as the machine shut itself off. Outside the kitchen window, a lone cardinal was chanting matins—*what-cheer, cheer, cheer . . . purty, purty, purty . . . sweet, sweet, sweet, sweet.*

Across the kitchen table from me, Rob Sims's breath rose and fell. It had the desperate calm of a man adrift alone in dark waters.

I did the only thing possible. I stretched out my hand across my grandmother's table top, its finish worn and scarred with use and time. It was a tenuous lifeline to offer at best, but the only one I had.

Rob hesitated before he reached out, cradling my hand in his like some precious object worthy of study. With a shock I realized what it was he was seeing, named it for what it was.

*A musician's hand.* Strong from all that keyboard training with the nails close-cropped and unpolished, devoid of any jewelry—the palms calloused now from moving all those boxes. Even at rest, the hollow of my hands tend to arch as if clutching at an invisible tennis ball, the legacy of teachers helping position my fingers on the keys.

When Rob looked up again, it was as if his eyes bored straight through me, weighing my reaction. I saw a hint of a smile tug at the corner of his mouth, indescribably sad.

"You ought to know," he said. "Yesterday, in that undercroft, was the closest I ever came, in all those . . . terrible years, to letting myself— "

"Admit that you're . . . *vulnerable*?"

Through the sting of tears, I forced myself to define it. It was that or risk harsher descriptions of the attraction that had surfaced between us. An attraction still there, my gut told me—if anything stronger—in spite of that sordid, agonizing confessional I had just witnessed.

"Char, I had . . . no . . . right— "

"Everyone, flawed and battle-scarred though any of us may be, has a right to know they're not alone. Or were you really that afraid someone finally got a glimpse behind all those masks you've created—raw and unguarded, no pretenses?"

He seemed about to react. Voice shaking, I cut him off. If I didn't say it now, I'd lose my nerve entirely.

"Make no mistake, Rob. I needed . . . *need* that affirmation as much as you do. What happened yesterday in that undercroft was *mutual.* And whatever happens next, I want you . . . need you to be my . . . *friend.*"

At that his fingers finally closed around mine, warm and steady—connecting. A muscle worked along the edge of his jaw and he swallowed hard before he responded. But his gaze never once faltered in the process.

"I'd never forgive myself if I hurt you," he said. "There's been way too much hurt already— "

I believed him. Still, there was one thing I had to know and that was what, between yesterday and now, had triggered this brutal moment of truth?

"Right now, if we're on the subject of pain," I told him, " I'd say you look like a guy with one . . . *heck* of a headache!"

The smile began with his eyes. In the end it lit his whole face from within. I heard the relief in his voice.

"Am I coming off a wild night on the town?" he said. "I'm still sober . . . if that's what you're wondering. Although—truth told—I spent most of the night on the phone with my sponsor."

I just looked at him. There was more.

"It always kept coming back to the same thing. I make no illusions about the future of my marriage—and on that score, a little unresolved guilt can be a healthy thing." Rob managed a strangled laugh. "But what I . . . couldn't face was the prospect of telling you the truth—not if it meant walking into that sanctuary week after week knowing that you were avoiding it . . . and me with it."

"Rob, I— "

"And then the unthinkable happened," he said. "Grace called crack of dawn. . . all in an uproar about some plan of yours to set up a sweat shop in the undercroft . . ."

"I told her not to present it as my— "

"Thank God, she did. Even though I went *postal* on you down in that basement, at least I knew now you weren't casting about for the first ticket out of town. Plus, knowing the idea came from you gave me the excuse, the hope, that we could somehow . . . salvage this mess, you and I."

"Who knows . . . *what* I was thinking . . .!"

*Or even, if.* I hadn't meant to sound so cynical. It felt good to admit what followed, even if I had to stare hard at the graining in my grandmother's tabletop to get it out.

"But I'm truly . . . *glad* you're here. Glad that you told me the truth." I hesitated. "Even if it means that I'll be going back to calling you . . . *Father Sims* . . ."

"Forget it . . .!" Rob laughed. "Non-negotiable. We've already had this conversation."

". . . Rob, then . . ."

When I looked up again, his smile faded. Slowly and with obvious reluctance, he shifted back in his chair. In the process, he withdrew his hand.

"Though don't misunderstand me," he said quickly, "On some level, nothing's changed, for me anyway. It's taken a lifetime of dumb choices to get to this point . . . way too little and way too late. But for the record, my mom was dead-right the first time she laid eyes on you—about hoping that I had the smarts to recognize a good thing when I see it . . .!"

*A dangerous admission.* Given everything that had preceded it.

The air in the kitchen felt suddenly hot and oppressive. With an audible intake of breath, I got to my feet intending to crack open the kitchen door. Through the screen, outside in her garden along the lot line, I could hear Grace humming away to the morning in that lush, just-let-it-all-out-there voice of hers.

The lyrics of the song played themselves out in my head, celebrating golden fields in the sunlight and timeless love—one of my favorite ballads, fairly recent as decades went, by Sting. I took my time coming back to the table.

"So, Rob . . ."

"So . . . Char . . ."

He had grasped the mug with two hands. I could see it was empty. With some difficulty, I managed to pour a refill without scalding him in the process.

Years ago, my own mother had given me one of those quote-a-day calendars about music. One of the entries had stuck in my head, by the poet Samuel Taylor Coleridge, whose life was a tragic downward spiral of spousal betrayal, addiction, madness and death. *No sound is dissonant which tells of life.*

For all my outward calm, I was feeling that clashing discord all around me—the strident reality of what was and the wistful counterpoint of what might have been. If I was going to draw my personal line in the sand, now was the time.

"Suggestions?" I said.

Rob stared at the mug in his hands, a murky crystal ball at best. "On that score . . . even my mother ran out of advice."

Grasping at straws, I came back to what I knew best. Shared work had been my bread and butter—finding opportunities for growth and change in the people I was trained to help. Only this time I was the one who needed it, frighteningly so.

It was tough to fake a smile, but I gave it my best shot. This was never going to get any easier.

"I meant what I proposed to Grace," I told him slowly. "But then it's your call—your undercroft full of rags and an awful lot of un– or underemployed parishioners. Fourth down and ten. Do we punt or do we go for it?"

Who was I kidding? Right now, I was thinking more along the line of cold showers than Hail Mary plays to help my hometown with an undercroft full of rag.

Rob's smile began with his eyes. "Who could argue with getting the town working again, Char?" he said quietly. "Though Grace was so busy arm-twisting on the phone, it was tough to sort out what it would actually take to get a . . . viable cottage industry going down there."

I felt like I had been holding my breath. Grateful, relieved, I let the momentum of my plan put some badly needed distance between us.

It was pretty much a rehash of what I had told Grace on the phone—what we needed to buy, what we could borrow or make, from glorified picture frames for the tapestry looms to my table loom and a couple of student model floor looms for the rag. From time to time, Rob broke in trying to put dollar signs on the catalog of equipment and supplies I was describing.

"Sounds a bit like Greek alphabet soup, all those shuttles, sley hooks and warping boards," Rob frowned. "Wouldn't the learning curve and start-up time be a problem?"

"We're going for folksy, not great art—plus we would be repeating the same simple patterns over and over. Folks around here are probably a pretty craft-savvy lot and rag weaving is fairly forgiving for amateurs. A month or two to train the weavers should do it. I've got some great design books and I know my teacher in Philly would help— "

"And when we run out of rag?"

"We can buy it," I told him, "pennies on the dollar, ready to go. Or keep on raiding the regional second-hand stores for their castoffs. Even purchasing rag, the materials in a pulpit or lectern hanging would cost less than ten bucks. Rug wool doesn't come cheap, but if we stick to small tapestries appliqued on solid-color brocade panels, it wouldn't take a lot."

Rob was adding it all up in his head. "I'm guessing a modest profit at best selling through retailers—potentially quite a while before we recouped the initial investment. It would be better if we could sell direct."

My heart sank as he laid it out there like that. I realized he was probably right.

"But then how do you put a bottom line on people feeling needed again?" I said quietly. "What price tag is there for discovering you're never too old to accomplish something meaningful . . . together?"

"Do all to the glory of God . . .?"

"Something like that." I nodded.

I saw the planes of Rob's face soften. His eyes glittered with a steady fire. He cleared his throat.

"So . . .," he said. "At first I assume we could just create a bunch of samples, enough to show galleries or create catalog photos—at least investigate the possibility of exhibiting at regional art fairs."

"You're the marketing guru. Tell me."

He turned the notion over in his head. "Position ourselves as specializing in 'folk art' liturgical designs for the country parish or back-to-the-basics suburban congregation. Make a plus of the negatives—that we're recycling the castoffs of a throwaway society. Develop a catchy logo, something that reflects our own church's personality. Maybe something like *Undercroft Art . . .*"

"I *really* like the sound of that." I said.

"We don't have to have an enormous stock on hand either—minimizing the risk if we misjudge and a particular product doesn't sell. When I went scrounging for cassocks and stoles, the church supply catalogs often required 4 to 8 weeks delivery, even longer sometimes."

"My friend in Philly and I could weave the prototypes—which could buy us the time to teach the other weavers and redo things if necessary on the client's nickel."

Rob nodded. "My thought, exactly."

"*What . . . exactly . . .?*"

I had seen it coming. Rob hadn't.

Barefoot and rumpled, clad only in ragged jeans that passed with him for pajama bottoms, Marty had wandered into the kitchen. The smell of coffee worked better to get my young friend moving than any alarm clock.

At the sound of another voice in the room, Rob whipped around on his chair like a bomb had just gone off in the kitchen. Marty chuckled.

"Mornin'!" he said, stifling a yawn. "I see Char's been overdoing it with the caffeine again."

Rob's laughter—to me, anyway—had the edge of a kid caught raiding the cookie jar. But then it could have been worse. Marty could have wandered in on us about ten minutes earlier, *holding hands across that kitchen table.*

As to what Rob Sims thought of a bare-chested young man clad only in blue jeans wandering into my kitchen at this hour of the morning, I couldn't even begin to speculate. Palms sweating, I made the introductions.

"Marty Santano . . . ," I stammered. "A former client of mine from Philly. He . . . Marty's helping me move— "

Rob's forehead had creased into a quizzical frown. I plunged ahead.

"Marty, this is Rob . . . Rob Sims— "

"As in . . . *Father* Rob?"

"The same."

"Mrs. Howard . . . Char says your church helps people who don't have jobs. Ya got any work for a carpenter?"

"If it hadn't been for a Carpenter," Rob chuckled, "We wouldn't even be having this conversation."

Poor Marty looked confused. Incarnation humor, I suspected, went way beyond anything he had learned in Sunday School 101. At least Rob seemed to have figured out the score card as far as my tenant and I were concerned.

"Father Rob and I were just talking about putting you to work," I explained.

"When?"

"Soon . . . we hope."

"You're joking, right?"

Marty's look shot from Rob to me, then back again. I tried not to read anything into the skepticism other than Home Boy street smarts. *When things seem too good to be true, hang on to your wallet.*

"I'm sure Char will fill you in." Rob had shifted into what had to be his counseling mode. "And yes . . . carpenters will be essential."

At that, finally, a grin began to spread across Marty's face. For the foreseeable future, Hope was exactly where my young tenant seemed prepared to set up camp. As for Rob, he was already half-way to the door—the back one this time.

"I'll cut through your yard and give Grace the green light about her getting something going in the undercroft—ASAP," he said. "Unless you'd rather do it . . ."

"Fine, go ahead. She'll know what to do about putting a committee together. If and when she needs it, I'm ready to help."

"Anyway, thanks for the coffee." Rob's hand was already poised on the porcelain knob of the screen door, when he half-turned my way and flashed a wry quirk of a smile.

"Though next time," he said, "the coffee's on . . . *my* nickel."

*Next time?* Taken out of context, to Marty sitting there half-asleep at the kitchen table, the offer must have sounded harmless enough. But then I knew better.

If Rob caught my frown, he showed no sign of it. From the porch, I could hear his laughter floating back at me, the sound of someone with a load off their mind. I wish I could have said the same for myself.

# Chapter Eight

Life has an unsettling way of taking with one hand and giving with the other. Rob Sims was off limits—our contact limited to only the most controlled and public of circumstances. Yet beyond my wildest imaginings, my minutes and hours in Hope were suddenly full.

Daily workouts on the tracker at Nativity and a grueling schedule of work on the Undercroft project proved to be as good a remedy as any for rampaging hormones whenever Rob was in my sight-lines. *Little or no will power required.*

Then, too, the cast of characters in my world was expanding exponentially. Second week in town I was alone at the keyboard, when out of the blue there she was—a frail little wisp of a thing in polyester slacks and a matching top with musical notes embroidered across the front.

*Wilma the organist.* I didn't need an introduction to tell me. She was clutching her needlework music tote against her with a look that said it all.

"Father Rob said we had a new . . . *organist* in town!"

Any invidious comparisons going on were her doing, not mine. Time to set things straight.

"Sorry . . . I'll get out of here right now so you can do what you came to do."

"No need. Just passin' through . . ."

"I was just about done anyway."

True enough. The sweat was running down my back and I felt that familiar ache that signaled I had been hunched on that bench in one position too long. It seems I had passed some kind of test. The woman smiled.

"Name's Wilma Smoller."

"Char, Char Howard."

She started to say something, then stopped—suddenly shy. "Ya love it, don'tcha?"

"Yes. Yes, I do."

"I knew your momma—all music that Grunwald girl. Got a kick out of watching her give you lessons back then. She kept those feet out there tapping, even though she played the classics when everybody else out there was singin' about how Jesus was their boyfriend. When she died, I was older than God but they got me back on that bench. Couldn't find anyone else."

"Tough finding organists these days."

Wilma nodded. "Who'da thought it? My cousin taught me. Eighty years ago. Same woman as taught your momma. Been playing ever since."

"Good for you," I smiled. "I took a little vacation for a bit there, but I'm getting back to it again, too. Not the easiest thing in the world."

While we were talking, I noticed her eye-balling the music on the organ rack. I could guess what she was thinking. It was tough as pieces go, but then apparently she had been listening for a while and I certainly had made my share of mistakes along the way.

"I never played that fast though," she said, "even in my best days. I figure one way or the other, we'll get there at the end."

I fought a smile. Half-knowing the answer, I still had to ask.

"What kind of music do you like best?"

"Old-time hymns." Her face scrunched as she thought harder about it. "But next I guess . . . I'd say that Methodist guy, Wesley. My son got me this book, *The Masters Made Easy*. Same pieces but a lot fewer notes."

Wilma was so dead-earnest, it took every bit of will power to keep from chuckling.

"I like the Brits myself," I told her, "modern composers like Vaughan-Williams and the earlier Baroque composers like Byrd and Gibbons, and from the Continent, Handel."

"My son bought me a lot of that B'roke music for Christmas one year, though it was a little fussy for me, all those notes running around. You're welcome to use my library any time, you know. My son just keeps it coming, stacks of it for Christmas, birthdays— "

"Thanks, I appreciate that."

Wilma frowned, like she was almost afraid to ask. "I was trying to figure out. How do you make that trumpet sound when you play? This organ doesn't have that Cornetto stop like my Hammond at home."

"Hautbois," I told her. "You put it together with that 2-foot on the Great. No 4's though. It's the distance between shrill and dark that gives that brassy edge."

"Tried that High-Boy stop once. Was afraid I'd blast 'em out of the pews. Alma Rogers keeps that hearing aid of hers turned up pretty loud—so she says she doesn't like all that noise in church. We had a sub one Sunday and Alma said she had to do her praying out in the parking lot."

I laughed. She was right of course.

"People get used to all that background music in elevators and supermarkets," I said. "When you really fire off a piece like it's supposed to be, some people start to get very . . . nervous."

"Or think you're showing off." Wilma sniffed. "Ya can't win, you know. It's either too loud or too fast or too slow or too something. By Monday morning the line outside the church office is a mile long with folks with an opinion, especially when ya slip and play the Gloria instead of the Doxology."

"I used to worry, too—a lot—about all the mistakes I made, all the wrong notes I hit. Mom told me if I wanted my playing to get better, I had to forget how many notes I play wrong and start concentrating on the ones I hit right."

Wilma shrugged. "Besides, at my age, what can the complainers do—shoot me? I'll just play for God and me . . . and to heck with 'em."

Our laughter felt good, reinforcing the tacit understanding between us. This was her bench as long as she chose to occupy it. By the time we left the sanctuary together, the elderly organist and I were on our way to becoming an Organ Guild of two, a dying breed in this little corner of the world. I had to remind myself the woman was in her nineties.

I also kept replaying that pep-talk I gave Wilma about taking chances as I went home and fired off yet another round of emails to my friend back in Philly. It finally did the trick. Undercroft Arts wound up with two floor model studio looms for teaching rag weaving, on more or less permanent loan from the area weaver's guild. Within the month both were set up in the church basement.

My partners in crime were busy on their own. After scouring my weavers' magazines for blueprints, Marty had put together a half-dozen workable and inexpensive picture-frame tapestry looms to start training the troops. Grace was out beating the drum for recruits. Rob was on-line doing market research. My email In-Box was flooded with updates.

Against all odds, it seems Undercroft Arts was off the drawing boards. In a go-for-it flash of optimism, the steering committee timetable gave me exactly a month to come up with viable designs, striking enough to sell yet easy enough to handle for novice weavers. It was enough to keep anyone up nights.

As the deadline approached, I hadn't unpacked a box from my move in weeks and my hastily thrown-together work space in the second spare bedroom of the homestead was littered with sketches. I was too tired even to take out the trash. With a lot of help from Grace, I had set up my looms in that impromptu studio, warped both the tapestry and table looms, and churned out a few small samples. For all that fussing, I felt more nervous about my upcoming show-and-tell than back in good old days, preparing for a budget hearing down at the job service.

The entire weekend before the deadline I holed up in the homestead, refining my work—missing church yet again. What anyone might make of my continued absence, never once occurred to me.

✣

*Monday morning.* A heck of a time for the alarm to malfunction. It was Showtime—the ceremonial unveiling for Grace's little committee of volunteers.

I couldn't believe it was 7:30 AM and I was standing in front of my bedroom closet, agonizing over what I was going to wear. But then office decorum dies hard after thirty years on the job—tempting as it was in retirement to settle into jeans and tee-shirts.

*Dress for success.* I had shed at least ten pounds thanks to the move, enough to wiggle back into a pair of tailored gray summer-weight slacks that hadn't fit in ages. I paired them with a coral sweater and a no-nonsense cropped blazer. After a touch of blush and lipstick to the hastily-applied foundation, I actually felt halfway human as I headed over to Nativity with my stack of drawings.

The chimes on the Nativity bell tower had already sounded eight o'clock—no time for roundabout routes. Head down, I was making a dash past the rectory, oversize portfolio with the sketches and samples under my arm, when a familiar voice stopped me.

"Char . . . over here!"

I looked up to see Rob standing on the front porch in running shorts and gray pocket-tee with a coffee mug in hand. Just the sight of him was enough to set off that ache of awareness building at the pit of my stomach.

"Getting your early morning caffeine fix, I see."

"Third jolt," he corrected me. "I was hoping to run into you on the way over to practice . . .!"

*He knew my practice habits and had been watching for me. For a good hour or more?* I made myself stay put on the sidewalk.

"Catch you later, Rob . . .! No practice today. I'm actually headed for the undercroft to show Grace and the guys my sketches."

Nativity's parsonage was set back on the lot behind a wrought-iron fence. Even from that distance, I caught Rob's frown and the pointed look that went with it.

"The committee will keep— "

"There's a problem?"

"You could call it that. I prefer 'unfinished business' myself."

His tone had an *I know what you're doing and I don't like it* edge about it. It would have been an insult to us both to pretend I didn't understand what he meant.

If there was a potential shoot-out in the making it was better to do it in private I decided, not right out there on the public sidewalk. Reluctantly I tightened my grip on the portfolio and started up the walk to the porch. As Rob held the parsonage door for me, I stumbled over the door sill trying to avoid ploughing into him.

His hand shot out and stopped my fall. This was not going well. Not well at all.

"Thanks."

"Excuse the mess."

By that, I assume Rob must have meant a laptop and stack of printouts piled inconspicuously alongside a Mission style chair off in the far corner of the living room. Everything else was straight out of an issue of *Country Living.*

I don't know what I was expecting, but it wasn't this. Against a backdrop of pristine flannel gray walls and super-white woodwork, the room was sparsely furnished with a collection of early 20th century farm-house antiques—any one of which could have come straight out of a museum catalog.

My attention settled on a delicate oak loveseat with scallop-shell carving on the backs upholstered in a subtle crushed gold velvet. Dominating another wall was a beautifully grained oak hutch with brass wire screen in the openings in the upper doors and pie safe windows below. On the gleaming bare wood floor lay an enormous deep red Persian carpet, obviously very old and very expensive.

"Wow," I breathed.

"I was thinking the same thing— "

If Rob was intending to clear the air in some way, it wasn't working. The comment could be dismissed as harmless, not so the look of awareness that went with it. He had noticed my modest attempts at a make-over.

"Rob, I really don't— "

He raised a hand, palm out, as if to fend off the protest he knew was coming next. "I know . . . I know. No PDA's!"

My face felt hot as I scrambled mentally to decipher the alphabet-soup. *Of course, idiot . . . Public Displays of Affection.*

"You haven't been at church," he said.

"No."

"You dash out of Undercroft meetings like a house on fire and practice next door at the crack of dawn. Apparently go blocks out of your way to avoid the rectory— "

"Not true. Walking helps get the kinks out of my back!"

"Relieved to hear it. I was beginning to think you're trying to tell me something."

Defensive now, I met his steady gaze. He was painting me into a corner and I didn't like it.

"I don't know what you— "

"I think you *do* know, Char—you know exactly what I'm driving at."

When I didn't respond, I saw a smile tug at the corner of his mouth. "Let me say it, once and for all…then be done with it. Were circumstances different, I wouldn't hesitate one second to take Mom's advice and beat a path to your front door on a regular basis. The alternative is *not,* however, to stay clear of each other as much as possible. Which— "

His eyebrow arched. What was about to come next, to his way of thinking, was not negotiable or in dispute.

"*Which* is what I think you have been trying to accomplish the past month. Major avoidance. Am I right here . . .?"

I caught my lower lip in my teeth. "True."

"It's working for you, then?"

"No."

The smile broadened. "Okay, then. I suggest we start over. I'm Rob Sims, priest at Nativity Episcopal and despite my mother's best efforts, I made a point of avoiding you in high school. My mistake. Things change. That said, I feel compelled to tell you, I'd be pleased to death if we would think about . . . becoming . . . friends— "

"F-friends . . .?"

"Friendship, Char. Your word, if I remember correctly. As I define it, it means public laughter and conversation without the assumption that something 'funny' is going on. It means wanting to know another human being as just that . . . another human being. It means telling someone they look great . . . when, doggone it, they do— "

"In a small town like— "

"I've got to believe we are old enough, wise enough, Char . . . to manage all that. Don't you?"

"Aren't there . . . rules about that sort of thing?"

Rob's jaw tightened. "And if friendship between a priest—married no less—and a widowed parishioner means automatically landing in the third level of Dante's Hell, I . . . for one, am willing to risk even that. If that's what it takes for you to stop putting three-quarter-mile crop circles between your place and Nativity—or me—every time you go out of the house . . ."

At that, and his deep intake of breath that followed, I couldn't help it. I finally laughed, out loud. In the process, the tension between us actually seemed to loosen a strand or two.

"So, I gather if I don't finally . . . show up in that congregation on Sunday, then you'll be . . . sending out the dogs?"

Rob shrugged. "A bizarre approach to evangelism. But if that's what it takes— "

"Not necessary."

"Good."

Time was passing. "But Grace will be calling search and rescue, if I don't show up next door— "

"I'll see you Sunday," Rob said. "If not sooner."

His hand was outstretched. Sealing the deal. My heart thudded wildly but I took it, shivered as his warm grasp closed around mine.

"Good luck over there," he said. "I'm mid-sermon or I'd join you."

*Thank heavens*—all I needed right now was walking into that undercroft with Rob as an escort. Even so, as I hastily beat a retreat out the front door of the parsonage, I found myself fighting a momentary relapse into paranoia, wondering just how my departure must look—as if my mere presence on Rob's porch crack-of-dawn like that could be potential headline fare for the eleven o'clock news.

Pulling myself together, I hurried across the lawn between Nativity and the parsonage. As I eased open the door to the undercroft, I caught the unmistakable sound of a meeting already in progress.

At first only Grace saw me coming. Her face lit up and she flashed a smile in my direction.

"She's here . . . ready to rock 'n roll, gang . . .!"

At that a dozen-odd faces turned in my direction. Hunkered uncomfortably on a semicircle of battered tablet-arm school desks sat a dozen potential weavers, a sea of very gray heads with the exception of Marty. Expectant or skeptical? I couldn't hazard a guess.

Grace did the honors. I already had met Wilma, of course. Next to her sat Lenora Frank, head of the altar guild, and then retired farmer Barney Clouter with a face wizened and weathered like one of those dried-out crab apple doll heads. That Holy Roller ball hat—a clone of the one Rob seemed to favor—had to be touting some sort of local club.

"Eighty and proud of it!" Barney interrupted. "And a die-hard football fan. If it's manly for that Rosie Grier fella to do needlepoint, well then it's sure okay for me—church sexton and all—to weave this rag stuff!"

The rest were women with gnarled hands and gardener-tanned faces, median age mid-eighties if I had to put a number on it. Several of them like Barney, Grace had warned me in advance, were on the church vestry. I hoped one of those church mothers wasn't the woman looking at me like I was about to propose burning down the church as a strategy for handling the heating bills.

*Perhaps,* I concluded, *I had been a tad too optimistic in my expectations.* I took a deep breath.

"Bear in mind, I'm no art designer— "

"We aren't weavers either!" Grace didn't beat around the bush. "Not yet anyway. Just go for it! We've already been organizing things down here as best we could."

It was only then I noticed. Along one side wall stood a row of cardboard boxes that hadn't been there before—from the labels on sides, the lot of them rescued from my front porch before my most recent trip to the dump. Each of the makeshift bins was neatly labeled, corresponding to the color scheme Grace and I had discussed. The same was true for that mountain of balled up yarn remnants.

That little team must have been working like fiends. Most of the bins were close to full and the omnipresent coat-racks full of clothes on the opposite wall seemed conspicuously more bare of content.

"Great—perfect!"

Okay then, no time to dawdle. Fumbling with the zipper, I stashed my portfolio on the beat-up work table in front of the group and began to lay out the drawings in sequence. Grace held them up one by one to give everybody a closer look.

"The first four sketches are meant to be seasonal pulpit and lectern hangings. In the trade they're called paraments. Liturgical colors usually change with the church year—purple for Lent and Advent, White for Christmas and Easter— "

I saw heads nod at that. Okay, so far so good.

"It would be hard to compete with traditional hangings. Instead, our versions are based on the liturgical symbols for fire, water, wind and earth. With careful color plans, Grace and I decided, these four basic 17 by 35-inch panels could fit with almost any season of the church year."

Grace was already holding up the first sample panel. The weaving was aflame with yellows, reds and oranges like a fiery lava field. Through the middle, horizontally, coursed a meandering river-like band of wispy blues and grays.

"Pentecost," Grace said.

Barney frowned. "Looks like my back forty down by the creek in November."

A chorus of protests followed. Mainly, I noticed, from Wilma and Leonora.

"Fire and water!"

"Crossing the Red Sea . . .!"

At least *they* got it. Barney—with a life-time of truck farming as a base for his aesthetics—still didn't look convinced. I flashed an encouraging smile.

"Weaving with rag," I told him, "isn't like using a paint brush. You have to tell the story with bold shapes and simple changes in color."

Barney squinted hard at the second sketch. "So then, that blue and green one's gotta be . . . earth and water . . ."

"You hit it right on the head. The presence of God moving over the waters in Creation."

Here the design depended on strong horizontal layers of color in a "hit and miss" pattern. Irregular diamond-shaped outcroppings of green on the right hand side of the panel thrust out into variegated blue diamonds of colors on the left. The result was meant to represent the place where earth and water meet, a lush Eden of a landscape.

"All that green makes it good for use in so-called Ordinary time."

Barney's frown was back. "*Ordinary* . . .?"

"No major festivals. Most of the church calendar fits that category. It's about our life together as a people of God, right here on earth."

"And the one that looks like a bowl of oatmeal?"

"Wind or Light, Barney."

"Looks hard . . ."

"Not really," I told him. "Good rag sorting is the main thing. Those horizontal layers of creams, grays and whites with just a hint of pale gold are meant to look like— "

"Genesis. 'And the Spirit of God blew across the face of the waters. The earth was shapeless, empty of life. And into the darkness God breathed,

*Let there be Light!* And there was . . .!'"

A conversation stopper if I ever heard one. Of all people, it was coming from that rather dour looking woman at the end of the row.

I just stood there for a split-second, dumbstruck. Up until now the name hadn't registered, but then something in the way the woman recited that ancient text finally made the connection. High School English. King Lear and Cordelia wandering the heath in that storm.

"*Right on*, Mrs. Brendorm . . .!"

So help me, I blushed—hadn't heard myself use that expression in decades. Marty was staring over at me as if I had just grown a third head. For a minute, I thought Grace was going to bust out laughing.

"Or then, too, Pentecost . . .," I stammered. "The rising wind of the Holy Spirit. Or a dawn sky at Easter. Take your pick. It's Grace's design, actually, and probably my favorite."

"You always had a way with words, Charlise Grunwald, ninety-eight average in composition your senior year. I'm happy to see you still got your wits about you." Mrs. Brendorm nodded benignly. "Call it what you want, to me that weaving of yours feels like rays of hope."

What do you say after something like that? I was having trouble remembering my new phone number and that woman remembered my grades from forty years ago. Good grief, the woman must be pushing a hundred by now. She seemed ancient even back in the dark ages when I sat in her classroom.

*Hope. Yes, absolutely. It certainly was.*

"Now . . . if we all look at these little tapestry samples I brought, too— "

Ducking my head, I scrambled to pass the swatches along to Grace for show-and-tell. "They're basically those same themes, just made with yarn not rag. We can do them on the lap-top tapestry looms that Marty has made."

"Kinda small aren't they?" Barney wondered.

"Not if we sew these tiny five-by-eight panels dead in the center of plain-colored red, cream, purple or green material."

I unrolled a crude sample I had put together with a glue gun—since my sewing machine was still MIA. "The woven pieces will look like they are set in a frame, just the size of a standard parament."

"Clever," Grace said. "They're classy but won't take forever to weave or need expensive looms like the rag panels do. Once we get the hang of it, we should be able to churn out those tapestry panels in no time flat."

That left only the fourth hanging—my toughest challenge, using that same simple horizontal layered rag-weave technique. The idea was to turn purples, blacks and greens into a symbol of the Lenten or Advent journey, a Brueghel-esque landscape that led the eye from hilltop to hilltop toward the horizon. The occasional white flecks in the rag almost looked like wandering shepherds under the night sky over Bethlehem.

In truth, most of the designs were as much about math as art. It took a lot of measuring and calculating to make sure the strips of color landed in just the right place to create the pattern. Marty stood for the longest time puzzling over that particular sketch.

"Been there," he said finally. "Seen that. I just can't remember where— "

I started quoting, "I will lift up mine eyes onto the hills, from where my help comes . . ."

"That's it!" Marty crowed. "In that blasted rental truck on I-80. I knew I'd seen that darn picture somewhere before."

I had been honestly thinking more of early Renaissance oil painting technique that used bands of color rather than vanishing points to establish perspective. All that, Marty informed me, was way too much information.

"Well . . .," someone chimed in softly, "I think it looks like those hills out there. Right in our own backyard."

Standing behind the knot of us was a young woman I had never seen before. From Grace's quizzical frown, I knew, neither had she. And Grace pretty much knew everybody.

Marty broke the impasse. "Can we help you?" he stammered.

I would have pegged her age at about thirteen, until it registered that the woman was balancing a toddler on her hip. With her pale hair and skin, dark luminous eyes and dusting of freckles, she could have stepped straight out of a Botticelli painting—except, of course, for her low-cut retro seventies cross-her-heart top and threadbare jeans with sizeable holes at the knees.

"I hear you find jobs for people," she said. Even her voice was more a girl's than a woman's. "I need one."

Marty looked over at me with the same expression on his face that my daughters had when they wanted a puppy. While I thought about my response, Grace took charge.

"We're starting a weaving studio down here," she said. "There's no money in it right now, but there will be. What's your name, dearie? Just call me Grace."

I thought the woman was going to burst into tears. Her lip trembled but I noticed she caught it in her teeth to keep from losing control.

"Leah."

"Do you live around here, Leah?"

The woman hesitated, sizing up the mountain of a woman in front of her. On the face of things, if anyone on the planet would be sympathetic to alternative lifestyles, it was Grace Alanson.

Finally, Leah shook her head, no.

"In Bartonville," she said. "But the cops picked up my boyfriend for passing bad checks and the landlord kicked me out. My folks live in Shaker Heights and they won't take me back. I hitched a ride north with a trucker but this is as far as I got."

"Do you have someplace to stay?"

Again, that defiant shake of the head. I had to hand it to her, the woman had guts. Still practically a child herself, she was scared to death, but too proud to admit it.

"I have an extra bedroom," I heard myself saying. "If it would help."

I thought Marty was going to kiss the ground at my feet—*a sure sign*, I thought, *I had lost it.* For all I knew, this angelic slip of a thing could be a scam-artist of the first magnitude.

At that, the dam broke and the woman began to wail. It so shocked the baby on her hip, that for a split-second I feared he or she would join in that desolate chorus. Fabric color of the baby's jumpsuit was no help at all in this instance for determining gender.

"Little Bart here and I've got n-nowhere else to g-g-go," Leah sobbed.

Launching herself like a missile, the woman hugged me so hard she nearly knocked me down. Over her shaking shoulder, I could see Marty was grinning from ear to ear.

"Ya'll like it," he rambled on. "There's lots of boxes all over the place, but you get used to it."

Reality set in. It hadn't occurred to me until that moment what I had gotten myself into.

With the Undercroft project kicking into gear, my timetable for settling in on Elm Street had hit a significant detour. Whatever the state of my house was, it wasn't child proof. And there was the little matter of coping with two more mouths to feed, when I wasn't sure I could keep even Marty and myself afloat.

Bless her heart, Grace must have picked up my rising panic—not hard, given my total disbelief at what I had just proposed. At that moment Grace crossed the divide once and for all for me, from neighbor to friend.

"Leah, I really think you and Bart would be more at home at my place . . . to start, anyway," Grace said gently. "I just rattle around all by myself in that big old house. You can visit across the back fence with Marty and Char any time you like."

Marty's face was a study in sullen dejection. Still, this time I wasn't about to be side-tracked.

"Grace is right," I said.

That settled, Grace was already moving on.

"So, dearie," she said, "Just give us a minute to . . . pack away some of this debris down here and I'll walk you right over to my place. Char, here, will take Wilma home— "

She looked at the baby, then at the huge backpack at the girl's feet. "And Marty, you can help schlep that bag over there."

Marty's grin was back with a vengeance. I can't remember when I saw him move quite that fast. He nearly ploughed into Rob who had chosen that moment to show up at the foot of the undercroft stairs. I assumed it was to check out how our meeting had gone.

He had changed from running shorts into a pair of khakis and that ubiquitous collar, which this time was slipped into a classic black clerical shirt that looked amazing against his tan. Flustered, I tried to slip a stack of the samples back into my portfolio, but quickly gave it up as a lost cause.

"Char, brief Rob . . . okay?" Grace threw out over her shoulder. "Show him the sketches— "

The baby had started to wail, loudly. Echoing in the deserted stairwell, the sound swelled into a kind of primitive chant, with the overtones spilling over each other.

*Waaaaa............na-na-naaah-na......Waaaaa....naaah.* A gasp for air and then the sequence repeated.

I smiled as Marty awkwardly leaned down to chuck the little guy under the chin—an exercise in futility that did nothing at all to dampen the baby's howling. The teeth-grating sound finally stopped only when the door in the narthex shut behind them with a thump.

*Silence.* My relief faded quickly enough.

Without quite knowing how and certainly without intending it, I found myself suddenly standing there alone in the undercroft with what had to be an even more unlikely entourage than the one that had just left. An odd little triumverate—Rob Sims and Wilma Smoller and me.

# ✣ Chapter Nine

Whatever uneasiness I personally was feeling about all this reluctant togetherness, Rob just looked amused. "I see that Marty's found a friend."

"Looks like it." I said.

"Barney will want to add two more to the head-count on that village limit sign."

Wilma frowned. "Way too loud, that baby."

I chuckled. "Another potential choir member, Wilma!"

Rob made eye contact—flashed a knowing smile in my direction. Marty finally may have found somebody his own age in the neighborhood, but then my young tenant wasn't the only one reaching out these days.

It didn't take grad school level courses in psychology for Rob to sense where things stood between Wilma and me. On the one hand, and not that long ago either, I would have given my eye-teeth to replace this frail little woman on the organ bench. Truth was, I had come to admire her courage and I certainly understood where she was coming from.

Her technical limits notwithstanding, Wilma at heart was an organist's organist. Once someone plays a mass or worship service, they never quite look at either church or God the same again.

The liturgy waxes poetic about prayers rising like incense. Sitting at that keyboard, the plaintive melodic lines, the shifting harmonies become the aural equivalent of that ethereal smoke rising heavenward. It is truly hard once a person has felt that to sit without playing in a pew on Sunday morning—detached from that precious spiritual centeredness.

It was her spiritual anchor Wilma was afraid I was threatening that day she first heard me practice. By now she knew I wouldn't mess with that for the world. And regardless of what he might feel personally about a change in personnel and what it might mean to the music program at Nativity, so did Rob Sims.

"You're going to let me get a look at those sketches?" he said quietly.

Hastily I retrieved the drawings for the liturgical hangings from my oversize briefcase and laid them out again on the table for Rob's benefit. One fluttered to the floor and he retrieved it for me, studying the row of sketches hard for a moment before sliding it carefully into place in the liturgical sequence.

*Good. He got it.* Without a word from me, I could sense Rob understood at once what the designs were intended to represent.

"Wilma's getting tired," I said. "I had better take her home soon."

Rob smiled. "We shouldn't be at this long. The designs are gorgeous, Char."

It was impossible to misread the surprise bordering on awe in his voice. I hadn't realized I had been holding my breath, waiting for his reaction. With his fingertip Rob traced the subtle gray ribbon traversing the Pentecost panel.

"You . . . like them, then . . . ?"

"They're so spiritually . . . rich, Char—on a lot of levels. The colors fit the seasons of the liturgical calendar, symbols of the Sacraments, reminders of milestone Biblical events . . . you name it. Churches in this Diocese tend to be fairly contemporary rather than high-church in their orientation. Unless I'm very mistaken, this earthy style will resonate well with large as well as smaller parishes."

"It was a struggle," I admitted, "to capture complex symbols with very simple weaving techniques. I was worried—"

"Well, you succeeded. They're . . . stunning. Unique."

I sensed the "but" in his reaction. It was the same as my own had been from time to time. After all, none of the team had ever done this before.

"The real beauty is how basic the techniques are," I smiled "The key is how we sort and pre-cut the lengths of rag to get just the right color sequences."

"And you really think you can teach Barney and the crew to do this?"

"Not me," I grinned. "Fortunately, help is on the way. After I emailed copies of the final designs to my friend in Philly, she was ready to come out overnight, if we needed it, to help Grace set up operations and train the weaving teams. She does this with school kids all the time. At least most of our folks are pretty savvy when it comes to sewing and/or fine motor skills—even Barney."

"We're talking about a pretty fragile age group here. Should we worry how . . . time intensive all this is . . .?"

"Not if we organize, assembly line fashion. Grace already has set up times later this week for folks to start sorting and cutting the rags into long strips, then boiling and drying them to get out the sizing. We need to lay out very precise patterns for the weavers to alternate the shuttles. Some volunteers can measure out the warp chains, dress the loom. You're welcome to join us— "

"Thanks, but no," he winced. "Football and computers aside, fine motor skills were never my forte."

I chuckled. "I'll admit, the terminology makes it sound like brain surgery. But remember, Rob . . . pioneers were doing rag weaving on simple looms in the wagon trains rolling West. We *can* . . . do this."

He was staring at the sketches again, as if trying to confirm his initial reaction. I could hear the rising excitement in his voice.

"I've never seen *anything* like this, anywhere. Once we get the samples done and photos of the product out to other churches, those panels should sell like hot cakes."

I laughed. "We should be so lucky."

The problem of getting slammed with orders seemed about as remote right now as a trip to Antarctica. Closer at hand, by now poor Wilma was starting to look as if she had already been to the pole and back again.

"You've been very patient with all this," I told her. "Sorry that Father and I got so . . . carried away here."

"I *was* thinking about walking home," Wilma sighed.

"No need for that— "

Her place had to be at least three miles from here. I started to stack the sketches neatly on top of one another, then stopped. In doling out the day's ride-share arrangements, Grace seemed to have forgotten one little detail.

"Oh-m'-gosh . . . senility strikes," I stammered. "I . . . *walked* over to Nativity myself."

Wilma just looked at me. *I didn't have a car?* Grabbing a chair, I quickly started to shove it in her direction.

"Stay put," I told her. "I'm sure Father Rob will keep you company while I run home and get Snaz."

A muscle twitched at the corner of Rob's mouth at my suggestion. "Snaz?"

"My hatchback." Embarrassed, I chattered away about the nickname and my car's license plate, SNZ-4222. "Though there is nothing whatsoever snazzy about the poor thing, especially since the previous owner smacked it into the side of her Philly garage every time she parked it!"

Rob was grinning outright now. His solution was a whole lot simpler.

"No problem, I'll drive you both— "

"Thanks . . . I really appreciate it, but just take care of Wilma. I can *walk*— perfectly fine!"

The words shot out of my mouth before I had time to think about how ridiculous my refusal was. Rob had made a sensible enough offer. What on earth about his intervention was making me so uncomfortable?

"Char, Elm Street is on the way," he said quietly "I'm sure Wilma won't mind. You've got that huge portfolio . . ."

Ensconced alone in the back seat of Rob's Hummer and with Wilma dead ahead in the passenger seat in front of me, I was already regretting my decision to go along for the ride, all half-mile of it. Even with the seat backs between us, I couldn't escape my fascination with the sheer physicality of the man.

That vehicle of his was massive and powerful enough to squash my poor old Snaz like a bug. Yet for all that, the only word to describe Rob's driving style was graceful, an athlete at play, from the way his hands gripped the wheel to the subtle flexing of his shoulders as he negotiated a turn.

He caught me at it, our eyes making contact in the rear view mirror. A hint of a smile teased at the corners of his mouth.

"Are those white knuckles I see glowing back there? Or just wild speculation about the choice of wheels? If it's any help, I bought the thing on a whim twelve years ago . . . "

Mercifully he misunderstood my interest, although it had occurred to me that it wasn't exactly what I would peg as the man's taste. *Expensive as impulse buys go.* But then from the model year, the purchase was made before his seminary days.

"You're kidding!" I flashed an awkward smile. "I was just thinking how easy you make handling this thing look. Whenever we rented anything bigger than a breadbox back in Philly, my girls accused me of driving like a scared rabbit. You're either quick-on-the draw in that traffic . . . or you're history!"

"You ever miss it—?"

"Philly . . . or the traffic?"

Rob laughed. I joined him.

Still our banter aside, his question was one of those 'ah-hah' moments that took me utterly by surprise. The issue hadn't popped up once since my move, not just flat-out like that anyway. I thought a while before answering.

"Seriously . . . no, I don't miss Philly. Though it's not as if I've burned my bridges either. Thanks to Undercroft Arts, I've actually talked more with my weaving buddies than I did sometimes when we were all up to our ears at our respective jobs, even with most of us living less than five miles apart."

"Good." Rob said. "Because once you trotted out those designs of yours this morning, fat chance you're getting out of here any time soon."

"Is that a threat?"

He shrugged. "Something like that."

Mercifully that beast of a car of his was already pulling against the curb in front of the homestead. Flustered, I struggled to wrestle myself and my oversized portfolio out of the back seat at the same time.

"Let me," Rob insisted.

Before I could get a word out, he had reached my door and was opening it. I just looked at him.

"Try to maneuver that portfolio my way," he said. "It's easier for someone outside to . . ."

"I could manage this— "

"Of course. But then I think you said the same thing about walking home."

Flushing, I finally let him pry the huge leather case out of my death grip. In just a few deft moves, he had eased it out the door and was waiting out there in the street alongside the Hummer for me to retrieve it.

"This will work, you know," he said softly, "if you give it half a chance."

I could tell he wasn't just talking about my move to Hope. Or about that blasted portfolio either.

"Thanks for the ride," I said.

"Now, was that so hard?"

Yes—yes, it was. But then, I was learning.

In passing I took a leaf from my good neighbor Grace's book and just hugged the guy—fleeting, awkward and totally out of character for me, but effective. For once the man was speechless.

"See you, Rob!"

I reached over to tap on the passenger side window.

"Bye, Wilma . . .!"

I don't think she heard me. Bless her heart soldiering on up there in the front seat, the elderly organist seemed oblivious to the whole business—an occupational hazard, given the decibel level and her proximity to the organ pipes all those years.

*Going deaf.* Something else I had to look forward to if I kept up practicing as much as I had since moving to Hope. But then there seem to be prices for everything we have the audacity to love.

Still chuckling quietly to myself, I turned and started up the front walk. Behind me, I heard the Hummer easing away from the curb.

The classical station was airing a program on madrigals, rife with gamboling swains and lasses, as I made myself lunch, then went online for another stab at googling sources for rag. I found myself humming along on the familiar melodies, strangely in tune with all that uncomplicated rusticity and *joie de vivre.*

I had to hand it to Rob and his off-handed way of pulling me up short—especially his shoot-from-the-hip speculating about my life back in Philly. He was right, of course. Not too subtle about it, but right.

I was finding a niche here and Undercroft Arts was a big part of it. But then so were those fierce, passionate, crack-of-dawn practice sessions over there in the solitude of Nativity's sanctuary.

The years may not have been kind either to my speed or flexibility. Still, in their place, miraculously I seemed to be finding something else—a determination and abandon in playing that I had never known before. Nothing I had ever experienced could match that almost desperate rush of energy and creative joy. Even Wilma sensed as much the first time she heard me play.

I had always told my clients that it is not the paycheck or the job title that determines our professionalism. I meant it then. I was learning to live it now.

Win, lose or draw, I was determined to give that precious practice time—a luxury all those years working at the employment office—the very best I had and more. And based on the reaction to my weaving dsigns for Undercroft Arts, there would be plenty to keep me and my new-found weaving buddies busy for months to come.

I would worry about surviving on a fixed income later. The goals I found myself setting may not have been the most lofty or even sensible, but right now, they were enough.

# ✣ Chapter Ten

I had made Rob Sims a promise, and for all my ambivalence about what it did or did not mean, I found myself making good on it. Next Sunday I showed up for church at Nativity for the first time. Though I tried to reserve judgment, I was prepared for just about anything.

Once I got over the shock of seeing him up there in an appliqued green chasuble and crisp white alb instead of the usual jeans and clerical collar, I had to admit I was pleasantly surprised. The love lavished on this tiny church was evident everywhere and a lot of that had to do with how people felt about Rob himself.

*Witness that chasuble.* Whimsical, almost Art-Deco swirls of vine-and-branches cascaded over the front and back of the vestment, obviously Grace Alanson's handiwork. Similar motifs appeared on the banners hung along the side walls of the sanctuary. It was a feast for the senses . . . in more ways than one and took someone as unabashedly masculine as a Rob Sims to pull off wearing it.

As a priest in front of his congregation, Rob was quietly confident and more at ease than I had ever seen him in his civilian life. His sermon was simple, direct and laced with humor and self-deprecating tales from his early years in Hope. He chanted the liturgy with a credible baritone and the children's sermon—albeit aimed at just three of them sitting up there in front on the chancel steps—had every adult in the place in stitches.

I stifled any lingering thoughts about the ambiguity of our relationship—even the difficulty of losing myself in the liturgy away from the organ bench. In the end, I succeeded.

One of the Lectionary readings for the week all but jumped off the page at me. *Whatever you eat, whatever you drink—whatever you do, do all to the glory of God.*

It was strange that as a career counselor, that particular text hadn't screamed out at me before. I found it percolating to the surface again as I filled the silence in the Prayers of the People with my growing list of friends and neighbors.

My thoughts went out for Grace and her boundless hospitality, for Marty and his hit-or-miss struggles to find his calling. I prayed for Leah and little Bart—whimsically named, I discovered, after a character on the *Simpsons.* And I lingered, too, on Rob at war with his demons and for my own, no less real and troubling.

I named them in my heart—*anxiety about change, my control-freak tendencies, fear of relationships even more powerful than my fears of being alone.* The list was considerably longer but by then we had collectively moved on.

For the first time in my life, I was starting to recognize and acknowledge at least some of those impediments to living. I owed a lot, if not most of that to Rob. Strangely enough, it even felt comforting to admit that I did.

Transported to this place by forces and circumstances beyond our understanding, we were choosing a common labor of love, flawed and glorious in our simple human concern for one another. My thoughts flowed into silence like the rise and fall of a hymn, at once an intercession, a confession and a thanksgiving. For the first time since my former boss Irene sat me down in that office in Philly, I felt—if not peace—then at least a tentative truce in my struggles.

As for what originated from the organ bench, Rob pretty much hit the nail on the head when it came to Wilma's pace and the speed with which she picked up on the cues in the liturgy. I couldn't miss the sound of the tremolo on just about everything.

That said, Wilma survived deer-in-the-headlights moments in two of the hymns and went on to play a lovely little interlude at the offertory. After the service, I waited until she finished the postlude, then I told her how much I enjoyed her playing.

The woman absolutely beamed. "Glad ya liked it," she said. "I went looking for one of those English guys, like you said. Can't tell by the name—but figured it had to be pretty close. Not one of those Germans or Italians anyway."

I wasn't going to burst her bubble and tell her the composer was, indeed, a good old born-and-bred Yankee. As we were talking, I noticed that Rob was heading back from the narthex, that gorgeous chasuble slung over the sleeve of his linen alb.

Wilma had her back turned, so she didn't catch the wink aimed in my direction. I read it as his way of telling me he was pleased that the two of us were making nice.

"Talking shop," he said, "or can a musical illiterate join in?"

Wilma laughed. "Sorry about that first hymn," she told him. "I know ya said only two verses, but I got carried away."

"No problem. We still made it through the service by ten. Old George Barker had his watch out once or twice, but when he shook my hand at the door he was smiling."

The parishioners of Nativity seemed obsessed by the immediacy of time. It was the only church I had ever seen with a wall clock hanging at the back of the sanctuary—a huge oak railroad clock right in the preacher's sight-line. As we spoke, Wilma's son was hovering in the background, consulting his own time piece.

I started to move aside as Wilma climbed down off the organ bench. Once on her feet, she reached over and retrieved a strange-looking waffle-weave pad from the spot she had been sitting

"Bad back . . .?" I asked.

"That bench slants forward so steep, I keep falling on the pedalboard," Wilma chuckled. "My boy Bradley, here, thought of getting me one of those mats they use to keep dishes from sliding around in the cupboards in motorhomes. Works like a charm."

We laughed, this tiny knot of liturgical insiders debriefing one of the most precious remaining acts of fellowship in this little town. For all the humor and behind-the-scenes logistics, this was life and death playing itself out inside these musty walls, the restless human search for the Divine and a sanctuary from the cruelties of the world out there.

Leaning heavily on her son's arm, the elderly organist shuffled off down the aisle in the direction of the front door. Rob and I stood watching her.

Bless her heart, I found myself thinking, that gutsy little woman even was beginning to have a profound impact on how I looked at my own daily practice regimen. With all her flaws as a musician, she still had the courage to hang on in her nineties, loving every minute of it—sciatica, arthritis and all.

Forget what you can't do and do what you can. She was a heck of a role model, if I ever saw one.

"Thanks for that," Rob said when Wilma was safely out of earshot.

"She's a neat lady."

He looked down at me, smiled. "Ditto."

"Some days more than others."

My mouth felt stiff. *Time to move on.*

I told him about my spontaneous offer of shelter to Leah, the utter stupidity of it on multiple fronts. Rob chuckled at Grace's intervention and Marty's daily treks across the backyards to report on the status of our newcomer.

"It's finally hitting home to me," I said, "how tenuous my situation is right now—what living on a fixed income means. My pension check doesn't show up for another week and my tab at Rutterbach's hardware has grown to two pages of a yellow legal-sized tablet. I've been eating into my savings like there's no tomorrow— "

"Sounds like you need a break," Rob said.

"Probably."

"It's Sunday," he said. "Mike's Eatery has a pretty good Sunday brunch . . . not just meat and potatoes lying there looking at you. A little high on the old carbs . . . but edible."

"Not in the budget, but thanks for the offer."

It wasn't totally fabricated as a way out. Marty just informed me I probably was going to have to replace the furnace before winter. I was still suffering from sticker shock as we did some online research.

"Mike's really isn't pricey . . . but then if it would help, this one's on me. Hey, I'm flush enough these days—just started drawing early Social Security a couple of months back!" Rob shrugged. "You can write this off as a welcome-to-Hope perk or one to celebrate getting those designs of yours off the drawing board. Take your pick!"

It was pretty plain he wasn't going to let me out of this. My instinct was to dig in my heels and beg off, but then—to my total surprise—I heard myself waffle.

"Dutch . . ."

He nodded. "All right then, Dutch."

Rob already was heading for the sacristy door. "Just give me a second to get rid of the outfit," he said, "I'll be right back."

It would make a fascinating sociological study to analyze what happens when a woman walks into a public place like a restaurant with a

man in a clerical collar. I had never really thought about it myself, but I couldn't help notice a strange lull in the natural flow of conversation, as if someone had momentarily pressed the mute-button on the remote.

My grandmother Grunwald used to share hilarious stories of family gatherings—laughter-filled affairs fueled with beer, tons of food and card games around the kitchen table—transformed in a heartbeat by the appearance of the clergyman's buggy on the road out front. With the dexterity of kids caught smoking behind the garage, away went the cards and the alcohol. The laugher metamorphosed into serious, hands-in-the-lap decorum. As soon as that buggy moved on, life resumed, loud and uncensored.

I told Rob about it as we settled into our window booth at Mike's. It was the only seating on that side of the door, set aside usually for the owner or restaurant staff on break. The area for patrons across the room from us was full. When I hit the punch-line about situational pastoral ethics, Rob's roar of laughter turned heads three tables away.

"So much for hiding in plain sight," he gasped.

"I suppose this means you'd better show up here with Wilma next week?"

"Heaven, help me . . . yes. I'll let her son pick up the tab, though. The guy's loaded. One of the few successful farmers around here. Summers he trucks his stuff down to the rest stop on I-80, makes a killing. Winters he drags rolls of barbed wire through the woods and opens the trails to cross-country skiers."

"Smart."

"Like a fox and cheaper than Midas. I've been working on him ever since I got here to help kick off a fund drive for the parsonage roof. The buckets have been salted like landmines around the attic long before I got there."

"How do you handle it," I wondered out loud,"elevating the Host one minute and agonizing over the budget, the next?"

"With difficulty sometimes. When I showed up at the seminary, it was partly to get as far away from the Board Room as humanly possible. Five minutes on the job in Hope pretty much shot that notion."

Rob hesitated, then shook his head. "If I had to put a label on it, I'd say , double-whammy—*compartmentalize* and *integrate.* On one side of the scale you put the people, the theology, the life-changing truth of what you can accomplish. On the other are the politics, the money, the fish-bowl lifestyle. Then you try over time to close the gap between your feelings about the two extremes."

I heard the frustration in his voice, but also the implicit love of what he was doing. "Biggest pet peeve?" I said.

"Accepting that people in the church are no better, no worse than anybody out there on the street you pass every day. And, too . . . that for some, the church is the one remaining place they can squabble to get their own way, let their egos flower while knowing that folks are supposed to love them for it."

I laughed. "As a sub, an organist can pretty much walk away from all that. But the sure-and-steady Wilma's of this world are right down there with you in that trench."

"Dodging the flak—and believe me, it's out there. Lots of it, despite those great folks who always have something good to say on the way out the door on Sunday mornings."

"Do you ever regret it?"

"The ministry? In spite of everything—*no.*"

He stopped. The waitress was headed our way, menus in hand.

"All in all, though," he said softly, "I'd say that this has been a pretty good month."

# ✣ Chapter Eleven

It wasn't easy sitting across the table in that restaurant from this man, Father Robert Sims. As we shared and laughed our way through brunch, the picture of discretion and respectability, I suddenly realized there were no words in my emotional vocabulary to express the intimacy that was building between us.

It was like suddenly being eleven again, when my mother announced—out of the blue—that she was going to let me play the prelude the next Sunday. She didn't have to ask me twice. Several anthologies of simple voluntaries tucked in my organ bag, I headed for Nativity after school to practice.

Preludes, I knew, were usually thoughtful and meditative, a musical invitation for people to settle down and start thinking about what God meant to them. It was up to me to choose the piece and set the organ so that I conveyed that mood.

Selecting the 'stops' for an organist is what choosing words is to a writer. The process is called setting the registration—deciding on the pattern of sounds for the piece. As I looked at the pull-knobs and their Gothic-scripted labels, I felt a heady sense of the possibilities. It was like being faced with a musical buffet. Alone and in combination, those lively reeds and flutes, mid-range 8s and 4s or 2-foots, the deep and growling 16-foot Bourdon, all had their own unique voice. I opened the bare little sonata in front of me on the organ rack and went to work.

It's safest not to trust memory, my mom had taught me. As I made my choices, I noted them down in pencil on the first page of the piece in my own bizarre notation system: DULC for Dulciana, LG for Lieblich Gedeckt, the "tenderly muted" 16-foot.

Sunday came and I slid on to the bench to offer up my handiwork. After the service, I had to know.

"Was it okay?" I asked.

My mother frowned. "Why the Vox Humana?" she said.

I knew instantly the stop she meant. *Vox Humana,* she had told me once, came from the Latin for *the human voice*—a stop developed ostensibly to recreate the tremulous sound of a voice in song. It is probably the most used and abused stop on the organ.

In my eleven-year-old's terminology, the 'Vox' had become the 'woo-woo' stop—my way of describing its distinctive trembling or vibrato. If I played loud enough with the Vox on, even the bench under me shuddered.

Mom had explained the mechanics of the thing. Hidden deep inside the heart of the tracker organ was a kind of flywheel that could interrupt the air supply and cause notes to vibrate. To my young ears, the sound was ghostly, mysterious, and despite my mother's dismissal of the Vox as a "favorite with little old ladies", I used it every chance I got.

"That piece is sad," I said. "I wanted people to feel that."

My mother's frown deepened. Then she shook her head.

"Charlise, honey, she said, "it's easy to pull out that Vox and let the flywheel do your job for you. But if you truly want to make those feelings real, *forget the Vox*. Instead, you need to work at how you time a phrase, where to pause and where you push ahead— "

"But that's so— "

"Hard? True. But it means you've learned to connect your hands and your heart to make the pipes sing. Expressing honest emotion is never easy, but that's just what a good organist does."

*Not just a good organist,* it seems. A lifetime later, here we were, Rob Sims and I—*living proof.*

Rob Sims was married. He was also caught in an emotional no-man's land, with a terrible disconnect between what he felt and what ought to be. Forget the ethics of his situation. Professionally, to react in any other way to the state of his failed marriage was, simply put, a career-buster.

But then I wasn't a child fooling around on the bench any longer either. Whatever my own feelings, emotionally I needed to slam off this particular woo-woo stop, once and for all. And yet—? My rationalizing began and ended there, at a question mark.

I had been widowed some thirty years—married less than four. I had long since learned to be alone.

Though early-on after Len died, men had come and gone in my life, I saw myself first and foremost as a mother. Once out of the nest and settled in their own lives, my girls subtly began urging me to date, even occasionally pairing me up with single friends at family gatherings. None of the relationships lasted longer than a month or so—awkward public encounters that never came within miles of a bedroom.

And yet here I sat, across the table from this relative stranger, palms sweating and a lightning-bolt shock of awareness every time I saw the guy's face crinkle into a smile. I hadn't felt this out of control since an adolescent crush on the postal carrier.

I was never a relativist when it came to relationships—had never been tempted to have an affair and wasn't about to start now. Rob was married. There was no justification here for anything but cold showers and cold, hard common sense.

"Have you heard from Karin?" I said.

Rob's face seemed to darken for a moment but then he, too, just went with the flow. It had to be asked. Friends would. And in this context, it was also a reality check.

"No. Nothing, although my son called last week."

I waited out the silence.

"Ted's back in college part-time," Rob said finally, "a step in the right direction. And apparently he has been seeing a counselor."

"I'm glad."

"You and me both. If he heard from his mother, he wasn't sharing."

My voice was low. "Have you . . . do your parishioners know about any of this?"

"The search committee had to hear some of it. But since then . . ., no. There's no point, really."

I nodded. "Tough, though—bottling it all up."

Rob had been working his way through his salad. Mid-bite, he chewed on the situation for a while. I had been pushing the mixed greens around my own plate for some time now without noticeable enthusiasm.

"I trust you, if that's what you're wondering," he said. "And I'm . . . grateful that I can."

The buffet was as advertised though noisy. Half the town wandered in and out as we moved on to our entrees. When I recognized a couple of parishioners waiting in the line to be seated, I caught Rob's eye.

By mutual consent, our conversation veered off to safer

pastures—kayaking, my career in Philly, more music and Rob's outrageous seminary stories that left me in stitches. I told him about my morning power walks, about my daughters and my theories about what makes music so compelling.

"It's not original, I'm sure," I told him, "but I've come to believe that part of the beauty of sound is the lack of it. If all music were just a solid wall of melody and harmony thrown together like stew, I think our senses would go on overload. It can be more powerful to wait for the music in the silence."

"Like that Biblical reference about looking for God's voice in the fire and whirlwind. But then in the end, finding it in that very still, small voice . . ."

I smiled. "Exactly."

"Have you ever walked a labyrinth?" he said.

"I've seen pictures. But no."

"Walking a labyrinth is a lot like what you're describing. Your body moves along a path, compact and circling toward a center. Your pace is measured and your breathing slows. At first every little sound interrupts that rhythm. But the longer you walk, the more your senses shut out everything around you but that simple curve of the journey."

"Beautiful. And when you reach the goal?"

"That's the amazing thing," he said, "the center isn't the end. It's only the beginning. As you retrace your steps, it is just a continuation of the path. And when you leave the labyrinth, you resume your life . . . but almost as if something has lifted— "

"Freedom. Peace."

"You've experienced it, then?" he said.

"Sometimes," I nodded. "I'll be playing a piece—technically difficult and so complex that the concentration becomes overwhelming. I start to lose myself totally in what I'm doing and then suddenly it's over. I didn't expect it to be. When I take my hands off the keyboard, I can feel the silence, the physical presence of it, come rushing in."

"The Eternal. And you don't want it to ever end."

"No," I said.

It wasn't the only leave-taking I was dreading. The waitress had brought Rob the bill. For once, I didn't argue with him when he reneged on his promise and insisted on treating me.

I didn't expect him to walk me home either, but he did. How much trouble can you get into in broad daylight on the way home from church and Sunday brunch?

Without fanfare, the rhythm of our strides adjusted to each other and the gaps in our conversations were more comfortable now. We had turned on to Elm Street, with just two blocks to go, when I asked. I couldn't help myself.

"How did you meet her, Rob?"

He broke stride, imperceptibly but I caught it. It was quiet a long time before he responded.

"Karin was literally a kid when I quarterbacked her dad's college team," he said. "Not that I noticed at the time. It was years later when I showed up at Coach's annual Fall alumni scrimmage, nineteen seventy-eight. I was mid-thirties and still single. My dad had died that summer and I had always looked on Coach as a mentor. His daughter Karin—as it turns out—was also home for the weekend."

He drew a harsh breath. Out of the corner of my eye as we walked, I could sense the tension as he picked through the wreckage of his past. I could have no doubts whatsoever this man was telling me the truth—things he had never shared with anyone.

"She was the most beautiful woman I had ever seen," he said. "Modeling at the time and taking courses at Carnegie-Mellon. On the way out the door, Karin slipped her phone number in my hand. One thing led to another."

"A long courtship?"

"Not long enough, apparently. But then it was easy enough to convince myself I was ready for marriage and that the age difference didn't really matter. Most of my associates already had taken the plunge."

"And afterward . . . she continued her career . . .?"

At that, Rob came to a dead stop on the sidewalk alongside me. Embarrassed at what might appear to have been prying, I joined him, woefully unsure of the ground under our feet.

"Was I in the market for a . . . trophy wife, is that what you're wondering?" he said. "Truth be told, I honestly don't know. It's hard to gauge when one or two of my married colleagues were already moving on—dating women Karin's age. Certainly she had witnessed one too many of my old game tapes and her dad's highly embellished tales of my daring-do on the gridiron. And then, of course, there was the vintage Porsche and the brand new Reserved-for-Partner sign on my parking spot at the agency."

He was looking at and through me now, caught up somewhere in the choices out there that had led him to this place. His voice was low.

"I do believe," he said finally, "that if Karin truly had wanted any of it—finishing her degree, the career—I would have supported her in all of it. But then I was making more than enough money for the house in Squirrel Hill, kids, the whole nine yards."

"You were happy."

"We were the golden couple. Karin took to the role readily enough, the perfect corporate wife—stunning, a formidable hostess . . . drunk or sober, she pulled it off. Two great kids, one of each—"

"The American dream . . ."

Rob closed his eyes. When he opened them, I saw nothing but pain behind them.

"Our daughter's death blew the lid off that fantasy," he said slowly. "After a couple of months of AA, it also hit me that the booze was a symptom, not just the disease. I was in the wrong profession. And the lifestyle that went with it, for me, was a disaster."

He must be a good six inches taller than my five-six. I had to look up to see his face. The anger was gone and in its place, a sadness so deep that it must have touched the man's soul.

"You blamed yourself for your daughter's death?"

Rob seemed about to respond, changed his mind. When he began again, his voice was taut—deceptively calm.

"I'm still not sure I'm capable of going there . . . not and hang on to any pretext of sanity. I do know that one morning I just looked in the mirror—sober for the tenth week in a row—and didn't like what I saw."

"You were in AA by then?"

He nodded. "On my lunch hours I started hanging out in the Episcopal cathedral for meetings. It was just blocks from my office and I got to know one of the priests pretty well. Eventually he suggested that I look into the seminary. At first I just laughed. So did the Diocese. Up until that point . . . the possibility had never crossed my mind. Not once. And certainly not Karin's."

"But you took him up on it?"

Rob nodded. "Not without a lot of soul searching. But then trite as it sounds, I had found my calling. And even the Diocese saw it. Karin was furious."

"Change can be wrenching— "

"Trouble is, I changed. Karin didn't."

I couldn't just stand there and let him think he had the monopoly on regrets. As confessionals went, mine was relatively banal. But then never, ever, had I consciously admitted my deepest doubts even to myself—to say nothing of a relative stranger.

"I wonder sometimes about my own choices, what my life would have looked like if my husband. . . if Len had come back from 'Nam," I told him. "He was so young and idealistic, gung-ho Army all the way—ROTC through college, while everyone around us was agonizing over the draft. Even when he died in those jungles, I never thought to question the 'why' of it."

My voice shook, steadied again. "And then . . . all those years with the Job Service, I saw so many of my young clients grabbing at enlistment to pull them out of poverty, fund their educations. But in the end, the price tag was horrendous . . . not at all what they expected. It made me . . . angry, for them . . . and at myself— "

"That you said nothing?"

Slowly, I shook my head, contradicting him. "That I . . . *did.* But to them, not my husband—not when it could have mattered."

I couldn't bear to meet Rob's steady, unflinching gaze.

"And when you go there," he said softly, "You still feel angry . . . even disloyal."

"That. And in my blacker moments, I ask myself if Len had come back, would we even have known each other by now. Or was ours just another one of those marriages destined to wind up a . . . grim statistic?"

The compassion in Rob's eyes was tinged with awareness. "Only hindsight is twenty-twenty. What drove Karin and me apart was there, always, in our relationship—from the very beginning."

"You must . . . I'd guess you must come across that sort of thing every day."

"Every time I do a wedding, I wonder." Rob chewed on his lip as he thought about it. "All those promises about health and money and death. I stand there and listen to couples repeating those promises—never realizing that they ignore one fundamental thing. You can't love someone else until you know and love yourself."

"And when a marriage doesn't start out on that foot—?"

"Is it still a marriage?" He flashed an awkward smile. "Don't misunderstand me, I'd be the first to say I respect denominations with zero-tolerance divorce policies. But when the bodies in the backyard start to pile up—usually because the relationship wasn't valid from Day One—let's just say, I'm not so sure anymore . . ."

"Or that 'life' is the appropriate sentence for . . . mutual stupidity?"

Rob laughed. "Not quite that blunt. But yeah . . . it can come down to that."

"I looked around that restaurant," I said quietly, "wondering just how much anguish was silently playing itself out in those lives out there."

"Judging by my pastoral counseling load, even in little Hope, PA . . . quite a few."

We had reached the front walk. It had to be done. The hug was quick and as innocuous as a handshake—good friends, taking their leave on a Sunday afternoon in late June.

Sheer instinct, when I hit the base of the porch steps I half-turned and in the process saw that Rob already had reached the corner. Irritated at myself, I didn't wait to find out if he would do the same. In a half-dozen brisk steps I was at the front door and fumbling for the key.

Feeling very vulnerable and stupid out there on the front porch, I finally managed, with difficulty, to wiggle that sliver of a key into the lock, stiff and intractable from under-use. My good neighbor, Grace, still laughed at me for that—locking the place up like Fort Knox every time I strayed from home and hearth, a carryover from my years "in exile down there in Philly", as she described it. *Old habits indeed die hard.*

# Chapter Twelve

In Hope, the Dog Days of late July can be steamy and brutal, wringing the get-up-and-go out of the hardiest among us. Marty Santano was in a funk. Preoccupied with my own *weltschmerz*, it took a while for me to notice.

In his casual truth-seeking around the edges of my life, Rob Sims seems to have set off some inner alarm system—if things seem to be too good, maybe it's time to break out the flack jackets. All the while my young tenant appeared to be charging ahead like some over-wound battery-bunny, I was finding it harder and harder even to roust myself out of bed in the morning.

Without a lick of maternal coaxing from me, my young tenant had started contributing modestly to our household kitty, landing what odd jobs he could, hither and yon, in between a steady agenda of fix-'em-up projects in the homestead. After hours he hung out every spare minute in the back yard with Leah and the baby. I really should have gotten suspicious when he abruptly shed the baggies for chinos, came home with a brush cut and again without prompting asked to use my computer to pump out a resume and started walking it around town.

All good stuff, but the implosion was quick to follow.

The mini-Mart interviewed him, just as the rise in gas prices started cutting into tourism traffic and the opening dematerialized. He didn't say much, but the hang-dog look was back. Marty was in a funk.

We were eating breakfast one morning—toast and eggs, his favorite.

Out it came.

"Char, what made you decide to be a counselor?"

I took another bite of toast, followed it with several swigs of coffee. The answer was not easily forthcoming.

"Nothing noble or spectacular. I was about to start my sixth semester of college and still hadn't declared a major much less thought about getting a job. Counseling seemed steady. I like working with people. Expectations in those days weren't a heck of a lot more complicated than that."

"Well, I took all those darn interest tests," he said, "and I flunked. Nobody seems impressed if you tell 'em you just want to slap a sign on your truck and see what happens. I mean . . . who's gonna say, Golly, I've just gotta hook up with a guy like that?"

"You're talking about Leah," I said.

Marty shook his head. "This isn't about her. It's me. After what she went through with little Bart's daddy, Leah thinks I'm a real Bill Gates. This is about what I want . . . and maybe, too, what I want to give her and that little guy . . ."

"Are you telling me you love her, Marty?"

"I don't know. I guess so." He raked a hand over that close-shorn haircut of his, visibly distressed. "When I drove Snaz over to the lumberyard in Bartonville last week, I went past where she and that . . . where she and Bart's daddy lived. Man, Char, what a dump! Tires in the yard and a burned out roof on the porch still half hanging there . . ."

"You worked in neighborhoods like that in Philly sometimes, Marty— "

"Yeah, well, I didn't have to live there. She did. My folks may not have had much, but they made me go to community college—get an Associate's degree in business. It was their dream, so it had to be the last thing in the world I wanted, right? I know they were pissed, thought I wasn't really trying, but they never gave up on me—saw to it that I finished."

"And Leah . . .?"

"That girl's old man is loaded. As a kid she had everything. Except the one thing she wanted—"

"Their time. Their approval."

Marty nodded. "You guessed it. So at seventeen she just took off—never finished high school. When they heard she was pregnant, her mom and dad really crossed her off their list . . ."

"And still, she went ahead and had the baby."

"It wasn't just an in-your-face thing, either. She said she loved the Bart-man from Day One, from the minute she knew. Whatever it took, she said, that little guy would know his mother loved him. No matter what."

I felt the sting of tears as I thought about how terrifying all that must have been. "And you're wondering if you have the courage to take that on, to be that support she never had?"

"Fat chance—without a steady income, no health insurance. It's a big deal when I even offer to take Leah over to the mini-Mart for a cappuccino."

It was the first time since I met him on my client roster that I ever heard Marty fundamentally question the course he had doggedly been steering for himself. I thought long and hard before I answered.

"Marty, that sweet girl has got to decide who she is and what she wants. You can't do that for her. And she can't do that for you, either. The best gift you can give each other would be if you helped each other learn to stop running *from* things and start walking *to*."

"Leah knows now quitting high school was a dumb idea."

"Not fatal. There are ways to get her GED, right here in Hope. And the community college offers night courses in Bartonville. You can borrow Snaz any time you want."

"I'm not much of a pusher, but if I really want to work for myself? I've got to be."

"Makes sense."

"Either I do that . . . or maybe it's time to just bite the bullet like my parents wanted and go to work for somebody else."

"Is that a question, or are you trying to tell me something, Marty?"

He looked at me, steady and intense. His voice was low.

"Do you think I can learn to . . . *hustle*, Char? Can you teach a guy something like that?"

I smiled. "Have you talked to Father Rob about it? He used to be in business, you know."

Marty shook his head. "Not yet."

"A famous writer George Bernard Shaw once said, that as people our job isn't to find ourselves, it's to create ourselves."

I could tell Marty didn't understand. "All that means, is we make a mistake just waiting around for a blinding flash of light on our road to tell us what we're supposed to do with our lives. Most of the time, it creeps up on us. We're working along, trying to be as good at what we're doing as we can, and one day it just occurs to us—*this is what I enjoy, this is what I'm good at, this is what I want to do with my life.* It can take a year. It can take a lifetime, even change over the years. Dreams like people, I believe, are resilient things."

"And if I think right now that maybe I want to go into business after all . . .?"

Marty listened intently as I told him about going on-line to learn more about business plans, about projected growth fields, about small business loans—firing off questions along the way. When I finished, he shook his head.

"Okay . . . , suppose I'm not ready for that yet on my own. Father Rob keeps saying we're going to need more retailers to buy our stuff. Say I go out on the road and find 'em. Leah can help over there at Grace's on the phone answering questions from customers, taking down the orders I get and still keep an eye on Bart—even go to night school . . ."

"Direct sales is really tough, Marty."

"So is sitting around waiting for somebody to hire me!"

His jaw tightened and for a split-second a subtle don't-mess-with-me glint flickered in his usually placid blue eyes. With a shock I realized my young tenant *already* had been watching Rob Sims at the helm during our Undercroft sessions an awful lot more than he let on.

Marty was on a roll. "If sales pick up . . . we'll need more of those lap looms. I'll build 'em, even recruit more weavers, take the supplies around to those who work at home and find out how they're doing and what they need. When one of those big floor looms breaks, I could fix it."

"Sounds like hustle to me."

He grinned. "You noticed. And I've been thinking . . . maybe after we get really good at all this, we even could invite people to come here to Hope and see what we do. They might buy stuff. Or we could teach them what we've learned."

"Workshops?"

"Over at Nativity I saw some brochures in the racks about these retreat weekends for men and women. Go off and learn all kinds of stuff. Why not weavers?"

Dumbfounded, I just looked at him. None of us had even talked about the possibility of value-added enterprises that could supplement our sales when the market was down.

I smiled. "That's a terrific idea, Marty. All of it. How about you and Father Rob, Grace and I sit down and talk about it."

"When?"

"Tomorrow . . . next week?"

"Tomorrow's fine!"

Springing to his feet, Marty excused himself and headed for the back door. "I'll be back," he said.

He didn't have to tell me where he was going. The screen door slammed and I heard his footsteps on the back stairs, quick and determined. Marty most definitely was a man with someplace to go.

I sat there in the kitchen alone for a while, listening to that relentless *drip-DRIP* of the kitchen faucet—that, despite at least two new washers since I moved in. It occurred to me maybe it was just time to replace the darn thing altogether.

Instead I picked up the phone and punched in my daughter Sarah's cell-phone number. She answered on the first ring.

"Mom, what's wrong?"

I looked at the clock. It was only nine-thirty.

"You're at work. Sorry about that. Everything's fine. If you like, I can call back later, when you get home tonight."

There was a frantic rustling of papers from the other end of the line, followed by a thud then a stifled expletive. I was just about to ask if my daughter was alright when I heard the sound of muffled breathing in the mouthpiece.

"No . . . fine, I can talk—sort of anyway, after dropping that humongous file I was trying to stuff back into my desk," Sarah muttered. "The boss is out of town, auditors are all over the place. I feel like I'm putting in 40-hour *days*, say nothing about weeks. Sometimes I feel as if I need a good dose of career advice, if you've got any to spare . . ."

I laughed. Sarah was carving out a niche for herself as office manager for a large wholesaling operation in Cleveland, not exactly what she had anticipated doing with a Master's Degree in English literature. But she was good at it, more to task than the owner and CEO from the sound of it.

"Join the club," I told her. "No boss, no deadlines and no darn excuse. The kitchen faucet is leaking again. I'm still tripping over unopened boxes, I haven't touched the keyboard in days—"

"Correct me, but I thought you retired from all that pressure?"

"*From* it or *to* it, I'm not so sure anymore."

"You volunteer for that weaving project, right? You talked about sending a couple of resumes to churches trying to snag some kind of organ job. And you haven't even been in Hope all that long. Maybe taking on more work right now is just too much."

"It isn't the organ—or Undercroft Arts either. I'm enjoying both more than ever, though I *am* trying to practice smarter lately not harder. My age is no time to start messing around with carpal tunnel. I've been lucky so far."

I hesitated. "And for the record, I didn't send out the resumes. Not yet anyway."

"Mad-money isn't a factor, then?"

"Depends on how many times I want to eat out a month or how many trips to Europe I'm planning. Besides, organists don't really make that much in the first place."

"Well, if it's our inheritance you're worrying about, forget it. That hubby of mine's family is richer than God, embarrassingly generous and can afford to be. You're on your own, have worked hard all your life for every cent of it. Get yourself one of those spend-til-you-drop bumper stickers and practice away forever if it makes you happy."

I laughed. "If I wind up out in some shack in the Baja with that tattooed biker that lives down my block, I'll remind you of that."

Even to me that sounded harsh, crabby. Apparently my young tenant wasn't the only one around here with issues. For a split-second I almost envied Marty for what he saw as his blank-slate of a past when my own was a thick-crammed file of choices made and roads not taken.

For all that, our respective futures were no less a mystery. And the Now—searching with two hands in the dark, both of us.

"Mom, you're just in a funk," Sarah sighed. "You enjoy playing. So, play. When you don't, stop. Heaven knows you tried hard enough to get me to follow in those sock-footed feet of yours. I hated every minute on that keyboard, with a passion. But stick me in a pair of track shoes and I'm happy as a clam."

There was no sense in tap-dancing any more around the bottom line. "Am I stupid at this late date, Sarah . . . trying to foist myself off on some parish like that . . .?"

I told her about Wilma, for better or worse, playing 'til she dropped. Much as I admired her spunk and though my own skills were well beyond that level and undisputedly were improving every day, the lingering childhood fear of making a fool of myself was very real . . . very much still out there.

My daughter laughed. "Since when are you the kind to pull the over-the-hill stuff, Mom? Besides, music isn't anything new in your life. You've been on and off one bench or another for—what?—fifty years now. Isn't it kind of late to start worrying about credentials now?"

*Longer than that—since Mom first signed me up for piano lessons at the ripe old age of four.* But I wasn't going to quibble.

"Your sister keeps telling me pretty much the same thing. And then too the parishes around here are hardly St. John the Divine."

Silence prevailed on the other end of the line. It wasn't like Sarah to hold back.

"Does it matter . . . ," she said finally. "I mean, maybe it's bothering you that your Mom worked at Nativity so long . . ."

Whatever I was expecting, it wasn't that. "I don't see how. Anyway the parish already has an organist. That's not even an option"

If she noticed I was begging the question, Sarah didn't call me on it. But I did, knowing she had hit a nerve. To send out those resumes would be to admit how badly I needed to play. And that yes, maybe some secret longing was indeed at work here, to close the circle and step into my mother's shoes.

But I had told it like it was. That door was closed to me, like another one I wasn't prepared to discuss either, with my daughter or anyone. It was the one with 'Rob Sims' emblazoned in big letters on the old mailbox.

"You realize, you're not making this easy, counselor!" my daughter sighed.

"Granted." I forced a laugh. "But then maybe I don't need solutions, just to hear you giving me hell. For old time's sake."

"Consider it given. I love you, Mom."

Amazing how those four little words can loosen the most gosh-awful knots around your heart. I choked on a response.

"I love you, too, honey. And if I thought it would make any difference, I'd be up there in Cleveland in a heartbeat and punch out that boss of yours for not recognizing a good thing when he sees it."

Small talk flowed more easily now, a healing stream through the shared wasteland of both our days. In the back of my skull I kept thinking, first Marty, now Sarah and me—maybe it was a full moon. But then who ever said life was going to be easy, whatever our age?

Eventually feeling a heck of a lot better—glad that my daughter seemed to be as well—I told her to give my best to Ryan and my grandchild, then set the phone back on its base. It would have been wrong to describe the act as breaking the connection.

# ✣ Chapter Thirteen

*Labor Day, how appropriate.*

I had been living in Hope four months now and retired or not, I had never worked so hard in my life. But then I was getting more or less resigned to the notion. Things were looking up.

For starters, Todd Rutterbach also had begun to hire Marty on a regular basis now for odd jobs—their own little informal contracting business. For the past month, my tenant had been paying close to the going rate for rent. I had subbed for funerals several times down in Bartonville when the regular organist was called away on business for her day job.

On the home front, we were finally settling in. Just last week, Marty and I had finally cleared all but a handful of boxes out of the homestead and hauled the flattened cardboard to the recycling center.

To celebrate on the official holiday itself, I went over to Nativity crack-of-dawn, before it got too hot and humid. It wasn't to collect my thoughts or practice as I usually did, but just to play—*for the sheer fun of it, flat-out, pedal-to-the-metal.*

Even at that hour the air in the sanctuary was close and still, so I was glad I had worn my gardening tank top and cargo shorts. The place was deserted—Grace had given her worker bees the day off—and the kayak was missing from the rectory porch. At least no one was likely to wander in and catch me in that otherwise inappropriate get-up.

I would have socializing enough before the day was out. Later in the afternoon, the village was holding its annual Community Homecoming and barbecue. Grace and I and our impromptu family of Leah, Marty and little Bart were planning to make a night of it.

The Hope village budget didn't allow for fireworks, but the local volunteer fire department had jerry-rigged a sparkler display in the city park, using as a base a homemade plywood version of the American flag. A local bluegrass band was scheduled to play for the dance that preceded the pyrotechnics—brief as that also might turn out to be, considering that two of the musicians were on parole from the nursing home.

Meanwhile this time was mine and mine alone, to pour out my passion and longing in peace in this holy space. Easing open the organ case, I settled down on the bench and started reading through the stack of music that Wilma had left behind from last Sunday's church service.

Performance is hard, physical work—just ask any orchestra player after a concert. For all the elegant black and white apparel, the standard anti-perspirant of choice is triple-X.

Fifteen minutes into my musical workout, I was sticking to the bench. Make a note, I told myself, to ask Wilma if I could keep a terry towel stashed around here somewhere for just such contingencies. Meanwhile, the sweat ran down into my eyes and stung as I squinted to pick my way through the tough passages. I felt like I was suffocating.

My modest expletive echoed in the empty sanctuary. *"For crying out loud . . .!"*

Time for some air, but the window on the side wall opposite the organ seemed hopelessly stuck. With brute force and much jiggling, I managed to crack open two of the hinged lower panels of beautifully leaded stained glass. A blast of cooler air spread over my upturned face like water out of a showerhead.

"Blessed relief . . .!"

I tried the same approach with the bank of windows on the wall closest to me. Eventually they, too, swung open. The net result was at least a five degree drop in temperature.

More or less resuscitated, I rooted through the file of music on the floor next to the bench and came up with a wild collection of "pipe dusters"—the organist's term for the flashy showpieces that literally blast out the lint collecting in the wooden and metal tubes. It looked as if Wilma had never even cracked the binding. Pedaling for all I was worth, I punched out staggered sets of chords with my hands, on the beat with the left hand and in sets of threes or triplets in the right.

*TA-ta-ta, TA-ta-ta-TA-ta-ta, TA-ta-ta*, shift the pattern up a fifth. Then repeat. *TA-ta-ta, TA-ta-ta, TA-ta, TA-ta-ta.*

I felt like I was under sail, dancing across a glassy harbor as effortlessly as a seagull in flight. The wind of the pipes above my head rushed against my face and I could imagine pale clouds scudding across an endless canopy of blue overhead.

From time to time, I felt a faint shudder as my fingers struck at a combination of notes. After the glitch, I heard a distinct wheezing puff of air as if the instrument were struggling to breathe.

*Rob might be right about the reservoir*, I thought.

But the piece was too powerful and compelling for me to linger long on technicalities. In a frenetic cascade of arpeggios, hand over hand and hitting more than I missed, I followed the notes along the staff to the great final crashing chord sequence. Like the roar of the ocean against the sand, the pitches soared wave-like upward on the staff.

Frozen in place, my hands held on to the final chord. As I let go, the sound ebbed away into a profound, almost disturbing silence.

"Right on," I exulted.

I was actually shaking with the concentration it had taken to traverse that final system. *Anybody hearing this, you sitting here wildly talking to yourself, would think you're nuts*, I told myself. In that moment, frankly, I didn't care about any of it.

Musical aerobics like that, from all I had read on the subject, were similar in a lot of ways to running a marathon. The closer to the finish line of a piece, the greater the chance of losing your concentration altogether and thoroughly botching the ending. Timing is all.

"First hit those triple bars at the end," my mother always told me. "Then tell yourself how good it was."

Easier said than done. But oh, how wonderfully good it felt when it all came together.

I played until my arms ached and my ears were numb from the overwhelming contrast between sound and silence. I played until I couldn't play any longer. And then exhausted, exhilarated, dripping wet in my shorts and tank top, I went home.

As I slunk past the parsonage, I noticed the kayak was back. *Give thanks for small favors*—Rob himself, this once, was nowhere in sight.

I didn't need the hall mirror to tell me the status of things. I looked like a wreck and a half. Cheeks flushed and hair glistening with sweat, I stared back at my image in the unforgiving glass.

For all the momentary wear and tear, I could have sworn, though the scale would argue against it, from the general state of things between chin and decolletage, that I had dropped another five pounds. *Great, if true,* though it was still going to take major surgery to get myself looking civilized again for the night's festivities.

More to the point, I had better take that power-nap I knew was on the agenda the minute the adrenalin high was over. That blessed twenty-minute grace period just barely would buy me the time to shower and wash my hair before I crashed.

I was sound asleep, dreaming about my mother. She was walking toward me through waves of ripening fields of rye rustling in the sun when my internal alarm clock shook me awake—five o'clock.

This blasted community picnic was *The* social event of the summer and, absent a hot date or not, I vowed I was going to enjoy it. By the time Grace hollered in at the back door at six, I had showered yet again, spent a good ten minutes in front of the mirror with the entire contents of my makeup case, and livened up my practical sit-on-the-ground black culottes and tank top with a garnet choker my grandmother had given me.

"Zowza," Grace whistled as she helped me haul my share of the picnic fixings to her trunk. "I hope you've tucked some Mace in all this luggage you're toting. When the male population of Hope—pitiful I grant you—gets one look at—"

"Yeah, well . . . thanks, I think. I was worried it was just a little too . . . Vampira for the occasion. But then there's not much color up there in the closet. One of these days I've got to start thinking about a mall run in Bartonville."

"Trust me, girl. If those threads of yours are any sample, you're doing just fine!"

We drove the few blocks to the park with our little crew fussing over logistics all the way. In the end we settled in on a blanket on the edge of the dance floor with just enough space between us and the fireworks, such as it was, to reassure little Bart. If Rob Sims was in the crowd already shoe-horning itself into the tiny park, I didn't notice.

The band was setting up—a process that took longer, I suspected, than their upcoming gig. In the fading light we enjoyed our little feast, supplementing the communal barbecue with some of the largesse that Grace had stashed in her cavernous picnic basket. My little 'extras" of hors d'oeuvres and a store-bought cheesecake for dessert just compounded the calorie count. At this rate, even my regular walking routine wasn't going to keep off the pounds.

The sun had fallen below the horizon by the time the band got going. After a shaky start, a fair number of couples took to the floor. Leah turned him down, but in my case Marty wouldn't take no for an answer.

Decked out in chinos and dress shirt open at the neck, my young tenant led me out on the cobbled-together plywood dance floor with the same self-conscious determination I had seen him apply to his venture as entrepreneur-in-training.

So help me, he was watching his feet. Marty's forehead knotted into a frown and I saw his lips move with the silent effort of deciphering the rhythm.

*One. Two. Three. One—*

"You've never waltzed before?"

He lost a beat, thinking about it. "Is it that obvious . . .?"

"Nothing ventured . . ."

"Well, your feet are sure going to regret this tomorrow."

I, too, was concentrating—in an effort to stay out of his way. So I didn't see it coming.

From out of nowhere, Rob Sims had made his way on to the floor and had tapped Marty on the shoulder, signaling his intention to cut in. The relief on Marty's face was unmistakable. So, I feared, was the reaction on mine, as Rob swept me into his arms.

"Subtle, huh?" he chuckled softly.

It wasn't the description I would have used as he whisked me off to a relatively isolated corner of the crowded floor. His hand was insistent against the small of my back, his body as lithe and expert as so many years ago maneuvering inside the twenty-yard-line. Whoever handled that knee surgery of his must have known their stuff.

Through clenched teeth and the smile that went with it, I put up what resistance I could, *given the obvious, that half the village was within earshot.*

"Is . . . this . . . wise . . .?"

"Probably not. I saw at least a dozen guys out there contemplating bludgeoning that tenant of yours with their walkers before I could get anywhere near you."

"Lovely—!"

"My thought, exactly."

Laughing, he coaxed me into a theatrical yet flawless turn. In passing, a sea of familiar faces swam through my field of vision . . . half of them on the vestry and all of them visibly amused at what was transpiring on that dance floor. I could only hope their reaction put the best possible construction on things, that totally out of character, their priest was making like Fred Astaire with the first handy partner.

Except Grace Alanson. I could have sworn our split-second eye contact had one thing written all over it—*well, now I've seen everything . . .!*

My world seemed to be spinning out of control. Without warning, Rob playfully swung us into another turn, a maneuver that closed the already marginal gap between us.

I did the only possible thing under the circumstances. Simply put, I followed him—would have through the jaws of hell, if that is where we were headed.

Heart thudding, I lost myself in the wild joy of the moment, the dizzying contact of Rob's body, cuing mine to respond. Mercifully at least, he had engineered his ambush mid-tune. After what seemed like a lifetime, I could sense the music slow, begin to taper to an end.

"By the way . . . for the record," he whispered just as the final note quavered and died, "after that workout you put the old Tracker through this morning, you sure clean up nice, lady . . .!"

I just looked at him. The other dancers were maneuvering around us now, jostling and talking on their way to the makeshift bar where a kegger was in process.

"You were *listening . . .?*"

"The silent stalker, is that what you're thinking?" He shook his head and if anything, that grin broadened. "It's pretty hard not to figure out something's going on next door with all the windows in the rectory open and the sound of leaded-glass popping over there in the sanctuary from the decibel level."

"Was it really that bad?"

"You're getting better all the time, Char. It's what I love about your playing. Technically you were always a cut above. But lately, it's been something else. Somehow more . . . fearless—"

So then, why was I so utterly, helplessly terrified now? Over Rob's shoulder, my favorite weaver Barney was offering a desperate way out. He was headed our way.

"You two sure look great out there, Father Rob," he bellowed.

I saw Rob's mouth twist into a smile. He didn't need to intone the response. *Amen, to that.*

With a last pointed smile in my direction, he let the retired farmer steer him toward a group of parishioners camped out in lawn chairs under one of the park's venerable oaks, ostensibly waiting for the fireworks. In my book, they already had enough for one night.

Still shaky and flushed, I joined Grace and the gang on the blanket. I was just glad that it was dark enough that none of them could see my face.

# ✣ Chapter Fourteen

*Come, labor on. Away with gloomy doubts and faithless fear! No arm so weak but may do service here . . . redeem the time; its hours too swiftly fly, the night draws nigh.*

It was the Sunday after the community barbecue and barely three dozen voices rang out over the sanctuary, mine among them. Inwardly, I was laughing—not just at Rob's choice of hymns but at the why of it.

The text wasn't in the official hymnal, so he had to borrow it from the Methodists and duplicate it in the bulletin. It was worth it, even when the wheezy old parish copier only feeds a sheet at a time and every other sheet jams.

Labor Day had never been a red letter day on my personal calendar, except when my daughters were young—when it marked the start of school and the end of my ongoing search for decent child-care. This year as it turns out, I had so much more to celebrate.

Not only were the sample liturgical panels done, but a team of a dozen weavers were hard at work on production—some at home and some, for the sake of companionship, at Nativity. Rob must have laid it on pretty thick with the powers that be. The diocese had engineered a small seed grant to help fund a more aggressive marketing campaign.

It was all the push Marty needed. He talked Father Rob into a crash refresher course in Sales 101. Then decked out in Dockers, that newly acquired blue button-down shirt and a Jerry Garcia tie salvaged from the clothing stash in the undercroft, he prepared to take off on the road four days a week. Plan was to pitch the Seasons of the Church Year panels and a Commemorative Wedding wall hanging to Christian retail stores from Toledo to Indianapolis on the west and from Buffalo to Allentown on the East.

Rob had coached him until he knew the whole shtick inside-out and backwards. To Marty, the modest salary courtesy of the grant from the diocese loomed larger than a million bucks at this point.

It had taken a bit of doing, but Rob also had talked Wilma's son, Bradley, into loaning the church's Undercroft project his mother's old station wagon for those road trips. The ancient vehicle was one of those classic "woodies" and on the back gate Rob fastened a simple but Gothic-looking magnetic sign that read, Undercroft Art.

Somehow the sign combined with the vintage wheels gave Marty's whole traveling-sales-persona a certain almost apostolic aura. With Bart in tow, Leah stood curbside with Marty watching wide-eyed as Rob and I double-checked the inventory.

"It's been sitting in the garage for twenty years. Is that thing really safe?" Leah said.

Marty flashed what was meant as a reassuring smile. "It's this or walk. Have you taken a good look at that church van lately? And poor Snaz would never hold all this stuff. I'll be fine."

Leah didn't look convinced. Rob was jockeying the last of the display boards into the cargo hold.

"I don't think even Paul heading off for Damascus could have had this much stuff," he grumbled.

"Shouldn't we christen this, maybe even Marty, with holy water or something?" I suggested.

Laughing, I was trying my best to help close the tailgate. Rob cocked an eyebrow as he weighed the possibilities.

"The Book of Common Prayer has a litany for just about everything. But it's hard to bless a fleet when there's only one of 'em!"

All of this wasn't doing a thing for Marty's deer-in-the-headlights mood. "Forget about it! I spent two days on that wax job! Knowing my luck, I'll probably blow a head gasket anyway the minute I hit the first interstate."

Rob clapped a reassuring hand around the young man's shoulder. "Just remember, Paul was a tentmaker—so trust me, he knew just how hard it was to make a buck. The guy wound up in jail a time or two, had to be smuggled out of town in a basket and ducked angry mobs throwing rocks at him. How much worse could it get?"

Marty didn't look convinced. In the end, waving and cheering, we all hung around—Rob, Grace, Leah and for moral support, even little Bart waving his favorite stuffed lion—out at the curb in front of Nativity until our new sales force of one was out of sight.

I wasn't thrilled at the straw I'd drawn in all of this. Waiting for me back at the homestead were three huge boxes of envelopes for our latest stab at a mass mailing. Still there was no sense in prolonging the inevitable.

"Back to the mines," I sighed. "I feel like I'm turning into the queen of the envelope stuffers."

I drew the line at tracking our rejection rate. That was Rob's department.

"Maybe this time's a charm." He hesitated, made eye contact.

"Though yesterday," he admitted, "we were turned down for the umpteenth time by a national church supply catalog. I didn't have the heart to tell you."

As his arm wound around my shoulder, I tried my best not to flinch. The gesture was harmless enough and he'd done the same for Marty. But as usual my antennas were up. Unless I was very mistaken, it seemed to me that Grace caught him at it, smiled.

Without making a big deal of it, I slipped out of reach. "Are you telling me maybe it's time to go back to the drawing boards? We borrow that digital camera again and revamp our whole package?"

Using that approach, we had created a fairly slick slide-show of our product for use on Rob's old corporate palm pilot so that Marty could hand off an instant digital catalog to a retailer on the road. We had even jazzed up the presentation with a soundtrack of me playing variations of "Restless Weaver" on the church's tracker organ.

"We've got every excuse." Rob shrugged."We're adding that Resurrection wall hanging next month with the sunburst breaking over that dark hillside."

It was just one of several of my new design experiments, including a labyrinth in pastel grays, turquoise and lavenders that we had rejected as way too confusing for our novice weavers. Rob and I had a good chuckle over the irony of that one. For some time now all those paths of his through the acreage behind the parsonage had been suffering from benign neglect. None of us exactly had a lot of time to meditate, to say nothing about fool around with precision lawn mowing twice a week.

The passage "fear not little flock" tacked up on the bulletin board in the narthex of Nativity, pretty much fit the prevailing mind-set. If one of those church supply outlets actually came through with an order, we were likely to find ourselves slammed—straining our current output to the max.

Or as Grace, ever the optimist, put it—"Brace yourself, kiddies!"

It was a colloquial but reverent doxology. For all the high anxiety surrounding our sales-force-of-one's maiden voyage, I hadn't felt this truly excited and hopeful about anything since my retirement.

Classical literature buffs call it the *music of the spheres*, the celestial harmony or glue that holds the universe together even through the most cosmic of storms and turbulence. Especially when hunkered in front of that keyboard at Nativity or sealing envelopes until my fingers stuck together, I had all but convinced myself that my life was under control and that occasional pain in the vicinity of my heart was just indigestion—that I wasn't falling in love with Rob Sims.

And then the unthinkable happened. Grace figured it out.

Marty was on the road, yet again. Grace and I were sitting together on a bench in my backyard, babysitting Bart and dissecting the draft brochure Rob and I had agonized over for the better part of a week The illustrations this time were not just of product, but of the production team as well.

Rob had caught a shot of the retired farmer Barney dressing a loom. Another photo was of an elderly former school teacher studying the Dove-of-the-Spirit pattern as it was emerging on her loom. There was a shot of the management and sales team taken weeks ago for the county weekly—with Rob in clerical collar and arm around my shoulder, Grace hefting little Bart, and Marty and Leah looking adoringly at one another down in the undercroft where it all had begun.

One photo in the brochure, of some of the recent downtown renovations, was paired with another shot of the lovingly-restored sanctuary at Nativity. The caption read:

**Undercroft Art Keeps Hope Alive**

The text went on to talk about domestic mission and the difficult problems of job loss and creation in rural communities.

It was a marriage of the best Rob had learned in his years at the ad agency in Pittsburgh and my own experience with public service hype slogging away at the job service in Philly. The pitch tied the uniqueness of the product and the uniqueness of the process to the very special character of the people of Hope itself.

And if I say so myself, it was good. Grace thumbed through the flyer one last time before handing it back to me. When I reached out to take the glossy three-fold, she chuckled—shook her head.

"You two make a heck of a team," she teased as only Grace can."And you don't have a clue . . . either one of you—!"

I couldn't pretend I was clueless about where her innuendoes were leading. Grace was putting one and one together and coming up with trouble.

"Since you won't ask," she said, "I'll tell you. Rob thinks you walk on water and you— "

"—are not going there, Grace! Father Rob and I work well together. That's the beginning and end of it."

"Little Charlise . . . I may be getting old and deaf, but I'm not dumb."

"Grace, he's married— "

"Separated."

"And he's a priest— "

My neighbor shrugged. "So . . .? Think Henry the Eighth. The Church of England. *E-pica-palians*— "

"And Murder in the Cathedral . . .!"

I was trying hard not to panic. Fresh from her wildly successful matchmaking with Leah and Marty, Grace was full of herself and not about to let it go.

"Grace, I love you madly. But trust me," I pleaded, "this is one. . . little project best left alone."

Something in my voice must have finally gotten through to her. Grace just looked at me, started to say something, stopped.

"Don't tell me," she said quietly, "I was right."

"Grace, don't— "

Tears were building up, hot and salty now behind my eyes, and I couldn't seem to stop them. My face worked.

"Oh, sweetie," Grace whispered. "Sweetie— "

I choked back a sob, gave in and let her hold me. Her big hands traced calming circles on my back. Like a mother murmuring to a hurt child, she kept saying it was going to be all right.

Desperately I wanted to believe her. True or not, the worst of it passed.

With a sigh, I pulled back and took a fierce swipe at my eyes with my sleeve. Grace looked so devastated, I tried to force a smile.

"Stupid, huh?"

"Me and my big mouth," Grace muttered. "I wouldn't hurt you for the world, kiddo."

I had heard those words once before, or something like them just feet away in my kitchen—only they were coming from Rob. I believed them then, I believed them now.

Grace Alanson might be loud to the point of overbearing, but she was one of the most warm-hearted women I had ever met. She didn't gossip and there wasn't a mean bone in her body. I had been carrying the burden of the situation alone so long, it felt like an enormous weight had lifted from my heart just to be able to admit it.

"I know that, Grace."

"You poor kids— "

I laughed, a wrenching explosion of sound that vented all the frustration I was feeling. Partly it was at the circumstances and mostly at my own inability to transcend them.

"Hardly, Grace. I was thinking, *old enough to know better.*"

Grace shot me a pointed look. "What makes you think love at sixty is any less painful than love at sixteen? For one thing, girlee, it's a heck of a lot tougher with kids and grandkids running around, and spouses and ex-es and a whole world of Thou-Shalt-Nots. Then, too, you've got a whole lot more experience to tell you how darn stupid you are . . ."

She shook her head, an emphatic negative. "Love is love. It ain't convenient, it ain't simple. But I gotta believe it's still the best thing we got going."

This time my burst of laughter was genuine and unrehearsed. Grace had a way of giving the truth a good clap aside of the head and waking it up once and for all.

"Do I detect a been-there-done-that tone creeping into this conversation, Grace?"

Grace looked down at her hands. "Caught me."

"Do you want to talk about it?"

"No. But I think I should . . ."

She did. And as she talked, I felt the familiar pain of her words pouring out over my own sadness with the miraculous healing power of loss shared.

"He was vice-president of the bank, served on the vestry down at Nativity, farmed one of the biggest acreages around here," Grace began. "A big, old hunk of a guy. I had been in town ten years—mid-forties at the time, and had gotten tired of dating local bachelors with 10-word vocabularies. He had traveled the world, spoke two-and-a-half languages, and miracle-of-miracles loved big-boned Hippie women. His wife, as it turns out, was a bitty slip of a thing with early on-set Alzheimers that tore the both of them to bits for twenty years."

Her smile was wistful, resigned to what was to come. "He never lied to me. He loved her and always would. Trouble was, he loved me, too— "

"How. . . what did you— ?"

"When it wouldn't go away . . . we took it out of town, the only thing you can do in a place like Hope. I loved that man like I had never loved anyone in my life. I'd have walked through hell-fire for him. So, I kept it close."

Grace stopped. "Finally, his wife . . . passed. You can't imagine the relief and the guilt, mountains and mountains of both. Terrible, either way. Six months later, he had a massive coronary and never made it to the hospital."

"Oh . . ., Grace . . ."

"Yeah. Well, it was the love of my life and I lived it. More than some folks will ever have."

I remembered speculating with Rob about the heartache flowering along Hope's quiet streets. All the time it was here, in my own backyard, with a woman I considered my best friend in the world.

*How little we really know of each other*, I thought. In rural and small towns, folk-wisdom says you better be careful what you hang out on the clothesline, because folk will still be talking about it three generations later.

I was never Char Howard here without the prefix: "Cecilia's girl—and wasn't that dad of hers, what-was-his-name-anyway, always a little shifty". And yet, here I was seeing a side of my neighbor Grace Alanson that I never even suspected. *Amazing what cruises along under the radar.*

Grace shifted in her chair. "So, you see, you two aren't the only ones around here loading a truckload of stupid."

"I'd be a lot more comfortable if you made that *one*," I told her. "I can only vouch for what's going on in my own head here."

"You and Rob haven't had The Talk, then?"

"Yes . . . no. Sort of . . ."

I gave her a highly censored version of the episode in the undercroft and the denouement in my kitchen. "As far as I know, the only runner out there on the road with that Olympic torch right now is me," I said.

"Have you taken a good look at that man's face lately when the two of you are pouring over all those pixels and proof sheets?"

I hadn't let myself. Maybe it wasn't the best way of coping, but it worked for me.

"I'm not sure, Grace, that I want to . . ."

She smiled. "I hear you," she said.

There was a lot at stake. I had to know.

"Is it really that . . . obvious?" I asked.

Grace shook her head. "It takes one to know one," she said. "You forget, I walked in those shoes. If I had to lay book on it? As far as the people of Hope are concerned, your little secret is just that. *Secret,* for better or worse."

It was the first and last time Grace and I talked about it. But especially when Rob and I were hashing out some problem or other, I sometimes thought I caught her looking at the two of us.

There was so much affection in that look and a sadness so profound, that I had to bite my lip not to respond. Instead, I found an excuse to recoup in the ladies' room until the moment passed.

# ✥ Chapter Fifteen

The October air was heavy with the smell of moldering leaves. My phone was ringing as I hit the front porch and I knew from experience that if I made a dash for it, I could catch it before the answering machine picked up. By now I wasn't locking the door which helped—yet another significant adjustment to rural life.

"Char Howard . . .," I gasped.

*Man, I must be slipping*, I thought. Mid-way through that perfunctory greeting, the darn answering machine activated and I heard a metallic clone of myself repeat the greeting.

"Hold on . . . I'll try to fix this."

The caller probably couldn't even hear me with that canned message droning away in the foreground but I went ahead anyway. Mercifully after a bit of muttering and fumbling on my part, the pre-recorded voice stopped.

"Char . . .?"

I recognized the caller with that single word. Rob and I had just wound up a six-hour marathon cranking out a whole box full of mailers to church supply houses. We were both tired and cranky.

Afterthoughts at this point were not on my agenda. I was thinking about a hot soak in the tub, a glass of wine and a heat-em-up-in-the-microwave dinner. Marty, of course, was over 'courting Leah', as Grace liked to put it.

"Don't tell me we forgot something," I groaned

"I just got a phone call. It was from Wilma Smoller's son . . ."

The words caught in my throat. "Oh, Rob— "

"She's had a stroke, Char. Massive. It doesn't look good. The doctors are saying hours, a day at most."

The questions flashed through my head, but went unasked. I already knew what was coming next.

"We need to talk, Char."

"I understand."

"Your place or mine?"

I thought about it before answering. A lot was riding on how we handled this, personally and professionally.

Rob called on parishioners all the time, was terrific at it. I accidentally had wandered over to a random neighbor's before and caught him in action. But this was different and there wasn't any sense pretending otherwise.

"Mine, I guess."

"A half hour?"

"Fine," I said.

The phone had already reverted to dial tone. Laying it on the kitchen counter, I found myself buying time by putting the coffee on to brew. I had come to care deeply for that feisty little woman. But there was no sense in pretending it was my sorrow alone that was at work here, fueling my rising sense of anxiety.

The bell rang just as the last of the water percolated its way through the filter. I had already set out the mugs on the kitchen table. As an afterthought, I set out a plate of homemade oatmeal cookies Grace had whipped up the day before.

"You have no idea," she told me once, "how great it is finally to have an army of folks to bake for. When it was just me, every time I opened the oven door I was heading for the record of World's Heaviest Woman."

Grace's infectious grin fixed in my memory as I took one last look around the kitchen. *Relax, you're among friends*, I told myself. I turned to head for the living room.

"Anybody home?"

Rob had already cracked the front door enough to make his presence known. It was a habit we had cultivated over the months of working together, one that saved a lot of scrambling. He now gave similar fair warning when I was practicing over at Nativity. We still laughed how spooked I was that first morning so many months ago when he showed up in the sanctuary unannounced.

"Here. In the kitchen. Just come on in!"

I heard the muffled closing of the door, then the rhythm of his stride on the bare wood of the living room floor. The shock of his face in the doorway was a function of my distress, nothing more, I told myself.

Rob was amazing in a crisis. I had seen him quietly helping families work through their grief in the narthex and cradling red-faced infants at the baptismal font. But Wilma Smoller was family . . . and one look at his face told me, all bets were off.

Whatever boundaries I had set for myself were irrelevant here. Whether he initiated it or I did, we found ourselves holding each other. Except for perfunctory co-worker hugs, it had been a while since I had felt a man's strong hands like this against my shoulders, fraught with the tension of love and loss, and unspoken need.

And still I clung to him, dry-eyed, every nerve ending on high alert. Gradually, his breathing steadied against my hair.

It couldn't last. Awkwardly, he levered a semblance of distance between us. His face was a quiet study in grief.

"She was . . . *is* a gutsy lady," I said. "I love her, too, Rob."

"You can know it's coming. And still . . . when it does— "

"I made us coffee."

At that, a hint of a smile tugged at the corner of his mouth. This was becoming our ritual, these quiet heart-to-hearts around my kitchen table. His eyes were as dark as the waters of the Delaware along the Philly waterfront. A whole lot of history in those troubled depths.

"We're likely to have the funeral before the end of the week—the whole town will be there. We don't have an organist for Sunday. Nativity is going to need you badly, Char. I don't have to tell you that."

He didn't. Hearing it, though, was difficult at this moment, on an awful lot of fronts.

"I'm more than willing to fill in, if it comes to that," I told him, carefully choosing my words, "until you find a permanent replacement."

He didn't respond at first. But I saw that familiar muscle tensing its way along his jaw, heard his frustrated outrush of breath as he pulled out a chair from the table and sat.

"Wilma would want you to follow her on that bench."

"I realize that . . . "

"Only you're afraid that we can't work together," he said slowly. "Even if we do every day now, or almost every day, down in the undercroft."

I just looked at him. "It's different and you know it, Rob."

Turning to the counter, I filled our mugs and brought them back to the table. Rob took one from my hand, gingerly—the stoneware was scalding hot. In the process, our hands never made contact at all. We were, despite all of Rob's protestations back when all this started, getting good at this avoidance business

"Different, how?" he insisted.

Even as gun-shy as I still was about calling much less thinking of myself as an "organist", Rob knew how I felt about music and the liturgy. That keyboard was the one place I could pour out my heart without worrying about vulnerability or exposing to the world my deepest emotions. I was offering it all up to God and whatever the motives or nuances, it was good and acceptable.

*Spiritually and emotionally, I needed that.*

"Some things are sacred, Rob. My relationship with that instrument—the sanctity of the liturgy and worship, for me, is one of them. I can't . . . won't risk tampering with that."

"I understand."

"Do you?" My mouth felt stiff but I needed to finish. "I've stuffed my feelings so deep inside myself that on most days, I don't even think about it anymore. Still . . . I'd be a liar of the worst kind if I tried to deny they weren't there!"

Char, you don't— "

"I've fallen in love with you." I looked straight at him and then down at the mug in my hands. "And I'm not sure I could sit on that organ bench every week, watching your face for every nuance as you recited that liturgy, listening for my cues—not and keep my head and heart intact!"

It was silent a long time.

"Char, I can't believe anyone could judge the way life threw us together. Not God, not anyone. You know I love you—more than I ever imagined possible. That may just turn out to be the greatest blessing . . . and *tragedy* of my life." His voice shook, steadied again. "Yet whatever you or I believe about . . . sins of the heart, we haven't acted on any of it."

"True—but not the whole truth."

There was no easy way for me to say it. But Rob had to know.

"Grace , for one, has figured it out," I said. "Heaven knows how. But she did. And fortunately . . . she loves the both of us enough to let it go at that."

"So you're worried the rest of the town won't be far behind?"

"You could lose your job here."

" There are worse things, Char, than losing a job—"

I shivered. Part of my economizing had been to turn down the heat drastically while I was out of the house. It took a while for the tired old furnace to catch up. Rob seemed mesmerized by the steam rising from the mug, ghostly waves rising like those flames on the Pentecost wall hanging.

"So, what better way to survive all this," he said, "than to offer up the truth together in that sanctuary? As is . . . every Sunday, it's your face I see in that rose window over the narthex with the angels soaring over Bethlehem, their music rising to the heavens. I always will . . . whether you are sitting on that bench or not."

He hesitated, staring deep into the murky liquid in his mug. "And I . . . thank God for that. You've changed my life, helped me find the music in it again—the faith in new possibilities, in spite of everything."

My face was burning, hotter than the glaze of that mug cradled in my hands. I began to count the rows of rag woven into my placemat, waiting for the calm I knew would come, if I could only gain enough time and distance.

"What are you suggesting . . .?" I said.

"I'm officially offering you the job as interim at Nativity. The vestry has to take it from there."

I set down the mug. My hands were shaking so hard that I had to steady them against the table.

"A month," I said slowly, "and then we'll see— "

"Make it two— "

"Fair enough."

"Done!"

Exhaling sharply, he ran the heel of his hand across the deep furrows that were creasing his forehead. I knew that gesture. It reminded me of the dull pain that was throbbing away at my own temple.

"More coffee?" I said. "Or a hefty sugar shock?"

"Don't tell me," he chuckled as he fished a nut-and raisin-laced oatmeal cookie from the plate. "Grace?"

I managed a smile. "Who else? I assume you'll want me to alert her so she can get the casserole squad going . . . for Wilma's family . . ."

"The minute I get the news about funeral arrangements, I'll call you. I suspect it will be mid-morning, followed by interment in the church yard and a luncheon for the family. If I had to guess . . . a cast of thousands. Everybody knows Wilma."

"Music?"

"Believe it or not," he sighed, shook his head. "I hadn't thought of that. But yeah, she was bound to have some strong opinions on the subject."

"If you like, when you talk to her son, you could let him know I'm playing the service and ask him what she would have wanted. He knows Wilma and I were close."

Rob nodded his assent. "Sounds good to me."

"I guess that's it then . . ."

When he made no move to leave, I got up and started busying myself with cleaning up after my coffee-making operations. No matter how hard I tried, there was always a trail of grounds somewhere on the counter.

"Char . . .," he said.

I looked up from what I was doing. But he just said my name again, smiled.

"I just wanted to hear your name," he said, "and to enjoy watching your nesting . . ."

"You can stay for dinner, if you like."

He shook his head. "Bad idea. If I had any say in the matter, I'd still be here in the morning. And what would the good citizens of Hope make of that?"

The community laid Wilma Smoller to rest on a bleak Saturday afternoon. A cold October rain had turned the church yard to mud where the grass was trampled from the shoes of the crowd gathered to pay their final respects. Rob's homily was enough to move a boulder field. The Biblical text was the Song of Miriam, one of the first hymns in the Bible.

Although her son had no idea what music to choose, Wilma it seems had already thought of that. Tucked in a stack of post-it notes on the ledge next to the keyboard was a list in that all-over-the-map handwriting of hers.

The prelude was the classic "Going Home" from Dvorak's *New World Symphony*. As an organist, Wilma had real trouble playing "Simple Gifts", but in death as a choral anthem, it was a perfect Eulogy:

> *'Tis a gift to come down where we ought to be. And when we find ourselves in a place just right, 'twill be in the valley of love and delight.*

We hadn't had a choir since I had been going to Nativity, but there had to be a soloist out there somewhere. Bless her heart, Wilma even wanted the contemporary worship setting.

I fought a smile when I saw her notes about the postlude. It was a piece I unearthed for her in that amazing music library of hers by Ralph Vaughan-Williams called, *The New Commonwealth*—one of my Brits. The piece quietly begins as a song to life and then soars upward as the theme repeats itself in another key.

I wept as I played it, the silent tears streaming down my face unchecked. Every note was for Wilma.

Rob caught my eye as he headed down the chancel steps toward the white-draped coffin positioned just off my left shoulder in the center aisle, scant feet from where I was playing. I must have looked a mess. By now tears were falling randomly on the keys.

If I was thinking anything, it was, *merciful heavens, if there's anything electrical down there under that keyboard, don't let me fry myself.* Lord knows, there wouldn't be a soul to play my funeral.

At the end of the service and just before Rob moved out of my sight-line, he gave me one of those hang-in-there smiles. A therapist couldn't have come up with a better antidote for what I was feeling. And so I played—played until the church was empty and beyond, played until the ache around my heart began to subside.

There was no point adding to the traffic jam in the church yard. Wilma's spirit was most at home here. Alone in the empty sanctuary, I was saying my goodbyes.

Finally, I took my hands off the keys and shut down the organ. Before I left, though, I needed to set up the music for tomorrow's service, routine and welcome housekeeping chores that helped me center myself again. I needed that right now.

Just as I was finishing, I heard the narthex door slam and looked up in time to see Rob wander back into the sanctuary. Droplets of water clung to his hair and glistened on the lapel of his jacket. He already had changed from liturgical vestments to his dark suit coat before he went out to the graveyard.

"Nasty out there," he told me. "*And the heavens opened* . . . by the bucketful."

"You seem to have picked up half the lawn out there on your shoes."

"The sexton is going to demand overtime."

It was an in-joke. Barney our master weaver was also the regular volunteer for sanctuary cleanup. The man loved vacuum cleaners and had a closet full of them, rescued from garage sales, for every conceivable purpose.

Our laughter took the chill off the sanctuary. The floor furnace was temporarily out of commission until a plumbing and heating guy from Bartonville could come out and tweak it back into service. I had been tempted to cut the fingers out of a pair of the gloves the altar guild used to polish the brass communion ware to make it through the service.

"With an Alaskan climate in here, Wilma's family decided to gather at Mike's Eatery instead of the undercroft," Rob reminded me. "You're welcome to join in if you want to . . ."

I knew Wilma's son. The booze would be flowing like water and tomorrow was Sunday. There's nothing duller than a church organist on a Saturday night under the best of circumstances. The routine is to stop drinking by eight and be in bed by 10.

"Thanks, but think I'll pass," I said. "Funerals like this one are pretty draining."

If Rob was disappointed, he didn't show it. "Truth is, I'm ready to drop myself. But I've got to be there."

"Give the family my best," I said.

"See you, then."

I did, the next morning for worship. Whatever anxiety I had about our working together, the liturgy flowed seamlessly from start to finish. My playing, if anything, was conservative. I was blind-sided by how nervous I felt.

Still, the congregation was stunned at the new tempo for the hymns and I had to assert myself to hold the pace steady and pull them along. At the end Barney and a few others came up and told me how glad they were that I was helping out.

"You're peppy," Barney said. "I like that."

Rob flashed a thumbs-up smile as he headed out with the Wallace's for Sunday brunch. As I closed up the organ case, I kept thinking of Wilma and her vinyl gripper pad on the bench. I could see the faint outline of the waffle-weave that had permanently pressed itself into the varnish.

Marty was waiting for me with Leah and baby Bart in the narthex. It was his first official visit to a worship service at Nativity and judging by that pinched ridge between his brows, he must have been having a fair amount of difficulty figuring out just what he had gotten himself into.

"Man, Char . . .," he told me, "you rock."

"Thanks, I think!"

"No. Seriously. I felt the floor shaking in that last tune. What was it . . .?"

"A toccata by a contemporary British composer. It's a kind of a showpiece intended to fire you out the door all ready to face the week."

"I got dragged to a church once," Marty said, "where everybody sat around at the end and watched them put out the candles and stuff."

"Ritual fire worship."

Marty looked so confused I had to explain.

"Years ago I was playing in a church that did that, so one Sunday morning the priest called them on it. Worship, he said, doesn't end with the blessing, it's just starting. When the priest says, Go out in peace to serve God and neighbor—that means, Go! ASAP! Do right by one another."

"It seems rude to walk out when somebody is playing."

I laughed. "Okay . . ., I'll admit, when a piece is really tough, it's flattering to have folks stand around and listen. But it's not what that exit piece or postlude is supposed to be about."

How lucky I was to have landed here, I told myself—in one of the few relatively liturgical parishes left in this little corner of the world. It was my mother's doing, in part. Her love of the classics had nurtured a generation that at least tolerated, if not understood them. Even Wilma had kept that precious seed alive.

I vowed then and there, budget or no budget, to insist on space in the weekly bulletin to explain why I chose the music I did for a particular week. It's hard to tell the players without a program. My to-do list, it seems, was getting longer by the minute.

*Why,* I found myself thinking, *had I worried how I was going to spend my days?* Time in retirement seemed to be taking on a strange flow that was vaguely unsettling after a lifetime of punching a clock.

If a person isn't careful, the sense of hours and days becomes so amorphous that weeks can go by without ever coming up for air, so to speak. Work and play, in fact, become indistinguishable.

Crack of dawn was spent on my solitary walks through the streets of my town, every sense coming alive with the stirring of life around me. By eight o'clock, alone in the sanctuary, I was reading through Wilma's repertoire and my own more modest music library, searching for the pieces to use with the upcoming services. Monthly, Rob left a schedule of hymns and sermon themes on the organ rack to help with planning.

By nine I was down in the undercroft with Grace and her crew. Business was still booming, and after the loss of faithful Wilma, we went out and recruited three new volunteers, one a laid-off secretary and two retired teachers.

The seasons were changing. A hard frost had taken out the annuals and all but the toughest of the perennials in my neighbors' gardens. My own had gone unweeded for a month.

Late November came and with it Christ the King, the Sunday marking the end of the church year. I greeted Rob with a "Happy New Year" as we got ready for worship. He grinned.

"I'm counting on it," he said, "a new church year, onward and upward. The vestry voted last night to offer you a fulltime contract. Fifty bucks a session and combat pay if you start a choir."

The thought was angst-producing on multiple fronts. I shot him an incredulous look.

"Choir? Heading into Advent and with only four weeks until Christmas?"

Rob shrugged. "We used to have one. Toward the end, poor Wilma just couldn't keep up. But if you're willing to risk it, I expect you would have enough bodies most Sundays to pull off singing in parts. I'm told your buddy Barney's a bass but when it comes to picking a vocal line, he tends to side with the sopranos most of the time."

"What ever happened to my two-month . . . grace period?"

Rob was giving me one of those "Who-me?" looks. "These folks may be living on the back burner out here, but they aren't stupid. Barney pretty much told 'em to grab you before the Methodists over in Harlan snapped you up. Word is out there that you're good."

"And I suppose you didn't point out that I had asked for time to think about all this?"

"What do you say to common sense? I just told 'em to go for it."

The maneuvering was so outrageous and blatant, I found myself biting back a smile. "In fact, I got a call from one of the choir members over at Harlan last week."

"You wouldn't desert the ship at Christmas."

He knew me too well. Organists tend to play sick or well year-round. It just comes with the territory. But if there's an absolute taboo, it's messing around with personnel changes at Christmas and Easter.

Over time, I was coming to believe, church musicians begin to feel the rhythm of the church year in their bones. Like the biological clock that makes us most vulnerable in the hours just before dawn, the liturgical calendar becomes a kind of spiritual tide-clock that pulls us with it. Even, it seems, in the shadow of death. Call it spiritual centeredness or just plain stress, I believe it's no accident that so many people in church work tend to give up the fight—quietly check out— just after those particular holidays.

"Does Nativity have a pageant?"

Rob winced. "Ten kids at most and a couple of live sheep. I'd say, any leadership you could provide in that department would be greatly appreciated."

A quick foray on-line turned up a viable version of Lessons and Carols that would fit our modest resources. Grace put out an SOS for bathrobes to costume the kings and ten yards of buck-a-yard fabric were quickly converted to one-size-fits-most outfits for the shepherds.

We decided against the live sheep and instead turned white sweatshirts inside-out to create credible sheep suits. Thank goodness for the inventor of hot glue. In a half-hour, Grace had turned out convincing wooly masks from recycled poster board and a leftover bag of pillow batting.

Never, we discovered, arm three eight-year-olds with shepherds' crooks. Still, despite their impromptu swordplay, the event was pronounced a rousing success. Our ragged little choir whipped the assembled parents and other relatives into singing along on the familiar hymns that are mainstays of the lessons and carols tradition. Grace coordinated a post-pageant coffee hour that would have fed half the county for a month.

Christmas was now only two weeks away—my first in my hometown in decades. Even with the relatively modest worship calendar in our tiny parish, spending the holidays in Cleveland or Pittsburgh with my daughters was unthinkable. Still, I couldn't bring myself to urge my girls and their families to make the trek to Hope. I was remembering those tense road trips I made with my daughters every Christmas, battling slick driving conditions and the back seat piled high with jostling kids and presents heaped well beyond safe sight-lines.

"Your kids deserve their own trees and their own customs," I told them firmly. Meant it.

"Well, then, we'll make the trek at New Year's," my oldest, Jen, told me. "I'll talk to Sarah and we'll make a whole family thing of it. Are you settled enough to put up the nine of us?"

I hadn't thought of that. Mentally matching heads and beds, I slotted Sarah and her husband into the back bedroom that was doubling as my work room. Their daughter was three and could sleep on a cot. Jen and her husband could take over Marty's digs with air mattresses on the floor for Nina and little Jeremy. If Marty didn't want the sofa bed in the living room, he would relish the possibility of bunking with Grace for a night or two.

"Tight . . . but I'll manage."

It didn't take the relief in my daughters' voices to tell me I had done the right thing. That said, I resigned myself to a table-top tree and a neighborhood progressive dinner late afternoon on Christmas Day with Grace Alanson, Marty and his beloved Leah.

A wide-eyed little Bart had learned a new word to celebrate the coming festivities. It was *Light.* And in spite of the lifetime of years between the Bart-man and I, I too had done some vocabulary-building in my own right. The word was *Organist.*

My name was running in the bulletin these days, followed by *Organist*—here on the bench where it all begun, where my mother had played those many years ago. Somewhere, I had to believe the two of them, she and Wilma, were watching this all, laughing.

# ✣ Chapter Sixteen

After about a half-day feeling sorry for myself and wallowing in post-pageant blues, I threw myself into getting the repertoire set and under control for the Christmas Eve and Christmas Day services. It wasn't easy, in an excess-of-riches sort of way.

Considering the brief stretch of time between Christmas and Epiphany, composers have had a field day over the centuries cranking out musical literature for the occasion. The smorgasbord is truly international.

Carols that began as pagan round dances were adapted by the church over the centuries into wonderful hymn settings. Pastorales originated in Renaissance Italy and then evolved into lyrical pieces that capture the piping of the shepherds in the lonely fields around Bethlehem. The uniquely French genre, the Noel, celebrates the angel choirs filling the heavens with glorious sound. Or who can imagine a Christmas without the majestic German chorales or the wistful beauty of *Silent Night*?

As all church musicians, I was facing a classic case of too many notes and too little time. For weeks I had been reading through Nativity's library of seasonal anthologies, trying to put together a plan.

Midnight was the time for shimmer and awe. On Christmas morning, literally, I was pulling out all the stops with a variation on REGENT SQUARE, *Angels from the Realms of Glory*, that used cascading sixteenth-notes to imitate the beating of angel wings, while the left hand and deep 16-foot pipes in the pedals intoned the familiar melody.

I had been practicing for about an hour, slowly working through and repeating the tougher passages time and again until I got it more or less right. When I finally slid off the bench, my intention was to get the kinks out of my back. Instead I stiffened, stopped mid-stretch by the sudden realization that I had an audience.

Hunched in the back row of the sanctuary was a man on his knees—literally and figuratively. His hands were braced against the pew back in front of him. I didn't need to see his face to know it was Rob.

I realized that I had been pretty much playing flat-out for the last twenty minutes. Something in the heavy silence when I finished must have disturbed his concentration. He raised his head.

"Rob—?"

At the sound of his name, he settled back on the pew seat. I stood there wanting to go to him, but not daring to risk it. He managed a wan smile.

"Thanks. I needed that."

I forced a laugh. "Still *way* too many rough spots—"

"You could have fooled me. From where I sat, it sounded . . . powerful, soul-shaking."

We were tap dancing around the bottom line. I had to know.

"Something's happened?"

"I got an email this morning . . ."

"Bad news—?"

Rob winced. "My son's on the way here as we speak from Cleveland, for Christmas. Part of his therapist's regimen, I gather. We haven't seen each other in a . . . very long time."

"Oh, Rob, that's—"

"Yeah . . . well. At least he's coming."

"He still blames you—for his mom?"

"Last count anyway." Rob shrugged. "For his sister's death. His mom. Bad genes. The state of the economy. The bank repossessing his Corvette. You name it . . . he's angry. And I can't say, I blame him."

"And all your *mea culpas* are helping—?"

"Physician, heal thyself?"

Rob grimaced as he nudged the kneeler upright on its hinges. As the heavy metal mechanism slid into place, it echoed like a gunshot in the empty sanctuary.

"You're right, of course, Char. Guilt only makes the situation worse, more fraught to handle. At twenty-three, Ted's an adult, capable of taking responsibility for his own stuff— "

"Great . . . in theory . . . "

"Well, as of six tomorrow, I guess I'll find out."

Three days until Christmas. To my knowledge, Rob hadn't even put up a tree. Marty had coerced me into it the day after Thanksgiving—tough with all those boxes of ornaments stashed willy-nilly in the attic.

*When in doubt, keep busy.* The motto had worked for me during my own Dark Ages as I learned to reconnect with my daughters without all the freight left over from adolescence getting in the way. Even when Jen and Sarah and I were at each other's throats, somehow we found common ground in something as banal as whipping up a batch of cookies together or blitzing a new paint job in the guest room.

I hadn't thought about it that way until this very minute, but it was shared work too with those around me that had turned my once fearful forced-retirement exile in Hope into something very different entirely. My status as Nativity's organist and designer for Undercroft Arts were not and had never been just about ways to occupy the hours from dawn to dusk or beyond. It was the human need for identity—that, and the search for collective human truth, in a word, Community.

In one of my collections of Shaker hymns recently I stumbled on the founding Mother's passionate formula for living and loving—*hands to work and hearts to God,* she told her disciples. As therapies go, father and son could hit on far worse to heal the breach between them.

"If it gets too . . . fraught," I suggested, "the two of you could always grab an axe and make a run out to Jensen's tree farm . . . "

Rob was looking at me strangely. I found out soon enough, why.

"Actually, I'd like you to meet him," he said.

"Me . . .?"

I felt like my lungs were imploding. Rob's jaw hardened and he got to his feet, positioning himself between where I stood in the aisle and the narthex behind him—as if he half-expected me to make a dash for the door.

"Think about it. Self-absorbed as they can be, our children can also have an uncanny nose for mendacity. Ted is no dummy. After all he's been through, I've got to believe my son will sense in the first ten minutes that something is very different in my life."

"I'm really not so sure that it's such a good idea—"

Rob raked his hand through his already tousled hair. "Neither am I, if pushed on the subject. I have no intention of getting in his face about our relationship, but neither will I lie or hedge."

"He could interpret all that as just one more betrayal of his mother."

"True enough. But if my son is still speaking to me by Christmas, I think it's important he believes me capable of more . . . emotional strength of character than he witnessed during the better part of his childhood. That includes admitting up front that I consider you the most wonderful thing that ever happened in my wasteland of an existence."

What Rob was proposing was a pretty harsh test of our friendship. It seemed flattering and frightening, in just about equal doses.

Still I had to believe, that he wasn't intentionally using me to manipulate his relationship with his son. Potentially, he was risking everything by letting Ted know where things stood. Question was, was I willing to do the same?

Rob's tone softened. "Besides . . . if that motivation makes you uncomfortable, let's up the ante and add sexual harassment to my tab. You *are* on the payroll. Coerced exposure to my cooking *could* be considered an incredibly inappropriate Christmas bonus— "

I couldn't help it. I laughed.

*Uncomfortable.* That certainly was among the words that came to mind. Still, to his eternal credit, Rob wasn't crowding me as I thought about it.

"Rob, I'm not . . ."

"Brunch. After church Christmas morning. My place."

"Are you sure— "

"Sleep on it."

Now that *was* an unrealistic option. It would be a long couple of days and even longer nights, wondering just what was going on between father and son in that parsonage.

The next few days started as replay of my first weeks in Hope . . . avoiding the parsonage at all costs. Though going without practicing wasn't an option.

In odd moments, I found myself trying to construct a picture of Ted based on the faded snapshots I had seen in passing in Rob's sparsely furnished living room. A soccer jersey and a shock of unruly dark hair stood out in my memory. A golden boy, like his father—if I simply took that cocksure half-smile at face value.

Once downtown on a shopping junket to the hardware for a last-minute Christmas stocking stuffer for Marty, I thought I spotted the two of them—Rob and son—at a distance, but I ducked into Rutterbach's before I was noticed.

Christmas Eve came and technically I still hadn't given Rob a definitive answer about brunch but then he hadn't pushed it either. I saw the questions in his eyes as our paths crossed getting ready for the service, but then the synchronize-your-watches routine ahead of me helped me focus on the task at hand.

I double-checked the registration I had programmed into the organ's primitive retro-fitted pre-sets and then flipped through the page turns in the solo and choral music. It was time to begin. After focusing on the first bar and then skimming ahead over the first system, I launched into the prelude.

*Divinum Mysterium. Of the Father's love begotten, 'ere the world began to be.* The words of the haunting ancient plainsong burned in my memory. *Of the things that are, that have been, and that future years shall see, evermore and evermore.*

*Of the father's love.* Strange what you encounter reflected back at you when you least expect it.

Like many organists whose instruments force them to play face-to-the pipes, I use a rear-view mirror to keep track of what is going on out there in the congregation behind me. Reflected back in my sight-line as the midnight service began was the same cynical hint of a smile I saw in that photo in Rob's living room—the unfamiliar face conspicuous among the otherwise usual cast of characters out there. It had to be Ted.

On the surface of things, up there in front of me at the altar, Rob was all business, intoning the liturgy with quiet conviction. But I could read the tension in his shoulders and knew it for more than the predictable High Holy Day jitters.

I picked Christmas Eve to venture into the realm of introducing an instrumental solo for the offertory. Barney's niece from Cleveland was there with her violin and despite a hair-raising rehearsal earlier in the day, she turned out a creditable duet with organ of "O Holy Night". Still I'll admit, for me the Doxology that followed was an especially timely act of thanksgiving—as in, sheer relief we actually made it through.

After the service, Barney came up to the organ bench, still mopping at his eyes with a red and white paisley farmer's "dew-rag". I was right in the middle of sending the chime rendition of "Bleak Midwinter" out over the church tower when he clapped me on the back in a heartfelt if ill-timed gesture of approval. For a second it was a case of Holst meets Schoenberg, but I recovered and went on to finish the delicate children's hymn.

"Beautiful," he stammered. "Just beautiful. Ain't my niece just wonderful . . .?"

"It was lovely, Barney."

"Not a dry eye in the place."

That seemed to trigger another wave of relational pride and emotion. Red-faced and fighting for control, Barney wandered off down the aisle again where a dwindling knot of parishioners was chatting away after church.

I shivered. The ushers had thrown open the church doors so the exiting worshipers could hear the tower bells. A veritable wind tunnel blast of icy winter air was inundating the over-heated sanctuary.

It was time to pack up. Tomorrow's service meant a whole new configuration of hymns and other music. Tired as I was, I wasn't about to leave until everything was more or less set for what came next.

The church's bottle-brush of an artificial tree—loaded down with a mismatched collection of hand-made ornaments from Sunday School classes past and present—stood immediately adjacent to the organ in the corner next to the outer wall. I leaned down awkwardly from the bench to unplug the lights, fumbling for the outlet before finally locating it.

As I straightened, I became aware of a familiar pair of scuffed dockers standing alongside the bench—and as my gaze moved upward, the incongruously elegant regalia that went with them. For a small congregation, the Christmas vestments at Nativity were spectacular. They would have done a cathedral bishop credit.

"Merry Christmas." Rob said softly.

In his eyes, I could read the things unsaid—the love and the longing that lay so close to the surface. Alongside them lurked the familiar sadness, no less real and just as difficult to articulate.

"You, too. Merry Christmas, Rob. It was a beautiful service . . . "

He nodded. "I'd like you to meet my son, Ted."

Liturgical vestments have a way of creating a larger-than-life presence. I hadn't seen the young man in a cashmere overcoat standing close behind his father until Rob stepped aside to introduce us.

"Ted . . . , this is Char Grunwald— "

Rob stopped, blinked. *My maiden name.*

I was surprised he even remembered it—a strange throwback to our adolescence and his mother's futile admonitions about "that Grunwald girl who plays so beautifully". Even in the heat of the introductions Rob knew a Freudian slip when he heard one.

"Howard now, actually," he corrected quickly. "She's an old school friend and our organist. Char will be joining us for breakfast after I finish officiating tomorrow morning."

I saw the resemblance even stronger now, down to the subtle flush spreading across the two men's features. Ted had his father's eyes, that same intense, bottomless blue. It was impossible to mistake the same tough-as-nails set of the jaw.

But despite Rob's take on his son's state of mind earlier in the week, it was not anger I read in the pinched set of the young man's brows. It was darker, harder to define—a kind of sullen awareness.

And then I sensed it. *Father and son had talked.* In fact, Ted already knew *exactly* who I was. I took a deep breath and plunged ahead.

"I'm looking forward to having a chance to get to know you," I said.

It could have been my imagination or more likely, paranoia. But as I extended my hand in greeting, I thought I sensed Ted hesitate a split-second before reciprocating.

"Your playing was everything Dad said it would be—emotive, *assured*." The way he lingered on the word made it sound vaguely distasteful.

I forced a smile. "I don't know about the 'assured' bit, but it's a great little organ. I learned to play on it . . . way too many eons ago."

"You've lived here all your life, then."

"I grew up here, then left when I went to college. I just moved back in Spring. From Philly."

*Eight months. Had it truly been that long?*

"The City of Brotherly Love." Ted's dry chuckle had nothing to do with humor. "Must be quite a switch, from that to Hope."

Not as much of a switch as I had once feared. Love and hope were both commodities in abundance around me these days.

"This place grows on you," I shrugged. "Although I'll admit, at one point in my life I couldn't get out of here fast enough."

"You weren't the only one." Rob chuckled.

Our laughter felt strained but nice. Like a quiet in-joke it momentarily calmed the stress of the job behind us and the even more potentially dangerous one that lay ahead—namely, somehow to connect with his son. Ted just stood there looking at his father like he had suddenly grown horns and a tail.

I tried to busy myself shutting off the organ's power switch, listening to the familiar sighing of the pipes as the reservoir deflated. The eerie whisper echoed in the by now all-but deserted sanctuary. Though I ached to feel Rob's reassuring hug, a lingering glance had to suffice.

"We'll see you tomorrow, then," Rob said. "Brunch."

I nodded. "Great to meet you, Ted."

Purse clutched under my arm, I turned and made a bee-line for the sacristy and my coat, leaving Rob to finish closing up. By now it was well past midnight—but then, muggers were in short supply in Hope. I actually found myself welcoming the walk home. We finally had gotten our White Christmas with a three-inch deposit of snow two days ago.

Still on edge, I picked my way cautiously along the deserted streets, the path illuminated by periodic star-burst glare from the street lamps. The sidewalks were clear but wet now with a film of ice. The temperature was dropping.

It was an odd time for a sociological study of rural Christmas customs, but I couldn't help noticing. About half the houses I passed were dark, devoid of obvious life. Snowbirds, I concluded, or the elderly—already retired for the night—with their families too distant to travel. Through the remainder of the windows I saw the gleam of candles, the bustling shadow-plays of families giving and sharing around their trees.

No Dickensenian fantasy here. Each one of those little tableaus was probably fraught with its fair share of tensions and flaws, I suspected—ambivalent memories to mar the still beauty of this night. *But comfort and joy nonetheless.*

A mere voyeur to those unfolding rituals, I walked on alone—walked on despite the quiet ache that settled in behind my rib cage. It wasn't just that brunch with Rob's son that was on my mind, but something just as close to my heart. Even with their New Year visit approaching, I suddenly found myself missing my own girls.

*'Round yon Virgin, mother and child. Holy.*

The quiet mantra repeated itself in my head. Gradually I felt my heartbeat steady, resigning myself to a dark house and empty bed.

But as I turned the corner on to Elm Street I stopped dead still, stunned at the multi-colored glow of lights reaching out to me from down the block in what had to be the homestead. The house was quiet, the living room deserted, though bless him, Marty had left the tree lights on before heading up to bed. A plate of Grace's fruit cake and solitary glass of wine sitting out on the coffee table were meant clearly for me.

Grateful—touched yet again by my young tenant's ongoing random acts of kindness—I settled into the wing chair closest to the tree. Picking up the portable phone, I punched in a familiar number.

My daughter answered on the fifth ring. From the background I heard high-pitched squeals of excitement that told me my grandchildren Jeremy and Nina were still in high gear, opening their presents.

"Jen? . . . Merry Christmas!"

"Same to you, mom. It's great to hear your voice."

# ✣ Chapter Seventeen

Christmas Day dawned clear, lashed by a wicked north wind that sent the few remaining leaves on the oak trees blustering across the empty streets. The sidewalks crackled under my feet as I headed over to Nativity for church. In spite of myself, I smiled as I passed the rectory.

In the front window, where it hadn't been the night before, stood an enormous tree covered in miniature white lights from top to toe. Apparently Rob had taken my advice and worked in a trip to Jensen's cut-your-own acres of evergreens after all. Nothing like a half hour in the biting cold on the business end of a saw to get a man's holiday spirit going.

The sanctuary was still deserted, although someone—most likely Rob—had turned up the heat. It seemed to take a good hour to get the space to a livable temperature and ten minutes beyond that to turn the place into a sauna.

I slid on to the bench and ran through the toughest hymns and a tricky spot or two in the postlude. That done, I settled down to wait.

It didn't take long. About five minutes later, what had to be Rob blew in—literally from the sound of it, through the sacristy entrance. I heard him stamping the snow off his shoes and the harsh slam of the door to the side yard, heavy, as if it had force behind it.

"Rob . . .?"

Silence. Then I saw his face and that shock of salt-and-pepper hair framed in the ornate wooden doorway.

"Man, it's cold out there. I made the mistake of charging over here without my coat. Holy Toledo . . ."

"And half of Cleveland and Akron—!" I laughed. "How are things over there in Mudville?" After last night, I wasn't so sure.

"Minimal weeping and gnashing of teeth . . . so far. Pretty much the occasional zings you caught last night," he muttered. "I just hope you're not on one of these low carb programs. It never occurred to me to ask. Ted pitched in yesterday but I've been alone in the kitchen since six . . ."

He stopped short, appreciatively taking in my tailored black slacks and tunic. "Not that you need to worry about it. You look . . . gorgeous. Merry Christmas!"

"*Et cum spiritu tuo!*" I flushed. "No problem with the menu. The alarm didn't go off and I didn't even get my usual caffeine-fix for the day. By the time we finish the service, I'll be so hungry I could chew on the wallpaper."

"You got some sleep—?"

"On and off. It's tough to wind down after playing so late." I wasn't entirely being honest about the cause of my short night. "Marty had left a bottle of wine uncorked for me and that helped take the edge off."

Rob looked pained. "Definitely not on the brunch menu."

It was only then I remembered. He was in AA.

"Sorry, Rob, that was tactless— "

"Don't be. It's been eight years, three months and twenty-one days. If I made it through the past forty-eight hours sober, I can make it through anything . . .!"

We hadn't been that skittish around each other in months. *Time to rein it in now.* With a quick intake of breath, I took the initiative and hugged him, forced a smile.

"I see Ted helped you put up a tree over there. Good for you! Looks nice."

That was a guess. But, as it turns out, it was a good one.

"Mostly lights and precious little by way of ornaments," Rob grinned. "But yeah, we took your suggestion and played Paul Bunyan yesterday morning. I had my doubts about the saw and axe business under the circumstances. But it was fun. Thanks. We hadn't done that since Ted was a kid."

"Is there . . . are we likely to be dealing with a crowd out there this morning?"

"Hardly. Fifteen last year, counting yours truly and Wilma. Mainly the very oldest folks who didn't want to venture out last night for the midnight service."

I still felt a quiet sadness whenever I thought of the former organist. She had given a good deal of her life to Nativity. I missed her.

"And Ted . . .?"

"Sleeping in. Twice in two days in this or any sanctuary is way off his radar. I'm honestly surprised he came last night."

Gun-shy, Rob and I both flinched when the narthex door swung open propelled by a blast of cold air that rustled the medieval-looking burgundy and gold-bead trimmed bows hooked over the ends of the pews along the center aisle that the altar guild had come up with for the occasion. But it was just Barney, the ever faithful, there to fold bulletins or do whatever had to be done.

"So, kids—we good to go, here?"

"Merry Christmas to you, too, Barney," I said.

"There were three cars turning behind me in the driveway. A regular traffic jam!"

"Time to suit up." With a lingering smile in my direction, Rob turned and headed back toward the sacristy.

*Onward and upward.* The music for the prelude was right on top of the heap on the organ rack. I eased into that lively little variation based on the familiar tune, FOREST GREEN, *O Little Town of Bethlehem.* From behind me at the back of the sanctuary, I heard the subdued buzz of voices, greeting one another.

I finished the prelude. With that gale outside and a dearth of altar servers, Rob had warned me he was going to forgo the usual procession and read all the Lessons himself. Evie, last night's violinist, had been recruited hastily to serve as acolyte.

Slamming on one of the most boisterous of the pre-sets, I began the opening hymn, *O Come, All Ye Faithful. Joyful. Triumphant.*

The more I threw myself into the music, the less I thought about what lay ahead when church was over. Before I knew it, I was winding down the postlude and Rob, Barney and I were shutting up the church.

I'd been taking my time, putting on my coat and bundling up for the hike over to the parsonage, short as it was. With the furnace off, the temperature in the sanctuary was already dropping precipitously. Rob just stood there in his shirt sleeves, looking all the world like a felon contemplating the guillotine.

"What say we make a dash for it!"

I feigned a frown. "That'll teach you not to try the old macho who-needs-a-coat stuff."

"You forget. I set the school record for the dash."

"A heck of a long time ago—"

"Wanna bet!"

With that, we were off, laughing and slipping on the slick curving walkway between the church and the parsonage, jostling one another for maneuvering room like two kids on the playground. Out of breath and flushed from the exertion we stumbled up the stairs to the front porch.

Rob was fumbling with door knob, stopped—and for a long second just looked down at me. His face was an open book.

"Merry Christmas, Char."

The words caught in my throat. "Merry . . . Christmas, . . . Rob!"

And then, mercifully, the door yielded to his touch and we found ourselves in the warmth of his living room. It was an odd sort of deja vu moment—what seemed like a lifetime ago since I first stood here in the parsonage. Then, as now, I found myself here more or less under duress.

Whatever my reservations about coming to grips with Rob's world—or better said, my place in it—one thing was indisputable. The smells emanating from the kitchen were incredible. Through the huge oak pocket doors open to the dining room, I caught a glimpse of an elegantly set table with festive clusters of cranberry-colored candles and what appeared to be a centerpiece of house plants nestled together in a rustic wicker basket.

Rob was helping me with my coat, innocent enough. But to my chagrin, what began as a casual Emily-Post-moment was threatening quickly to become something else entirely. I shivered at the closeness, the contact of his hands as I maneuvered out of the tight-fitted sleeves. My teeth were chattering.

"This is d-dangerous . . .!"

"You said it," Rob exhaled sharply. "Duty calls. I think something out there might be burning— "

With obvious reluctance, my coat still in hand, he made a dash for the kitchen. Son Ted was nowhere in sight.

At loose ends and on my own, I settled to catch my breath in a Morris chair that had been re-upholstered in a bargello print of subtle turquoise, gold and rust. It was a mistake. The antique recliner was way too comfortable. Despite myself, I was starting to doze off. The combination of two days of stressful playing and a short night was taking its toll. I closed my eyes.

"Coffee . . .?"

Rob's voice startled me. I yawned, stretched and peered around the chair back to see what was going on.

He was standing in the kitchen doorway, shirt sleeves rolled up and wearing a *Have-You-Hugged-an-Episcopalian-Lately?* apron. His intervention couldn't have come at a more fortuitous time. Any longer and I would have been out for the duration.

"How long have I been in a coma?"

He smiled. "Not long. Ten minutes . . . less."

"It's so cozy here compared to that organ bench. I could sleep sitting up. If you've got a cup of that black stuff, I'd love some."

As I watched, Rob disappeared again and quickly reemerged from the kitchen with two oversize mugs of scalding brew. Together we stood looking at the tree, reveling in the caffeine and the prospect of a week until the next gig over at Nativity. This time we had the sense to keep a bit of distance between us.

The tree was enormous and it still had that wonderful fresh-cut smell, pungent and green. The decor was as advertised. Except for the lights, the main trimming was what had to be at least a forty-foot paper chain, in every color of the rainbow and then some.

*Obviously home-made.* I fought a smile as I thought about Rob sitting there with a shears, forehead knotted in concentration, cranking out one construction paper strip after the other.

"What's so funny?"

"You." I told him what I had been thinking.

"Touching . . . but not quite accurate. The paper was commandeered last minute from the Sunday School closet and I borrowed the church's paper cutter to mass-produce all those blasted paper links. Ted wielded the stapler— "

"You had a regular sweat shop going over here."

"Quick and dirty took on a whole new meaning. By the time the midnight movie was over, the chain was done and on the tree. It took more time to vacuum up the shards than to make the crazy thing."

"That's cheating, you know."

"Probably. I'll replace the kids' paper supply once the holidays are over."

Old houses have at least one advantage. The subtle shifting of wood alongside wood on the stairs told us we were about to have company. I turned in time to see Rob's son rounding the landing from the second floor.

As preppie as his father was oblivious to fashion trends, Ted had pulled on a pair of dark flannel slacks and a button-down shirt topped with a subtle moss-green cashmere sweater. From highly buffed shoes to his high-price-spread haircut, his whole aura—trendy to a fault—smacked of wannabee. That, or a desperate holdover from his childhood lifestyle.

Rob had explained his own transformation when he first told me about his daughter's death—about priorities changing when your back is to the wall. Even coming out of that same terrible crucible of experience, father and son couldn't have been farther apart at this point in their lives.

Rob had been there. He had done that, embracing the posh neighborhood and all the trimmings. Quietly and without fanfare, he had come to the conclusion that tee-shirts were fine with or without the requisite logos.

"You're admiring our handiwork, *Ms. Howard*?"

It seemed politic to ignore the sarcasm in Ted's tone. Apparently between now and last midnight, something had transpired to set him off.

*What*, I couldn't pretend to guess. From Rob's scowl, I could tell he was as clueless as I.

"The early American look," I said. "Nice."

"Yeah . . . well, it's all about lemons and making lemonade. Right, Dad?"

Rob shot a pointed look in his son's direction. "Good morning to you, too, Ted."

"I just got off the phone with Mom. Your nickel. Hope you don't mind."

"Of course not."

His jaw set, Rob looked over at me as if to say, *Brace yourself.* I had already gotten the message. Ted was just getting warmed up.

"Mom and . . .*Sean* are down in Boca for the week. I caught her on her cell."

I couldn't tell, from the way Ted let slip the name of his mother's companion, whether he was expressing veiled disapproval, needling his dad—or both.

"Good for her. It's warm down there, anyway." Rob sounded gruff, uncomfortable—with the look of someone trying their best not to overreact. "Ted, I could sure use a hand . . ."

I knew better than volunteer. Whatever was sticking in Ted's craw, Rob was not going to let it pass. Right now that kitchen was the last place any sane person wanted to be.

"Don't mind me," I said, "I'll just hang out here enjoying the tree."

"There are CD's in the changer. Feel free to browse."

*A good idea*, I decided, given the tense set of the two men's shoulders as they disappeared into the kitchen. *When in doubt, drown it out.*

Although a number of Christmas CD cases were stacked next to the changer, I opted for potluck with whatever Rob had left behind. I hit the Power switch, then Play.

The crystalline tones of an English boys' choir filled the room. I recognized the recording. My oldest daughter had given me the same CD for Christmas last year. Reclaiming my spot on the Morris chair, I sipped away at my coffee and tried to concentrate on the music, not the hushed voices or the sound of clattering pans and utensils coming from the kitchen.

Although distance masked the details, the occasional recognizable word was enough to catch the unfortunate gist of things.

"She thinks . . . I'm . . . *what*—? Ted . . . surely you can't— "

"Damnit, Dad, . . .?" The rest was lost, inaudible. "What do you . . . *expect* me to think . . .?"

Again, the voices dropped to an agitated whisper. From the CD player, the music flowed out in a passionate stream. The boys' choir had moved on to the beloved noel about shepherds camped out on the hillsides over Bethlehem.

"You think that . . . *matters*? Ted, *I love you.* You're my *son!*"

Some things between husband and wife are too volatile, too dysfunctional for an outsider to comprehend. Even children raised under that same roof have trouble coming to grips with it. I could only guess at what followed next in that kitchen from the punch line.

"If that's what she *wants* . . .? All your mother has to do is ask. This isn't the Middle Ages. And the church or church policy has got . . . *nothing* to do with this."

It was pretty obvious that the D-word finally had found its way into the conversation. Karin really wanted a divorce?

After a few muffled comments, a silence ensued—worse almost than their heated exchange. Finally I heard footsteps heading from kitchen to dining room.

"Brunch'll be ready in a minute."

Rob's announcement was aimed in my direction. But before I could react, his footsteps retreated again.

Tentatively, I stood up—waiting for a cue whether to stay put or head toward the dining room. Instead, from behind that kitchen door, I heard Rob's anguished undertone, every painful syllable of it.

"Face it, Ted . . . we're here. Your mother is . . . not. *Her choice.* Meanwhile, that woman out there in the living room deserves your respect. Whatever you might think of me, Char is . . . "

The rest was lost in the rising chorus from the stereo. *Gloria. Gloria, in excelsis Deo.*

And then above the triumphant angel song, I heard Ted shouting and the unmistakable slamming of a door. The silence was deafening.

*"Sonofabitch . . .!"*

I had never heard Rob resort to expletives, not even in his bleakest moments. My chest felt as if my heart was about to beat its way out of my rib cage. I stood there, believing the worst—confronting the obvious.

Much as I bled for Rob and his son, with a shock I realized that could be me out there. If this were my daughters, how would *they* react to the bombshell that after all these years of more-or-less single life, their mother had fallen in love again? With a priest—and a married one at that!

Rob was right. Whatever ground-rules applied as far as our lives and work in Hope was concerned, this was different. This was family.

If I was going to maintain any pretext of integrity at all, I was going to have to be honest with my girls as well, and *soon.* The clock was ticking. New Year's Eve they would be here, both of them, complete with kids—and in Jen's case, I had been forewarned, with the new kitten my granddaughter had gotten for Christmas.

Much as I hoped my daughters could rise to the moment, I knew I couldn't be certain they would embrace this man I loved. Or that they would comprehend the boundaries we were setting for ourselves, any better than Ted was doing. I had never even considered it before. Truth was, it was high time I did.

When Rob strode back out of that kitchen, he had the look of a man pushed to the brink. Ashen and stony-faced, he looked straight through me, a platter of freshly-cut fruit in his hands.

"Rob, are you all right . . .?"

He drew himself up short. Even from that distance, I heard him steadying his breathing. Mentally counting way past ten.

"Sorry about that . . .!"

"No need. You forget. I have two daughters. That could have been me out there."

A hint of a smile twisted at the corner of his mouth. "Hope you're still hungry. We've got enough here to feed an army."

"And . . . Ted . . .?"

"He'll join us eventually, I suspect. After he has a chance to cool off. Meanwhile . . .," Rob nodded in the direction of the table, "this is getting cold as we speak."

I let him hold my chair, knowing it was part of his coping mechanism. In Hope, the ethos was and is a simple testament to a kinder, gentler time. Liberation or not, a gentleman still holds doors for a lady. You avoid airing your dirty linen in public and you always change your underwear, never knowing when that unforeseen car wreck is going to leave your lapses in judgment exposed to public view. And you redefine your identity in generations—aren't you Cecilia's daughter, the one who kept playing the piano all hours of the day and night?

That was not the prevailing culture of the world from which Rob—and even I, to some degree—had most recently come. In the business world he had taken what he wanted, fought for it with his bare knuckles if need be. My career may have been at the far end of the alpha spectrum. Still, was my life truly all that different? From 8 to 5, I had defined myself as a got-her-stuff-together counselor. After hours and outside the safety of the client-relationship, I was the woman who avoided commitment at all costs.

Urban warriors, both of us, we were just trying desperately in our own broken fashion to survive. And yet here we were, back where we started, lo those many years ago. Only this time there was enough baggage between the two of us to accommodate a multitude of regrets.

Just when my mood hit rock bottom, I heard faint sounds of life emanating from the kitchen. Rob heard it, too.

"Ted . . .?"

"Coming."

He did. But even as he settled down at that empty place at the table, I sensed the change. This was not the same cocky, judgmental Ted who had walked down that staircase to meet me, what seemed like hours ago. This was a desperately confused young man trying to face head-on the end of the world as he knew it.

*Shell-shocked.* Those up-scale clothes and even the attitude, in retrospect, had all had the earmarks of a lost little boy thrust into a man's world. Whatever animosity I might have felt vanished in a heart-beat. I laid down my fork.

"I suspect you had a hand in this, too, Ted," I told him. "The brunch is wonderful."

As he looked up his smile seemed strained, awkward. But he plainly was making an effort and right now that was a lot.

"Dad's the cook. Always was. I just . . . stepped and fetched."

"Well, congratulations. Everything is great."

"He says a lot of the herbs came from your garden."

"Just a sawed-off barrel full of the basic greenery outside my kitchen door," I said. "But yes, I flash-froze a lot of them before the frost hit. There was way too much just for me."

"It must be tough cooking alone all the time."

I fought a smile. Unless I missed my guess, in spite of himself Ted was setting off on a subtle fishing expedition of his own. Rob was right—this son of his was no dummy.

"My neighbor Grace, your Dad and I have a kind of weird casserole club going. We independently go on these cooking jags, freeze the leftovers and then divvy up the wealth."

Rob shifted in his chair. His scowl was pure theater.

"You know, all this third-person stuff?" he said. "It's getting a bit *tedious*, you two."

Father and son made eye contact. It was Ted who flinched first. Especially when he smiled like that, the resemblance between the two men was uncanny.

As if someone had thrown a switch, the tension began to drain from the room like the steady whisper of the air leaving the organ's reservoir. Gradually, the conversation shifted around to the vicissitudes of small town living. Rob and I started swapping stories and laughing about some of the more interesting moments we had experienced.

Ted's laughter was polite enough. But for some time now, he seemed intent on chasing a hunk of melon around his plate. He gave up.

"You two put a good face on it. But I can't even imagine what it's like living here . . .!"

Rob had been replenishing the water in my goblet. He stopped, looked quizzically at his son.

"The fish bowl—?"

"That. But also this whole . . . priest thing." Ted shook his head. "I can't even imagine what it would be like running around in that collar, dealing with all those expectations . . . *alone*—without something, without someone to tell you when you're out of line. Anything that helps to keep you . . . *real* . . ."

I just stared at him, fork poised in my hand. It was obvious who Ted had in mind, that it was my presence he seemed to see at work here. An hour and change ago, this reaction from Rob's son would have been unthinkable.

For a split-second I thought I was going to lose it. Through a sudden welling up of tears, I looked down at my plate—the Florentine strata with three cheeses and prosciuto in the layers, the bread tomato compote and last few bites of sauteed mushrooms. Every bit of it was Rob and his son's gift to me, that and so much more.

Rob cleared his throat. "Ted, I . . . thanks, for that."

I sat watching the silent communication between the two men, intense and raw. The vulnerability was out there—quite literally on that table. As homecomings go, this one could have been an awful lot worse.

"My mother had a saying," I said softly. "When in doubt . . . there's always the dishes— "

We laughed, the three of us. After lingering over our coffee, we eventually took Mom's advice, clearing the vestiges of that feast together and loading the dishwasher, not just once but twice. In the process, conversation veered off in less emotionally charged directions.

I could see Rob was exhausted and I wasn't feeling too perky myself, but no one seemed in a hurry to call it a day. With the housekeeping out of the way, at Ted's suggestion, the three of us sat down for another round of coffee in front of the fireplace. Rob and I were together on the sofa. His son had perched on the window seat, watching the showers of snowflakes that had begun to drift down from the leaden sky.

The crackle of the logs, the candlelight and the shimmering simplicity of the tree were straight out of a Victorian novel—the classic trappings of a family Christmas. Just last night on my solitary walk home, I was on the outside of this world looking in.

What a difference a day makes. I, too, had found my place in the story.

Reluctant as I was to spoil the moment, it had to be done. Grace and Marty and the gang would be expecting me soon for our own Christmas festivities. Rob offered to walk me home, but I declined—willing him every possible moment to spend with his son.

Still, if I was going to make it through yet another feast, I had better get myself moving. Ted said his goodbyes and headed upstairs. I soon understood why.

On the way to the door, his father stopped at the tree and fished around under it before coming up with an elegant burnished gold gift bag with a cascading platinum bow on its handles. Suppressing a smile, he held it out in my direction.

"Just a little something," Rob said. "I saw it in one of those online catalogs while I was doing all that website research. It seemed to have 'you' written all over it."

"Rob . . ., you shouldn't have— "

"I'll decide that *after* I see your reaction!"

He expected me to open it then and there. I did, cautiously feeling my way through the tissue paper to a small black velvet box, on the cover of which was embossed in gold the name of a prestigious church art supply company. Removing the lid, I looked down at the contents—speechless.

"Oh . . ., Rob . . .!"

Lying there on its cushion of velvet was the most incredible piece of wearable art I had ever seen. Worked in 10 carat gold, the tiny oval disk couldn't be more than three-quarters of an inch across. But on its face was carved the image of St. Cecilia, seated at her organ, with the ranks of pipes towering in front of her and above her head, a shaft of light descending.

The patron saint of musicians, in the world of religious art Cecilia is conventionally pictured in that setting, sometimes even with angels bearing garlands hovering over the source of the light. Here the oval of the medal was so small and the workmanship so exceptional that it took my breath away. It was fastened to an equally delicate gold chain made up of multiple strands spun together for strength.

I could sense Rob watching my reaction. Something he saw in my expression must have given him his answer.

"You like it, then?"

"Do I . . . *like* it . . .? Oh, Rob— "

"Read the inscription," he said.

Carefully, I turned the tiny medallion over. On the back, I read the simple engraving. *Love always, Rob.*

My eyes were misting with tears. "I'll . . . I'm almost afraid to wear this."

"Why don't we give it a try?"

Rob reached out. Gently he took the medallion and chain from my hand.

"Let me help," he said.

The clasp was so small. As I turned and bowed my head so that he could fasten it around my neck, I could feel the gentle touch of his fingers working at the mechanism, felt his breath warm against my skin as he bent closer to see how the fastener fit together.

The medallion in place, it would have been the most natural thing in the world to turn into his embrace. I was working so hard to hold back the tears, I didn't dare risk it.

"I have . . . something for you, too," I managed to stammer.

Rummaging in the organ bag at my feet, I found the cylindrical package with the single tartan ribbon holding it together. Rob fumbled with the knot—finally gave up and slid the whole ribbon off one end. The shiny red foil crinkled in his hands as he undid the wrapping.

Anxious, I tried to gauge his response. It was the best tapestry weaving I had ever done—a prototype for that liturgical panel that I had given up on last Fall as way-too-complicated for our little Undercroft team. Executed in blues and grays and lilacs, Rob's favorite colors, it was a labyrinth similar to the classic Chartres design. If you looked at it a certain way, the central image had the same contour as the mystical ancient near-Eastern Tree of Life. On the back I hand-stitched a label with the single word, the ancient Hebrew blessing, *L'chaiam . . . to Life.*

"This is not for Nativity," I told him softly. "It's for you."

"I thought you had already given me the best possible present anyone could wish for. My son—!"

Rob's eyes glistened with unshed tears. My own had finally begun to fall, unchecked.

"Char . . ., sweetheart— "

It was an invitation and one I could not refuse. I knew I was inundating his shirt front as he held me. His lips were moving against my hair, shaping my name again and again—the kind of inchoate sounds that soothe a child overwhelmed by the realities around them.

But then, we were children no longer and the intimacy between us had taken on a whole new meaning. *In joy and sorrow.* We were there for each other, the most precious gift of all.

As the tears subsided and I began to distance myself, I could finally see his face. I didn't need words to tell me what I read there.

"I wasn't intending to set off a . . . flash flood," he told me.

"I'm not . . . *sad.* I'm h-h-happy— "

"An alarming way of showing it."

Still laughing, I let him escort me down the hall to his study. There was a spot on the wall that would be absolutely perfect for my panel, he assured me. I had never been in his inner sanctum before, but the room was vintage Rob—very different from the more austere public rooms he shared with visitors.

Book shelves were crammed full floor to ceiling and a battered leather desk chair served a desk the size of a football field. Amid the genial clutter, safely tucked away next to the base of the banker-style desk lamp, I caught sight of a small, delicate silver frame and in it a faded black-and-white photograph of a young woman I had never seen before. Freckled, her pale shoulder-length hair loose except for a single beaded braid to one side, she smiled out at the camera.

*Lily.* Rob's daughter. It had to be.

With a shock of recognition, I dropped my gaze—steadying myself on the back of Rob's chair. Mercifully Rob didn't seem to notice. As my heartbeat slowed again, I noticed that he was holding my tapestry thoughtfully against a vacant spot on the wall.

"Perfect," he said quietly.

I sensed the rationale immediately. Just below the spot for the panel was an ornate Florentine-style icon of Christ the Teacher and alongside it, in a dark wooden frame, hung a piece of charred parchment with calligraphy in some unfamiliar language. My woven panel would complete the iconography—the mystical grouping of three.

"I don't recognize the writing," I told him, "or the script."

Rob smiled. "A Muslim proverb and a present from a friend in the seminary. *Lilah al bāqī.* My pronunciation is probably atrocious— "

"Translation?"

*"What remains belongs to God."*

I struggled to make the connection. "The Cross would have to be the power of sacrifice, alongside the labyrinth as the symbol of eternal renewal or the life journey. And that calligraphy text . . .?"

"Commitment. When we let the holocaust of experience burn away the unwise and unnecessary, what is left is not dust and ashes, it's love and beauty. If we have the courage to see it, to sanctify those last precious truths of our life— "

"Then we find God."

Rob nodded. "A survivor's mind-set, I suppose, but— "

"It works for me."

In the one hand I was still toting around my heavy organ bag. With the other, I found myself cradling between finger and thumb the tiny image of St. Cecilia now suspended at the base of my throat.

"You told me Cecilia was also your mother's name," Rob said softly.

I nodded. "I keep her picture in my wallet opposite a Holy Card depicting the Saint that a Roman Catholic colleague gave me."

Rob, too, was part of the equation now. Every time I reached up and felt that precious symbol of my life coming full circle in this place, his love and support would be there behind both the sound and the silence.

*What remains belongs to God.*

"If I don't leave soon— "

"If I had any choice in the matter," he said quietly. "I would never let you go like this— "

"I'm glad I came."

Rob nodded. "Thank you . . . for everything."

"You raised a good son, Rob. I hope you know that."

He followed me out on the porch, shirt sleeves still rolled to the elbows though he had shed that crazy Episcopalian apron of his. The wind was howling and the wind chill had to be at least minus ten. Long goodbyes were not a good idea. I was in the process of turning to go when he reached out and snagged my hand.

"We . . . need to talk, you and I. Soon."

I didn't trust myself to speak. As we hugged, I felt his lips, fleeting and gentle, against my hair—discreet and yet unbearably intimate. We drew apart, still connected by the reality of what we felt. His voice was barely audible over the rising wind.

"I love you, Char."

It was then that I did the unthinkable. With my free hand, I reached up and laid it alongside the chiseled plane of his jaw. Without a thought for the consequences or who might be out there around us, I just kissed him—full on the mouth. It couldn't have taken more than a second, the length of a quarter note *a tempo*, if that.

*Stupid, stupid, stupid. What in the name of all that's holy were you thinking?*

I didn't wait for Rob's reaction to register. As I tore down the steps, all I could think was the utter folly of what I had done.

We weren't kids any longer, flirting with disaster in the back seat of Dad's Chevy. All it would take was one neighbor at the window at the wrong time—the fallout could be horrific.

Frigid air was making it tough to catch my breath. And still, I stumbled ahead. It took a good half block for my pace to slow—a half block beyond that for the erratic pounding in my ears to subside. I didn't dare look back.

*Stupid.* Absolutely.

I kept telling myself that over and over again. When all along I knew. If I had it to do over again, I wouldn't have changed a thing.

# ✣ Chapter Eighteen

"Your son thought you're . . . *WHAT* . . .!"

Rob winced. Then he slowly repeated what he had just told me.

"That I'm *gay*."

"But how on . . . earth would he—?"

"Courtesy of Karin's phone call on Christmas morning." His voice hardened. "Her rationale, it seems for demanding a divorce."

It was the morning after Christmas and Rob's son had just left on his return trip to Cleveland. Within the hour, Rob and I were encamped around the kitchen table—*his* this time, to minimize unexpected visitors.

We were deconstructing, as Rob put it, what had happened over that Christmas weekend with his son. Pretty heady stuff.

"Karin told Ted that she left you, that you went into the priesthood because you're . . . *gay*?" My voice dropped to an incredulous whisper. "And Ted *believed* it? That's *impossible*!"

"Thanks for the vote of confidence, I think."

"Rob, I'm *serious*. How *could* she—?"

"Put yourself in Karin's shoes. She doesn't understand why I'd give up a successful corporate career, for what she considers a morally hypocritical lifestyle. Put that together with the media war about closet homosexuals in the clergy . . ."

"Still, why on *earth* would she—?"

"Why not . . .!" A pained look on his face, Rob kneaded at the knot of tension at the base of his skull. "Our marriage was in shambles even back then. As explanations go, that is certainly more palatable than blaming the booze and lack of shared values— "

"And Ted just . . . bought it—!"

He exhaled sharply. "Unfortunate but understandable, given his current doubts about his own sexuality . . . !"

"He . . . your son thinks he's—?"

"It's not unusual for young adults to question their sexual orientation. Under the circumstances Ted just may be facing the possibility later than most— "

"That he *really . . . is . . . gay.*"

"Given his mother's accusations about me, it's tempting to make a link. Dear old Dad's been in the closet all these years—*ergo* . . ."

Rob paused. "You add it up. He's angry and scared, prepared to blame the gene pool yet again."

Finally, the fragments I had heard through the door that morning made sense. "And when you told him you didn't care—that you loved him . . . regardless?"

"Ted lost it. Especially since his mother had painted me pretty much as the anti-Christ for what she told him was my 'deviant lifestyle'. For a minute there I thought the kid was going to deck me— "

"Oh, God, Rob!"

"Pretty much sums it up," he shrugged. "Somewhere out there between a prayer and a swear. Much as I would like to get her alone in a dark alley, I have got to assume Karin didn't know what she was unleashing. In high school Ted never dated much, though at the time I just chalked it up to all the tension at home. Not much of an example of budding romance . . ."

I kept turning the dynamics over in my mind. "No wonder Ted was so . . . hostile. As he saw it, either you were just using me as cover, yet again. Or I was living proof his mother wasn't telling him the truth."

"A no-win situation if I ever saw one."

"But Ted came back." Against all odds, I realized. "And somehow you . . . *knew* he would rejoin us at that table."

Rob smiled. His voice was low.

"Hoped. But, yes. It's amazing what human beings can rise to, given half a chance."

*A miracle?* I stopped short of naming it.

Miracles were burning bushes and manna from heaven, not human love accomplishing the impossible or at least the unlikely. Not in little Hope, Pennsylvania.

"Just before I decided once and for all to enroll in the seminary," Rob said quietly, "my friend and mentor, the priest at the Cathedral, preached a homily. It was on the text of the loaves and fishes."

I knew the text. It was the miraculous feeding of the five thousand out on that barren hillside.

Rob chuckled, remembering. "It was my first exposure to non-literal theology. *Did the Great Magician wave his wand and save the starving masses*, my friend said. *Or when that little boy walked forward with his miserable loaves and two scrawny minnows, could the compassion of the Suffering Servant—consecrating the gift—have triggered an even more amazing miracle?"*

Rob paused. He shook his head.

"Maybe that mob on the hillside, though selfish and afraid like the rest of us, dug down deep into the sleeves of their tunics and pulled out a loaf here, some cheese there, a precious handful of figs—and they shared. Enough to feed that crowd twenty times over."

Rob had taken my hand in his. I felt his thumb tracing the length of my fingers, as if searching for the music he knew was lurking there under the tissue, the bones, the pale veins just beneath the surface.

"Love, Char. In spite of everything—because of everything . . ."

From habit we had put the table between us. But Rob stood, moved around to where I sat and then drew me into his arms. Under the soft fabric of his gray turtleneck, I felt the strength of his body holding me. His eyes glittered with a quiet fire—then with agonizing certainty, his mouth found mine. I closed my eyes.

We had fought this intimacy for so long. The time for restraint had come and gone. Trembling, I felt our bodies fitting together as we kissed, until even that closeness was not enough. Light-headed I thought I heard Rob whisper my name and then for a split-second, he awkwardly levered enough distance to see my face.

*Rob . . .?* By way of answer, with a groan he buried his face against my shoulder. Mercifully, it seems, one of us had summoned up the force of will to stop it. It wasn't me. In slow shuddering gasps, Rob's breathing began to steady itself.

"No cold shower on the planet is going to handle this—," he growled.

Shaky attempts at a laugh seemed to catch in my throat. "Serves us r-r-right . . .!" I said.

"I won't lie to you, Char. This could get a whole lot. . . *tougher* before it gets better."

He wasn't just talking about what months—longer—of this sort of thing could do to our libidos. Short of "taking it out of town", there was no way on earth we could finish what we had started, not without risking everything. It was just a fact.

"We're painting ourselves into a corner, Rob—you see it. I see it. And if we're not careful, the whole town— "

He didn't let me finish. "If Karin wants a divorce, as my son says she does, I'm going to give it to her. *Whatever* it takes!"

"But . . . that still doesn't mean the Diocese will agree to . . ."

"We'll cross *that* bridge when we come to it."

*We.* I knew that Rob did not toss words around lightly. What was he trying to tell me?

"A priest can divorce and still remain a priest."

Rob nodded. "In most cases, yes. But if there's re-marriage on the horizon . . . it's not always that clear-cut."

He didn't have to spell out chapter and verse. Given where and who we were, I had to hope Rob was right about miracles. For a control freak like me to admit even that much was a leap of faith beyond anything I had ever managed in my lifetime. I needed him to know it.

"I love you, Rob."

His answer was far simpler. It was, quietly and without fanfare, to kiss me again.

With that, post-Christmas burnout had risen to drastic new levels. Partly I was feeling the lingering fallout from that emotional encounter with Rob's son and, indirectly, the painful glimpse it gave into the state of things between his parents. In part, too, I was thinking about my own daughters and their pending visit over New Year.

Both girls had been nothing but supportive of my move to Hope and all that went with it. All they knew about, that is. Music and rag looms were one thing, Rob Sims quite another.

The next few days passed in a blur of food and neighbors and a lot of sleeping in. I was welcoming any and every excuse to avoid thinking about what I was, or was not, prepared to share with my progeny about my feelings for Rob.

My daughters arrived with entourage—Jen and company around noon and her sister and family within an hour of that. I felt like I was running a B & B. But then at least this was family. I couldn't even imagine having the patience to play hostess-with-the-mostest like this for a houseful of strangers.

We exchanged gifts, pigged out on turkey and the fixings. Then of course, Marty eventually wandered back with Grace, Leah and little Bart in tow. My girls seemed more uneasy about the comings and goings than I was.

My daughters and I had long since resolved most of the mother-daughter stuff that goes on in adolescence. Still as the day wore on, it was becoming pretty clear that despite all our upbeat chatty phone conversations, both Jen and Sarah had been nursing the stereotype that in my dotage I had exiled myself to outer darkness here in Hope—a regular nun in a nunnery.

*Little did they know.* But then, I wasn't in much of a hurry to enlighten them.

The moment of truth came early that evening when my sons-in-law took over kid-patrol so that Jen, Sarah and I could have some face-time alone in front of the fireplace. On some level, it was hilarious. Whether they realized it or not, my daughters were doing a pretty credible re-enactment of the inquisitions that routinely had played out between us when they were growing up.

"So, mom . . .," Jen led the charge. "you're really settling in here!"

It was uncomfortably like watching a clone of myself staring back at me, younger of course and with gray eyes, not that strange burnt amber I had inherited from my own mother. As I had in my middle years, Jen even wore her hair in that same austere up-do that enhanced her strongest asset—those taut facial bones that showed every promise of holding up well with time.

With a half-smile I watched her slip into her counselor-client mode, wondering if it was my own style of mothering she was replaying for me here, or something all her own. A little of both, I suspected.

"I've made a lot of friends," I told her. "Surprising, I know, in a closed little community like this, but— "

"Frankly, we were . . . we thought you might find it hard. This *isn't* Philly."

Our roles seemed to have undergone one heck of a reversal. *How odd and wonderful it is,* I found myself thinking, *to find the tables turning.* You actually reach a day when your children start to worry about you, instead of the other way around.

"You're worried the natives might not be friendly?" I chuckled. "In a way, I *am* one of their own, as they see it. That helps."

It was as good a time as any, I also decided, to drop the proverbial shoe. I took a deep breath and plunged ahead.

"Then of course, getting to know Rob again has been a big part of that . . .!"

Silence followed that pronouncement, but I caught the I-told-you-so look that passed between the two girls. Jen's eyebrows shot up like the Arch on a postcard she had sent me from a family trip to St. Louis a couple of years ago.

"Rob . . .?" she said.

"Rob Sims, a friend from high school. We've been spending a lot of time together— "

"He's retired here, too . . .?"

"The priest at Nativity."

Jen's intake of breath pretty much said it all. "Isn't that the Episcopal Church where you're . . . playing the organ . . .?"

I nodded. "Rob and his wife have been separated for over three years now— "

"Good grief, *mother* . . .!" My unflappable eldest looked as if I had just hit her with a shovel. "You can't be *serious* . . .!"

This was not going well at all. Stony-faced, my younger daughter just stared at her sister, then at me.

Sarah was all Len, her father—fine-boned with a mop of curly sandy hair. Tight-wired that girl, with a lightning wit and penetrating way of getting to the heart of things. That was strange, since she was too young to remember her Dad's take-charge personality.

Under normal circumstances Sarah would have verbally shot from the hip by now. Could it be that for once she too was flustered, caught off guard? Apparently enough to give her pause anyway.

"Isn't . . . doesn't the church . . . *frown* on divorce?" she stammered.

"For crying out loud, mom!" Jen chimed in. "You *work* for the guy! There's gotta be some rules against that sort of thing."

"Probably. But then it isn't as if either one of us . . . planned this."

Sarah's eyes narrowed. "Planned . . . exactly . . . *what*?"

There was no sense in beating around the bush. "We're in love with each other."

"Holy . . . shit . . .!"

An explosion of sparks from the fireplace cut short whatever was coming next. A log had shifted and in the process, imploded with an ominous crackling and hiss of pent-up energy releasing itself. Sarah straightened in her chair.

"Don't tell me, mom, you . . . you're—?"

"Sleeping with him?" My face felt hot, as flaming as my new deep wine velvet pants suit, a gift to myself for their visit. "No. I'm not."

"Good grief! At your age, women— "

"Should behave as if they have one foot in the grave?!"

"That isn't what I meant. "

I decided it was time to lay out the ground rules once and for all. On that score, anyway.

"Well, for the record, I'm not dead yet," I said stiffly. "Not that it's anyone's business, but Rob's and mine. I realize you're surprised by all this— "

"Try . . . *shocked* . . . !!"

I bristled."Okay, *shocked, stunned.* If it's any comfort, so am I. I loved your dad and after all these years alone, I wasn't looking for a change in status. But then I wasn't planning on early retirement or coming here either. Not Rob—not any of it."

"So then, why . . . on . . . earth—?"

"Sometimes, life happens," I said. "Like jazz. One minute you play a note and then another—and suddenly . . . you're somewhere else."

That finally got Sarah really going. "So, that's what this is all about! Some late-life music, romance, fantasy thing . . . !"

"Finding your voice has *nothing* to do with age," I corrected her. "For years I never gave any of that much thought. I was a widow. I was a mother. I did what had to be done. Well, times—it seems—have changed. I'm trying to change with them."

Sarah's mouth curled in disgust. "Obviously! I suppose at least we should be grateful it isn't that *tattooed biker* down the block you're always threatening us with!"

"Are you going to let us meet him?"

*Dear Jen*, I thought—*ever the pragmatist.* I chuckled softly.

"I thought you'd never ask. But yes, if that's what you want."

She shook her head. "*Want* has got . . . very little to do with this."

"I understand. Believe me, I do." The words were coming easier now. "Rob's son came home for Christmas. He hadn't seen him in years. It was rough, but we got through it— "

"I can imagine."

"Call me naive but I was hoping, just maybe, that we might fast-forward a little quicker than that. Contrary to what the two of you might be thinking, *I am not senile.* I am not in my second childhood. Rob is a wonderful man and despite all the . . . logistical stuff, we love each other.

I hope that once the shock wears off, maybe you might even be . . . happy for me."

Footsteps on the stairs—from the sound of it at least one and maybe both sons-in-law returning from a bed-check upstairs with the grandkids—interrupted my train of thought. More to the point, the commotion stifled any comebacks from my daughters.

"Break out the champagne, ladies . . .!"

Jen's Jason—all lean, extroverted energy—bounded into the living room, followed closely by Sarah's husband, Ryan. As restrained and reserved as my youngest was volatile, Ryan was a gentle bear of a man. I liked both men immensely. My girls had done well for themselves and I told them so whenever I found the opportunity.

"We've got two hours 'til the Ball drops," Jason crowed, all but beating his chest with fatherly pride. "*Les enfants* are out for the duration."

Collectively my sons-in-law seem to have achieved the impossible. Despite all the sugar they ingested and mayhem of opening their presents, the grandchildren had zonked out in record time.

"Don't get up, Char, I'll get the glasses . . .!" Already en route to the kitchen, Jason called back over his shoulder. "Right or left of the sink?"

"Right. Top cupboard," I said.

"Pliers, something to deal with the cork?"

"Left of the sink. Second drawer down."

My daughters just sat there. A sullen calm had settled over the room. Ryan, a psychiatrist, picked up on it first.

"Why do I get the feeling we've got a . . . *situation* going here?" he said slowly.

Sarah frowned. "Later . . .!"

No sense beating around the bush. "I'm seeing someone, Ryan," I told him.

"Good for you, Char!"

The look my youngest daughter shot in her husband's direction would have frozen water. His hands full of glasses, Jason had wandered back into the room.

"A little help here!" he said.

Ryan scrambled to comply, but I saw the arched brow exchange that passed between the two men. While the rest of us sat there with my delicate stemware in hand, son-in-law Jason once again beat a hasty retreat to the kitchen for the bottle of champagne. That accomplished, he filled the glasses and settled down on the love seat next to his wife.

He, too, picked up the strained silence in the room. "Is there something I ought to know?"

"Not now . . .!" Jen muttered through clenched teeth.

There we were. It was up to me to lead the toast.

Glass raised, I looked around the room at my daughters and their husbands—happier than most, as near as I could tell. *Give them a chance*, I told myself, as I confronted the confusion and anxiety I read in their eyes. If Rob could handle what his own son had come up with, I had to believe that he could deal with my skeptical and fiercely protective brood as well.

"Happy New Year!" I said quietly.

Their voices weren't in synch as they repeated the traditional salute—I wasn't sure my youngest had responded at all. But for all that, there was a comforting, almost liturgical feel about the moment.

The search for happiness may begin as an isolated cry to be heard. But we yearn for the reassuring affirmation that follows. *And also with you.*

I had never been superstitious about grabbing at the good things that life had to offer. But then, had I ever truly wanted as much? If Rob was right about what the New Year might bring, we were going to need that unlikely benediction and then some to weather what loomed ahead.

# ✣ Chapter Nineteen

It didn't start out that way. But simply put, on New Year's Day Rob charmed the pants off 'em. And he did it over coffee and fruit cake, stone cold sober with three grandchildren more or less terrorizing the bunch of us the whole time.

And with precious little help from me. As it turns out, I was out of the room at the moment of truth.

From the get-go Sarah particularly started quizzing the guy with such tenacity that after a few unsuccessful attempts to get a word in edgewise, my two sons-in-law exchanged eyebrow-raised glances and wandered out into the kitchen where they proceeded to hunker down in front of my pitiful counter-top TV to watch whatever bowl game was in progress. Anything to get out of the line of that blistering fire.

The twenty-questions pretty much started with that clerical collar of his and went downhill from there. I knew better than to try to intervene. Finally in quiet desperation, I drew my eldest, Jen, aside at the buffet in the dining room to plead for a truce.

"Enough, already. Your sister keeps pouncing on every word out of the man's mouth like he's a parole violator. It's really very simple. Rob doesn't drink because he's a recovering alcoholic. He doesn't smoke because, blast it all, he knows better. And why on earth he's still here with the two of you tag-teaming him like the Spanish Inquisition, beats the heck out of me."

Jen grimaced. Her pale eyes—my husband Len's contribution to her double helix—crackled with annoyance. It was the look someone gets when they're busted and aren't about to back down.

"Why don't you tell us what you really feel, Mom?

"I love him. Will that do?"

"Mom, we only want what's best for you."

"Believe it or not, honey, so do I!"

She looked so righteous in her indignation, I couldn't help it. I laughed.

"Trust me, Jen. I think I've found it. What's best for me, that is. Is it so unreasonable to ask you to give that—give us—half a chance!"

Jen bristled. "You're asking a lot!"

"I'm sure. Now how about we go out there and see what waving the white flag for a while might do, okay? That is, if he hasn't already left."

It had gotten way too quiet in the living room. Whatever I was expecting on our return, it wasn't the sight of Rob and my youngest side-by-side on the sofa, silently convulsed over the Hilltoppers yearbook.

From the snippets of conversation still intelligible through all those gasps and sputters of laughter, I guessed it must have been the edition from my freshman and Rob's senior year. Jen just looked at me and then back at her sister like a volcano was erupting in the living room and somehow we had missed it.

"Good grief, Mom," Sarah gasped, "were you ever a ... dork! Where have you been hiding this all those years? And take a look at that . . . *hair* . . .!"

"I'll match you and raise you ten," Rob casually flipped through the pages toward the back where the athletic department carved out photo space for highlights of all their events.

"That's . . . *you*?"

More laughter. By now even the grandkids were clamoring to see. Over the melee, Rob made eye contact. Message sent, message received.

So much for their "lunatic" mother's "religious nut of a boyfriend". We had become people to them, a major breakthrough if I ever saw one.

By evening's end, we had every family album in the living room piled in one corner or another. Crack of dawn both daughters and their retinues departed for Cleveland and Pittsburgh, respectively—if not still totally thrilled at the changes in my life, at least more or less in agreement not to have me committed.

I stood on the porch waving until the tears blurring my vision started to freeze on my face. Then I went inside and started looking for the phone. In the process, I encountered a still-half asleep Marty back from his exile at Grace's. When I tried to thank him for giving up his bed for the sake of my girls and their families, he just grunted and kept going.

Someone, most likely a grandchild, had been playing hide-and-seek with the phone. After an extended search and a lot of help from the locator on the base, I finally found it under a couch cushion.

"Rob?"

"Hi, sweetheart!"

"They're gone."

"I'll be right over."

"Bad idea. I'm not alone."

"Marty?"

"Uh-huh. He got back from Grace's a few minutes ago."

"So, phone sex is going to have to do."

I laughed. "That's allowed . . .?"

"Probably not. But I'm open to suggestions."

"I plan on practicing tomorrow."

"Twenty-four hours from now. Outrageous!"

"Best offer."

"Listening to you let off steam from the back row of the sanctuary isn't exactly a hot date either."

"I recall a conversation not too long ago about how tough this was going to be."

"True." He cleared his throat. "For the record, I loved your family."

"I've never seen Sarah on the warpath quite like that before. And Jen—"

"They're funny, bright as heck and fiercely protective of their mother. Especially Sarah."

"We survived it."

"Yes." His voice was low. "Yes, sweetheart, we did."

Sounds of life were stirring from the direction of the stairway. In another moment, this conversation would be impossible.

"I've got to go— "

"I love you."

"Me, too."

I clutched the phone with two hands, listening to the buzz of the dial tone. It took me a second to fumble with the Talk button and silence it.

"The natives are sure restless early—who died this time?" Marty shuffled back in to kitchen, obviously in search of caffeine.

"Wrong number," I said.

Puzzled, Marty stared blankly at the phone in my hand. "I didn't hear it ring."

"Me. I was trying to catch Jen, but I forgot and dialed her home not her cell. You just missed them—"

"Don't mind me." Distracted, Marty was fumbling in the cupboard, trying to find a mug. "Go ahead and redial if you want to."

"Not important. I'll call later."

My heart was in my throat. Lying was never my stock in trade and I was lousy at it. When I told Rob about the incident in our fleeting contact next morning in the sanctuary, he was silent a long time before responding.

"We're caught, you realize. With families who know how we feel and a community around us that doesn't— "

"And can't."

Rob sighed and with aching tenderness cradled his hand against the curve of my cheek. "Sweetheart, I don't like living a lie any more than you do. But what alternative is there?"

Trembling, half fearing even that fragile intimacy would betray us if somebody walked in that narthex door unannounced, I grasped at the only solution I knew—*work*. And lots of it.

If the fever pitch with which we threw ourselves into the Undercroft project in the weeks that followed bordered on the desperate, Grace Alanson was the only one who seemed to notice. And to her eternal credit—except for a quirked eyebrow now and then—she didn't call us on it.

I found it almost scary watching Rob in his pre-seminary mode, the tough marketing exec who wouldn't take 'no' for an answer. By Valentine's Day he single-handedly had pushed, pressured and hustled one of the smaller, though up-and-coming church supply houses into finally stocking some of our product in the upcoming Spring catalog. Turnaround time on orders would be eight weeks. Cautious but hopeful, we braced ourselves for what we hoped would be a grand slam.

It was poor Leah who turned out to be the bearer of bad

tidings. Pale and shaking, she came charging through the snowbanks in the back yard one late February morning.

Over the weeks and months, Marty had worn a considerable swath of bare ground into the snow piling up between Grace's backyard and mine. But the drifts sometimes made his vital lifeline impassable. Little Bart was walking now and as he and his mother stumbled into my kitchen, his snowsuit was wet to his armpits from the effort.

"I tried to carry him," Leah gasped, "but he is just too . . . darn . . . heavy now . . . !"

"Leah, is something *wrong*?"

The young woman just looked at me. *"WE'RE GOING TO JAIL . . . all of us . . .!"*

Her face crumpled. But she pulled herself out of it.

"Honey, what on earth happened?"

I caught the gist of the problem if not the details. Internal Revenue had called from the regional office to demand proof of compliance with tax code.

As our more or less official Undercroft answering service, Leah got hit with enough legal-speak to scare anybody, starting with Undercroft Art's legal status. Is this a for-profit or a not-for-profit business? Is it operating out of a church? Did we submit the proper forms?

The list, I had to admit, potentially spelled major trouble. While Leah struggled to take off her boots, I was tackling little Bart's galoshes and snowsuit. Once both were settled down at the table with juice and cookies, I got on the phone to Rob.

"How's it going over there?" he said.

I still couldn't get used to the fact that Rob had caller ID. There was something unnerving about being a giant step beyond "hello" before I as the caller even had time to say a word.

"Trouble in Dodge."

"Not the girls—?"

"Worse. The IRS."

Quickly I filled in as much as I could glean from what Leah had remembered. Rob listened, from time to time popping in with a question to clarify some detail. More often than not, I didn't have a clue what the answer was.

"Did the caller give a contact name or case number?"

I relayed the question to Leah. Scrunched in her jeans pocket was a pink phone memo which she unfolded as best she could and handed to me.

"Laville. he agent's name was Laville. No case number that I can see, but here's the phone contact."

Rob asked me to repeat the number. I did.

"Tell Leah not to worry," he said. "I have a friend in Pittsburgh, a lawyer, who can get to the bottom of this."

"Call me!"

"The minute I know anything."

The phone went dead in my hands, then dial-tone. Wide-eyed, Leah had been listening to the whole conversation, or at least my end of it.

"Father Rob is going to handle this," I told her. "He says not to worry. You did fine."

Leah didn't look convinced. "It's been an . . . awful week, Char. Just awful."

"Do you want to talk about it?"

When she didn't respond, I poured myself yet another cup of coffee and sat down at the table with her. Within seconds, Bart was on my lap, his chocolate-chip-smeared hands playing with my shaggy cut hair. As salon visits went it was pretty primitive, but I suspected by the time he was done, my hair would have acquired some pretty interesting highlights.

"Yum," he laughed, "yum-mee-in-the-tummy."

"Cut that out, Bart!" Leah's smile wavered. "It's about my folks, Char."

"I remember you were telling me they were coming out to visit."

Her face morphed into an uncomfortable frown. "Two days ago . . . *came and went.* It was the first time I've seen them since Bart was born."

"How *wonderful*, after all that time. They must have been excited— "

"They took Marty and me out to dinner. At Casa Blanca in Bartonville."

I had never been there myself. But for the area, it was supposed to be pretty up-scale.

"Was it nice . . .?"

"The food or them? The food was so-so and the tab could have fed little Bart and me for a month. Dad put down my GED, mom hated the way I was raising Bart. The both of them made Marty feel like road kill . . .!"

Leah's voice quavered and trailed off.

"Oh, honey, I'm so sorry— "

"I wish you or Grace were my mom. From the beginning, even when I didn't have my stuff together at all—you never made me feel . . . small, or stupid. I saw you with your girls at Christmas. They are *so* lucky. "

I'm not so sure her version of that family reunion quite dovetailed with my daughters' take on things. Still, it was touching anyway. I wasn't about to rain on her parade.

"Leah, you've got so much courage," I said slowly. "Keeping that baby despite your parents' disapproval, finishing your diploma, working with Undercroft, giving Marty more confidence in himself. And Bart is one cool little guy. You're a wonderful mother, should be very proud of— "

"Yeah, right. Tell my folks that!"

Her voice was low. "Marty had cooked up a surprise. He told my parents he wanted to marry me. Right there in the restaurant. It was so sweet. My father just looked at him as if Marty was planning to . . . rob a bank. My mom cried for an hour!"

"Oh, honey— "

"Char, I couldn't have wished for someone better than Marty. He's kind, smart and works like a dog to take care of little Bart." Leah shot to her feet. "How could they do this to him? To me? . . . To us?"

Leah looked so lost, sounded so desolate. Her son took that as his cue to try wriggling out of my arms. I set the little guy on the floor, and walking over to his mom, gave her a lingering hug.

"I'm being . . . stupid, aren't I?" she said.

Retrieving a towel from the oven door, I started to dab at her tears as best I could. All eyes, Leah let me.

"You're not stupid, honey. And trust me, nobody's parents are perfect either. We all want the best for our kids—even when we don't always know what 'best' is."

I hesitated. Still, it had to be said.

"I've let my girls down—messed up royally sometimes. I'm sure Grace would say the same about her nieces and nephews. It's tough to forgive the times we disappoint the people we love. But I believe we've got to try. We all want those we care about to think we're doing the right thing. Just trust yourself, honey. *You* know what's right for you and your son. And somehow . . . it'll all work out. I'm sure of it!"

"*Hard.* When what kept me going through all this, even deciding to go through with the baby, was just sheer cussedness—never, never, ever to wind up like the two of them!"

My heart bled for her. Leah seemed such a delicate flower, but then maybe I had misjudged that, too. She had grown so much in the past few months, that I had assumed first Grace then Marty were her anchors. In truth, with that childhood of hers, she was and had been on her own—at an age when a lot of her peers still were playing at being fashion dolls.

Platitudes aside, I was finding it hard to be as charitable toward her parents as I was urging her to be. By comparison Rob and I were lucky. Though our recent run-ins with our offspring had been traumatic, emotionally we had come through relatively unscathed.

Too bad no one had primed me with that pep talk before our Christmas moments of truth. It would have saved a lot of fretting.

"More yum . . . yum-yum-yumee."

Tired of trying to get his mom's or my attention, Bart was straining to get at the plate of cookies—just out of reach on the kitchen table. I was worried he would pull the whole thing over on himself. Leah looked disapproving but too tired to deal with it.

"We better go . . .!"

I wasn't about to let her walk home in that mood. Snatching Bart from the edge of calamity, I balanced him precariously on my hip and headed for the living room.

"Father Rob should get back to us any minute," I called back over my shoulder. "Hold on, honey. I've got something I think Bart will like."

Thanks to my grandchildren's recent visit, I still had a modest stack of toddler-age toys heaped at the bottom of the stairs waiting to go back up into storage in the attic. I hauled a building-block farm set into the kitchen and little Bart set to amusing himself and us by assembling shaky structures and then—crowing proudly as he did it, knocking them to pieces again. Leah and I chatted through the din, about our work, Christmas and her obvious love for Marty.

Technically, I hated to admit, Leah's parents were right on one score. The young couple's fiscal situation was well beyond precarious.

Still, I had to admit a touch of envy. They were so hopeful, so full of plans, despite life doing its best at the moment to kick the stuffings out of their hopes and dreams.

Leah sighed. "Was it always so . . . tough to fall in love, Char. I mean, when you were young . . .?"

*When I was young.* If it weren't so ironic, I might have found it funnier.

"When I was young, I put aside my dreams without a qualm," I told her quietly. "My husband and I were still practically kids ourselves when he died. There were two daughters to raise. So I just took . . . romantic love and packed it away in the box with my wedding veil. Still, if I've learned anything over the years—love is never easy. The best things in life rarely are. Your work. Your family. Any of it."

"You . . . never fell in love again . . .?"

Her eyes were sad. I looked down at my hands, clutching a silly jointed animal that Bart had handed me.

"Believe it or not, honey, sometimes the older you get, the tougher relationships get. You become cynical, afraid. You worry that if you risk and trust, in the end you'll wind up even more *alone* than before."

Little did Leah know how desperately I needed to hear the very advice I was dispensing in her direction. What had Rob said that first day we really started to get to know each other, out there on the steps of Nativity? I paraphrased it as best I could.

"Still, even toothless and doddering, I've got to believe I'm still young enough to risk, to grow."

It was what I had told my girls at Christmas. And it was what I kept reminding myself when Rob called, twice in less than fifteen minutes. Call number one was benign enough—to say he had reached his friend in Pittsburgh. *The cavalry was on the way.*

At least with that news, Leah was considerably calmer on the way out the door than when she showed up on my back porch. I offered to feed Bart and Leah lunch, but she declined.

"Gotta get back to the phone," she said. "Don't wanna lose a customer 'cause I'm not on the job," she said. "Marty would just shoot me!"

Together we stuffed little Bart back into his snowsuit. Looking all the world like a marshmallow-man, he toddled alongside his mom through the backyard in the direction of home. I waved to them from the porch, until I heard the sound of the phone ringing in the distance.

As I scrambled to find the receiver, I was half thinking that Rob's friend in Pittsburgh might have had second thoughts. My shoes left soggy gray imprints on the kitchen floor.

It was Rob on the phone alright. But the news was not quite what I was anticipating.

"Are you alone?"

"Leah left a few minutes— "

"She called, Char."

*She . . .?* Karin, it had to be. Out of breath, I steeled myself for what was to come.

Rob chuckled, a desolate rumble of sound. Like a tidal wave on the horizon, it threatened to sweep with it everything in its path.

"It seems she talked with Ted, finally connected the dots and realizes I'm seriously seeing someone," Rob said. "My son hadn't exaggerated one bit at Christmas. More than ever and bizarre as it sounds, Karin would rather peg me as a . . . 'flaming faggot'—a direct quote, by the way—than to concede I could be in love with another woman."

"Oh, Rob . . .!"

"Yeah." He let out his breath in a rush. "I can't even imagine how Ted reacted."

"It's possible . . . maybe your son will call— "

"And then again, he might just crawl off in a hole somewhere and write the both of us out of his life. I couldn't blame him if he did— "

"And Karin?"

He hesitated before answering. "Breaking out the heavy artillery, as we speak. She wants a divorce, a chunk of the corporate pension among other things—and if she thought she could get by with it, my head on a platter."

"Rob, you don't think she'd do something *really vicious*?"

"I can't imagine that. But it's one thing for her to walk out and quite another to hear that I'm capable of moving on with my life. If Karin's feeling cornered, I'd say all bets are off *what* she might do!"

My voice lowered to a whisper. "When can we see each other?"

"Now—?"

I managed a weak smile. "Seriously."

"I've got a vestry meeting at six. How about dinner afterward, out somewhere? Bartonville. I shouldn't be too late."

Right now, I didn't care if it would be midnight. "Fine. I'll be waiting."

# ✥ Chapter Twenty

It was a long afternoon. Anxious and jittery, I settled in for a long soak in the tub and then took extra care with wardrobe and makeup. It may not have changed anything to feel the silk of that new blouse caressing my skin or to assess the impact of those well-tailored slacks on my less than youthful figure, but it passed the time. And right now, I needed that.

Marty came home from Grace Alanson's house around seven. He had stopped to see Leah on the way back from a half-day trip to Pittsburgh to check on a couple of religious book stores in the area that had stocked our hangings on a trial basis. When he dragged into the living room, I had shifted to killing time waiting for Rob by working on some new sketches.

Just one quick glance at his face told me Leah had been dead-on accurate about my young tenant's mindset. But then under that raw veneer of despair, I also sensed something else—a change that had crept up on me so gradually, I still couldn't fully appreciate its significance. Sometime in the past eight months, my young friend and tenant Marty Santano had become a man.

"Rough road trip?"

Marty sighed and let himself down gingerly on the sofa. "Not half as rough as that run-in with Leah's parents. I hear she told you about it. Thanks for being there."

"I feel bad for both of you," I told him. "You don't deserve that."

"Yeah, well, stuff happens."

"What are you going to do?"

"What *can* we do? It would be easier if Leah didn't care so much what her folks think. But she does. And the harder she tries to please them, the worse it seems to get."

Marty hunched forward and buried his face in his hands. When he finally straightened, his eyes were red-rimmed, his voice shaking.

"Damnit . . . I love her, Char!"

"I know."

"Are we crazy?"

"You're good to and for one another. I don't call that crazy. Not at all."

"Then why does it hurt so . . . damn much?"

"I don't have the answer to that question. Believe me, if I did— "

Marty laughed. "I'd buy whatever you were selling."

"Do you think . . . would Leah marry you, even without her parents' approval?"

"I don't know. I'm almost afraid to ask." Marty hesitated. "You were married, Char. Would you do it again—if you had a chance, I mean?"

I took a deep breath, exhaled. "That's a pretty big 'if', when at my age there are more women than men out there—not counting the ineligible, the disinterested and downright comatose."

"You're cool . . . and fun. A great cook— "

"A regular Emeril, that's me." I winced. "Are you sure you don't have me confused with that neighbor of mine, what's her name . . . Grace?"

Marty laughed. "Trust me, I've met your fan club— "

"I'm afraid to guess."

"Father Rob."

My heart leapt into my throat. "Where on . . . earth did you come up with *that*—?"

"For starters? The two of you laugh a lot when you're around each other— "

"Friends, Marty. Good friends."

He shrugged. "I just call 'em like I see 'em."

"One small hitch." It came tumbling out before I had time to think. "Father Rob's *already married*."

I sensed immediately that Marty didn't know. He would have

cut off a limb rather than say anything that could hurt either one of us. He was also well aware by now what the rumor mill in small towns could do. Grace Alanson made that pretty clear from the get-go when Marty and Leah started dating. Grace might have been a flower child, but as a landlady, as far as Marty was concerned, sleepovers were out.

"So much for that idea," he muttered. His gaze was riveted on his shoes.

"Not that I don't appreciate your matchmaking," I told him quickly. "Only this time, it's a tad . . . off target— "

It was a forgivable lie, considering there was more than an undercurrent of truth in it. Unfortunately, the timing didn't help its credibility. In the background, I heard the sound of footsteps on the front steps, followed by stomping noises as someone cleaned the snow off their shoes.

"Expecting company?" Marty said.

He might not have known what was coming, but I did. Although the station wagon with the Undercroft Art sign was parked in the driveway, at this hour Marty normally would still be hanging out with Leah and the baby. The door flung open and I heard the familiar voice.

"All set to go, lady . . .?"

At least Rob hadn't called me something more intimate. Still, given where our conversation had been going, it was impossible for Marty not to do the math. I saw the puzzled knot tighten between his brows.

"Father Rob, hey!"

"Marty. Back from the wars, I see."

Rob wandered over to the couch and Marty stood to greet him. The two men shook hands. I sat there in the wing chair as if glued to the cushions.

"How are things in Pittsburgh?" Rob said.

Marty shrugged. "Looks like we've sold another four sets of paraments, probably a regular dealer from now on."

"Great. Wonderful. I suppose Leah or Char filled you in on the excitement around here in your absence."

"That thing with the IRS?"

"Apparently a lot of tempest in a teapot. So much for the myth about the kinder, gentler IRS. Char and I were just going out for steak down in Bartonville. I'll fill her in about what the legal eagles are saying— "

I felt the air rush out of my lungs. Marty's brows had now fused into a single line. Something had to be done and fast.

"We'd love to have you join us, Marty." I offered quickly.

At that, if anything, Marty looked even more confused. He wasn't the only one. Safely out of my young tenant's sight-line, Rob's eyebrows shot up and his lips shaped a single question, *What?*

"Sorry," Marty said. "The Bart-man will be in bed by now and Leah and I were planning a little quality time over at Grace's. It's been a heck of a week."

I hope I didn't sound too relieved. "Sounds like fun. We'll keep you posted if we come up with anything."

Bolting for the front hall closet, I grabbed my coat and awkwardly maneuvered into it before either of the men could offer assistance. I was nervous as a cat and was doing a lousy job of concealing it.

Once outside, I practically ran down the front walk. Rob was still fumbling with the front door, which had been badly in need of a locksmith for some time now. I could see Marty through the front windows, standing where we had left him in the living room.

"Are you planning on walking . . .?"

I finally ground to a stop, my hand on the door handle of Rob's Hummer. It wasn't until then I realized he was still a good thirty feet behind me. Truth was, I had enough adrenalin going to run a half-marathon.

"Sorry. I thought you were right behind me— "

Gently, Rob eased past me to open the passenger door. I could hear the worry in his voice.

"Either you're starving, have one monumental case of cabin fever, or something was going on in there that has gotten you pretty spooked . . .!"

"Try all three."

Rob hesitated, then as I settled in the passenger seat, closed the door behind me. Fumbling with my seat belt, I watched through the windshield as he picked his way around to the driver's side through the slush. His mouth set in a tight line, he worked the key into the ignition and then just sat there, the motor running.

"Bartonville?" he said. "I was thinking Casa Blanca. It's not quite as . . . crowded as Mike's or that farmer's bar, Woody's."

"Fine."

It occurred to me as I said it, that Casa Blanca was the scene of

Leah and Marty's recent fiasco with her parents. I had to hope the place wasn't jinxed.

Silent, my heart still thudding like a trip-hammer, I took stock of the familiar route leading to the highway. I guessed by the lights who was still awake and who was out for the evening. Those signs of life also were clues to whose kids still had homework around the dining room table and which basement laundry rooms were in operation.

Rural people all do it, it seems. We know the rhythm of our lives. We know each other. Sometimes too well for comfort. "Are you going to tell me what that was all about?" Rob said quietly.

I shivered. "Marty suspects—*knows*—we're an *item*."

"Smart, that kid!"

"It started out, I think, as some harmless matchmaking on his part, but then your . . . showing up when you did tended to confirm it. I tried to muddy the waters—though I just might have made things worse in the process. He knows you're *married* . . ."

As objectively as possible, I filled him in on the conversation. Rob took a while to think about it. Traffic was heavy and the glare from oncoming headlights was making it difficult to see.

"Char, you could be overreacting— "

"True."

*But doubtful.* I remembered Marty's face when Rob walked in that door.

"But then, that's not the point is it?" Rob waited to finish until he passed a slow moving pickup. "Add up Marty's suspicions and the phone call from Karin and we've stirred the hornets' nest, sweetheart. I guess we can't be surprised if we find things stirring back."

The parking lot at Casa Blanca was virtually empty. On the cusp of the mid-West, restaurant-goers in these parts were early eaters. After all those years in Philly, I was still having trouble redefining what qualified as a civilized hour for dining. As it turned out, we were the only customers and the kitchen was planning to close in fifteen minutes.

Rob ordered a steak. I kept my choice to lite-bite sauteed sea scallops on a bed of julienne zucchini, penance for way too many of Grace's home-baked "yum-yums" as little Bart called them. The scowling waitress returned with our salads in record time, clearly more eager to get off shift than collect one last tip for the night. From the kitchen, the muffled clank of metal on metal must have meant the clean-up crew was on overdrive.

"Maybe we should have gone somewhere else," I speculated out loud.

"Any port in a storm. Most places have probably closed by now."

"The vestry meeting was pretty short."

"No biggies on the agenda. Just the perpetual roof on the parsonage and whether we do or do not have the money to fix it."

As if by mutual consent, we were running circles around Karin's phone call and the whole business about Marty that had popped up on the radar from out of nowhere. The cast of characters aware of my relationship with Rob was growing—just a little too quickly for comfort. There was no use delaying the inevitable.

"With Karin on the warpath," I said slowly, "and now Marty wondering what's going on, maybe it would be a good idea if we cooled it for a while."

"Which means . . .?"

I couldn't read Rob's tone or expression, any more than I could come up with a suggestion. Short of quitting my job as organist and pulling back from the Undercroft project, there wasn't much I could offer up on the altar of discretion.

"I don't know."

"Well, I do. And it took that phone call from Karin to make me realize it."

I just stared at him. Rob slowly reached across the table and caught my free hand in his.

"I can't do this any more," he said. "Hiding how I feel about you, obsessing about every unguarded word or look. By all rights on that phone today, I should have been furious, outraged at what Karin is trying to do. And yet, when she finally hung up on me, all I felt was a bottomless . . . *sadness* that it had to come to this— "

He closed his eyes, remembering. When he began again, his voice was steady. Despite the obvious signs of exhaustion, his was the unmistakable look of man who had gone through the fire and emerged unscathed.

"By any sane definition, Char, *I haven't been married in a long, long time.* I realize that from the outside looking in, there are those who might . . . dispute or misunderstand that All they see is that piece of paper. But *perception* is not *truth*— "

"Perceptions still can have an enormous price tag, Rob."

"And if I'm willing to . . . pay the piper?"

"I'm not talking about Karin or the money. You love your work. That congregation at Nativity loves you."

"There are other congregations."

"Not if the bishop pulls the plug."

"So, I'll drive a bus, if I have to."

"Oh, Rob!" My voice wavered, dropped to a whisper. So it could come to that. "How would you expect me to . . . live with myself?

"Wrong pronoun, Char. *We. Us.* That's how we'll deal with it. One day at a time. And for openers, we make truth and fact come together as quickly as possible— "

"Surely not by *intentionally* going public about. . . !"

"Divorce is one of the most . . . public things I know, sweetheart. I'm driving down to Pittsburgh to talk to my friend Barry, that lawyer I was telling you about, first thing tomorrow—about giving Karin what she wants. *A way out of this marriage.* And I want you to come with me."

After a sleepless night I did just that—went along for the ride, keeping my qualms to myself as best I could. The day began overcast and by the time we were on the road, it had started to snow. Not quite as bleak as my mood but close.

Crosswinds shook the car and sent dry showers of white flakes swirling across the slick pavement in front of us. I stared out the passenger side window of Rob's Hummer, still half asleep, watching the western Pennsylvania landscape drift past. At the edge of the white-washed fields, bare stands of trees lifted their branches heavenward in mute appeal.

*Winter's last gasp*, I found myself thinking. The change of seasons was proving to be anything but a graceful one.

Rob's hands flexed on the wheel, diverting my attention. *Beware the Ides of March.*

"Where are we?" I yawned.

"An hour out of Pittsburgh," he said quietly. "And about that long since you said a single word. I understand, Char. You're not sure you wanted to do this. But talk to me . . .!"

Rob had succeeded in jarring me awake. I felt my forehead

crease in a frown.

"You sound like my boss Irene, or should I say *ex-boss*, the day she laid me off at the Job Service. *And what do you plan to do with your life now, sweetie . . .* ?"

My tone matched the words, testy—inappropriate. I had agreed to go readily enough. With a good chunk of the trip behind us, this was a lousy time for second thoughts.

Rob shot a quick glance in my direction. I sensed he was choosing his words like he was navigating that slick roadway—practiced, wary.

"Why do I think I'm picking up some not-too-subtle, *Nobody's-OK* vibes here . . .?"

"You forget, I know the drill." I bristled. "Two counselors on a road trip—minus clients. A bad idea, that's all."

I hadn't noticed we were within inches of a rest stop—not until Rob's controlled but abrupt deviation from our dead-ahead course told me he was pulling off the four-lane. A hollow feeling at the pit of my stomach, I burrowed into the seat cushion while he eased the Hummer into a parking spot at the far end of the passenger lot. Ours was the only vehicle in sight.

Rob cut the engine, then slowly straightened and made eye contact. His eyes were as steely blue and troubled as that roiling sky out there.

"What's wrong, sweetheart?"

"I'm not the nine o'clock appointment on your counseling caseload, Rob— "

"I never thought you were."

"You could have fooled me."

For a split-second Rob just stared at me. His voice was as tight as the set of his jaw.

"Are you trying to . . . pick a fight, Char? Because if you are, you're doing one heck of a job."

"I shouldn't have come. "

"Judging by what's going on here," he said quietly. "I beg to differ."

I started to protest, then my mouth clamped tight. He was right, of course.

My being here wasn't just about supporting him—although I couldn't imagine pacing out the day back in Hope, powerless, wondering what he was up against. He knew me well. My biggest fear was and is the unknown. Whatever lay ahead of us, the more I knew, the more likely I could weather the storm.

My mouth felt stiff. "I'm scared to death, Rob."

"Understandable."

"You had a life there, in Pittsburgh, I know very little about."

"And it's one thing to hear about it. Something else to . . . be there."

"Yes."

Every street we traversed or every storefront or office building we passed, it would be impossible not to speculate about the memories they held for him—memories which were not a part of my emotional experience. I was about to meet his long-time friend, a go-for-the-jugular lawyer, intimidating even under the best of circumstances. This man also had known Karin.

And here I sat decked out in my austere organist's wardrobe—the tailored gray flannel slacks, off-white easy-wash jewel neck blouse, and the black sweater-coat my daughters had pitched in to give me for Christmas. It was anything but the picture of glamour and chic that surfaced whenever I thought of Rob's ex.

*Scared?* I was shaking from my towel-and-go hair to the scuffed toes of my ten-year-old leather ankle boots.

Rob was looking at me strangely. His face was as inscrutable as granite on a mountainside, but I sensed something flicker in his eyes. It wasn't anger.

"This really isn't about us at all, is it?" he said slowly. "It's about . . . her. *Karin.*"

It wasn't a question. I felt my face grow hot.

"You're wondering what my friend Barry's going to think when we walk into that office together. Anticipating comparisons, or that he'll misinterpret your being there. You're afraid you can't handle the . . . dirt under the rug, up close and personal. You're wondering how you'll respond to all those questions my friend is bound to ask—? "

"Yes. If you need to hear me admit it, yes."

"I only need one thing from you, ever!" Rob said quietly. "That's to know you love me, at least enough to let me . . . *love you.*"

"To *let* you *love* . . . ?"

I felt my voice break off, half sob and half cry. Rob's eyes widened, then narrowed to glittering pinpoints of light. Bucket seats or not, he reached out and pulled me into his arms. With a stifled groan, his mouth found mine.

*Passion.* I had presumed to know what it meant. But then, I had presumed, believed, assumed a lot of things. *That time blunts the senses. That I had mastered the art of suppressing intimacy.* I was wrong, on all counts.

As if caught in a rip-tide, every touch, even the most inadvertent contact of our bodies, was pulling me into deep and unfamiliar waters. Were these my hands, controlled and disciplined from years at the keyboard? They seem to have acquired a will of their own, tracing the lean muscles along the small of Rob's back, urging him closer.

His breath was coming in long, shuddering gasps. I recognized the words, but not their significance.

"Char . . . oh, Char . . . , sweetheart . . . "

His hands had gone dead still, cradling my face. My mouth was still upturned toward his, lips parted—hungry, waiting.

"We have got to *stop* this. Right now. Unless you're prepared to wind up in the back seat like a couple of teenagers."

Disoriented, I opened my eyes. *The back seat of the Hummer?* Holding that thought, I blurted out the first thing that popped in my head.

"Is a *room* . . . out of the question?"

"The cell phone's on the dash." Laughter rumbled in his chest. "Do *you* want to break the bad news to Barry, or should I?"

It finally sank in how impossible this was. The gear shift was wreaking havoc with my left kneecap. I could feel the pretzel twist of each and every vertebrae and by ten o'clock we had to be in Pittsburgh. With a nervous laugh, I awkwardly began to disentangle myself.

"Where . . . did . . . *that* . . . come from?"

"Nothing I haven't been fantasizing about. For months, sweetheart."

With a free hand, Rob gently brushed at the film of sweat glistening along the curve of my cheek. I shivered.

"I'm . . . I must look like the wrath of God— "

"Like someone who's loved," he corrected me.

"I've been a . . . *jerk* all morning, Rob. I'm sorry."

He shook his head. "Don't apologize. It could have been worse. You could have told me you had decided to walk home. And I would have had to chase you down."

My power walks were a standing joke between us. Despite the difference in our heights, I routinely gave Rob a run for his money when we went anywhere on foot together. Fiddling with the mirror on the passenger-seat sun visor, I caught a glimpse of my reflection—the look of someone just back from an hour on a treadmill.

"Damage control," I muttered.

Rummaging at my feet for my purse, I retrieved a comb and lipstick. Rob's hand was poised over the ignition key.

"Do you want me to wait?"

"Not necessary. Short of a soak in the tub and a hefty supply of patching plaster, the restoration prospects are pretty limited."

Still chuckling quietly to himself, Rob restarted the engine and eased us back out on to the highway, headed south. The sky seemed to be brightening, along with my mood.

For the first time since we left Hope, I took a good hard look at us—as a couple, the way his friend Barry was bound to do. I already had voiced my misgivings about my organist's black-and-white fashion statement. But then here sat Rob in his graveside-use-only black suit, matching dark shirt with a clerical collar, and totally out of character, even black shoes.

"You realize," I told him, "the two of us are going to be wandering the streets of Pittsburgh looking like a couple of. . . penguins."

"A couple of. . . *what* . . .?"

I spelled out my take on our inadvertent wardrobe coordination. Rob laughed so hard the tears were rolling down his face.

"I can see by your outfit that you are a cowboy . . . !" he gasped, making total hash of the facetious children's nonsense song. "Well , if thing go *badly*—at least we're already set for the funeral."

# ✣ Chapter Twenty-One

The city crept up on us. One minute we were surrounded by rolling farmland and the next we were winding through a starkly-lit tunnel under the ridge of hills surrounding downtown Pittsburgh. As we emerged into daylight, the view was enough to take my breath away.

Rearing up in front of us was the Three Rivers skyline, imposing in its compactness, like a fantasy building-block city set down at the point where the Allegheny, Ohio and Monongahela meet. The way the pristine white of the snow cover on the grassy park of the Triangle jutted out into the sullen gray waters, tone-on-tone, reminded me all the world of a page of music, stark and beautiful, waiting to be played.

Barry's law firm occupied a suite of offices in one of the tonier of the high-rises. The elevator music was a subdued string quartet rendition of Vivaldi's *The Four Seasons* and the ambiance went upscale from there. While Barry finished up with a client, Rob and I settled in on the delicate mauve watered satin Queen Anne sofa in the waiting room.

I could have sworn that the receptionist was checking us out, big time. But then, it couldn't be every day of the week that what looked like a priest and a nun showed up together in the offices of one of the toughest law firms in Pittsburgh. In an undertone, she communicated something via the intercom and within a few minutes, a tall man in his mid-sixties showed up at her desk and handed her a thin stack of file folders.

*Barry*, I assumed. Rob shot to his feet. In a few quick strides, he closed the gap between the couch and his friend, hand extended in greeting.

"Son-of-a-gun! Rob, or should I say Father Sims. . .?"

"If you mean the get-up?" Rob winced. "It seems to work wonders landing a great table in restaurants."

The two men laughed, hugged in an awkward guy sort of way. By now I was standing as well. Barry didn't wait for an introduction.

"Char, I assume," he said. "Rob has been telling me so much about you . . ."

I found my hand enveloped in his. "I've been looking forward to meeting you."

Not exactly accurate, based on my melt-down on the trip over here, but so far so good. Rob was at my elbow and before I had time to react, he had wound an arm around my shoulder.

"I told Char that if anyone can make some sense out of the situation, it was you," he said evenly.

Rob had never pulled that kind of territorial stuff around me before and for a second, I resented it now. Slowly I let out my breath, time enough to put the gesture in perspective. Bottom line, not too subtly Rob was telling his friend he was prepared to protect my interests at all costs. I caught Barry's curt nod.

"How about we set up camp in my office," he said.

Barry Federson pretty much fit my stereotype. From the breadth of his shoulders, I concluded he and Rob had spent quality time together tossing a football around during their college career together. His pinstripe suit had to be tailor-made and his cuff-links were embossed with the Congressional seal. The look of the man had "Power" written all over it.

As he got down to business, I saw why Rob trusted him. Barry went at Rob's history with the deft thrusts of a surgeon. When and how had Rob's marriage to Karin gone on the rocks? Awkward, but just as relevant was when had I come into the picture and how. The lawyer also probed Rob's experience with past cases like this and how the Diocese handled them. Terse and matter-of-fact, Rob told it like it was.

Ultimately, it was Barry's turn to react. To my dismay, the issue quickly became one of dollars and cents. How ever I imagined myself fitting into Rob Sims's world, money never once was part of the picture.

"You retired from Dulles and Cochran three years ago," Barry said, "so I suspect Karin's pretty much got a lock on your pension. A chunk now— "

"And the full amount if I drop dead mid-sermon?"

"Tough to dispute."

"And the investments, the monies from the sale of the house in Squirrel Hill. . .?"

"You're what, sixty-two?" Barry chuckled. "Episcopal priests, to my knowledge, don't take some vow of *fiscal insolvency.* Your current income makes the poverty level look like a small fortune. No court in the land is going to take a look at that collar of yours and allow Karin to leave you starving under a bridge or on welfare. "

"I just want to make sure that if anything . . . *happens* to me, my son and Char are covered— "

"No need," I said more forcefully than I intended. "I have a pension and— "

"Independent. Feisty." Barry's eyebrows shot upward. "I admire that."

Rob chuckled. "After all that keyboard practice she indulges in, I've seen her break the top off of Mason jars. Talk about scary . . .!"

I frowned, not at the humor but his attempt to duck the issue. Before I could get a word in edgewise, Barry whipped out a crisp monogrammed handkerchief from his breast pocket and waved it facetiously overhead.

"Truce, white flag—time out!" he protested. "I'll leave it to you two to duke it out over the details. *Later.* But if you're planning on kicking off any time soon, old buddy, I'd think hard about changing your will. And if you haven't traded in your old credit cards for ones issued solely in your own name, sooner is wiser than later."

We moved on to less odious topics. I admired the blunt and easy communication between the two men, tangible signs of their longstanding relationship and trust.

It was Barry who proposed lunch, at the old railroad station, the Grand Concourse, known for its seafood and unique ambiance. I had eaten there many years ago with one of my girls on my birthday and had vivid memories of a spectacular stained glass ceiling, potted palms and a harpist playing the classics at Sunday brunch—and food cascading down a central staircase like a gigantic horn of plenty.

Rob hesitated, but then seemed to shake off whatever reservations he had about the choice. *Of course,* I thought, he must have gone there with Karin.

The Hummer was on the street, close at hand, so Rob offered to drive. When we arrived at Station Square, it was still early enough that the lunch crowd had not yet materialized. The host knew Barry well, and after one of those who-knows-who-knows-who exchanges, guided the three of us to a table near the grand staircase, seating that gave us a magnificent view of the elegant hall.

I hadn't had this choice of fresh things-aquatic since I left Philly. Barry and Rob went for surf and turf, while I settled on an interesting cold seafood platter. Our conversation had moved on to books we had read and the state of the Union. Barry was planning a month-long trip by boat along the rivers of Europe. Midway through a synopsis of the itinerary, he paused, scowled, muttered an expletive under his breath.

"You were right, Sims. And I was a . . . worse than stupid to recommend coming here. Don't look now, but I spotted a bogey at 10 o'clock."

*Bogey?* I followed his clock-face directions and even from this far end of the enormous hall, it was hard to miss an ultra-slender woman in a massive fur, and with her a younger buff-looking man in a suit that must have cost more than six months of my income as organist at Nativity. Her face was model-thin, impeccably made-up, and her frosted hair had been cropped short enough to qualify as a crew-cut.

Judging by the look on Rob's face, it had to be. *Karin.*

I was suddenly, woefully conscious of every single ounce of cellulite I had accumulated over the past thirty years. This woman would have pinched substantially less than an inch on just about any part of her anatomy.

"Brace yourselves." Barry winced. "We're about to have company."

On the verge of allowing the maitre 'd to seat her, the woman saw us, paused. Leaving her companion behind, she began to thread her way through the crowded tables toward the three of us. Barry scrambled to his feet, and more slowly and with visible reluctance, Rob joined him, his hands balled into fists at his side.

"*Fa . . . ther . . . Sims. Amazing . . .!* How good to see you again."

Karin's smile was tight, forced. When Rob continued to stand ramrod stiff, showing no sign whatsoever of making a move in her direction, with a swift, fluid motion she hugged him.

Rob flushed and his jaw clenched. "Karin. You know Barry—?"

"And this must be *the organist* I've heard so much about." Visibly amused, she extended her hand my way in greeting. "You'll have to help me with the . . . name . . ."

"Char," I said. "Char Howard."

"Robert's old . . . school chum, I understand. What a *coincidence.* The two of you and our favorite legal-eagle Barry. Sadly though, prepared to go for the jugular, if I'm not mistaken, old *friend.* Well, good for you."

"Karin, this is not really— "

Her laughter cut short whatever disclaimer Barry had in mind. "But then stuff happens to the best of us, doesn't it Robert? Life moves on."

I was beginning to believe there is no such thing as a "coincidence" Like the subtle interplay of themes or melody lines in a fugue, our lives weave together, seemingly random and disconnected. But in the end the pattern is there, if we only manage enough distance to see it.

So often in my heart of hearts I had wondered what this other woman in Rob's life was like, and suddenly as if bidden, *here she was. Be careful what you wish for.*

It was getting harder to ignore the paranoia that was rearing its ugly head with every syllable coming out of the woman's mouth. And then it hit me. I had seen those dilated pupils before, the manic speech and twitchy aura about her. It was with clients who later wound up in rehab for methamphetamine use.

Karin Sims was high as a kite. Rob and I made eye contact. *He knew.*

Fidgeting from foot to foot on her strappy sandals, Karin's glance darted quickly back toward her table. From the look of it, her companion had seized the moment to chat up the young woman charged with the beverage orders.

Karin frowned. "I'd introduce all of you to Sean but he's a little . . . skittish around strangers. Poor baby— "

Our own awkward little assemblage was growing. The server had arrived with a gleaming silver pitcher of water that by now was sweating profusely on to her shoes. I could identify totally with the young woman's predicament.

"Oh, I'm so-o sorry, we're holding you up here," Karin

murmured. "Well, maybe you can toss off some . . . reassuring little Benediction, Father. Or whatever it is that . . . *you people* do on public occasions like this— "

Her laughter floated back to us like ice tinkling in the crystal glasses on the table, as Karin turned and floated back from whence she came. She never looked back.

It was the longest three minutes of my life. Without making eye contact, the two men and I resumed our places at our table. The entree would be arriving any minute.

"I thought that went well," Barry muttered. "A little . . . fraught. But well . . ."

He was making an art form out of repositioning the oversize linen napkin on his lap. Rob drained his lime-flavored water in a single swift motion, down to the last dregs.

"Thank God, the two of you passed on the booze," Rob muttered. "I can't vouch for any self-restraint right about now."

I managed a wan smile. "Well, at least I won't be bugging either one of you about what Karin thinks of me."

The two men laughed, a tension breaker of sorts. After that, there wasn't a heck of a lot more to say. Lunch passed in a blur and it was not until Rob and I took our leave and headed back through the tunnel toward home, that the terrible knot around my heart began to ease.

"So, you've met her," Rob said finally.

"She's . . . truly beautiful."

"That hasn't changed. As for the rest, I'm sure you sensed it was the Drug-du-jour talking, not Karin. Although the contempt for what I put her through, as she sees it, is certainly real enough."

"It must be hard— "

"Hard to see her like that?" For a moment, a shadow fell across Rob's features. "It was certainly a wake-up call—a brutal reminder how badly we hurt each other. I'd like to think, back in that restaurant, it wasn't malice or spite fueling all that anger of hers. On some level she, too, recognizes the tragedy of it all. That in the end, it had to come to this."

"She's going to . . . you think she's going to contest the divorce?"

"No. Everything short of that, maybe." Rob's voice was incredibly sad. "That little . . . performance back there was about as close as Karin gets to throwing down the gauntlet."

Thrust and run. Rob didn't have to tell me how ugly this all could get. I already knew.

There was more. Better as news went, albeit not by much.

"You ought to know," he said, "I spent two hours last night on the phone with the Bishop. Would have headed over there today if the guy hadn't been flying East to a conference."

"And?"

"I told him about the divorce and my plans to meet with Barry. Old news, really. We went through all of this, in spades, for years now, starting with my admission to the seminary. It could have complicated my assignment to Nativity when Karin left—calling or no calling to the priesthood, the church is most reluctant to aid and abet home-wrecking. Fortunately, nobody else wanted that parish and the Bishop was convinced more or less our marriage was a lost cause at that point. I promised to keep him informed if anything changed. I did. It's done."

"And us?"

It was tough going with the slick roads and heavy traffic. Hands clenched tight on the wheel, Rob just stared straight ahead into the distance. I took that for all the answer I needed.

"You didn't tell him?"

"No."

"Hedging your bets!?"

For a split-second Rob shot a look in my direction that stopped my rising anger and paranoia cold. I regretted the words as soon as I spoke them.

"Just trying to be honest, Char," he said softly. "Because in my heart and head, the decision to dissolve my marriage and my relationship with you had—and have—absolutely nothing to do with each other. To even have spoken of you in that context would have implied a link that for me simply does not exist. I was not willing to give the Bishop a . . . *single shred* of a reason to assume it does."

For a split-second the roaring in my ears succeeded in drowning out the throaty sound of the Hummer, the traffic and even the persistent gusts of wind buffeting the vehicle. We could have been in a room somewhere, the two of us, alone in the world.

A watershed. And Rob was waiting for me to come down on one side or the other. My hands were shaking as I clutched at the shoulder restraint.

"Rob, I'm . . . sorry. Truly sorry. That was uncalled for."

"Apology accepted."

He shifted in his seat. He wasn't finished.

"And for the record?" he said softly. "I love you, Char—more than ever. Just in case you were wondering."

# ✣ Chapter Twenty-two

Spring was coming. The daffodils in the side yard at Nativity were in full, glorious flower. At the rectory, the kayak was back on the front porch and Rob was making threatening noises about borrowing a second one from a neighbor and taking me out in it one of these days.

I was in love. And right now even a kayak sounded great—if it meant a rare but precious opportunity to be together. Publicly. In the clear light of day.

How I envied those young lovers holding hands and laughing as they hung out on weekends in front of the mini-mart. By default it had become the rendezvous of choice downtown when Rutterbach's sidewalk became an obstacle course of planks and trenches as crews did battle with a shifting foundation.

"Those kids keep complaining they're bored out of their skulls," Marty grumbled as he came back from gassing up the Undercroft station wagon in preparation for yet another one of his epic road trips. "The whole spoiled-silly lot of 'em. What I'd give for two hours down there every afternoon, if it meant spending more time with Leah and Bart."

I smiled, shook my head. "No way! You can't quit now, Marty. A dozen retailers are carrying our paraments and that up-and-coming little catalog has picked up our line. You're the best salesman we've got."

"Try the only one!"

I laughed, but with a heavy heart. The truth was, I knew exactly how he felt.

Just last Sunday one of the older couples had lingered behind at Nativity, fussing over one another before braving that nasty descent down the front stairs. Did he have his cane? Did she have her purse? I saw Rob notice them, too, and for an agonizing moment, his glance flickered in my direction.

"How you holding up?" he said as he wandered over to where I was struggling with the hinged lid of the tracker. But then, he already knew before he asked.

Laying his briefcase down on the organ bench, Rob reached over to help. It took no small amount of finessing on both our parts to ease the cranky mechanism back into place enough to close up the instrument.

"It just occurred to me—a year ago next Friday," I told him, "I was sitting in my boss Irene's office as she gave me my walking papers."

"And here we are," he said softly, "watching Earl and Eunice out there in the narthex. A living reminder, if ever I saw one, that Love—writ large—is in the details."

"I can think of a lot worse ways to spend my retirement, Rob. If that's what you're wondering."

As his hand lingered on mine, I steeled myself—assuming it couldn't last. Instead, on a sigh, he pulled me gently into his arms. Silent, we stood there holding each other for what seemed like a long time.

"At the rate we're going, Rob," I said finally, "the vestry is going to show up tomorrow night and still find us here. Like two pillars of salt. I don't know about you, but the old adrenalin is going fast!"

As I spoke, my eyes were already flickering closed. I felt Rob's reluctance, but he began to pull away.

"Spoilsport!" he yawned.

We were both yawning now, laughing with the release of tension and sheer exhaustion. With our last reserves of energy we collected our coats, shut off light switches and handled all the routine housekeeping chores that usually made these weekly partings more bearable.

"You also should know I talked to Barry last night," Rob said as we headed down the steps. "Karin's apparently . . . madder than a hornet. Apparently her attorney told her any illusions she had about making sure I wound up living under an overpass were just that, *illusions.* He also told her the pension agreement is more than fair and is urging a sign-off."

"I'm glad."

*Sorry, too.* But too tired to discuss it. The adrenalin rush was all but gone. If I thought too long or hard over what all that might mean for the future, I would never make it home.

"In any case, it's almost Holy Week," I said. "At least Easter's almost set. With you in the choir to keep Barney in line, we're up to eight now. I actually found a trumpeter to play fanfares, a little old guy—a retired barber—who learned the instrument years ago as a military bugler— "

We had reached the walk leading to the rectory. Rob hesitated. I could tell it was taking every bit of will power the man had not to invite me in.

"I'm sure Easter will be wonderful," he said. "But right now you look exhausted—a good power-nap would take the edge off. I'll call you later."

*Thank God*, I made a mental note, *for email and unlimited calling plans.* We had another long night ahead of us.

*Two weeks now to Easter.* The countdown to Holy Week had begun.

It was a Tuesday and I had been practicing about a half-hour when I heard the door to the narthex slam—hard, as it usually did for those unfamiliar with its hair-trigger. Turning on the bench, I saw a stout, balding middle-aged visitor, clad in chinos, a tweed jacket with leather elbow patches and a clerical collar, heading down the center aisle in my direction.

"Charlotte. Charlotte Grunwald, I assume."

"Charlise. But yes. I'm Char."

Stunned, I let the Grunwald part stand. How on earth he got my maiden name or from whom, I couldn't even pretend to speculate. Either he had been prowling around in old church records or he had been talking to someone.

One thing was clear. He seemed to know something else far more disturbing, something he wasn't prepared to share.

"Father Dennis Wills." He hesitated. "I was hoping to catch you here!"

Something in his brusque, guarded introduction set off even more alarm bells. As we shook hands in greeting, I racked my memory banks unsuccessfully for the name.

"Have we met, Father Wills?"

"I'm with the Diocesan administrative staff. Father Sims told me you usually practiced around this time."

I nodded. "True. Is there . . . a problem?"

"At Father Sim's request, I'm going to be covering for him here at Nativity for the foreseeable— "

"Impossible. Rob would never choose to leave his parish hanging with Easter just . . ."

But apparently he had. The conversation was becoming more and more uncomfortable. I tried not to let my rising anxiety show.

"I'm sorry, Father Wills, but I . . . I'm simply not . . . following you . . .!"

"The Diocesan offices received a letter several days ago. Father Sims is in Pittsburgh as we speak, discussing its contents with the Bishop."

My heart sank as I sensed where Father Wills was headed. It wasn't hard to suspect not only the contents of that document, but its likely source or sources.

"Challenging Father Rob's . . . fitness for ministry," I said.

Father Wills just looked at me, hard. "You have reasons to assume that could be a possibility."

It wasn't a question. Panicked now, I took a deep breath to clear my head.

My mouth felt stiff. "I think, Father Wills, we are all aware of the ongoing media concern for gender-related issues and the clergy."

The priest appeared to be turning something over in his mind. From his obvious caution, I concluded we were straying into matters that he had not come here intending to discuss.

"The Diocese received an anonymous letter," he said finally. "Charging Father Sims with sexual harassment and impropriety with an employee."

I felt my face grow hot. But then at least it appears the document wasn't playing the *gay* card or didn't pull out a Scarlet Letter and add *adultery* to the list.

Suddenly lightheaded, I slipped into the closest pew and sat. For some reason, I kept fixating in my mind's eye on that hateful sheet of bond on the Bishop's desk as if maybe, just maybe, if I willed it hard enough, the vicious and damaging accusations printed there would vanish into thin air.

All the while, I could sense Father Wills watching me, my every reaction. My hands were shaking.

"Serious charges," he said quietly, "if true."

"Fiction."

"I assume, Ms. Grunwald, that the staff member mentioned in the letter is—?"

"Me?"

I fought the irrational urge to laugh. Did two people count as 'staff'? The church sexton was Barney, my buddy from the Undercroft weaving team, and the volunteer secretary was an eighty-year-old choir member. Which left me, the only person at Nativity except Rob formally on the payroll—if you could call it that at fifty bucks a session.

"What apparently the letter fails to mention is that Rob Sims and I were *friends,* before I ever darkened the door as a parishioner again—or started working for Nativity."

"And you met, how?"

"We went to the same high school, years ago. When I moved back here last Spring, he gave me permission to practice on Nativity's organ. The previous organist died and as a courtesy, I agreed to stay on for two months, as *interim,* until the vestry found a replacement. They offered me the job and I've played here ever since."

"You knew Father Sims is married?"

"Yes. He and his wife had been separated—though recently, she filed for a divorce. She, Karin . . . is an . . . addict."

"He told you—?"

"I met her."

"*Here*, in Hope?"

"Pittsburgh."

The priest frowned. "So, in this *interim,* prior to his divorce you and he—?"

I had to believe it was accidental on the part of Father Wills to play that language back at me. But inadvertent or not, it felt ugly, cheap.

"In the interim we *what* . . . ? What . . . *exactly* are you suggesting, Father Wills . . .?"

The priest looked uncomfortable. "I didn't come here, Ms. Grunwald, intending to launch into some inquisition—"

"The answer is, *no.* We were never . . . intimate. Father Sims was and is one of the most decent, principled men I have ever met."

"You're saying then . . .?" He hesitated. "There is *no relationship* between you and Father Sims?"

I just looked at him. Define . . . *relationship?* He had to be kidding. It took every bit of willpower not to just turn around and walk out of there.

"I can't, *won't* speak for Father Sims." But then, I could not, would not, lie either. "I can only speak for myself. I consider Robert Sims my dearest friend. I love him . . . deeply."

"Ms. Grunwald, I— "

"Let me finish!" My voice broke then steadied again. "That said Father, I'm sure you would agree, how love is expressed takes *many* forms, not all of them . . . sexual. No matter what that letter claims."

The priest cleared his throat. "Be that as it may, Ms. Grunwald, you need to understand that the Diocese is not inclined to give credence to unsigned correspondence— "

"But nevertheless you've suspended him."

Father Wills just looked at me. "No. Father Sims has been an excellent priest in this parish. The Bishop is also fully aware that Father Sims has been under a great deal of pressure and that his family situation is . . . most difficult. So when Father Sims asked to take a . . . temporary leave of absence, the Bishop chose to send me to— "

"So, you really are going to do it . . . replace Father Sims at Nativity? With Holy Week just *days* from now . . .?"

The Diocesan representative flinched. "Unfortunate timing but, yes. At his request."

"Then you'll be wanting my resignation as well."

"That isn't necessary," Father Wills said quickly. "At worst, if there is unprofessional conduct at stake here, as an employee, one would consider you to be an . . . innocent *victim* of— "

"*No!* Whatever spin you ultimately choose to put on this situation, I am *not a victim*. Of anything. Much as I love serving as organist at Nativity, much as I love the liturgy, love playing that keyboard, I love other things more. The truth is one of them. I'm giving notice to the vestry as of close of business tomorrow that they should start looking for a replacement as soon as possible."

"Unfortunate, Ms. Grunwald. I hope that you might decide to *reconsider*. With Father Sims on leave, the parish is going to need every bit of stability possible— "

"Stability? This is going to tear the heart out of these people. In one of the holiest seasons of the Church Year. For no *damn* reason at all. If Diocese wants my opinion, there it is!"

Swallowing hard to hold back tears and chin high, I turned and headed back to the organ console. The more or less steady wheezing of the reservoir shuddered and died as I hit the Power switch. Closing the case, I stacked my music together in a ragged heap on the bench. By the time I turned to leave, Father Wills was gone.

I didn't know at whom I was more angry, Rob, Wills or that nameless, faceless church hierarchy whose role it was to pass judgment on all of this. Then too, was Wills telling me the truth, or was all this just some sort of code for having engineered Rob's suspension?

Confused and disoriented, I stumbled out of the sanctuary and into the side yard of the parish house, with a single syllable repeating itself in my head. *No. No.* And yet there it was, that unfamiliar car parked in front of the rectory.

I looked for Rob's Hummer. It wasn't there. My pulse working double time, I all but ran the half-mile home.

Marty was on the road and the house silent and empty. Slinging my coat on the back of the sofa, I sat down in the wing chair within sight of the door and within reach of the phone. I waited.

The days were growing longer now. The sun had already begun to set before I noticed how chilly it was getting in the house. Shivering, I adjusted the thermostat upward and then, pulling a throw around me, sat down again in the darkening living room.

At six I clicked on the end table lamp. At seven I lit a fire in the fireplace and got comfortable in my favorite wing chair watching the dance of light in the firebox. I must have dozed off, because when I heard the sound of the door, I thought I was dreaming. It was ten o'clock.

Haggard and unshaven, Rob Sims was standing in the front hall, minus overcoat and clerical collar. One look at his face was enough to drain the anger from me in a heartbeat.

"I've been waiting," I told him.

Without a word, he came to me and as involuntarily as breathing, I slipped into his arms. For a long time we just held each other as if his life, and mine, depended on it.

"Rob, I'm sorry. So very, very sorry— "

At something in my voice, he stiffened. Reaching down where my hands were circling his waist, he caught them in his and cautiously shifted so that we were standing at arms length. It was impossible to evade his steady, questioning gaze.

"He . . . Father Wills . . . talked to you . . .?"

"Y-yes." My voice shook, but steadied again. "Yes, he did."

"Sweetheart, I wish . . . I wish to . . . heaven you didn't—that he didn't have to put you through that."

"*Us*, Rob. We *are* in this *together.*"

I thought I saw the tension in his face ease, if only a little. My heart felt as if it were beating its way out of my chest.

"I don't think . . . in all fairness to Wills, I don't think he came up here to read me the riot act. I sort of pried the truth out of him. Rob, I can't even . . . imagine what your end of that *conversation* was like in Pittsburgh." I hesitated. "Father Wills told me . . . he said that you— "

"I asked to be put on emergency leave," Rob drew a harsh breath. "When I got back from seeing the Bishop, I packed some stuff and planned to head up to the retreat house on Lake Erie. Getting out of Dodge. A friend of mine runs the place—a refuge for enthusiastic lay groups and burned-out clergy. Wills or one of his staff will be staying in the parsonage along with a supply priest if needed until the Diocese finishes its inquiry and I get my head on straight— "

"You know what the parish is going to think."

"That they axed me?" Rob shook his head. "No. Believe me, I thought of that. Wills isn't going to make that hate letter public, just share the issues privately with the vestry. I know those good people. Any one of them would reassure the rest of the parish that this isn't a witch hunt, that I was not forced out, by anyone. My request for a leave is exactly what it says it is—a plea for support as I try to cope with some very serious . . . family problems."

"These people need you here. I need you."

Rob sighed. "Were it that simple. You know as well as I do that hate letter was someone's desperate cry for help. I'm sure also you know at least two likely sources . . .!"

"Rob, I don't— "

"Either way, whoever wrote it didn't hesitate to go to the top—as in, my boss. Pretty gutsy as opening salvos go, I'd say, intended obviously to inflict damage on a mega-scale. And especially fraught since I made what may yet prove to be a colossal blunder of two-stepping it with the Bishop— "

"I don't understand."

"That junket to Pittsburgh to see Barry," he reminded me. "And the two hellish hours I spent on the phone the night before with the Bishop. Lousy timing, since we couldn't talk face-to-face—the guy was on the way out of town. I told you that I stopped short of informing him about us. It was on the agenda to set him straight, in person this time. Unfortunately— "

"Somebody beat you to it."

"Yes. And who *knows* what the next target might be if there seems to be no response! Somebody out there obviously is out for blood— "

"Never give in to blackmail."

Rob winced. "That's what the Bishop said. But in the end, he understood my scruples about taking a chance and ignoring the situation. *Not at the expense of the parish.* Still, I can understand if you're finding it hard to— "

"I told Father Wills I'm submitting my resignation to the vestry tomorrow."

"Char . . . *no*!"

"That's what *he* . . . what Father Wills said!" My laugh ended on a rising note. "Stay the course. Pin a target on my back and die at the keyboard, face to the pipes. For the good of the parish . . . "

"Wills is right and not the . . . ogre you're making him out to be," Rob said slowly. "Gruff, maybe and even occasionally, clueless. But he means well and the poor guy is going to need you, big time—especially now at Easter. In the name of heaven, why would anyone pick *now* to start something like . . .?"

He broke off, as if sensing the futility of where his thoughts were headed. Was there ever a *right* time for what was happening?

"And your leaving is going to fix all that?" I said.

"Char, I can only do what I can do. I'll go up to Erie and think this through, let the dust settle—hope that my old friend Barry succeeds in pouring some oil on the waters, persuades Karin's attorney to get her to listen to reason. Something. Anything. A better solution, I believe, than tearing down to Pittsburgh and duking it out with either Karin or worse, with . . ."

*With Ted?* Rob's expression was an open book as he struggled even to grasp the possibility that his son could have done something so utterly, terribly hurtful. I felt the sting of tears behind my eyes.

"And so you're just locking yourself away up there. Alone. Letting everybody think you've been exiled to outer darkness."

"Anything but," he said softly. "Because I know you'll be here, the woman I love, pouring out all our grief on that poor tracker, looking our friends in the face and helping them get through this. I think we always . . . knew it could come to this, sweetheart."

I looked down at my hands, unable to meet his steady gaze. "Do you . . . did they tell you *anything* that would help figure out who might have . . . "

"Sent the letter?" He shrugged, shook his head. Calmer now. "I'd stake my life that it wasn't a parishioner, regardless of who knows or suspects how we feel about each other. Probably not Ted either. Maybe it's just wishful thinking, but I've got to believe that my son's incapable of that. My money is on Karin or that junkie boyfriend of hers, ticked off at all the lawyering going on. But on some level . . . I don't want to know."

"Rob, I can't just let you *go* like this . . . "

"I told Wills I would be out of here by tonight."

"Tonight. Just like . . . *that*?"

His voice was a hoarse whisper. "Trust me, it's not what I want, Char . . .!"

"For the record? *I want* what I've wanted for as long as I can remember. I want you to . . . " I took a deep breath, then came right out with it. My voice was low. "I want you to make love with me . . ."

Rob's smile began with his eyes. Deliberately, he raised both my hands—palm open, to his lips. It was more intimate than if he had kissed my mouth.

"Tempting," he said softly. "But then I keep butting heads with that quote from the gospel according to Joplin . . ."

"Scott?"

"Janis. *Me and Bobby McGee.* I think you . . .we both have learned more than enough about both, *freedom and loss,* in the last few hours to last a lifetime. We can look anybody in the eye right now, Char, because we know who we are and what we have or have not done. In spite of anonymous slings and arrows."

"And you're wondering if maybe I'm just hurt, angry. Looking around for some. . . *in-your-face* gesture to get back at—?"

Rob winced. "It had occurred to me."

"What I feel has nothing to do with Wills or the Diocese," I said, a heck of a lot steadier than I felt. "I love you, Rob. And I told Father Wills as much. Loud and clear, to his face. He knows point-blank we were never . . . intimate. Not the way that letter apparently meant, anyway. Though the way we left things with Wills, I was making no guarantees things would stay that way . . ."

My voice shook, but I forced myself to finish. "If I had . . . any . . . choice in the matter, that is."

Rob's eyes had begun to glitter with a dark fire. I sensed him shaping the question in his head.

"No regrets, Char? Whatever comes, after. I need to know."

"My grandmother's brass bed is pretty intimidating. But that aside . . . "

His hands were already clutching mine. Only this time, it was I who was taking the lead.

"Upstairs," I told him. "First door on the left."

For all my bravado, it was not until we stood facing each other in the subdued lighting of the bedroom that I realized how nervous I was. As many other women in my generation, I had married the first man with whom I was physically intimate. And in the years since his death, the dating scene had gone from moonlight and roses to singles' bars and the terrifying realities of STDs and HIV.

Somehow Rob sensed it. He coaxed me into his arms with a look that would have melted the polar cap. Then instead of heading for that brass bed, he eased us toward the bedroom mirror.

Standing behind me, his arms wrapped around my shoulders, he drew my gaze outward toward our reflection caught in the subtly crackled, out-of-focus surface of the glass. The instinct was to flinch from the image, to avoid the telltale evidence of the passing decades. But Rob persisted.

"Reality check," he said quietly.

I had found the ornate gilt antique in the attic of the homestead a couple of months ago. As a mirror it left a lot to be desired, but its frame fit perfectly over one of the faded patches in the wallpaper. Like I felt, now, in Rob's arms—*at home, where I belonged.*

"Do you have any *idea* how beautiful you are?" he said. "The set of your mouth, the way the curve of your cheek sweeps toward your hair. Your eyes— "

"The crow's feet . . ."

"The honest, unvarnished truth, of a caring life."

I forced an anxious laugh. "Now you're scaring me— "

"I certainly hope not, sweetheart. Though I'll admit, I've had my moments when I could have said the same of you."

"That first morning in the undercroft."

"That, too." He smiled. "And all those years, when we were kids, watching you on that bench. Hearing the truth about what my life could be, what love could be, and running away from it as fast as I could."

I dropped my gaze. "That . . . *girl* is gone, Rob."

"Is she . . .?"

Gently he turned me in his arms so that he could look down into my face. "That intensity—looking beyond the surface at the things, especially at the people you love. The music in that smile. Take a good, hard look, sweetheart. I wasn't flying blind on New Year's when I hauled out that yearbook of yours. I'd already checked, your freshman year. *Grunwald, Charlise Amelia.* There it was."

My breath caught in my throat. I tried again. "You did . . . you did . . . what . . .?"

"The small town public library is a wonderful invention," he chuckled. "But there was more. On page 27, unless memory fails. It was the fall choir concert with you at the keyboard, your face radiant in the lights flooding down from the stage into that orchestra pit. I've seen that look . . . every week. In the chancel, and now, in that mirror in front of us . . ."

"Thirty pounds heavier— "

"A woman."

I felt his breath moving against my face as he lowered his head. His mouth was warm and insistent. And then my fingers were twining themselves in his hair above the crisp edge of his shirt collar, the hunger for closeness unbearable.

Laughter carried us through the awkward moments. A habit from my years on the bench, I kicked off my shoes, trying—not entirely successfully—to keep my footing. All arms and elbows, I helped him ease off my sweater, anticipating the touch of his hands moving over my bare shoulders and down the exposed skin of my back. My imagination was working overtime, willing his body to respond and take control.

*Come then, my love; my darling, come with me. The winter is over; the rains have stopped.* The familiar rhythm of the Song of Solomon flashed through my head, its lyrical poetic meter soaring heavenward. *The time for singing has come; the song of doves is heard in the field.*

And then my body was becoming the song, ebbing and flowing with raw desire. Rob and I were on the bed, together, moving as one—in a dance of passion as old as Eden. I saw his face, poised for a split-second over mine, snapshot fashion. The truth was written there . . . the love, the heartache. All of it.

"Yes . . . ," I whispered. "Oh, love . . . yes."

His mouth fitted itself gently to mine—then, in an agonizing rush of sensation, we lost ourselves in each other. I wanted to cry out but there were no words, only the wild siren call of life coursing through every cell and fiber, spending itself gloriously in the silence.

It couldn't last. Shaking, our bodies glistening, we lay in each other's arms, measuring out the passage of seconds and minutes with the gradual slowing of our breath. *Decrescendo and diminuendo.* The music of my heart was playing itself out—every quaver and subtle breath mark, and the fierce spiritual hope and longing behind them.

"I love you, Char," he breathed.

It could just have been the night breeze stirring outside the window, anticipating the summer to come. My ear tuned my body to the sound, waiting for a sign that I had truly heard. And then magically, he began to love me again.

# ✣ Chapter Twenty-three

We finally slept. The cold pre-dawn light had just begun to cast pale shadows across the bed when I sensed Rob stir alongside me. Fitted together like proverbial spoons, I could feel the quickening rise and fall of his breath as he freed a hand to check his watch.

"Sweetheart . . ., I've got to go."

My response was to snuggle closer, reveling in the warmth of his body cradling mine. Still, I was awake enough, I had to ask—even knowing, fearing what the answer would be.

"Rob, when will we . . . see each other again . . .?"

He sighed. "No clue. If it gets too bad, the Diocese won't have much choice but transfer me."

"And the people of Nativity can't do . . . anything—?"

"Unlikely"

"But possible. And then, too, whoever wrote that letter might retract it."

He hesitated. "Char, it would be . . . unwise to get our hopes up. Either way."

Unwise, but human. While he pulled on his jeans, I snagged my robe from the antique brass hook behind the bedroom door and slipped into it. It was strange to watch this man I had seen so vulnerable and open, preoccupied with the buttons on his open-necked shirt—all the mundane civilizing logistics that were about to take him away from me, for goodness knows how long.

He looked up from lacing his running shoes. "I'll phone when I get there."

"I'll be here," I nodded.

"Char, *don't resign*. Promise me."

My teeth caught the inside of my cheek as I processed what he was asking of me. Finally, reluctantly, I nodded my assent.

"Rob, I'm frightened."

"*Go where the music takes you. Forget the angst and the mistakes.* Till the day she died, Wilma remembered you told her that. Sweetheart, she wasn't the only one who needed to hear it. It changed my life."

His eyes were dark and the smudges below them darker. "I've seen you play like that," he said. "The way you lose yourself in the moment and the love you pour into every note, *fearless*. More so, with every phrase and passage you transcend. We *will* get through this, sweetheart. I'll email as often as I can— "

A faint smile tugged at the corner of his mouth but faded as quickly as it began. Before I realized what was happening, Rob pulled me into a powerful embrace. Then, just as abruptly, he was gone.

The bedroom floor was cold under my feet. I stood where he left me, listening to the deliberate rhythm of his footsteps on the stairs. Then from farther away, I heard the heavy sound of the front door closing behind him.

*Closure.* I had never realized how glib, how ugly the word was until that very moment. In a few hours—whenever Father Wills had finished briefing the vestry, my phone would be ringing off the wall. For now, I heard only the harsh finality of that door, replaying itself in my head.

I would worry later, give in to the tears that so badly needed to fall. *Go where the music takes you.* Right now, I needed to savor the last, lingering sense of his presence. Slipping between the sheets, I curled my body around his pillow—holding the memories tight in the circle of my arms.

The coverlet on the bed was still crumpled, as we had left it, with its wild garden of cabbage roses, wide black borders and trailing ivy and leaves. The music of our love was there all around me, in that tapping of a branch against the window and the quiet whisper of linens rustling—in the inaudible beating of my pulse.

My body ached with the lingering sense of his presence. I closed my eyes and breathed in the bitter-sweet scent of our bodies, no longer certain where his life ended and mine began. And over time, mercifully, sleep came—filled with half-dreams that scattered like spring mist before the morning sun. In those dreams, I was not alone.

✣

"Char . . .! Are you here . . .?"

It took several repetitions and variations on that general theme for me to realize I wasn't imagining it. Someone was downstairs in the house, looking for me.

"Char, sweetie . . .!"

I recognized the voice. "Upstairs, Grace."

After a time, I heard the creaking of the treads on the staircase, ascending now. Their pace slowed halfway near the first landing and then again near the top. The bedroom door was still standing open as Rob had left it.

"Sweetie, are you . . . decent?"

An unfortunate choice of words. In spite of myself, I chuckled—a bleak, dry-bones rattle of sound that did nothing to ease the terrible tightness in my chest. *Decent?*

"No. But come ahead."

"Stay put— "

It took Grace a split-second to figure out where I was. Half-propped up in bed, I pulled the sheet tight around me and the movement caught her attention. We made eye contact.

"Oh, kiddo. You look . . . awful."

Dry-eyed and disoriented, I blinked—tried to focus. "What time is it?"

"Two in the afternoon. How long have you been—?"

"Rob left crack of dawn. I've been here, ever since."

If Grace caught the gist of my admission, that we had spent the night together, she showed no sign of it. Her forehead morphed into an epic frown.

"I just got out of a meeting over at Nativity with . . . that guy from the Diocese— "

"Father Wills."

Grace nodded. "I wanted to punch him in the mouth. But then, Barney pretty much took care of that. Verbally, of course."

Easing alongside me on the edge of the bed, she sat there for a long time before either one of us said anything. After a while, her hand snaked out and awkwardly began to kneed at the vicious knot of tension at the base of my skull.

Poor Father Wills. I was finding it hard to swallow much less speak.

"He told you about the anonymous letter . . ."

"Trash."

"I can't imagine what people think of me—us . . ."

"The people of Nativity are *not* going to let this stand, kiddo," she said firmly. "But then, they aren't blind or stupid either. Of course you two love each other. If that's a firing offense—shit, sweetie, what are we preaching week after week over there in that sanctuary anyway?"

*Love one another.* Unfortunately, I wasn't convinced that was the way someone out there was interpreting the New Testament mandate.

Grace frowned. "Do you know where Rob . . . has he left?"

"I couldn't stop him. H-he . . . drove up there alone."

"*There* . . . as in . . .?"

"Lake Erie. The retreat house."

"Leah can alert Marty. If he knows, he can pass through there on the way back from— "

"Bad idea, Grace. Rob needs his space right now and I think we need to give it to him."

"Rob really asked for a leave then? This isn't some life-and-death battle with the powers of darkness—as in, Wills or the Diocese's idea? So help me, if I thought that, I'd go over to that rectory and— "

"Oh, Grace . . .! "

I couldn't help it. I laughed, although more a strangled half-cry.

"Rob is so lucky," I said softly, "truly lucky to have parishioners like you."

"C'mere you," she said.

I did, my head resting on her ample lap like a wounded child while deep, aching sobs shook my shoulders. But still, the tears would not come. Muttering soothing nonsense, Grace used her strong and knowing hands to bring the trembling under control.

"I . . . love . . . him, Grace."

"I know, sweetie. I know."

"What's . . . what will happen to us?"

Grace hesitated. "You're going to hang on, get through this. You are not alone in this. Not by a long shot."

It was silent for a long time. But as my friend, I needed her to know.

"Until last night, we . . . never . . . ever— "

"Trust me, old Gracie knows when someone's 'getting it', kiddo. If you ask me, it's . . . high bloody time! Nobody with half a brain in their heads around here is going to be shocked or surprised."

Gently Grace urged me to a sitting position. She gave me my marching orders with the same read-my-lips bedside manner I had seen her use with her Sunday School class.

"Now, I'm going to make up this bed and you're going to climb in that shower down the hall. You're going to get dressed. Then we're going over to my place so Leah can call Marty. Barney and the vestry are coming over to my place for a potluck and you're going to tell them exactly what they need to know to help you. Easter is coming!"

I went, as ordered, one foot in front of the other. Grace hadn't exaggerated. I looked a fright—almost unrecognizable from that glowing, breathlessly happy woman who had stood in front of my bedroom mirror last night. For starters, this time my reflection in the glass was conspicuously alone.

While Grace paced in the hall outside the bathroom door, I showered and washed my hair. Judging by the cloud of steam that whole process generated, I must have been at it a long time. A rattling sound from the door knob told me my friend was getting impatient with my progress.

"Makeup," she barked when she caught me standing in my bathrobe zombie-fashion at the sink, toothbrush in hand.

Hands shaking, I applied the base, the highlights under my eyebrows, the hint of blush along the curve of my cheekbones. Waterproof mascara followed and then some of that two-coat lip color, both layers designed to withstand a hurricane.

Grace watched, finally nodding her approval. "Better."

"I feel like— "

"You just had the crap kicked out of you. I know. Point is, you don't show it. Barney and those guys on the vestry are going to be worried enough, without you looking like you're about to succumb."

Trailed by Grace, I wandered back into the bedroom and stood in front of my closet. I was clueless where to begin.

"None of that black Harpie-on-the-lintel wardrobe of yours either, like a spectre out of Edgar Allen Poe," Grace ordered. "Jeans and that turquoise cashmere sweater Rob likes so much— "

"Grace, don't tell me . . .!" I sucked in my breath. "Were we all that . . . transparent?"

She chuckled. "Now that's better—dander up and ready to go

out there swinging. Kiddo, you two were so *damn discreet* there were times I wanted to light a fire under either one or the both of you. But then I gotta say, whatever else that letter did, it brought things out in the open. Thank God. Now let's go out there and deal with it."

All Grace needed was a bullhorn and some flowers in her hair, and she could have been out there leading a protest march, shades of the sixties. For a split-second, I felt tears swimming to the surface again.

"Grace, in case you haven't noticed. I love you . . .!"

So help me, she blushed. "Mutual, I'm sure. Now, have ya got a pair of boots somewhere? That path through our backyards is still pretty muddy."

Just as we were about to head out through the kitchen, the phone rang. I hesitated, wondering if I should answer it.

"Better get that," Grace advised.

Stumbling to the wall phone next to the door to the dining room, I grabbed it mid-ring. "Char Howard— "

"Hello, sweetheart."

*Rob.* I felt the word stick in my throat.

"Where *are . . . you*?"

"Erie. My friend just helped me get settled in one of the counselor's rooms." He hesitated. "Unfortunately, the only phone is in the hall and my cell's out of juice . . ."

I chuckled, trying to envision Rob conducting surreptitious phone sex camped out in the male wing of a retreat house. "Cramping your style?"

"You have no idea. There's a whole squadron of Boy Scouts up here working on their Pro Deo et Patria badges!"

"Well, you always wanted to visit the monastery at Taizé. Here's your chance."

Grace had moved out on the porch, bless her heart, to give us privacy. I told Rob about her visit, omitting the part about dragging me out of bed in the middle of the afternoon. I didn't want to worry him.

"I tried my best to make a case for leaving you alone, but you know Grace. She insists that Marty stop at the retreat house on the way back from his sales route. In case you're feeling . . . neglected up there."

I heard the laughter in his voice. "Ya gotta love 'em . . .!"

"True."

Grateful as I was for their support, it was not our friends' affection I was thinking about at the moment. Rob read the silence for what it was.

"But then, you know, sweetheart, what's . . . really churning around in my skull right now!"

Also true. "Take care of your head and your heart," I told him. "I assume you had better cut this short . . . and on my end, Grace is waiting . . ."

"Understood."

"I love you."

"Check your email when you get home tonight."

The line went quiet in my hands, followed by dial tone. Re-cradling the receiver, I joined Grace on my back porch.

"Atta girl," she said. "That's the old fighting spirit."

As I slid down on the step alongside her, I added the silent prayer. Amen. *May it be so.*

# ✠ Chapter Twenty-four

Our grieving little parish and I went into Holy Week as best we could with Father Wills and a nervous young priest-to-be at the helm. The only thing that kept my sanity was the sheer quantity of the playing and the knowledge that I could go home afterward and pour it all out via email to Rob in self-imposed exile on the shores of Lake Erie.

> Palm Sunday, dearest Rob, and you aren't here. All dozen of the Sunday School kids processed around the sanctuary with a surprising amount of enthusiasm even though Grace bought those fan-like palm fronds for them to wave this year instead of the light saber variety. By all accounts, the previous model led to way too much violence on an already very ambivalent religious holiday.
>
> You were right about Wills. He's a decent man, though I'll admit, I'm glad he's not our parish priest. Just a bit too high-strung for my taste. I've been trying to help him as much as possible, but he hasn't handled the whole Easter week worship sequence in way too long for comfort (not start to finish, anyway).
>
> For a recessional I chose that Entrada you heard me practicing, very contemporary and full of dark premonitions. Coming up with the emotional edge, unfortunately, wasn't hard under the circumstances. I miss you.

At least as I signed off, I consoled myself that we were in the same climate zone.

From Rob's descriptions, the shores of Lake Erie were no less damp and depressing than parts south where I was. Still, he had not lost his capacity for ferreting out silver linings.

> Sweetheart. I chuckled when I thought of you dodging that razor-edged palm jungle whipping around in the aisle behind you. I can empathize. At the moment I am limping myself and covered in calamine. Monsoons or not, my Maundy Thursday devotional was to strike out cross-country through a wooded area on the grounds I had never explored before. About the same time I ran into a dense stand of wild raspberries or something equally thorny—and was about to retreat (bad pun, I know), when I literally stumbled into an enigma.
>
> At first I thought it was a patio or foundation from an old building, but as I followed the flagstone rubble through the undergrowth, it became clear the debris was scattered in more or less concentric arcs. Over lunch my friend confirmed that there had once been a Peace Grove somewhere out back, obviously in the form of a labyrinth. For lack of money for maintenance, the entire installation had fallen into major disrepair.
>
> I quickly decided to make my personal Easter Vigil a blitz to clear as much of the labyrinth paths as I can. The only thing two hours of hacking away at the underbrush produced were some prodigious blisters, a mild case of poison ivy and a good idea how nasty the job is going to be.
>
> At least I'm tired enough to sleep for a change, no easy business without you. Funny, how quickly the simplest things can become a necessity.

My throat felt tight and I read the last paragraph over a couple of times. Just this morning Grace had made a not too subtle comment about how late my lights were on all week. I fibbed—told her it was just a night light when Marty was on the road and I was alone in the house. Somehow, I don't think she believed me.

On the home front, we ran into logistical nightmares of our

own—first my home computer meltdown, then a sit-down-strike by two of the Undercroft weavers who vowed they wouldn't move a muscle until Rob was back in the rectory. When I finally connected to the internet again, I had some catching up to do:

> The Big Three (I hate using Tridium) have come and gone without a word from me. Maundy Thursday to Easter Sunday sound so long. *Mea culpa.*
>
> But mid-stream my computer crashed big time and it took Marty until Easter Sunday to get me up and running again. As for our liturgical countdown at Nativity from darkness to Holy Fire, we didn't crash and burn although we came close several times.
>
> Father Wills reluctantly agreed to carry through with the Thursday Tenaebrae service you organized, though I thought the poor man was going to lose it once or twice. Despite recent events at Nativity and all that Biblical precedent about betrayal in the Garden and all that unleashed, poor Wills unfortunately has very little sense of drama—at least when it comes to liturgy. Fortunately the readings speak for themselves and the stripping of the altar and that desperate slamming of the narthex door at the end pretty much summed up everybody's mood. Rutterbach's teenage nephew was on door detail and got so carried away that the gale blowing through the sanctuary snuffed out the Christ candle—an unsettling moment. Right now, there isn't a soul at Nativity that doesn't get the part about being forsaken of God.
>
> But then our Good Friday vigil came off without a hitch. Your little flock is getting pretty fierce about standing at the foot of crosses.
>
> On Saturday even the rusty barbecue grill we retrieved from behind the rectory lit on the first try before the Easter Vigil (and didn't burn down the church either). So to celebrate, we popped a bottle of gosh-awful cold duck in the Undercroft after the service and toasted the Resurrection. Don't be disgusted with us for backsliding to our quasi-pagan roots. With you gone, your *ersatz* tradition of sparkling juice just wouldn't cut

> it. And face it, everybody was pretty much in the mood for the real McCoy.

That odd local custom of hailing the Risen Christ had pre-dated Rob but on his watch, the festivities had mutated to nonalcoholic. I didn't feel it necessary to add that afterward Grace and I went home to my place and polished off yet another bottle of the high-test on our own. It was already getting light when I finally went to sleep.

Dumb, I concluded, with another Easter liturgy to play at ten o'clock in the morning. But not as dumb as trying to play with a hangover. Gritting my teeth, I vowed if I lived, it was the first and only time I would pull that stunt.

I also left out of my email that part about the Undercroft protest strike. Grace and Marty were working on it. No sense, I thought, in worrying Rob until it became an issue.

Rob's email came within an hour of mine. I was right to exercise caution. Between the lines, I sensed he had been watching for it.

*A blessed Easter, sweetheart*, I read:

> I was worried all that playing over Holy Week had done you in, but then your email came through. How great to hear all is well.
>
> *Came the Boy Scouts to the rescue.* Turns out, my Easter hall-mates were looking for a service project and restoring the labyrinth seemed as good as any. By the time the troops cleared out late on Sunday, at least two-thirds of the paths were cleared of enough errant foliage to think about resetting the flagstones. So, although once again I'm on my own, the impossible is seeming considerably less ridiculous.
>
> I've already broken two shovels and a saw—necessitating a run into town for reinforcements. While I was at it I got a tetanus shot at the clinic thanks to a minor run-in with an axe. My friend who runs this place thinks I'm nuts. But then you know how much mowing it took to keep those modest paths cleared behind the rectory.
>
> I look forward to walking the finished labyrinth with you before we get appreciably older. I love you.

I couldn't reconcile my picture of him out there in the brambles with a gang of gung-ho adolescents, aching and covered with sweat—with the reality of another priest conducting worship in his church, on one of the holiest days of the church year. And yet, I searched his words in vain for a drop of self-pity.

Still, I must have sounded depressed when I shared Rob's travails with Marty after work on Monday. He listened, commiserated, then after rushing through dinner, disappeared for two hours.

When he finally staggered back, he was red in the face and drained an entire bottle of spring water in one sitting. Whatever he had been doing, it hadn't been playing with little Bart.

"You're going to pass out, Marty," I fretted. "What on earth have you been doing?".

"Tell Father Rob not to worry," he gasped. "We're . . . on top of it."

"It . . .?" I probed.

"His labyrinth. Out in back of the rectory . . . that crazy pedestrian dirt-track of his. I got Rutterbach to open up the hardware and help me. We laid down landscapers' cloth and started to mulch it. The whole darn thing—until we ran out of wood chips. Rutterbach's got an order for another load of free ground-up bark from the county. Enough to cover those paths at least six inches deep. By the time Rob gets back, the darn grass will be too *intimidated* to grow."

I laughed out loud, grateful for the depth of my young tenant's friendship. His sales calls around the area were proving to be the parish's best excuse—and mine—for keeping the precious contact with Rob going. Grace had already sent up a half a trunk-full of baked goods, ranging from home-made Easter bread to pies, brownies and cookies of every variety imaginable.

Late morning on the Tuesday after Easter I finally wandered back over to sanctuary to clean up the mess around the organ from Holy Week and try out a few pieces for the upcoming Sunday. My heart wasn't in it. I was barely two bars into a reedy little hymn prelude in the style of a *pastorale* when I heard the narthex door slam.

Barney repeatedly had promised to fix the creaky old mechanism, but I wasn't encouraging him. The racket it made was more effective than a watch dog.

Turning on the bench, I half expected to see Father Wills on one of his periodic inspect-the-troops tours. Instead, I saw a tall sweat-suit clad young man standing in the narthex . . . visibly hesitant about whether or not to come into the sanctuary itself.

"May I help you . . .?" I called out.

The visitor turned and stepped out of the shadows into the sunlit aisle of the sanctuary. With a shock I realized, *I knew him.*

"Ted . . .! What are you *doing* here?"

The young man's face tightened in a frown. "I'm not sure."

"If you're looking for your dad—"

"He's not here. I heard. I just stopped at the rectory and ran into this guy— "

"Father Wills."

Ted nodded. "Yeah. He says that dad is away on . . . some kind of . . . leave somewhere . . ."

"The retreat house on Lake Erie." I hesitated. "You . . . didn't know?"

"Know . . . *what*? That guy Wills was being pretty creepy. What in the heck is he doing in Dad's house?"

I told him. "The Diocese received a letter . . . accusing your dad and me of an affair. It was ugly enough to assume there could be more to come. Your dad was worried about the parish—decided it was best that he keep a low profile until things sort themselves out. I tried to resign, but your dad advised against it."

Ted paled, then his face turned a fiery red. He swore softly. "Who on earth would have—?"

He stopped. I didn't have to say a word. As the silence stretched out between us, a strange look of awareness spread over his features. It was amazing even in that light how much he resembled his dad. Still silent, I waited for the other shoe to drop.

"You don't suppose—dad doesn't think that . . . I sent that letter?"

"Did you . . .?"

"No, hell no." Ted ran a hand over his close-cropped hair. "If I thought for one minute, he believed that . . . I'd—"

"You'd what, Ted?"

"I need to see him. Now. He's got to know. I would . . . never . . . ever— "

By now it was obvious that the young man was telling the truth. He looked too distraught, too angry to believe otherwise. With an abrupt movement, Ted turned and let himself down heavily into the closest pew, his hands braced on the pew back in front of him. They were trembling.

Ted shook his head. "No wonder that . . . Wills guy was so . . .

weird."

Still, it was too much of a coincidence—Ted's coming here out of the blue like this. I had to know.

"Ted, why now . . .? What made you decide to come up here?"

For a split-second, he just looked at me. I could see the answer fomenting in his brain. It took a considerable passage of time to shake it loose.

"I spent Easter with mom," he said softly. "Just something . . . something about what she said, made me think the divorce was all but signed, sealed and delivered. Still, it got pretty. . . tense. I decided to make a detour on the drive back to Cleveland and get Dad's take on things— "

I needed every bit of my counselor's skill not to maneuver him the rest of the way into the corner. If Rob's suspicions and my intuitions were right, what possible purpose would it serve to force Ted to discredit his mother now? In front of me, of all people.

"Do you have a map in the car?" I said quietly.

"Map—?"

"A Pennsylvania road map. Preferably with a lot of detail, not just the interstates."

"Yeah . . ., of course. I guess so."

Ted made no move to go.

"If you get it," I said, "I can mark the route to the retreat house. It's along the lakeshore but a bit off the beaten track."

When Ted still sat there on the pew—unmoving, I took a chance. Cautiously I eased over and laid a hand on his shoulder. The young man stiffened as if I had struck him.

"I understand how . . . awkward it is. But I'm sure, Ted, your father would be . . . glad to see you. Really glad. The last weeks have been— "

At that he stood. In the process he shook off my hand—rude on the surface of it, but clearly unintentional. His furtive eye contact smacked of embarrassment not hostility.

"Sorry. I'll go get the map."

Heart pounding, I watched him go. It was only when the narthex door whipped shut behind him that I realized I had been holding my breath.

The seconds ticked past, then minutes. Where on earth had Ted parked? Eventually he returned, an atlas in hand.

"This way's a little longer," I told him. "But you'll save time in the long run."

With a fingertip I traced a series of secondary roads feeding on and off the interstate that led to the lakeshore. My awkward stream-of-consciousness directions must have been tough to follow but Ted nodded, letting me know he understood. He frowned, obviously calculating something in his head.

"Driving time?"

"About two hours. Maybe less."

"Thanks. I appreciate this."

I hesitated. "Tell him . . . give him my best, will you . . .?"

I extended my hand. Without making eye contact, Ted shook it.

"I interrupted your practicing," he said uncertainly.

"No problem. I was finished anyway."

One thing was clear. After what just transpired, I wasn't about to go back to it. My thoughts were racing a mile a minute, my concentration shot to heck. After Ted left, I finished cleaning up the random music strewn around the organ console and got ready to head home.

To my surprise, when I got outside, I noticed that Ted was still sitting in his car parked in front of the rectory. If he wanted to make it to the retreat house before the mid-afternoon commuter traffic started clogging those secondary roads, he had better get going.

But then I had decisions of my own to make. To email or not email? In the end, I trusted my instincts to let Ted's pending visit remain unannounced. I crossed the street behind Ted's car and headed home the long way.

He still appeared to be studying that map. I don't think he even noticed I was out there.

Rob's email showed up around midnight. I knew because I was on-line, writing to him when it came. Clicking my way into the in-box, I highlighted the Sender-line and waited for the message to down-load.

> Sweetheart. It's late. You're probably sound asleep but I needed to get this off my chest. Ted showed up. But then you know that.
>
> Suffice it to say, my son was confused and furious and afraid I blamed him for the fiasco with the Diocese.

We settled that in the first two seconds.

I'm not sure who is prodigal in this particular parable, but after that the two of us spent the last few hours of daylight hauling flagstones—not bad as bonding experiences go. At the moment Ted's asleep in the cell of a room next door. I wasn't about to let him drive back to Cleveland tonight.

He didn't elaborate much on what you told him, but reading between the lines, you must have been incredible when Ted showed up in the sanctuary. In the dead of night and way too many miles away, I again find myself thanking you for giving me back my son. It took a lot of tears and shouting, but he understands his mother is ill. As a recovering alcoholic, I am not claiming some monopoly on virtue here either.

What you don't know, is that after he left you, Ted went back and talked to Wills. I gather he gave the guy quite an earful, none of which fit with the stereotypes someone might have been tempted to cultivate about either you or me after that letter showed up. I told him it took a lot of courage for him to do that. It is a touching thing when a son becomes adult enough to care whether or not his dad is happy. He genuinely likes you, Char—knows how much you have changed me, have changed my life. There's still a mountain of hurt to shovel our way through, but we've made a healthy start. I ache for you, sweetheart, more with every passing day. Feel loved.

I clicked the Print option, read the email again. By the third time through, my face was wet with tears.

Midnight or not, I picked up the phone. Going on autopilot, I punched in the familiar number.

# ✣ Chapter Twenty-five

When the phone rang the sixth time, it finally occurred to me to look at my watch. *Twelve-eighteen.* My oldest would have been in bed hours ago. I half-contemplated hanging up when I heard someone pick up the receiver.

"Jen . . ., it's mom." I said.

"Mom . . .! What's wrong? We got your Easter package with the stuff for the kids—thanks." She fumbled briefly with the receiver. "But you . . . it's after midnight."

"I've . . . I haven't wanted to worry you. But I just . . .can't any more. It's been awful. Rob has asked to be placed on personal leave. Very worst case scenario, he could lose his job . . ."

"Why, for goodness sakes?

"*Us.*"

The alarm in Jen's voice had ratcheted up considerably. "Mom, slow down! Back up—."

By fits and starts, I explained, with my rambling confessional punctuated by terse questions from my daughter. Eventually, the lay of the land became less obscure.

"Why . . . why didn't you tell me?" Jen whispered. "I'll be up there in the morning."

"You can't . . .! Your job— "

"Forget the job. I've got personal time. Mom, I'm coming. Now, try to get some sleep."

It was like telling a waterfall to stop falling. But after what seemed like hours wide-awake staring out at the darkness, I must have finally dozed off. At first light, I woke to the sound of the doorbell, interspersed with a rhythmic hammering on the door itself. Grabbing my robe from the foot of my bed, I shuffled downstairs in my bare feet.

There on the front porch stood Jen, hair tousled, devoid of makeup, bleary-eyed with concern and lack of sleep. I opened the door and she flew into my arms, almost knocking me over.

"Mom . . ., you're barefoot. For crying out loud—you'll get pneumonia."

I couldn't help it. I lost it. Half laughing, half crying, I let her drag me into the living room and deposit me in my favorite wing chair.

"Coffee. I'll make it. You? Sit . . .!"

I sat. From the kitchen, I heard her banging around looking for what she needed.

"Sugar? Cream?"

"You're kidding . . .! Have you taken a look at my waistline lately?"

Jen popped her head out of the kitchen door. "Mom, thin isn't everything! Apparently Rob likes you the way you are."

*Odd as compliments go, but well meant.* I took the steaming mug she offered me, warming myself on the feel of the stoneware between my hands.

"Mom, Sarah and I have been thoughtless . . . awful. That's over now."

"You haven't been awful. Just busy, concerned that I was making a . . . foolish choice. I understand— "

"Well, I don't. You've always been there for us. And the first time in your life you start thinking about what *you* want and not what everybody else needs, where are . . . *we, your family,* prepared to support you?"

"You were here at New Year's. You made an effort to get to know Rob. I couldn't ask for more."

"Well, I could have given a heck of a lot more, without your asking. Think about it, mom. For the first time since Dad died, you were trying to be happy under very fraught and difficult circumstances. Not for us. Not for the grandkids. For you. And we just show up and chuck you under the chin like some funny uncle, and go back to business as usual."

"Jen, I think you're being rather hard on— "

"I should have told you how glad I was for you. I should have looked for ways to show Rob we wanted him to be part of our family.

And that's just exactly what I intend to do."

The sting of tears told me I was headed for a major meltdown. Closing my eyes didn't seem to help. By now the coffee was sloshing in my mug, scalding hot and dangerously near the rim.

"Oh . . . shit . . .!" I muttered.

"Mom . . .! You're gonna kill yourself. Here, let me!"

Dropping to her knees alongside my chair, Jen took the mug out of my trembling hands like a psychiatrist disarming a deranged patient. I let her. When she set down the mug and awkwardly tried to hug me, I gave in to that as well.

"Mom, what can we do? There has to be something."

I told her just enough about what had happened to let her know where things stood. Under the circumstances, the Diocese was being more than supportive. We were just going to have to wait and see what Rob's friend Barry is able to do on the legal front.

"Mom, when did you last see him—Rob?"

"Not quite a month."

Unfurling the paper napkin Jen had brought with her when she served the coffee, I blew my nose. The threat of a potential emotional shipwreck seemed to be subsiding.

"Mom, we're going up there."

I just looked at her. My daughter's forehead scrunched into a frown.

"Where did you say that retreat place is?"

"North. Two hours from here. On the Erie lakeshore. But really, Jen, politically. . . really I don't think it's— "

"Don't think. For once in your life, don't think. Just go!"

I knew it was futile to argue when her chin jutted out like that. She looked like she did when she was thirteen and spoiling for a fight, as only daughters can.

"And Mom, I'll drive. In the shape you're in, you'd wind up wrapped around a tree somewhere."

When I gave in, nodded my assent, the decision had more to do with loving my daughter than how reasonable I thought her idea was. *A scary business, letting yourself be loved,* I decided. But then was it any odder than Rob, out there in the middle of some bramble patch, letting his son help him move a ton of flagstones.

As ethical human beings we can become so obsessed with how blessed it is to *give*, that we forget how—or even, why—to *receive.* I had been there, done that and I was tired of the tee-shirt. Whatever a relationship based solely on giving may be, *it isn't love.*

Rob had challenged me to let myself be loved. It was time we both took that advice.

*Forget the mistakes and become the music.* While Jen waited in the front hall, I ran upstairs and threw on jeans and a sweater, tossed a change of clothes, hairbrush and makeup in an overnight bag. My daughter was right. The balance in my life had been out of kilter so long, I truly believed I was standing on level ground. It was time to stop limping and start living.

"I'll be right down," I called to her from the landing.

My daughter looked up at me. She was smiling.

It seems road trips were becoming milestones of sorts in my life—unsettling, though not necessarily unwelcome for all the changes that seemed to come in their wake. I was thinking partly of that fateful trek West with Marty in the moving van and partly too of my ambivalent junket with Rob to Pittsburgh.

And here I was, on the road again, not at all sure how I got there. This time it was alongside one of my grown daughters hell bent on abetting my transformation to a woman for whom "love" abruptly had moved up in rank-order before "motherhood" in my emotional vocabulary.

Jen had settled in behind the wheel, clocking off the miles to the retreat house with what seemed like a heck of a lot more chutzpah than I would have mustered under the circumstances. At loose ends, I tried to keep my mind off everything that possibly could go wrong with this little outing of hers by engineering some major transformations of my own with blush and lash lengthener. No easy business even on terra firma.

"I'd . . . love to get my hands on the . . . genius who apparently decided to cut . . . pothole repair out the state budget." With my teeth clenched I tried to brace myself as we maneuvered around yet another gigantic crater in the asphalt. "This is ridiculous . . . !"

"Do you want me to pull over, Mom? I can, you know. There's a rest-stop coming up ahead."

"Thanks. I'll manage."

*Sheer bravado.* If I wasn't careful, I was going to wind up looking like one of those racoons splayed out as road kill along the shoulder. *Lovely.*

Hands shaking, I made one last ditch effort to use highlighter to improve on my technique with the mascara. Against all odds, this time the results were marginally better.

"Finally." I snapped shut the case to the eye shadow and called it good. "Up from the grave she arose— "

"Atta girl, Mom!"

A low whistle of approval followed that pronouncement. Startled, I stopped trying to stuff my cosmetic bag back into my purse. Out of the corner of my eye, I caught my daughter watching me—half amused and half uncertain what to make of my wildly fluctuating mood.

"And to think," I sighed and shook my head, "you used to be grossed out at even the *idea* of my having a love life."

Jen chuckled. "Live with it, Mom. You spent a decade railing at Sarah and me for chasing everything in pants. Hard for anyone to put that together with good old mom getting it on with some guy, ya gotta admit."

"Was I really all that hard on you two?"

"Hard enough. But then as near as we could tell, you never seemed to let guys within ten feet of you— "

"A bit of an exaggeration."

"Seriously, Mom—either you were the most discreet single mom on the planet, some kind of nun or— "

"A starry-eyed idealist holding out for the love of my life?" I shrugged. "For all I know, there could have been other men like Rob out there. If I was looking, I wasn't really seeing. Goodness knows, he called me on it quick enough. Question was, was I finally ready to stop playing super-woman and let someone love me."

Jen looked pained. Like that spin on things was not quite what she had hoped or expected.

"Touché," she muttered. "If it's any consolation, my Jason keeps saying the same thing—followed by a pointed reminder that I am *not* his mother. Why is it so . . . darn hard to get out of that role once you're typecast in it?"

"You're asking me? At least in my case, something pretty darn drastic. Try unemployment, early retirement and a trip down memory lane that reminds you just how far off the track the old train seemed to have wandered."

"Rob understands all that?"

"Lived it. His own version, anyway."

I told her if not all of his life history, then at least the high and low points—starting with his mom pushing him my direction all those years ago, his booze-driven marriage, his daughter's death, and my run-in with Karin in Pittsburgh. Jen listened without comment to my rambling narrative. Her reaction, when it finally came, revolved around the *now* not the *then*.

"Did his ex . . . do you think it was Karin who sent that letter to the Diocese, Mom?"

"Likely. Yes. But Rob hasn't come out and said so. Apparently he doesn't need or want to know, and I've got to respect that. There was no signature."

"And if in the end the Diocese sends him somewhere else?"

"What will I do?" My chest felt tight. "I don't know. We both love this place, it's home."

"Would Rob . . . give up the priesthood . . .?"

"It has taken him a lifetime to find his calling, Jen. I don't know. But one thing is certain. I would never expect that."

There was a lot, I had to admit with a shock, I didn't know. *A scary thought.*

I was used to living alone, controlling how much I let myself want from life. My choices were just that—my choices. In this strange new world of love and relationships, I was becoming painfully aware how very different, how complex things became when you factored words like *yours* and *mine* into the mix.

Deciphering the state map Jen had jammed in the glove compartment was just about as arcane and puzzling. I had never been to the Kerygma retreat house, but I vaguely remembered pictures from a brochure tacked to the bulletin board in the narthex at Nativity.

Red brick and limestone buildings nestled on a high outcrop of land along the shimmering waters of Lake Erie, bounded on three sides by a decaying fieldstone fence. Apparently some of the considerable acreage was being rented out and farmed. There was a photo of wide open vistas of prairie grasses and a beautiful stand of birch and evergreens.

Unless I had gravely miscalculated, the complex was just up ahead. In the distance across a recently sprouted field of winter wheat glistening in the sun, I could see a cluster of mismatched structures that more or less resembled those in that crumpled flyer. Jen clicked on the turn signal and just when I thought she was going to ease the car through the half-dismantled fieldstone gate, she instead pulled off on the shoulder. Stopped.

The motor was still running. As I turned in her direction, I noticed my daughter was just sitting there behind the wheel, staring straight ahead off into the distance.

"Car problems, honey . . .?"

She shook her head. "We're fine."

Shifting in her seat, she made eye contact. For a split-second she had that same fierce and determined look she had on her face that day I walked her down the aisle. My little girl, a woman now, stepping off into an unknown future.

"You two are going to want time together," she said. "But first and foremost, I want you both to know that Sarah and I support you a thousand percent in whatever you do. I'm telling you that. I need to tell Rob that as well."

I felt a sudden tightening in my chest—the gut response of a parent unexpectedly thrust into a major role reversal with their offspring. Jen obviously had been rehearsing this little pep talk, meant every word of it.

"I . . . appreciate that, honey. And I'm sure Rob will, too."

"Will he think we, Sarah and I, are being pushy . . . messing with things that are none of our business?"

"I think he'll sense you're loving kids who are trying to be there for their parent. And how could anyone fault you for that?"

"Good," Jen nodded.

I fought a smile. For all her take-charge aura, my oldest was far more anxious about setting the record straight than she had seemed to be.

Chewing on her lower lip, she slipped the car back into gear and turned into the winding road leading up to what had to be the main administrative building and commissary of the retreat house. At the far end of the huge and all-but-empty parking lot, I saw Rob's Hummer nosed into a stall. Rob himself was nowhere in sight.

Cutting the engine, Jen stretched the kinks out of her back. As she fished under the seat for her purse, she stopped long enough to glance my way.

"Do you want to go on ahead, Mom?"

I smiled. "Let's go together. I really have no idea where the office is. But then there seems to be posted signs."

As we debated, I noticed a wisp of a man around Rob's age in jeans and a plaid flannel shirt had appeared on the front porch and was looking our way. I took the lead, with Jen close behind, toward the wide staircase leading to the massive central doors.

"You lost . . . or retreating?" the stranger called out to us.

Both, I was half-tempted to say. But my daughter beat me to it.

"Neither," Jen said. "We're looking for Father Rob . . .!"

"Out back. Hauling rocks. Be careful, or you'll wind up getting roped into manual labor yourselves."

"I'm Jen and this is my mom, Char Howard. She's a friend of Rob's and I'm along for the ride."

"Father Tom Gillespie. Welcome to Kerygma House."

It could have been my imagination, but when Jen mentioned my name, I thought I caught a look of recognition flash across the priest's face. He started down the staircase in our direction.

"Why don't I walk you back there? I need the exercise."

"Great," Jen said.

Together the three of us walked around the side of the rambling brick structure and its afterthought out-buildings. The unfettered view beyond it was breathtaking—a lush sea of greens rolling placidly outward toward the glistening waters of Lake Erie. Off to our left, Father Gillespie pointed out an odd little hillock, topped by a dense knot of trees.

"The Peace Grove, though a week ago, you'd have never known it. Rob has been pretty much moving heaven and earth to restore a labyrinth up there."

Through the trees, I caught a flash of movement. *Rob.* It had to be. As we drew closer, I could tell he was in the process of leveling a huge flagstone with the help of several crowbars.

"Hey, Sims!" Father Gillespie shouted. "Company— "

The sun was behind us. I saw Rob straighten and shield his eyes, trying to pick out just who his friend had in tow.

"Char . . .!"

He had already laid down his tools and was making his way briskly down the hillside in our direction. Leaving my companions behind me, I helped close the distance between us. He looked thinner but tanned, fit. Despite my misgivings, hard physical labor, it seems, was just what the doctor ordered.

"Char, what on earth are you . . .?"

"Surprise—!"

I barely had time to get the word out before he swept me into his arms. Laughing, I felt my feet leave the ground momentarily—the abandon of a child twirling in the spring sunshine.

"Been lifting weights, I see."

Rob laughed. "You look . . . gorgeous."

"Better than I did a couple of hours ago. Jen came up to Hope to visit, took one look and decided I needed some R-'n-R."

"Post-Easter stress. It'll do it to a guy every time— "

"Try missing you."

"Ditto— "

The rest was lost in the gentle touch of his mouth on mine. It was painfully brief—we had an audience. But I read the unmistakable promise of more to come in his smile.

"Okay, you two, break it up . . .!"

Jen had joined us on the hillside. She extended her hand Rob's way, then changed her mind and opted for a hug.

"I haven't seen Mom smile like that all day," she told him.

"Why do I think I owe you one for engineering this little field trip?"

My daughter blushed. "Guilty."

"Although, penance in this case is totally unnecessary. I'd call your jaunt up here a stroke of genius."

Jen's laughter faded. "I'm . . . I was shocked, saddened to hear what happened, with that letter."

"All in all, I've been pretty fortunate. Both the parish and the Diocese have been nothing but supportive. But thank you."

"Are . . . is this likely to—?"

"End badly?" Rob shrugged. "It's unlikely I'd lose my job over this. More likely, I would wind up in another parish."

"Would you . . . go?"

I didn't know where to look first, at my daughter's face or Rob's. Leave it to a child, even an adult one, to ask the difficult or unanswerable. I was about to protest when Rob broke in.

"Hope is home. I don't think anything would be served by running away from the situation." He stopped. "I've got to believe at the end of the day, the Diocese won't go that route. Nativity was priestless for five years before I came."

The bunch of us settled down around a battered old wooden table in the retreat house dining hall for coffee and sandwiches. Father Gillespie regaled us with stories of "retreaters" he had known over the years. Rob had slid into the folding chair next to mine and though I couldn't see his face, I felt his presence. There were no overt gestures of intimacy. Yet from time to time, we reached for a glass or pitcher at the same time, laughing as our hands brushed and touched.

Across from us, I could see the awareness tempered with caution in my daughter's eyes. If I had to peg Father Gillespie's mood, for all the hail-fellow conversation, it was guarded too, even sad. He and Rob, I learned, had been friends for a long time, back in the Pittsburgh days.

In the afternoon, Rob planned to show us the labyrinth. Curious, Jen peppered him with questions about both the spiritual dimensions of the devotional practice and the technical logistics for restoring the one at the retreat house.

When his cell phone rang, Rob frowned, mid-sentence into a description of his strategy for resetting the massive limestone slabs.

"Hold that thought." He was already on his feet, phone in hand, squinting to read the caller ID in the glaring sunlight. "This is Ted. I probably ought to get this."

Identifying himself, he listened while the caller did the same. All the while he was moving out of range of our conversation, but not quick enough for me to miss his sharp intake of breath and verbal response to whatever it was the caller had shared with him.

"Ted. I'm so . . . God, I'm so very sorry."

Rob's face grew still. His knuckles white with the effort, he clutched at the case of his cell phone while his son poured out his heart on the other end of the line.

"Just tell me what you want me to do. Anything. I promise you."

Silence. Rob looked slowly down at his watch.

"I understand. It's a four-plus-hour drive from here. I'll start within the hour, stop off in Hope to talk to Father Wills, so calculate forward from there."

Hand shaking, Rob hit the End button. The way we were standing, I was glad my daughter and Gillespie couldn't see his face.

"Rob . . . what is it?"

"She's dead, Char."

She? I could think of only one possibility that would have fit Rob's reaction.

"Karin."

"She drove her sports car into a bridge abutment—midnight or thereabouts. Apparently massive head and internal injuries. The first responders couldn't do a thing."

"Oh, Rob, *no*!"

Instinct told me to go to him. But something in his face stopped me. Eyes wide and not totally comprehending, my daughter had been standing there watching the both of us.

"But how . . .?" Jen breathed. "How in the world would anyone know to look for you in this godforsaken—?"

Rob managed a wan smile. "My son. Ted said the identification in his mother's wallet listed him as an emergency contact. Apparently he jumped in the car middle of the night and drove to Pittsburgh. I promised him. . . well, you heard . . ."

"Of course, you have to go," I said, finding my voice at last. "Is he—is Ted . . .?"

"Coping."

There was more. "Char, Ted decided he wants the funeral at Nativity. And he wants me to officiate. He already spoke with the Bishop's secretary and has an appointment within the hour."

Rob didn't have to tell me how bizarre or desperate the request was, or what an untenable position it would put Rob in if he were to honor it. Forget the fact that I was the church's only organist.

I took a deep breath. "What are you going to . . . do?"

"Unless the Bishop and Father Wills object?" Rob's voice was hard as flint. "God help me, I'm going to conduct that service."

# Chapter Twenty-six

Questions and tears, the reality of grief would come later. For now life seemed to be carrying us forward filmstrip fashion—frame after frame lurching awkwardly ahead into the unknown. While Gillespie helped Rob collect his belongings, my daughter and I stood on the porch of the retreat house and wrestled with the logistics.

There were three of us and two vehicles. Jen was determined that I keep Rob company on his trip back to Hope. I wasn't about to let her make that drive alone.

"Halfway," I said finally. "I'll start off in the Hummer and we can switch at a rest-stop around the halfway point."

Rob just listened without comment. *In shock*, I decided, understandable enough under the circumstances. And so we set off, caravan fashion with Jen out front and Rob and I following a cautious distance behind in the Hummer.

Our glorious sunshine was gone, pushed aside by a front that brought with it a bleak, sullen gray sky and the smell of rain. Silent and ram-rod stiff, Rob sat with his hands clamped tight on the wheel, battling the gusts.

I had seen him this shut up inside himself only once before. My heart sank as I remembered. It was months ago alone together in the undercroft, when he was moving heaven and earth to put emotional distance between us—Rob, the married priest, and the woman I had become, the woman who had learned to love him.

There was no safe way to reach out, given his mood. But I had to try.

"Did Ted . . . when did your son hear about the accident?"

"Early this morning. A witness called it in just after midnight. In that convertible of hers neither one of them, she or Sean, had a chance. They aren't really sure who was driving."

"Rob, I wish there were something I could say to— "

"This was always a possibility." He exhaled sharply. "Still, if and when it actually comes . . ."

"Was Ted . . . how did he—?"

"Half in shock. Angry. Shaken. But I'll hand it to him, he grabbed hold of himself, the situation—had the presence of mind to come up with the name of the funeral home where we . . . the one we used for his sister . . ."

"That kind of thing can stick in your memory. Hard as you try to forget."

"When they asked him about arrangements, it seems Ted got on the phone and rousted Wills out of bed at the rectory. He told him flat out what he wanted and that he expected Wills to make it happen. That he was prepared to go to the Bishop, what ever it took to make it possible for me to officiate at that service."

"It's human to want closure. The three of you together, for better or worse, one last— "

"A heck of a way to create the illusion of family."

"He loves you, Rob."

"I know. Thank God for that."

His hands flexed on the wheel, agitated, impatient even. Time was passing and we were here cooped up in the Hummer, in this frustrating no-man's-land. Not where he needed to be.

"I told Ted I'd stop off at the rectory," Rob said. "Thrash things out with Wills. By dark I should be meeting Ted in Pittsburgh."

"I could go with you if— "

"No. Not necessary. I can't ask that of you. And if you're thinking about playing the funeral, that's . . . *absolutely* out of the question. We'll scare up an organist in Bartonville."

Silent, trying desperately not to overreact, I stared out the windshield. I could understand Rob wanting to be alone with his son, understand wanting to spare me the terrible awkwardness of participating in that funeral. But there was more at stake here than just finding someone to play that service.

"Don't you see, it completes the circle?" I told him. " Rob, I *have to do it—have to play that service. Want to.* I'm certain Ted expects that. If I don't, your son will never forgive me. More to the point, I wouldn't forgive myself."

"This is *not* open for discussion. It stops here and now, this . . . whole business. I've been unfair to you—dragging you into this mess. *No more.*"

He bit off the words, syllable by syllable, with the intensity of a quarterback calling out play numbers, leaving no doubt in the world who was in charge. It was a side of Rob I had never seen before, determined and unrelenting. With a rising sense of alarm, I tried not to respond in kind.

"I'm a big girl, Rob. You can't protect me from life. I don't want or expect that. Life is messy. Relationships are messy. "

"True enough. But there are some things that appear to defy redemption. And this, yet another *misguided* attempt to get my life under control, is one of them. The body count is rising and anyone with a grain of sense would know when it's time to just . . . hang it up."

My heart froze. *I hadn't imagined it.* Something was horribly wrong and I needed to figure out what, before one or the other of us said something we would regret.

"You don't really . . . believe that," I said softly.

Rob shot a glance in my direction. His face had the look of a man staring into the abyss.

"Right now, I'm not sure what I believe."

*Take nothing for granted. Life is fragile. Precious.*

That desperate little litany kept replaying itself in my head. My daughter and I began this day with one set of expectations and suddenly we found ourselves somewhere else entirely.

"What are you trying to tell me, Rob? Because if it's what I think it is— "

"I love you. I'm telling you to get out while you can. And if *you* won't walk away from this . . .!"

He left the rest unsaid. *Then he would* . . .! It was about as brutal as a brush-off can possibly get. Like a slap in the face, unambiguous.

Through the shock, my hurt and anger, I told myself this was his guilt talking—guilt and a despair deeper than anything I had ever experienced. I had not tried to stop my husband when he went off to war those many decades ago, putting my life on the line along with his own. I was not about to make that same mistake twice.

"You expect me just to turn my back, leave you to face all of this . . . *alone*? Rob, I am *not* going anywhere."

"I can't . . . won't be responsible for trashing your life."

"*My life*—!" My voice broke but steadied again. "Decades alone, without passion and commitment, without even the courage to risk it. Bland as oatmeal, drowning in a sea of it— "

"Sweetheart, Char, please try to understand— "

"Believe me, I do. I understand guilt and what it can do. Say what you will, I can't regret loving you. No matter how it ends. And if it ends here . . . *if that's what this is about* . . . then yes, *you* are going to have to do it. We may make our choices for all the wrong reasons, struggle over the consequences of our folly for a lifetime—awful, but human. But if anything the last few hours should have taught us, life is short and in the end, only love— "

"Remains? Would it were so."

I clenched my hands into fists in my lap, willing them to stop shaking. Rob stared straight ahead out the windshield.

"Where, Rob? Where is the integrity, the principle in throwing away warmth, intimacy, even the simple need to connect?" I said. " I tried that most of my adult life. You asked me once if avoidance and denial worked for me. They didn't then. They don't now."

My timing was working against a response. A truck was passing us on a steep and winding hill with a wide load. Out of the corner of my eye, I caught the hard set of Rob's jaw as he concentrated on holding the Hummer in our lane.

"I've been a party to destroying one life, Char. You don't deserve that. From Day One I promised you I'd never hurt you—just another vow I've broken, repeatedly, ever since we met."

"But you haven't— "

"No. Whatever face you put on the past twelve months, it's true. You know it is. I've put you through hell. Hope is your home, you belong here. I'm going to ask the Diocese to transfer me. It's over."

The wake from the passing semi hit us in that moment, an ominous rush of sound and energy that shook the vehicle like a leaf in a summer storm. And yet not half the force of the shock-wave those words set in motion.

Rain had begun to fall, hard and persistent. It was only then I noticed the radio was on, tuned to Public Radio and the music of Copland's "Appalachian Spring". Numb and shaken, I listened as the Hummer's windshield wipers beat out the rhythm of the piece like the steady motion of a conductor's baton.

Ta-ta-thwack, ta-ta-thwack-a. *'Tis a gift to be simple. Tis a gift to be free.*

"You . . . *really* . . . *mean* it." My mouth felt stiff. "You're ending this."

It wasn't a question. Still, Rob's silence gave me an answer.

The branches of the oaks along the roadway seemed to be reaching skyward in mute appeal, the neon green of their leaves a garish reminder of that first hopeful flowering of spring. Tears had begun to trail down my face, hot and stinging. I closed my eyes.

Dark-shaped images welled up, the vacant stare of the rectory windows looking back at me, row after row of taut-to-breaking warp threads stretched across a loom as rigid as the metal shafts of the organ pipes rearing up in front of me. I was seeing my life without him—devoid of joy and music and the reassuring whisper of my name in the night.

"Char, you'll thank me for this, trust me."

I laughed, more an anguished cry. "Believe that," I said, "if you have to. I don't for a minute."

There was nothing more to say. The landscape sped past in a dizzying blur, isolated houses and endless stretches of woods and marshland. Out ahead of us, I watched my daughter expertly navigating the curving and narrow roadway while in the Hummer, the silence grew more formidable and ominous with every passing mile.

The rest stop, our agreed-upon rendezvous point, had come upon us without my noticing it. Rob was already maneuvering into the parking lot. As he eased the Hummer into the stall alongside my daughter's waiting car, he didn't cut the engine. Instead, he stared straight ahead out the windshield at the sheets of rain washing across the glass.

"Y-you . . . you're just going to leave things like this?"

At that, Rob shifted enough in his seat that I could see his face. Pale and drawn, his eyes red-rimmed with grief, the love and longing I heard in his words cut me to the heart.

"Char . . . I . . . for what it's worth, this is the hardest thing I ever had to do. I love you. Always will."

I choked back a sob. Whatever it took, I was not going to let him see me fall apart. Fumbling with the door latch, I managed to stumble from the Hummer and shut the door awkwardly behind me. I didn't look back.

Hand on Jen's car door, I heard the sound of the Hummer behind me, shifting into reverse. By the time I settled in the front seat alongside my daughter and engaged the seat belt, Rob was gone.

"Mom, what in the world—? You look like death!"

Jen was staring at me, eyes wide and questioning, her hand on the ignition key. The tears had dried on my face. It felt stiff, like a lacquered mask stretched over a mold. I forced a smile.

"Probably."

"Weren't we going to—? Rob just . . . left."

"Yes."

I saw my daughter's brows tighten into a single line, read the unspoken questions there. There was no sense avoiding the inevitable.

"It's over, Jen. He . . . Rob broke it off."

"You and he . . . just like that? Did he tell you, why?"

"Guilt. An ugly mountain of it."

"He blames himself for Karin's death—?"

"For starters."

"And so he's crawling off like he did to that retreat place. Penance. All of it self-imposed, like one of those medieval monks flagellating himself, and for *what*? And in the process not just hurting himself, but you . . ."

I found my hand straying to that tiny medallion at my throat. *Saint Cecilia—martyred rather than give herself to a suitor.* But then it wasn't the intent of Rob's gift to me to remind me of that woman's choices. It was his inscription, the love behind it engraved there, the letters barely traceable under my fingertips.

*Love. Always.* Choosing my words carefully, I forced myself to project a calm I did not feel.

"Rob doesn't see it that way. He gave me the chance to walk away and when I refused, in his eyes he's only trying to save me from myself."

"Mom, you don't deserve this . . .!"

"Funny, that's just what he said."

"Typical take-charge, I-know-what's-best-for-you . . . alpha male . . . *jerk* . . .!"

At that I laughed, couldn't help myself. Though to my chagrin the sound trailed off in a sob.

"How easy it would be if only that were true, Jen. Then I could have stuck out my chin and resorted to a shouting match to shame him into realizing how ridiculous it was."

"But you didn't."

"No."

"So, what are you going to do?"

I flinched. "Tell him I love him. Pray for both our sakes he exorcizes whatever demons are eating away at him."

Even to me that scenario sounded feeble, an exercise in futility. But it was as far as I was prepared to go without losing it. Distracted, still caught up in what I had told her, Jen ground the transmission but managed to get the car in gear.

"And if he doesn't?" she said. "If he doesn't come to his senses?"

"I hang on long enough to play Karin's funeral, if Rob will even permit it. Then start looking for another job. If Rob leaves that parish, I simply can't chain myself to that organ bench until I'm too feeble and addled to care. Then, too, it's very possible they would simply close the church. Without a priest again . . . I just don't know how they'd kept it going."

Jen's hands tightened on the wheel. "You're kidding. You're just going to sit there in that sanctuary looking straight at the guy and playing his wife's funeral as if none of this mattered."

"Tough, I'll admit. But you just go on autopilot and do it. Rob's in the same boat, after all. Worse. Under the best of circumstances, it's unusual for a close family member to conduct a funeral. Rob's son must have been pretty darn persuasive."

*Best of circumstances* was hardly a term that came to mind when I thought about what had been happening at Nativity during the past month. I shivered.

"You're cold, Mom. Do you want me to turn off the air conditioning?"

"I'm fine. Just tired."

As lies went, it was so outrageous that at first, Jen didn't even dignify it with a response. I could hear the rising anger in her voice, looking for someone or something to blame.

"Mom, how could he? You loved that man . . ."

"Love. Present tense. Hard as that may be to believe."

Good old Jen, my first-born, always the counselor, probing for the truth of where things stood—an argument for the power of the gene pool if I ever saw it. I could have hugged her, but then the rain was falling harder now and traffic was heavy. She had her hands full.

I clicked on the radio, heard the familiar strains of a Brandenburg Concerto spilling out over the airwaves, cutting in and out the way stations do in our part of the world. Foothills have a nasty habit of rearing up out of nowhere to block the signal. I strained for a while to piece together what I was hearing, but the musical theme, hence the concerto number, eluded me.

*Give it up.* A cautious probing of the radio dial turned up nothing but announcers intoning the ethical virtues of family and abstinence, dark country tunes about lost loves or hard rock rhythms that struck in the cramped confines of the front seat with the relentless fury of hammer blows. Out of synch with road sounds and the windshield wipers, at that.

Again I hit the Power button. The silence was even more unsettling.

"Put yourself in Rob's place, Jen," I said. "Imagine yourself days, weeks at the most from signing the divorce papers, still blaming yourself for the failure. And then after all the pain and anger that went into the settlement, suddenly everything's moot. Senseless. Violent. Final. How would you feel under the circumstances?"

"Tough to live with."

"Exactly."

"But Mom, it's not . . . fair. That man loved you."

"Still does."

Jen had begun to let out a muffled stream of expletives, choked and fitful, like the rain coursing down the windshield. They seemed fueled by frustration more than anger—a sense of helplessness and the knowledge that solutions are often anything but simple and in the end may be no resolution at all.

The landmarks around us were becoming more familiar now. I saw the still-boarded-up farm market standing forlorn and badly in need of a paint job, awaiting the first influx of local produce. At the pump-your-own gas station, someone had tied down the mountains of soda cartons with cord and mismatched tarps to fend off the rain.

In Hope the streets were rain-swept, littered with small branches and matted clumps of half-opened buds from the canopy of trees overhead. Triggered by the prematurely darkening sky, porch lights and an occasional street light flickered in the eerie half-light.

"You'd better keep right on going," I said as my daughter swung the car into the driveway. "We're likely to get another downpour before the night is out."

By way of an answer, Jen cut the ignition and started to open the door. "I'll head back in the morning. I'm not leaving you alone tonight."

"Not necessary. Really, I'm fine. Your husband is holding down the fort all alone down there."

"He'll manage."

"So will I."

Another lie. But they were becoming easier now. As the evening wore on and the phone didn't ring, I almost fooled myself into believing it could be true.

Marty was on the road on a sales swing through Ohio. Jen and I were alone. The two of us worked side by side putting together a modest supper, then settled down together in the living room staring at the empty fireplace and making small talk. Anything but revisit the 'biggies' still out there. Starting with, *what's next?*

I saw the question in my daughter's face. It took a while for it to surface.

"Something wrong, honey . . .?"

"Just thinking We talked about this once before, Mom. But I still think it's important— "

Jen hesitated. "I know I probably sound like a shrink, but looking back, what has meant the most to you? What have you wanted most in your life? Truly wanted."

As I wracked my brains to remember that earlier conversation, I drew a blank. A frown had begun to settle in between my brows and I found myself rummaging through the attic of my memories for a response.

"I wanted to have a family. To work at something that lets me feel needed, useful—that uses my gifts."

"And?"

"Health. I suppose everybody wants that. Enough money to be comfortable or at least not worry about winding up under a bridge somewhere. Then too I keep hoping my hands hold out so I can go on playing the organ without the fear of carpal tunnel surgery."

"And . . .?"

I was starting to become vaguely annoyed at my daughter for slipping into her social worker mode. Where on earth was she headed with this Grand Inquisition of hers?

"And so far, so good. Most of the time anyway."

"You lost Daddy."

"No one expects or wants that."

"And all those years alone, you never wanted to find someone again?"

"I wasn't afraid to be alone."

"Maybe . . .," Jen started to say something, stopped. "Has it ever occurred to you, it might have been the other way around?"

"That I'm afraid of another *relationship*, you mean?" I bristled at the thought. "What about Rob—about everything we've been going through . . .?"

"What about him!"

"Jen, how can you . . . even—!"

My daughter's sad little twist of a smile stopped me cold—that, and the awareness in her eyes. With a terrible shock I replayed my pitiful attempt at a grocery list of priorities and what it meant. In fact, Rob Sims' name was nowhere on that list.

"I mean loving that man enough," Jen said softly, "to really, truly . . . fight for him, enough to help him work through his hang-ups and yours. To leave this place, give it all up if it comes to that rather than lose him."

"Jen, I— "

"You've already written him off, Mom. And heaven help you if you do."

Was I really so transparent that even my daughter saw through it? That powerful urge to pull back inside myself, to control what I needed and expected from life, was what it had always been, a prelude to my letting go. It was the conditioned response of a lifetime, my modus operandi for coping with the unknown, the emotionally dangerous and my own vulnerability.

For all my righteous indignation, the distancing had already begun. Practice, it seems, makes perfect.

Slipping to the floor alongside my chair, Jen clutched my hands in hers. "Mom, you say you know that man loves you. *What does that . . . mean to you*? I think . . . I truly believe you know that, too. Twelve hours ago you certainly did, loud and clear. I've never seen you happier. The real question is, what are you going to do about it?"

My throat felt constricted and the words did not seem to want to come. "It's not that simple. "

"Yes." Jen nodded. "Yes, it is. Mom, you have a real chance here . . . a wonderful chance to find a life that is good for you. Not just for everyone around you. For Sarah and me. Your clients. Or even those Undercroft buddies of yours. By the time this week is out, I truly hope you'll pick up that phone and tell me you've come up with an answer."

Moved and shaken, I pulled her to me and hugged her as if my life depended on it. As we held one another, the tears I sensed against my face were hers as well as my own.

"Jen. Jen, honey," I heard myself murmuring again and again.

I was so unsteady and exhausted, I couldn't put one foot in front of the other much less think straight. Grateful beyond words, I let my adult daughter take charge as I half talked, half cried myself to sleep. We hadn't snuggled together in my bed all night like that since she was ten.

In the harsh light of day, it was easier to laugh about it. We did, even when she sternly reminded me once more of our conversation on the way out the door next morning. Still, through that laughter, I saw the thinly veiled worry in her eyes.

She already had the car in gear when she rolled down the window one last time. Her voice was low, trembling.

"Whatever happens? Remember, Mom, I love you—"

"And I you." I told her. "I'll call, honey. I'll call, already. I promise."

My hands clutched tight around my bare shoulders against the early morning damp, I stood vigil on the porch watching until her car turned the corner headed for interstate. The house had never seemed so empty.

# ✣ Chapter Twenty-seven

Numb and bereft, I settled down at the kitchen table with my coffee. When the outside world finally intervened, it turned out to be Grace pounding on my back door. At something she read in my face, she swept me into one of her Momma-Cass hugs and didn't seem to want to let go.

"It's true then? Rob's wife was . . . that Wills guy called me a half hour ago and asked if I would get our usual little brunch going after the funeral. And Rob apparently is still in Pittsburgh with his son— "

"You . . . obviously know more than I do."

Grace just looked at me. Hard.

"You're not telling me something, kiddo."

"He's leaving."

"Who?"

"Rob."

"Leaving . . . as in . . . exactly *what*?"

"Hope." *Me.*

I heard Grace draw a harsh breath.

"In heaven's name, why?"

By fits and starts I told her, about the impromptu trip my daughter and I made to Kerygma and threw in a highly-edited version of what followed with Rob's phone call from Ted and that terrible drive in the Hummer back to Hope. When I finished, Grace just stood there in my kitchen looking at me as if I had told her I had robbed the mini-mart.

"God save us from control freaks and martyrs!" she snapped. "You and Rob off in your respective corners, ramming your heads against the wall, as if somehow when you hurt enough you just might knock some sense into those duty-bound skulls of yours. Forget who else the two of you separately and collectively batter to pieces in the process . . .! Do you have any idea what this little mutual suicide pact of yours is going to do to this town, any idea at all?"

I flushed but stood my ground. "You're not being fair, Grace. Rob and I— "

"Are flawed? You forget. I sat on the search committee that brought Rob here. As for you, it's also amazing what you can pick up when your back yards butt up against each other. I love the both of you, sweetie—even if you can't seem to fathom that there are times when two wrongs *do* make one right, any way you slice the pizza!"

"Grace, you don't— "

"I understand we're all broken people, kiddo. We all leave our share of wreckage in our wakes. What's new? Let it go. With all that love and forgiveness stuff you two dish out week after week in that sanctuary, you'd think some of it would have stuck. But then what's the old saw about physicians taking their own medicine?"

It was pretty much a variation on a theme. My daughter had told me the same thing, only Grace was a whole lot less subtle.

"All the guilt trips in the world, Grace, are not going to turn this around."

"Wanna bet? Just let me at him and you next. Face it, kiddo, sometimes guilt is the only thing we've got going for us. Provided we use it as a reality check. Whatever else Rob Sims may feel obliged to beat himself up about—? Ancient history. But if that man leaves, Nativity dies. We'll never get another priest. And he knows it!"

As she came up for air, her chin jutted out. Her voice was shaking, rare for go-with-the-flow Grace.

"As for *you*? I'd give an arm and a leg, walk on hot coals and back again to be in your shoes, to have some guy looking at me again the way Rob looks at you. Granted, he let you down—but if you are prepared to let that be the final word, let that — "

"Grace, this is *my* life you're— "

With an impatient wave, she cut me off.

"Yes. Yes, it is. That's the whole point here. Life. Love. To separate them is unthinkable!"

Through the terrible pounding in my ears, I felt the anger and frustration slipping away. Eyes wide, I searched my friend and neighbor's face, knowing full well Grace was right. Even my own daughter had said as much.

Any answers to be found would have to come from me. And me

alone.

"For starters? I guess . . . even if Rob objects, I know I'm going to have to find a way to play that funeral, Grace. I know it's what Ted wants and no matter what anyone says, I'll do it. I'll go talk to Wills."

"When?"

I hesitated. "Now."

Grace nodded. "That's better. And Rob and the two of you?"

Going on sheer bravado, I threw it out there. The words sounded steady and sure.

"I'm going to find a way to . . . look him in the face and tell him this isn't over, not by a long shot."

"Good for you girl!" Grace nodded sternly. "It isn't . . . and won't be *over* until the Fat Lady—me, in case your wondering—belts out that aria. In the case of you two, we haven't even made it through the first six bars yet."

She shot an impatient glance down at her watch."Okay, then, synchronize your watches. I'll give you exactly one hour before I stomp over to that rectory and let Wills have both barrels. That if and when Rob is transferred, this entire town will picket the Diocese until they drag him back, whatever it takes. And I'll personally lead the ticker tape parade when they do."

For a long, hard moment I thought she was going to threaten that if I waffled, she would force-march me down to the rectory herself. I found myself fighting a smile.

"Have you ever thought of a second career as a parole officer?"

Grace glared at me. "Not funny."

Maybe, but I couldn't help chuckling anyway. "Sorry Grace, but for the record, I thought it was hilarious."

I half-turned toward the living room, trying to get myself moving before I lost my nerve entirely. Out of the corner of my eye, I noticed that my friend and neighbor's frown had tightened a notch again in intensity. There was more?

"You have problems with that?"

Grace shrugged. "Before you get too far, I was just thinking you might want to rethink that wardrobe."

It was only then I realized I was still barefoot and in my oversized and way-overwashed nightshirt with the penguins on the front. Our laughter filled the kitchen.

"A *hair shirt* maybe," I teased. "And sandals?"

Still laughing, Grace by now was at the back door herself. "Call me?"

"Of course."

Before or after my daughter Jen, I wondered. My to-do list was growing by the minute. Still, whatever lay ahead of me down at the rectory, at least on the home front I knew I wasn't alone.

My closet was a disaster area, but I rummaged around and came up with a pair of black performance slacks, turquoise tank top and matching overblouse. A pair of my favorite museum reproduction Egyptian earrings were lying on top in my jewelry box.

The *udjat,* symbol of the eyes of God. *Perfect.*

I caught Father Wills in the middle of a phone call but stood there patiently on the rectory porch, watching him through the screen for signs of his wrapping it up. For once as he pocketed the phone and held the door for me, the good Father seemed flustered.

"Ms. Grunwald. Sorry to keep you waiting."

*There it was again.* You'd think after all the earth moving, digging and probing the guy had been doing, at least he'd get my name right. But then this was no time for niceties.

"I'm sure things are . . . difficult right now.

Wills looked uncomfortable. "You've heard then."

"About the funeral, yes. It's why I came, to let you know I'm available to play it."

The priest seemed puzzled. "I was talking about Father Sims. I just faxed the Diocese his request for a transfer."

"And you didn't try to—?"

My mouth clamped shut. Rob had done exactly what he said he would and apparently Wills hadn't tried to stop him. I had to know.

"I hope, trust they didn't accept it," I said slowly. "If anything should prove to you that the man's integrity is beyond question, the last 24 hours should have done that."

"We're in an awkward spot, here, Ms. Grunwald. I shouldn't have to tell you that."

My mouth felt stiff. "Not half as awkward as if this entire parish gets up in arms. These people have banded together against all odds to get not just Nativity but this whole town to redefine itself. I don't have to tell you what courage that took, or how much they depended on Father Rob to lead them through that crisis."

Wills nodded. "True enough."

"Under duress, the parish also withheld judgment and trusted you to handle those harassment charges fairly and without prejudice. If you accept his request for a transfer, no one is going to believe it wasn't coerced. Regardless of what you say or do."

"Also true."

Suddenly light-headed, I forced myself to focus—in the process, saw Wills' silence for what it was. A willingness to listen. Really listen.

"Your agreeing to that leave of absence started all of us on this course, perhaps out of the best of motives. Only you can end it," I told him, "for that good priest and for this parish. You wanted evidence of his integrity. He offered up his career to oblige you. But nothing on the planet says you have to let him do it."

"You love him."

"Yes. But then you already knew that."

"And unless I misread the situation, thanks to the man's 'all for the good of the parish ethic', he has added your relationship to the casualty list, along with his job at Hope."

"Yes."

"Before he left for Pittsburgh," Wills hesitated. "Rob put out a call to an organist in Bartonville to handle the funeral service."

"I see."

"But then nothing says I can't override that either."

"You won't regret it."

"I already do, Ms. Grunwald, a lot of things. A rural community can be a fragile thing. Vulnerable. This whole situation has been . . . most unfortunate."

"I'm just a church musician, Father Wills. But in even the simplest piece, I start with the premise that each of those notes is connected, dependent on the one that came before, impacting the ones that come after."

From his expression, I gathered I had just gone up a notch or two in his estimation. "Well said. Unfortunately, I can't promise you, though, what the Diocese will decide."

"I understand."

"But I can promise you this. If it were up to me . . . "

"Thank you, Father Wills."

He flashed a wan smile. "Just one favor in return."

Suddenly exhausted, I braced myself for what came next. Heaven knows, the situation was about as bad as it could get.

"On the caller ID while I was on the phone to the Diocese, I spotted the number of that neighbor of yours— "

I fought a smile. "Grace, Grace Alanson."

"That's it. Unless I miss my guess, she will be over here within the hour."

"I'll run interference, talk to her."

With a sigh, Wills ran his hand over his bald spot. The relief on his face was so profound, I chuckled. He laughed himself, sheepish at having shown how relieved he was to have ducked the fireworks.

"By the way, on the way out the door Father Rob also left a list of music," he said, "for the funeral. I assume it would help if you had it in advance."

The priest rummaged in his pocket and pulled out a crumpled stick-em note with several hymn numbers and a date and time scrawled on it in Rob's unmistakable, nearly illegible handwriting. Two days from now, I read.

"You'll call me if anything changes?" I said.

Wills nodded. It was pretty obvious I wasn't just talking about hymn selection.

"Take care," he said. "You've been most helpful, Ms. Grunwald."

But then this was not just my future on the line any more and Wills knew it. Escorting me to the door, he stood there on the porch steps while I struck off in the direction of home. Hymn list or not, I was simply too emotionally drained, my concentration too shot, to practice.

At the corner I looked back toward the rectory, half-expecting to suddenly see Rob's Hummer miraculously snugged in at the curb. Instead I caught sight of Wills, still standing there on the porch where I had left him, watching me.

Once again, I had misjudged the man. Under that hapless even imperious and unctuous exterior, the man was decent enough. The good folk of Nativity could have done one heck of a lot worse than having Wills as their advocate.

My neighborhood was quiet, that small town pre-noon-hour calm when it's possible to roll a bowling ball down any random street without making contact. But when I caught sight of home, I saw that the Undercroft-Arts-mobile was out front and in the shade of the porch roof, I could make out Marty and Leah camped out on the front steps, holding hands. From the look of it, they were waiting for me.

I waved and they responded in kind. But even from that distance I could read the anxiety and tension in their faces. The rumor mill obviously had been grinding away in my absence. *Time to put a hale-fellow spin on things.*

"Marty, welcome home! Good trip?"

He stood, forcing a smile. "Better than what's been going on here, apparently. Grace says we may be losing our priest."

At something in my silence, Leah headed down the steps and toward me on the front walk. Shyly she coaxed me into a tentative hug.

"Oh Char, we're so sorry," she said. "About Rob. About . . . everything."

"I know, honey. I know. Thank you for that."

She began to detach herself—a radiant young woman, almost unrecognizable from that desolate and frightened girl who had popped up in that undercroft so many months ago. As we moved apart, I eased myself down on the steps between the two young people.

"Where's my little man, where's Bart?" I teased.

It was as good an attempt as any at a change in mood. My companions exchanged glances, tough with me sandwiched in between them like that

"Bart's out back with Grace, digging in the garden. Last time we saw him he was ear to ear in mud." Marty looked down at his hands. "We had planned on waiting for you, hoping to share some good news. But then we heard about Father Rob and— "

"Is it true that he . . . that Rob might be leaving Hope?"

"Only time will tell."

I tried not to overreact, but then I couldn't lie to them either. Whatever Father Wills recommended, there were no guarantees. And this was no time to speculate. The disappointment in Leah's voice was all too apparent.

"We were hoping, Marty and I, that Rob would be back, so that he could *marry* us next month."

My heart leapt at the announcement. It was a long time coming, with so much heartache en route.

"Oh kids, I am so very, very happy for you. If anyone deserves to be happy together, it's the two of you. Congratulations."

Beaming, Marty started to shake my hand. Instead he opted for a makeshift bear hug.

"By the way, you're going to be a grandma. Leah and I are arranging for me to adopt the Bart-man."

The pride and love in Marty's voice brought tears to my eyes. If he were my own son, I couldn't have respected him more than in that moment.

"Fair warning then. You're going to have to whip up some signup sheets for babysitting. Lately Grace has been having all the fun."

"And you? What will you do if Rob—?"

"I don't know. Honestly, Marty . . . I don't. Keeping Undercroft Arts afloat is going to have to be a pretty big priority with all of us I think."

"Is there . . . if there's anything Leah and I can do, all you have to do is ask. You know that . . .!"

"Yes. I do. And that means more than I can say. But right now there doesn't seem to be much anyone can do. I told Father Wills this morning I would play the funeral. Barney may need your help organizing the men in the parish to help Rob."

"Done."

"But what about you, kids? How has your family responded to the news about the wedding, Leah?"

I fought a smile as Marty subtly flashed a take-charge glance in Leah's direction. The gesture was vintage Rob. Apparently it wasn't just a crash course in sales and marketing on the agenda when I steered my young friend Rob's way those many months ago.

"We made every effort," my young friend said quietly. "It's all we could do. Now it's in their hands. We hope they will be there with and for us. If not, we have family here . . . you and Grace, Rob, Barney—more than we could ever hope or want."

He chuckled, shook his head. "And of course my folks love her. Anybody who could get me in a suit and off the unemployment rolls is going to get their seal of approval, big time."

"We wanted to ask . . . we would really like it if you played for us, for the wedding." Leah said. "Grace is doing the food and the flowers. Over the past couple of months, she has been hiring Marty to turn that huge space over her garage into an apartment . . . so we have a place of our own to live, afterward. It's not like we're moving to the moon or anything."

"Of course. I'd be honored."

How simple, how natural it all felt. The love radiating from those two wrapped itself around my aching heart.

"But right now, we're taking you out to dinner," Marty said, "to celebrate."

I went, while Grace pulled the Bart-detail. The choice was theirs—Casa Blanca, the site of ambivalent memories for me as well as them. Months ago. A lifetime ago.

Things change. "To love", we toasted. I wished them every good thing, from the bottom of my heart.

# ✣ Chapter Twenty-eight

Morning—the day before Karin Sim's funeral—dawned to another dull and leaden sky. Storms were forecast for later in the afternoon. True to his word, Rob hadn't phoned or emailed. I had no idea where arrangements stood for the funeral service beyond those sketchy details he had left behind with Father Wills.

One thing was certain, I couldn't put off organizing the music any longer. Half-dreading that Rob's Hummer would have shown up by now at the rectory, I decided to drive over to Nativity as a way of minimizing potential contact. It was one thing to sit there on the bench tomorrow and listen to him intoning the funeral liturgy—quite another to cope with this pervasive, terrible silence between us.

My daughter's soul-talk notwithstanding, any kind of attempt to deal with what had happened would have to wait. Now was not the time for either one of us, Rob or I.

The sanctuary was deserted, the air heavy with the scent of lemons—evidence that Barney and his cleaning crew already had been hard at work. Father Wills had given me Rob's note with the list of the music. As I slid on the organ bench, I tacked it on the clip I used on Sundays to keep track of the service order. "Amazing Grace" was pencilled in as the processional, the hymn of choice at many Twelve-Step funerals.

My fingers had a will of their own as they began to run through the familiar hymn. The second time, unexpectedly, they faltered—as I found myself caught up, distracted by the powerful text.

*Through many dangers, toils and snares.* All three certainly had become a persistent leit motif in my relationships ever since I arrived in Hope, none of it intended.

But then the no-fault principle in law and life assumes a level of responsibility simply for being there, for turning up in a particular spot at a particular date and time—for the air we breathe and the footfalls however gentle we leave behind on the earth. *Existential guilt*, theologians call it, *original sin, as old as the Garden.* At its heart lay the temptation to play God, one transgression Rob and I certainly knew up close and personal as we fled from grace and each other.

But then the hymn was drawing me on to its powerful close. *I once was lost and now?*

Both my daughter and my pull-no-punches friend and neighbor had called it like it was—that in the human hunger for intimacy and love lay not a curse, but one of our greatest blessings. The choice was mine. It was time to let go and let God, to embrace the gifts I had been given, all of them.

*First things first.* I had a gig to play.

Still on autopilot, I played through the list for the rest of the funeral service to make sure the music was stacked in more or less the right order. That done, I began to sift and read my way through the heaps piled on the floor next to the bench, flagging suitable pre-service music, here and there, with my omnipresent stack of stick-em notes.

Time was measuring itself out in the poignant configurations of quavers and phrases coming to life in my hands. I already had played most of these classics at one time or another—Bach, Faurè and all the blockbusters of the funeral repertoire. Only this time it was my own losses, my own nameless grief I was pouring out into the holy space around me.

Finally, physically spent and my concentration shot, unable to play any longer, I listened as the music quavered and hung there in the silence. Feeling bereft, blankly staring at the music on the rack in front of me, I felt a sudden chill—the eerie sensation that someone was there with me in that sanctuary.

I half-turned on the bench, assuming it was just paranoia—that I was imagining it. Instead, to my shock and distress, I made eye contact with Rob, sitting in his favorite spot in the back of the sanctuary.

"I thought I'd find you here," he said.

"You're . . . back."

By way of confirmation he stood, gingerly easing the kneeler in front of him upright in the process. Even from that distance, I saw he wasn't wearing the collar, just a black turtleneck and jeans. His hands clutched at the pew in front of him so hard that the knuckles stood out ashen white against the age-darkened wood.

"I'm back," he said.

"I see that."

"For keeps, if you'll still have me."

It felt as if some unseen hand had cut off my air supply, robbing me of speech. My eyes felt gritty, making it hard to see. Behind me I heard the soft purr of the tracker organ's motor, waiting.

"I assume," he said, "Wills told you . . . about my request for a transfer?"

"Yes."

Rob winced. "Stupidity. Pride. You want a catalog of all the mortal and venal sins a man can commit in 48 hours? I'm not sure I can count them all—the ones aimed your way being among the very worst."

"You were hurting. I understand that."

"Well, I don't, not by a long shot. Not after all those years in AA, the seminary and all that lofty rhetoric about turning your life over to a Higher Power." His voice broke, steadied again. "Not when the truth was here in front of me all along inside these four walls, where I could have found *you* even back then, all those years ago . . .if I hadn't been too blind to see it."

And *now*? I thought but didn't say it.

"I love you," Rob said. "I've been a fool— "

"Yes."

But then so had I, contributing more than my share of foolishness, shutting down my heart, or at least trying to. The habits of a lifetime die hard.

"*Absolvo te.*" It came out a whisper, but true just the same. "If you need to hear it."

I saw the awe, the disbelief in his face as it registered what he was hearing. *Unqualified forgiveness.* Sacred. Healing.

There were no flaming swords in my world any more—or angels with faces set like flint. Unless, mercifully, it was to block the legacy of the past for once and for all.

"What I need to hear," Rob said, his voice raw with longing, "is that you love me. That you'll be with me on that bench on Sunday mornings, be with me—in that rectory—when all of this is behind us."

I just stood there, looking at him. "And the transfer?"

"Wills told the Diocese to forget it. The powers that be down there pretty much told me the same thing. If I intend to stay in the priesthood, then my place is here—in Hope."

What was he telling me? Impossible as it seemed, they were actually . . . *forcing* him to stay at Nativity.

I exhaled sharply, twice, trying to clear my head—so stunned that for the life of me, I couldn't say a word. Rob smiled.

"Pretty much my reaction, sweetheart. Disbelief, followed hard by a heck of a lot of gratitude. From what Wills said, your heart-to-heart had a lot to do with all that."

"We talked."

"So did my son, apparently. It seems his little phone call to Wills was just a warmup for his run-in with the Bishop, starting with an impassioned blow-by-blow about his mother and me, my tenure here and us, as he saw it. He urged them to make their decision not on appearances but the truth— "

"Courageous— "

Rob shook his head. "You have no idea. I went down to Pittsburgh intending to help him cope. What incredible hubris on my part, from the get-go! When I got done openly congratulating myself to my son for what I had done on that drive back to Hope with you, let's just say he had a very different take on things entirely."

He drew a harsh breath. "*Dad, what do you expect from that God of yours,* my son asked me. I started to unload the usual answers about love and absolution. He just listened, shook his head. *Hope, Dad,* he said. *Of all things, you forgot Hope. Odd . . . when you finally seem to have found the way back there . . .*"

Literally and figuratively. In so many words, it was that moment of truth with my daughter all over again, just a day before and under pretty much the same circumstances.

Bizarre what one remembers at times like this. I was thinking of that story Rob shared with me when we were first getting to know each other. It was his friend's sermon about miracles and the story of the loaves and the fishes—that little boy standing there with his hand out, offering up everything he had.

We all have our stories. I was starting to understand that—and more important, that it is in the sharing they become holy, even life changing. We had been pursuing our peace, our salvation alone for so very long, Rob and I. How humbling it is to find that, if and when redemption finally comes, it comes in community.

"We both know the text," I said softly. "*And a little child shall lead them*—I think I prefer that one immensely to ones about *sins of the fathers*, Rob, don't you?"

He seemed about to say something. Instead, his face transfixed with the clarifying calm of a man seeing his whole life suddenly flash before his eyes, he sank down slowly on the bench behind him.

"Char—dear God, Char . . .!"

The words were almost indistinguishable. Reaching out blindly to brace himself against the scroll work of the pew in front of him, Rob slumped forward so that his forehead was resting on his hands. Then shoulders shaking with the effort, in virtual silence except for that first soul-wrenching outcry of awareness—he wept.

All of that had happened as if in stop motion, image by agonizing image. Instinct told me not to intervene. This man had bottled up his despair and grief, the guilt and self-loathing for so long that this freedom to let it go was truly precious, a blessing.

Hard as it was, I just stood there alone in the aisle of the sanctuary and let that outpouring of emotion run its course. Although my heart was aching for him, I had cried myself out what seemed like a very long time ago.

Outside the sanctuary, a branch was scraping against one of the stained glass windows, a ragged rhythmic tapping, and I could feel as much as hear the sighing of the wind against the roof above the exposed wooden trusses of the sanctuary ceiling. Judging by the waning light, that storm we were expecting seemed about to break. Somewhere in the shadows a cricket was droning out its plight, exiled alone in this alien landscape.

This was the heartbeat of my life I was hearing, that quiet rhythm reminding me there is a time for and a music in all things. I knew it for what it was—a triumph song of sorrow and joy, of brokenness and healing.

"For what it's worth," I said softly. "All those years I never saw what was right here in front of me either. But once I did, I never stopped loving you, never will. No matter what you choose to do, about the priesthood, about any of this."

At that, eyes dark-rimmed with spent anguish, Rob raised his head. "I don't deserve that."

"Do we ever . . . ever expect grace when and where we find it? No love is easy, if it's real. I told Marty that once when he was trying to figure out what to do with his life. I really should have been telling myself. But then my daughter pretty much did that for me, a little late, maybe—the night we came back from Lake Erie, in fact But then, I guess, we just have to take things when they come."

And how far we truly *had* come, Rob and I, from that first walk together from the hardware to the undercroft, by fits and starts sharing the failures and doubts that had crippled our respective lives for so long. I held his words from those Spring mornings in my heart, the wistful hope that it is never too late to begin again.

In the end, it seems, our sacred calling—our life's work—had found us, in spite of all our groping and searching for it. Not the job I had lost to retirement or even the peace I rediscovered at the keyboard, not the clerical collar that Rob had grasped to center his floundering life, we had found our vocation in the business of loving, pure and simple. It was a task that had been waiting for us all the time, here in this place, from the very beginning.

Rob was looking at me strangely. "What's so funny?"

"Nothing, really."

But I told him—told him, too, what my daughter and Grace had said. If we are open to it, life can teach us to rethink our equations. Against all logic and conventional wisdom, even two wrongs, it seems, can make a right, and of that we stood here together, living proof.

Our laughter felt good, cleansing. And it was the only invitation we needed.

As Rob began to maneuver out of the narrow space between kneeler and bench, I came to meet him. We slipped into each others' arms as if we had never been apart.

"Remind me never to use Grace as a reference!" he teased. "When the best she can manage is, *You two really deserve each other*!"

"Apparently our kids sure seem to think so."

At that he started to pull back enough to see my face. I smiled up at him, tucking away in my memory the love in his eyes and the promise of better days to come.

"Speaking of kids," he muttered. "Ted's been over in that rectory this whole time with Wills. Lord, help him. Wills, that is."

I laughed. "I can almost feel sorry for him."

"I'm not sure I'm prepared to go quite that far yet, sweetheart, but we've really got to get over there. There's still a lot to *do* before tomorrow."

Yes, there was. And it was time to get on with it.

# ABOUT THE AUTHOR

## Mary A. Agria

**The Vox Humana is a stop on a pipe organ meant to imitate the sound of the human voice. It is never meant to be used alone.**

Thrilled with the overwhelming response to her novel, *TIME in a Garden*—which in summer of 2006 wound up on numerous best-seller lists, garnered four and five-star reviews online and from book groups, and which sold out at signings on Long Island and in Michigan—Mary Agria has responded to requests from readers to "keep it coming" with *VOX HUMANA: The Human Voice*. A story about community and personal growth, VOX also combines two of her personal passions: liturgical music and weaving.

They are worlds she knows well. Ms. Agria has performed professionally as an organist ever since she was a teenager growing up in Wisconsin. Though only a recent member of a Long Island weavers' guild, she has learned to appreciate deeply the skill and artistry of the craft and its power as a metaphor for life in human community.

Ms. Agria earned B.A. and M.A. degrees from the University of Wisconsin in literature and linguistics, then spent much of her career as a technical writer and counselor in the field of community development and work force issues. Her syndicated column on work force issues ran in newspapers for 20 years. In her first "retirement" to Long Island's North Fork, she served and continues to serve as organist and music director at both Protestant and Roman Catholic congregations. She has begun publishing *TIME in a Garden*, a newspaper column dealing with community gardening and its connections to spirituality.

Together with her best friend and husband, retired university president Dr. John Agria, Ms. Agria enjoys traveling the globe from Europe, to China, India and the ancient civilizations of Central and South America; tends their gardens; and looks forward to quality time with friends and family at home in Michigan and New York. She is the proud mother of four daughters and five grandchildren.

# DISCUSSION QUESTIONS
## for Mary A. Agria's VOX HUMANA: The Human Voice

1. In one way or another each of the main characters—Char, Rob, Marty, Leah, Grace, and Rob—are "broken" people. With which of them can you most identify? What in their particular "story" intrigues you?
2. Secondary characters like Rob and Char's children, Todd Rutterbach, Wilma and Father Wills all make unique contributions to the novel. Single out the one that resonated most with you. How does that character impact others in the story?
3. What are the strengths in Char Howard's character? What weakness(es) helped fuel the crisis in which she finds herself? How does she learn to transcend her past?
4. What is Rob Sims' greatest strength? What character traits keep him from moving beyond his past failures? What event(s) prove key in changing that?
5. Why did early retirement hit Char so hard? How did her view of work contribute to limiting her growth and undermine her sense of self-worth? What events most help her see what it truly means to find her vocation or calling?
6. What factors caused Rob to make the personal and professional choices that proved so disastrous for him? Discuss key events that helped him begin to change.
7. What role do the generations play in the novel? How is "family" defined in a place like Hope? Point to a single incident in the novel that for you reflects the best or the best in family/community life.
8. What would you describe as the strongest positive aspect of life in a rural community like Hope? The most negative one?
9. Music in VOX is both solitary and communal. Discuss the connections Char feels between her art and her spirituality. How does that impact others? eg., Wilma, Rob.
10. How does a visual art like weaving enrich the lives of people in the novel? Discuss "Undercroft Arts" in the context of rebuilding struggling communities.
11. What role does the institutional church play in the unfolding novel? How do characters like Wills, the Bishop, the retreat house director Father Gillespie or the members of the congregation at Nativity contribute to the novel?
12. What single episode in the novel had the greatest impact for you and why? What single episode was the most surprising or disturbing?

**READER AND CRITICAL PRAISE FOR MS. AGRIA'S NOVELS:** "Fresh language and images"..."Richly drawn, wonderfully engaging characters, haunted by ultimate questions of mortality and spirituality"

**TO MEET THE AUTHOR:** arrange for a phone "Author Chat" for a book group; schedule a signing or reading; follow Ms. Agria's monthly online "Reflections"; or learn more about her other novels/books, by visiting her website at www.maryagria.com

✣

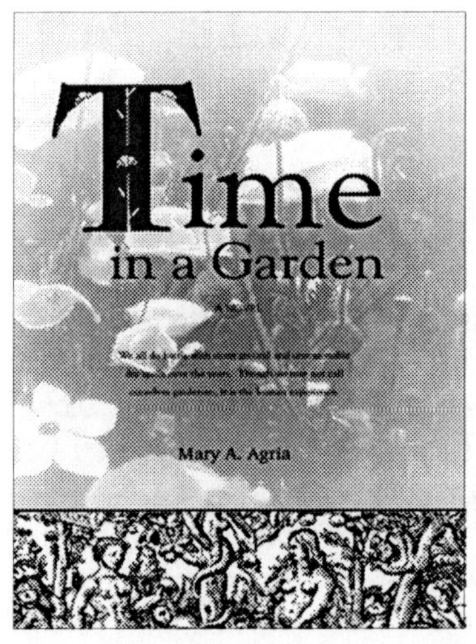


"A must-read for the contemplative gardener . . . "

New in summer 2006 . . .a best-selling novel about the search for meaning in the changing seasons of our lives,

by Mary A. Agria

Laced with gardening tips, wit and wisdom, *TIME in a Garden* is an inspiring story of emotional and spiritual growth for gardeners of all ages, mothers and daughters, and anyone struggling to bloom where they are planted. Retired and in their sixties, Eve Brennemann and Adam Groft find themselves in an unlikely Eden . . . helping a crew of senior citizens beautify their dying rural Michigan community by creating a perennial garden along an interstate off-ramp. Eve's marriage was saved from divorce only by the accidental death of her husband. Her daughters are estranged and living elsewhere. Adam has spent a lifetime avoiding relationships and expectations that he run the family nursery business. When Eve begins writing a garden column in the local county weekly, these unforgettable characters embark on a heartwarming, poignant journey to discover love and meaning as they cope with growth and loss in the changing seasons of their lives.

"From the very first paragraph until the very last, I was hooked. Ms. Agria captures the very essence of life and its connection to a garden" ... "Richly drawn characters who continue to be haunted by ultimate questions of mortality and spirituality. Agria's timeless garden metaphors are pure wisdom." **5-star Amazon.com** reviews - 2006

"Wonderfully engaging main characters!" **...** "One of my top ten best reads. The characters are beautiful. I loved this book and it garnered positive reviews from our book club." **BARNES & NOBLE.com** reviews - 2006

"A must-read for the contemplative gardener", *Suffolk Times*, May 2006

**Summer 2006 "Top-3" best-seller lists for paperback fiction, McLean & Eakin Booksellers, Petoskey and Horizon Books, Traverse City, MI**

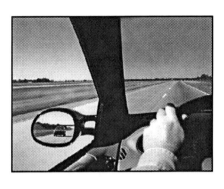

CPSIA information can be obtained
at www.ICGtesting.com
Printed in the USA
FSOW01n2026030816
23425FS